W9-CHF-503

The Trail of Blood . . .

"Hello?" Gretchen asked quietly into the wind. "Anybody there?"

Finally she sighed and shook her head, taking one last look across the driveway. The house was just creeping her out. She was going to have to get used to all the strange noises that came with living out in the middle of nowhere.

But as she was closing the door, something small and white on the top step caught her eye. She bent down to look at it more closely.

It was a sealed envelope. Gretchen picked it up and turned it over in her hands. Funny. She hadn't remembered seeing it there before. She held it up to the light and saw that there was something inside—a note of some sort. Had somebody left it there?

Suddenly Gretchen froze. Somebody *had* left it there. Somebody had walked all the way down the dirt road, dropped the envelope on the front step, and left without saying a word. Tonight.

The paper inside was heavy and yellowed and the words on it were stenciled in black ink:

To Adam's baby-sitter,
   Go home. Get out while you can. Nothing will stand between Adam and us. Stay and you will suffer the consequences. The Trail of Blood ends in blood. Adam is ours.

Baby-sitter's Nightmares

Alone in the Dark
The Evil Child
Lights Out*
A Killer in the House*

*coming soon

Available from HarperPaperbacks

BABY-SITTER'S NIGHTMARES

ALONE IN THE DARK

Daniel Parker

HarperPaperbacks

A Division of HarperCollins*Publishers*

HarperPaperbacks *A Division of* HarperCollins*Publishers*
10 East 53rd Street, New York, N.Y. 10022

Cover illustration by Bill Schmidt

First printing: June 1995

Printed in the United States of America

HarperPaperbacks and colophon are trademarks of HarperCollins*Publishers*

❖ 10 9 8 7 6 5 4 3 2 1

This book is dedicated with the utmost respect to George "smooth like butter" Wallace

PART 1

The flames rose high into the black night.

Around the fire stood seventeen men, women, and children. For eight hundred years, in many places and in many times, a circle such as this had been drawn from the legions of believers to tend the sacred fire. They stood hand in hand in robes of shimmering white, chanting in a language long dead, their energy focused on the flickering heat in front of them.

"The Trail of Blood ends in blood," the High Priest cried, his whispery voice barely rising above crackling flames.

The High Priest was old; his life ebbed from his broken body with each wheezing breath he took. A flowing snow-white beard partially obscured the sullen face that had been shriveled by time. He leaned heavily on his staff. Centuries of waiting were drawing to a close. . . .

"The Trail of Blood ends in blood," echoed the circle.

Everything the prophets had written had come to pass. Now only one thing remained.

"Bring forth the initiate," called the High Priest.

A small earthen temple of thatched wood and mud stood in the eastern corner of the clearing. From its blackened doorway three figures emerged. A pale, ash-haired girl stepped foward, wrapped in robes of bright red. Two tall figures in white followed, their faces hidden by ornate masks of wood and glittering jewels.

"You will bring the child to us."

"I will bring the child to you," she answered.

"We will see the Fiery Dawn upon his sacrifice. It has been written."

ONE

"Do you think I need to bring my own towels?" Gretchen Childs stood next to her bed, folding clothes into a suitcase. The telephone receiver was wedged in a mass of chestnut curls between her shoulder and her ear.

"Give me a break," Lacy answered dryly. "These people have a mansion on the beach and you're worried about towels?"

Gretchen laughed. "I guess you'd only bring some suntan lotion, huh?"

"Not even." A wistful sigh came out of the receiver. "I can't believe you're leaving today. You must be so psyched. Did, uh, the Wollmans happen to mention anything about you having friends over—you know, to help with household chores?"

"Nice try, Lace," Gretchen said, tossing a last pair of socks into the suitcase and slamming it shut. "No, they didn't mention it. Anyway . . ."

"You just want to be left alone," Lacy gently finished for her.

Gretchen smiled. Lacy knew *exactly* what she was thinking. "No offense," she said softly.

"None taken. Listen—give me a call when you get there, okay? I want to know every detail about the place."

"You got it." Gretchen was just about to hang up when she heard Lacy's voice again.

"Hey, Gretchen!"

"Yeah?"

"Have fun, okay?"

Gretchen smiled to herself. "I will."

She was finally on her way. But Gretchen wasn't nearly as excited as she had imagined she would be.

She was nervous.

Gretchen stared out the window as the scenery rushed past—the scrub brush, the evergreens, the turquoise ocean far below. The late afternoon sun hung just above the water at the horizon, casting long shadows across the highway.

Beautiful.

And every turn of the wheels carried her farther away from home, from school, from everything that had made spring semester of her junior year a complete disaster.

So why did she feel so strange? She had felt it all afternoon. A gnawing ache in the pit of her stomach. Maybe she had forgotten something . . .

"You're awfully quiet," said her mom.

Gretchen glanced at her mom, hunched forward in the driver's seat. "I'm just trying to remember if I packed everything."

"I wouldn't worry. If you forgot anything, I'm sure you can always borrow something from the Wollmans." She smiled wryly. "Something tells me it won't be that hard to make do."

"Yeah—I guess you're right." Gretchen rolled her window down a little, letting the wind whip through her shoulder-length chestnut hair. She stole a peek at herself in the rearview mirror. The sunlight made her blue eyes sparkle, but the expression on her face was unreadable, even to herself. She was probably just excited. Her mom was right—there was nothing to worry about. The Wollmans were going to have everything she needed.

"Did I remember to tell you that Lacy called last night?"

Gretchen rolled her eyes. "No, Mom, you didn't remember. But I spoke to her this morning."

"Whoops." Her mom grinned and bit her lip. "Sorry. I hope it wasn't anything too important."

"She just wanted me to call her when we get there—so she can make me feel guilty about having the summer job of the century."

"I hope you don't plan on spending the next three weeks running up the Wollmans' phone bills on calls to your best friend," she teased. "You are going to have *some* responsibilities, you know."

7

"Sure." Gretchen smiled. "Let's see—hanging out in the Jacuzzi, joyriding in the Wollmans' Mercedes, getting a tan . . . that about covers it, right?"

"Gretchen! I'm serious—"

"Mom, c'mon. You know I'm the greatest, most responsible baby-sitter who ever lived. The next three weeks are going to be the best weeks of Adam Wollman's life."

Her mom laughed. "At least you aren't lacking any self-confidence." She raised her eyebrows. "But then again, neither is Adam. You two are going to make quite a pair."

Maybe *that* was the reason she felt nervous. Adam Wollman. His mother had volunteered at the women's shelter her mother ran, before they'd moved out of San Francisco. The last time she had seen Adam was about six months ago, when the Wollmans had driven up to visit Gretchen's mom at Christmas. Gretchen had never met any kid quite like him. He had just turned seven, but the way he spoke and behaved was so . . . *mature*. It was almost as if he were an adult trapped in a little boy's body. And she remembered feeling vaguely unsettled by the way he had stared at her with those intense black eyes. She shook her head. He was probably just one of those boy-geniuses who spent all his time reading and building model airplanes.

"I think Adam is adorable," she said aloud.

"I know," her mom said. "That's what I told the Wollmans when I volunteered your services.

Of course, I wasn't expecting the Wollmans to let you use their Mercedes, but that's another story."

Gretchen smiled. She knew her mom had organized this whole baby-sitting job because she had been worried about her. It *had* been a pretty miserable spring. Her smile faded. She had promised herself she wasn't going to think about Todd. But it was no use; the memories came flooding back against her will, as they always did.

Dana. Gretchen could have handled being dumped—even being dumped for someone else. But Dana! Why couldn't Todd have seen her for the conniving jerk she was? She was a manipulative—

"Gretchen, is anything wrong?"

Gretchen suddenly realized she was clenching her fists. She forced herself to relax. "Nope. I'm just psyched to leave San Francisco behind for a few weeks. The only things I'm gonna miss are you and Lacy," she said flatly.

"I think it'll be a good thing for you to get away for a while, too."

"So that about covers it." Mr. Wollman tossed one last suitcase into the trunk of his Jaguar and slammed the door shut. "You know where everything is, you've got the house and the car keys, and you've got the hotel numbers in case anything comes up."

Gretchen nodded. She looked around, still unable to believe it. For the next three weeks, she was going to have all *this* to herself.

After she and her mom had arrived, Mr. and Mrs. Wollman had given them the grand tour of their house. Palace was more like it. The Wollmans' home was a colossal structure of white stucco and glass that sat perched above the ocean at the end of a tiny peninsula. It was the only house on a one-lane dirt road choked with trees; the nearest neighbor was a quarter mile away.

"We moved here for peace and quiet," Mr. Wollman had explained.

The inside of the house was like nothing Gretchen had ever seen—ultramodern, softly lit, sparsely furnished with lots of open space. At the far end a large sitting room faced the ocean. Its glass doors opened onto a broad patio into which was built a Jacuzzi. From there a long wooden staircase ran down a sharp incline to the beach below.

As far as Gretchen was concerned, it was paradise.

"I can't thank you enough for watching Adam for us, Gretchen," Mr. Wollman said.

"Believe me, it's my pleasure. Where *is* Adam, anyway?"

Mr. Wollman glanced at the house. "I thought he was in his room, but I guess not." He shrugged. "Maybe he's in the basement. He's pretty shy."

Just then Gretchen's mom and Mrs. Wollman walked out the front door.

"We'd better get going, honey," Mr. Wollman called to his wife. "Have you seen Adam?"

"Here I am," said a boy's voice.

Gretchen spun around. There he was— leaning nonchalantly against her mom's car. He was just as she remembered him: small and skinny with smooth dark skin, jet black hair, and those piercing black eyes.

"Well, there you are!" Mr. Wollman exclaimed. "We've been looking for you. Adam, you remember Gretchen, don't you?"

Adam raised his eyebrows. "I saw her at Christmas, Dad. Of course I remember her."

Gretchen stifled a giggle. "You ready to have fun for a few weeks, Adam?" she asked, putting her hand on his shoulder.

Adam shrugged. "Yeah, I guess," he said in a bored voice. "You don't have to worry about me, though. I can take care of myself."

"Adam, please," Mr. Wollman said sternly. "That's not a very polite thing to say. I think what Gretchen is saying is that she's excited to have you as a playmate for the next three weeks."

Adam locked eyes with Gretchen. "She's seventeen, Dad. I think she's a little old for a playmate." He abruptly walked up the front steps and disappeared into the house.

Gretchen looked at Mr. Wollman. Suddenly they both started laughing. "Bright kid," Gretchen said.

"Adam's just up to his usual tricks—showing off for our guests," Mr. Wollman said. "I'll admit that he acts—well, older than his age. But don't worry, Gretchen. I know he likes you a lot."

"That's good," Gretchen said. She glanced at her mom. "It's nice to finally meet a boy I can talk to."

Mr. Wollman smiled. "I'm sure you two are going to get along great." He glanced at his watch. "We should really be going. We don't want to be late for our flight."

"I'll follow you out," said Gretchen's mom. "I want to get home before it gets too dark."

Gretchen gave her mom a quick hug before she got into the car. "Thanks again," she whispered.

"You're going to have a great time." Her mom smiled. "I'm sure this is going to be something you'll never forget. This will be something you'll remember for the rest of your life."

Mr. and Mrs. Wollman slammed the doors of their Jaguar and the car rolled across the gravel of the driveway toward the front gate.

"Don't you want to say good-bye to Adam?" Gretchen called.

Mr. Wollman poked his head out the window. "We did earlier. Anyway, Adam hates long sentimental good-byes. Have fun, Gretchen!"

Gretchen glanced at her mom, who shrugged.

Her mom got into their old VW bug and started up the engine. "Remember, honey, I'm only two hours away. If anything happens, I can be down here in a flash."

"I know, Mom. I'll be fine. You'd better get going. I'll call you in a few days."

"Bye, Gretchen!"

The Jaguar eased out the front gates, followed by the VW. Soon the dust of their departure settled and the hum of the engines faded into silence.

Alone at last, thought Gretchen. All she could hear was the monotonous sound of crickets and the distant crashing of waves against the beach below. *Peace and quiet.*

The sun had now sunk below the horizon and the sky was a deep, rich blue. Gretchen shivered in the late evening breeze. She turned and walked up the front steps. But just as she was putting her hand on the big lacquered wooden front door, she heard something that made her pause—a small scuttling sound in the bushes by the garage door.

Gretchen peered into the shadowy tangle of evergreens and hedges, but the failing light made it impossible to see anything. She swallowed. This house *was* pretty isolated. Were there animals around here she should know about? Bands of rabid raccoons? She laughed suddenly and her laughter cut into the silence, expunging her fear. She pushed the door open. So what if there were wild animals? They were probably easier to deal with than muggers or drunk drivers.

The door opened into a two-story foyer with a floor of polished oak, lit by a hanging chandelier. A spiral staircase stood in the far left corner that led to the wing with the bedrooms. An arch on the right side opened into the living room.

"Adam?" Gretchen called. Her voice sounded hollow against the bare walls and floor.

"In here," came the faint reply. "In the back."

Gretchen walked through the living room into the sitting room at the back of the house. The sunlight was fading. Adam was slouched in a leather couch, his eyes glued to the bands of fiery red and orange across the horizon.

"Wow," Gretchen murmured. "It's beautiful."

Adam said nothing. Gretchen stole a glance at him. His expression was unreadable; his pupils were two pitch black orbs. Gretchen turned away quickly.

"This view is the only thing I like about this house," he said finally.

"Why's that?" Gretchen asked, sitting next to him.

"It's weird here. It doesn't feel like a home." He shrugged. "But Mom and Dad love it."

Gretchen glanced at Adam out of the corner of her eye. He was right. The house was beautiful—but she could never feel comfortable living in a place like this all the time. It was more like a museum than a home.

"How long have you been living here?" she asked.

"We moved here last summer. I had to switch schools and everything. I didn't want to move."

"You don't like your new school very much?"

"Not really. The kids there are all dumb jerks."

"I know what you mean." She sighed. "I have a lot of dumb jerks at my school, too."

He turned his eyes away from the view. "You know, I meant what I said earlier. About being able to take care of myself. You don't have to worry about me while you're here."

"Well, what if I *want* to worry about you?"

In the twilight, Gretchen could just discern a small smile curling at the corner of Adam's lips. "I guess there isn't much I can do about *that*," he said.

Gretchen put the last dish into the dishwasher, turned it on, and went into the sitting room. It was almost eleven o'clock. She flopped down on the big leather couch and gazed at the stars out the huge glass doors. It had been a long, exhausting day.

At least Adam had finally warmed up to her.

Gretchen laughed to herself. The kid certainly *was* odd. After having prodded him for almost an hour, she had finally gotten him to tell her that his favorite meal was spaghetti and meatballs. Did he want to have some for dinner? Maybe. Did he want to help her make it? Sure—if she wanted him to. It seemed he never used two words when one would do. But when they had finally gone into the kitchen and started preparing the food, Adam had relaxed a little.

Mostly he talked about how much he hated the house—and how much he wished his parents had taken him with them on their trip.

Why *hadn't* the Wollmans taken Adam with them? The whole thing seemed strange. They hadn't even been that concerned about saying good-bye to him. Oh, well. It was none of her business. She only had to worry about making Adam happy for the next three weeks.

The house was another thing. Sitting alone in the vast darkness of the sitting room, Gretchen began to understand why Adam hated living here so much. Everything was starkly perfect— cold and antiseptic. She thought of her small, cluttered town house in San Francisco, with its cozy little kitchen—

Just then she heard a sharp rustling of leaves outside. Her ears pricked up.

All was quiet for a moment.

There. She heard it again. This time it was more faint, followed by a soft rapid thumping, like footsteps running across a lawn.

Gretchen began breathing faster.

Was that an animal?

Adam had told her that he had seen raccoons, possums, even an occasional deer. But she knew that sound couldn't have been made by any of those animals.

That sound had been made by two feet.

Gretchen bolted from the couch and ran to the front door. She flipped on the outside lights and looked into the night. The harsh pale blue bulbs illuminated the gravel of the driveway, but beyond that, the bushes and trees were a wall of shadows. She stood in the doorway for several seconds, wrapping her arms around herself. Her teeth were chattering.

The night was silent again.

"Hello?" Gretchen asked quietly into the wind. "Anybody there?"

Finally she sighed and shook her head, taking one last look across the driveway. Why was she getting so nervous? The house was just creeping her out. She was going to have to get used to all the strange noises that came with living out in the middle of nowhere.

But as she was closing the door, something small and white on the top step caught her eye.

She bent down to look at it more closely.

It was a sealed envelope.

Gretchen picked it up and turned it over in her hands. It was blank—no label on it, no postage, no return address. Funny. She hadn't remembered seeing it there before. She held it up to the light and saw that there was something inside—a note of some sort. Had somebody left it there?

Suddenly Gretchen froze.

Somebody *had* left it there. Somebody had walked all the way down the dirt road, dropped the envelope on the front step, and left without saying a word.

Tonight.

Gretchen slammed the door shut behind her. She rushed into the kitchen and tore the envelope open.

The paper inside was heavy and yellowed and the words on it were stenciled in black ink:

To Adam's baby-sitter,
Go home. Get out while you can. Nothing will stand between Adam and us. Stay and you will suffer the consequences. The Trail of Blood ends in blood. Adam is ours.

TWO

Gretchen's hands trembled. Her eyes frantically raced over the strange paper again and again. Finally her hand shook so violently that the note fell to the kitchen floor.

Adam!

Gretchen bounded up the spiral staircase and sprinted down the darkened hall to Adam's bedroom. She burst through the door.

Oh, no . . .

Adam was squirming under his covers, moaning in a low voice. "Adam!" Gretchen cried, flipping on the lights and rushing over to the side of his bed. "Adam, are you okay!"

There was no response. She could see that his face was bathed in sweat and that his eyelids were fluttering, revealing only the whites. He twisted slowly, mumbling something incomprehensible.

"Adam," she pleaded desperately, shaking him. "Adam, wake up!"

Suddenly his eyes popped open and he stopped moving. He blinked a couple of times. "What's going on?" he croaked.

Gretchen opened her mouth, then hesitated for a moment. Should she tell him about the note? It would probably just frighten him. "Uh—you . . . you were having a nightmare."

Adam stared at her for a second. His eyes narrowed. "Was I talking in my sleep?" he asked sharply.

Gretchen paused. *Talking in your sleep?* His question didn't make any sense. "Uh . . . nothing I could understand."

"Oh." He looked relieved. He turned over on his side and closed his eyes. "I'm fine. Don't worry, Gretchen. Good night."

"Are you sure?"

"Yeah, yeah," he said impatiently. "Just turn off the light, please."

Gretchen stood and hurried from the room, flipping off the light. She closed the door and leaned against it, breathing a heavy sigh. Her heart was pounding so loudly it sounded as if it was coming from outside her body.

What had been going on in there? Why had Adam been so worried about talking in his sleep? Gretchen began to feel goose bumps rise on her arms. Adam wasn't behaving the way a normal seven-year-old behaved. . . .

Relax, she told herself. *Adam is fine. He was just having a nightmare. Whoever left the note is gone.*

After hurrying through the house and making

sure all the windows and doors were tightly locked, she returned to the kitchen. The note was laying in the middle of the floor. She stared at it for a moment before picking it up and putting it on the kitchen table.

What was going on? What would anybody want with Adam? She paced up and down the kitchen floor before finally heading over to the phone.

She needed to talk to someone who could calm her down. Someone down to earth. Someone who never let her imagination run away with her.

She quickly dialed Lacy's number.

"Hello?" asked a sleepy voice.

"Lacy!" Gretchen hissed into the phone. "It's Gretchen."

"Gretchen?" Lacy sounded confused. "It's almost midnight. Where are you?"

"I'm at the Wollmans'. Lacy—I'm scared."

"Scared?" Suddenly Lacy's voice was awake and alert. "What's going on? Are you okay?"

"I'm fine. Adam is upstairs asleep. But something really freaky just happened. I heard this noise outside, and then I went to the front door to see what was out there. I found this envelope. It doesn't have an address or anything. The note inside says I have to get out quick because they're going to get Adam—"

"Hold on—Gretchen, slow down. Start from the beginning."

"Some lunatics dropped off a note on the

front doorstep that says they're going to get Adam!"

"Take it easy, Gretchen," Lacy said. Her voice was soothing. "Read me the note."

Gretchen gripped the paper again in her sweaty palm. " 'To Adam's baby-sitter, Go home. Get out while you can. Nothing will stand between Adam and us. Stay and suffer the consequences. The Trail of Blood ends in blood. Adam is ours.' "

There was silence at the other end of the line. "That *is* pretty freaky," Lacy said finally.

"It's written on this really weird paper, too. It's like parchment or vellum or something. And it's written in fancy script—almost like calligraphy."

"Any strange neighbors you noticed while driving in?"

"That's the thing. The Wollmans live on this peninsula. There isn't another house for at least a quarter mile."

"Maybe Adam did it."

Gretchen paused. She hadn't even considered that. He was a little peculiar—but she didn't think he was *bad*.

"No, he couldn't have. He hasn't been out of my sight all night, except when he went to bed. I would have heard him coming down the stairs. I'm gonna call the cops."

"Gretchen, I know you're freaked out, but don't you think that's a little drastic? Okay, so some weirdo is playing a sick practical joke. But believe me, nothing is going to happen. The last thing you want to do is scare the kid to death by having a bunch of cops show up at the house in the middle of the night."

"But what if—"

"Trust me," Lacy interrupted. "Weird stuff shows up on my doorstep all the time." She giggled. "Remember that time I found all those drawings of . . . oh, never mind. Some bored loser knew the Wollmans were going away and decided to scare you. If I were you, I'd just throw it away and forget about it."

"Maybe you're right," Gretchen said doubtfully.

"Gretchen—I know I'm right." Her best friend's voice was firm and confident. "What a way to start off the best three weeks of your life, huh?"

Gretchen sighed and ran a hand through her hair. "You're telling me."

Lacy laughed. "Look, go to bed and get some rest. Don't give it another thought. Call me tomorrow night, okay?"

"Okay. Thanks a lot, Lacy. Sorry to wake you up."

"Hey—that's what friends are for. Whenever you need to know that you're blowing something way out of proportion, give me a call."

"Gee—that's nice, Lace," she said dryly. "I know I can always count on you to say the right thing at the right time."

"Don't mention it." Lacy laughed. "Good night."

*   *   *

Gretchen woke up the next morning at the crack of dawn. She'd managed to sleep, if somewhat fitfully. The sunlight streaming through the windows cast a soft, warm glow across the guest bedroom, and the memory of what had happened last night seemed faint. Lacy was right—it was probably just some weirdo with a sick sense of humor.

After showering and getting dressed, Gretchen headed downstairs to the kitchen.

Today the fun began; she was going to make sure of it.

A few minutes later, Adam stumbled through the door in his pajamas.

"Hey, there!" Gretchen said. "Sleep well?"

Adam slumped into a seat at the kitchen table and yawned. "All right, I guess."

"Want some breakfast? How does scrambled eggs and bacon sound?"

"Okay."

Gretchen went to the refrigerator and took out a carton of eggs. She began cracking them into a bowl on the counter. "I was thinking about going into town today to run some errands." She turned and smiled at Adam. "I figured it would be a good excuse to drive your parents' car. You can be my tour guide."

"If you want," Adam said shortly.

"Any local hot spots I should know about?"

"Nope."

"Any good beaches?"

"There's a beach in our backyard."

"I guess you're right." She turned on the stove and pulled a spatula out of a drawer. So much for small talk. Obviously Adam wasn't in the mood for conversation—*any* conversation. She began slowly stirring the eggs in a frying pan.

"Hey, Gretchen?"

"Yes?"

"Don't worry about that note. Like I said—I can take care of myself."

The spatula slipped from her hands and fell into the eggs. "How—how—what are you talking about?" she sputtered.

"Just don't worry about it, okay?"

She quickly reached over and turned off the stove, then turned to face him. Her mind was racing. How did he know about what had happened last night? Maybe if . . .

Her eyes narrowed. "Adam, are you playing a joke on me? If you are—"

"I'm not playing a joke," he said. His gaze locked onto hers with an odd intensity.

He's not lying, she thought. *Then how . . . unless he listened to my phone conversation—*

"How dare you!" she shrieked.

"No, Gretchen, I didn't listen in on the phone, either."

"Then how did you know I was even going to bring it up?"

Adam shrugged.

"Look, Adam, we need to lay down a few ground rules here. *Don't* listen to my phone conversations, got it?"

Adam was silent. Gretchen walked over to the kitchen table and slid into the chair across from him. "Adam, I don't mean to get angry with you," she said softly. "I'm just a little worried, that's all. For the next three weeks, *I'm* responsible for you. Do you understand that?"

Adam nodded.

"Good. I'll forgive you for listening to my phone call. Just don't let it happen again, okay?"

His face was blank.

"Now do you have any idea who could have left that envelope on the front door step last night?"

Adam hesitated for a second, shifting uncomfortably in his seat. For some reason, his silence made Gretchen nervous. It was the first time she had ever seen him look unsure of himself.

"Adam, is there something you want to tell me?"

He looked her in the eyes. "I don't know who it was exactly," he said. "But I have an idea."

"Who?" She leaned across the table. "Who, Adam?"

"These people . . . they want to use me for something. They know what I can do."

Gretchen felt a slight tingling at the back of her neck. "Adam, what are you talking about?"

"I can't tell you." His voice was suddenly loud.

"Why not?"

"I just can't, okay?" He got up from the kitchen table and headed for the door.

"Adam!" Gretchen shouted. "Where do you think you're going?"

"Upstairs to get dressed," he called, disappearing out the kitchen door into the front hall.

Gretchen leapt up from the table and ran after him, catching his arm just as he was about to head up the spiral staircase. Of all the nerve! She spun him around and held him between both hands. "Adam—"

But then she stopped.

A tear was running down the side of Adam's face.

"I don't want to talk about it anymore," he whispered. "Okay?"

"But—" Gretchen sighed. "It's okay, Adam." She brushed the tear off his cheek. "We don't have to talk about it if you don't want to. It's okay. It's okay."

They spent the rest of the morning in silence.

Finally, at about ten-thirty, Gretchen began to get antsy. The big, stark house was too cold and too empty. She'd been lying on the leather couch in the sitting room for the past hour, staring at the ocean below.

Adam had gone straight to his room after breakfast and shut the door.

What was going on here? This was supposed to be the best job ever. *"The best three weeks of my life,"* she'd told Lacy. The thought made her laugh out loud—a short, harsh laugh that echoed across the bare walls.

Gretchen abruptly sat up straight. Enough was enough. A beautiful, cloudless day stretched out before her. It was time to get going. It was time to have fun.

"Adam," she called loudly.

"Yes?" She could barely hear his voice coming from the other wing.

"You want to go into town with me?"

"Okay."

A few seconds later she heard his feet bounding down the steps of the spiral staircase. She got up and grabbed the keys to the Mercedes off the kitchen counter.

"Let's go!"

The car was in the garage: a beautiful two-seater that was a brilliant, shiny red. The top cover had already been pulled down. It was sleek, low to the ground, almost like a racing car.

"Pretty cool, huh?" Adam said as he hopped into the passenger side.

"You got that right." She slid into the driver's seat and slammed the door, pressing the garage door opener. Sunlight slowly filled the garage. She revved up the engine. "Here we go!"

The convertible sped out the front gates, down the dirt road, and onto the winding two-lane road that led to town.

"It's so nice up here," she said, taking a deep breath of the crisp ocean air. The sun felt warm on her back. The car glided around the curves as if it were floating. "Yee-haw!" Gretchen yelled into the wind.

Beside her Adam giggled, hair flapping in his face.

Now this is more like it.

"Let's go to the mall first," said Adam. "There's some cool stuff there. There's this antique shop with these really cool old books."

"Really cool old *books*?" Gretchen started laughing.

"No, really. They have all these incredible drawings and designs in them."

"Whatever you say." Gretchen grinned. "You must be a genius or something, Adam. I think I was reading Dr. Seuss when I was your age."

Before she knew it, the road had straightened and the forest on either side had thinned out. Houses appeared. Gretchen slowed the car.

"Take a right at the first light," Adam said. "The mall's down that road."

Gretchen rounded the corner and downshifted. Ahead of them she could see a sign: OCEAN VIEW MALL.

Gretchen pulled into the parking lot and eased the car into an open space next to a green Volvo station wagon. The two of them got out and slammed the doors.

"Antique books, huh?" Gretchen said as they walked away from the car.

Suddenly she stopped in her tracks. A bumper sticker on the Volvo caught her eye.

BORN TO SHOP.

Gretchen laughed. *Dana.* What a coincidence!

"What's so funny?" asked Adam.

She shook her head. "This girl I know has the exact same bumper sticker. . . ."

All at once her smile faded. She felt sick to her stomach.

No. It couldn't be.

Dana also had a green Volvo station wagon.

"Gretchen, do you feel okay?" Adam asked, touching her arm.

"I-I'm fine," she said. She grabbed Adam's hand and hurried toward the mall's big glass doors. *It's just a coincidence. There's no way Dana could be here. We're two hours south of San Francisco in a tiny town that nobody's ever heard of. Somebody else just happens to have the same car and the same . . .*

"Gretchen Childs!" shouted a girl's voice from across the parking lot. "It can't be—is that you?"

Gretchen froze. She squeezed her eyelids tightly shut. There was no mistaking that high-pitched, flutey voice. Adam's hand dropped from hers, forgotten.

"It *is* you!"

Her head swam. Fate couldn't be that cruel. It couldn't. Slowly she turned around and opened her eyes.

No!

Her jaw fell open.

Walking toward her across the parking lot was not only Dana, but Todd—and some other boy she didn't know. It was unreal, a vision out of a horrible dream: Dana, in a short flowery skirt, her long black hair hanging in her pale, almost white face; Todd, with his curly brown hair, smiling broadly in a T-shirt and cutoffs; and the other boy, some tanned, good-looking kid with longish blond hair and blue eyes in a bathing suit and sandals. They drew closer and stood around Gretchen and Adam in a semicircle—bright-eyed and smiling, relaxed, eager to talk.

"What are *you* doing here?" Dana asked.

"I . . . I'm baby-sitting," Gretchen answered inanely.

Dana laughed, a rich, musical laugh that instantly set Gretchen's teeth on edge. Something wasn't *right* about Dana. Something was terribly wrong. . . . Gretchen knew it from the moment Dana had stolen Todd from her. Mostly it was the way she had gone out of her way to become friends with Gretchen after. It was baffling—but more than that, it hurt. Dana had always been there, around every corner at school, trying to make small talk, trying to act as if nothing had happened. And Todd, too—Todd had just behaved as if he and Gretchen were great buddies, as if they had never been involved. Well they *had* been involved. Why couldn't they just leave her alone and let her get on with her life. . . .

"Gretchen, this is my friend Zander." Todd's voice snapped her back into reality.

"Oh. Hi."

The boy nodded. At least he seemed uncomfortable, too. He shifted nervously on his feet, his bright blue eyes darting from Dana to Gretchen and back again.

"And who's this handsome little boy?" Dana flashed a wide smile at Adam.

"My name is Adam." He paused, fixing his black eyes intently on each one of them for a few seconds. "And your names are Dana and Todd," he said in a strange voice. "You're staying for a month at a cabin on the beach here in Madison, next to your friend Zander."

"Wow!" Todd said, glancing at Gretchen. "How'd you know that?"

Adam was silent. He fixed his eyes on Dana. Gretchen noticed that his eyebrows rose slightly.

"Maybe he's a psychic or something." Dana laughed again. "What an *interesting* little boy, Gretchen."

Gretchen's mouth opened, but nothing came out. Not only was the whole situation unbearable—it had suddenly become very weird.

"Sorry, guys, I can't really talk right now," Gretchen said quickly, grabbing Adam's hand again and backing away from them. "I just remembered I left my wallet at home." She turned and began running toward the car, pulling Adam along beside her.

"Gretchen, wait!" Todd called. "Don't you want our number? We should all hang out sometime."

"I'll get it later," Gretchen mumbled over her shoulder. "I'm sure I'll see you guys around. It's a small town."

Gretchen flung open the door and fired up the engine, roaring out of the parking lot before Adam even had a chance to shut his door all the way.

In the rearview mirror, she could see Todd, Dana, and Zander staring at her.

Their smiles were gone.

THREE

"So what was that all about? You know, at the mall this morning."

Adam shrugged. "What do you mean?"

"You knew my friends' names. You knew where they were staying, and for how long. *I* didn't even know that."

"Those people aren't your friends," Adam said. He lifted the last of his hamburger off his plate and stuffed it in his mouth, chewing slowly.

Gretchen stood up from the kitchen table. She walked over to the door and looked into the sitting room for a moment, watching as the sky began to cloud over. It would storm tonight, but now the ocean looked as calm as a pond. After she had bolted from the parking lot, she had driven straight back to the house, where they had spent the rest of the day outside on the beach in the backyard. At least she had enjoyed *that* today.

And what fun that had been. Gretchen laughed

34

to herself. She and Adam hadn't said a word to each other. Not on the beach, not while Gretchen had made hamburgers for dinner, not while they had sat across from each other and eaten them.

Now it was almost seven-thirty.

"No, they aren't my friends," Gretchen said. "You're right about that." She began clearing the table in harsh, jerky movements, slamming the silverware into the sink. "But that still doesn't answer my question."

"You went out with Todd for six months, three weeks, and two days. Then he called you up and said he couldn't go out with you anymore. A week later he started going out with Dana. You hate her."

Oh my God.

Adam was staring at her from his chair at the kitchen table, his black eyes bright, his face an expressionless mask. For a moment, time stood still; she was aware only of the two of them in the vast silence, their eyes riveted to each other across empty space. . . .

"How do you know all of this?" she whispered. "How?"

"Dana was right."

"What do you mean?"

"Today. At the parking lot. She said I was psychic." He tore his gaze away from her and looked down at the table. A bitter laugh escaped his lips. "I hate that word. It sounds so bad. I'm not a freak. It's just that . . . I can see things other people can't see."

Gretchen stood motionless by the kitchen sink. She suddenly found it hard to breathe. A dizzying blackness formed at the edge of her vision. "I-I don't believe you," she stammered.

Adam turned to look at her again. "Yes, you do."

She reached out and gripped the countertop, forcing herself to take slow, deep breaths. *Just take it easy. Relax. Somehow he must know Todd or Dana.* "Prove it," she said.

Adam's eyes bored into hers. "Your best friend's name is Lacy Stewart. She lives five blocks away from you. She is two inches shorter than you, has straight brown hair that comes to her chin, and brown eyes. You met her when you were seven. It was on the playground near your school—"

"Stop it!" Gretchen shrieked. She buried her face in her hands. "Stop it, please. Just go away. Go away!"

All at once she felt his hand touch her side. He was standing next to her. She uncovered her face and saw that his eyes were welling with tears.

"Don't be scared, Gretchen," he sobbed. "I don't want to hurt anyone. I swear. But I don't know how to tell anyone the truth without scaring them."

Gretchen gazed at him. Right now, Adam looked like any other ordinary kid whose feelings had been hurt. She was suddenly ashamed.

"I—I'm not scared," she managed finally. "I

just need to think. I'm sorry for screaming, Adam. It's just that I'm—I have a lot on my mind."

He clenched her hand tightly and sniffed. "Gretchen, I think I may be in trouble."

She led him out of the kitchen and sat him down on the big leather couch in the sitting room. "Why don't you tell me what's going on, okay?" she said gently.

Adam stared out into the darkening evening sky. A few raindrops pelted the big glass window. "These people want to get me. Somehow they've figured out what I can do."

Gretchen's skin crawled, but she forced herself to appear calm. "Who? And why?"

"I'm not exactly sure. It's a secret group. They're sorcerers." He closed his eyes tightly as if he were trying to remember. "And . . ."

"Yes?"

He hesitated and turned to face her, looking frightened of what he was about to say. "Dana's with them."

Gretchen swallowed. "How do you know?"

"See, this thing that I have—it only works a little bit sometimes. It's like I look at a person, and I concentrate real hard. Sometimes it works easy, like with you." He gave her a curious half grin. "That's because you're . . ." He seemed unsure of what word he wanted to use. "You're *open*. You know?"

Gretchen didn't know. The thought of being "open" to Adam's omniscient eyes filled her with a sickening numbness.

"When you found that note, all I knew was that people were looking for me," he went on. "I learned that from *you*—by looking into you. I just figured it was because they just wanted to use me for something. But when we were at the mall today, I looked into Dana, and I saw bad things."

"What kinds of things?"

"I'm not sure. It's fuzzy. That's because she's not open. She's hiding stuff. But I know she's with this group. And these people don't just want to use me—they want to hurt me."

"Why, Adam?" Gretchen grabbed both of his hands. "Why?"

His eyes were fearful. "I don't know."

"I'm calling your parents right now." She leapt off the couch. "They need to come home."

Adam shook his head. "You can try, but it's not going to work. I'll bet you anything the numbers they left aren't even real."

"What? That can't be right, Adam."

He clenched his teeth. "My parents just learned the truth about me a few months ago. That's why they planned this vacation without me. They're scared of me. They don't want to think about me for the next three weeks." His voice grew shaky and his eyes clouded with tears again. "They just want to be alone."

"Adam, that's not true." Gretchen sat back on the couch and wrapped her arms around him, letting him cry into her shoulder. She softly patted his black hair. *What a poor, lonely, scared kid*. She thought of her own mom. Her mom would never shut Adam out. She would try to help him—to figure out how to cope with this thing, this gift he had. But the Wollmans were different. They were cold and unfeeling, just like the house they lived in—

Just then the phone rang.

Gretchen flinched, holding her breath. A second harsh ring filled the silence. Her heart pounded furiously. Maybe it was her mom, calling to check up . . .

She dashed for the phone.

"Hello?"

"Gretchen?" asked a boy's voice. "Is that you?"

"Yes. Who's this?"

"Gretchen, it's Todd." His voice was strained; she could scarcely recognize it.

"Todd? What's wrong? How did you get this number? Are you okay?"

"Look, that isn't important. Gretchen, you've got to listen to me. You're in danger. You've got to—"

The line clicked.

"Todd?" Gretchen whispered desperately. "Todd, are you there?"

Then all she heard was the dull buzz of the dial tone.

Her fingers flew over the buttons. She had to get in touch with her mom. Her mom would know what to do.

One ring. Two rings.

Please.

Three rings.

Click.

"Mom!"

"Hi, you've reached the Childs's residence," her own voice said back to her. "We can't come to the phone right now, so please leave a message."

Gretchen waited an eternity for the beep. "Mom, call me right away. It's an emergency. I'm—just call me, okay?"

She slowly placed the receiver back on the hook.

"Adam, everything's going to be okay, right?"

"I can't look into the future," he said quietly. "It doesn't work that way."

"It doesn't?"

"No."

Outside, the skies opened and the rain began to pour.

FOUR

"What do you mean you can't do anything?" Gretchen shouted into the phone over the pounding rain. "A kid's life may be in danger!"

"Look, ma'am, I know you're upset." The scratchy voice at the other end sounded as if it had reached the end of its patience. "But a note on the doorstep and a phone call isn't enough to merit police protection. It may be hard for you to believe, but we have our hands full—even in these parts."

"I'm telling you, something's going to happen. And it may happen tonight."

"And *I'm* telling *you*—nobody, not even a homicidal maniac, is going to go out in this weather tonight. The roads around here are just too dangerous. So sit tight. You said you know the caller, is that correct?"

"Yes—I go to school with him. Why?"

"Any possibility he's pulling a prank on you?"

41

"No! We used to go out, but now he's with his new girlfriend and—" Gretchen realized she was sounding hysterical.

"Calm down, ma'am. It sounds like there's some history here. Look, if you still feel so sure about this note in the morning, come down to the station and fill out a report. But don't try to go out tonight, got it? Now snuggle up and sleep tight. If anything happens, call us. We'll be here."

Gretchen slammed the phone down on the hook. "Idiot," she muttered.

She glanced up at the clock. Twelve-fifteen. Adam had been in bed for two hours; she'd poked her head in an hour ago and he'd been snoring soundly. At least *he'd* sleep tight.

Gretchen sat down at the kitchen table and stared at the phone. Why hadn't her mom called her back yet? She almost never stayed out past midnight. Maybe she'd been been trying to call while Gretchen had been talking to the police. . . .

She walked over to the phone and lifted it from the receiver one more time.

Nothing. Not even a dial tone. Gretchen jabbed at the receiver with her hand, but it was no use.

The line was dead—just like that.

Her hand quivered slightly as she put the receiver down.

I am not *going to panic.*

Had somebody cut the line?

Gretchen's eyes were locked on the phone. Her mind raced, but her thoughts kept coming back to the same undeniable conclusion: she was truly alone—cut off from everyone and everything.

Rain pounded against the house.

In a daze, she wandered into the sitting room and sat on the couch.

"Nobody, not even a homicidal maniac, would go out in this weather tonight." What about lunatics who believed in black magic? *"The Trail of Blood will end in blood."*

A flash of lightning briefly illuminated the swirling ocean below, followed a few seconds later by the low, loud rumble of thunder.

The weather *was* pretty terrible.

Gretchen forced herself to relax. The storm must have knocked out the phone lines; that was all. The cop was right—*nobody* could possibly go out tonight. She would just have to wait until the morning. Then she would go into town and fill out a report at the police station.

No problem.

In the meantime she was on her own until the storm passed.

Fine.

Gretchen got up and walked determinedly across the long, bare wood floor into the living room. There was no reason to panic. Her eyes fell on the wide-screen television sitting in one corner. Perfect. She looked at the clock. Twelve-seventeen. If she were watching television, time would fly by. Before she knew it, the storm would be over and the sun would be coming up. She picked up the remote control and flopped down on a sofa.

". . . severe thunderstorms along the coast," said a weatherman in front of a satellite map. "A flood advisory is in effect for low-lying regions. Several towns report downed phone and power lines—"

Gretchen flipped the channel.

A group of five middle-aged women with heavy makeup were sitting in a circle talking. A 900-number flashed on the bottom of the screen. Their smiling faces looked dreamy and vacant in the cheap, fuzzy light, and their voices were muffled—almost as if they were talking under water.

Gretchen managed a half smile. Even Madison, California, smack in the middle of nowhere, had infomercials. What a relief. More than once she and Lacy had stayed up half the night together in hysterics, watching as some burnt-out, formerly famous actress pleasantly discussed facial cream or cellulite. This would be just the thing. . . .

"So, Janet," said one of the women. "Tell us how your life changed when you first called the Psychic Soul Connection."

"I've never felt better about myself," the woman replied with a yellow grin. "My own personal psychic has guided me to a whole new level of self-awareness. . . ."

Gretchen suddenly found herself unable to listen. The woman's voice melded with the rain, becoming a senseless babble of background noise.

Psychic.

Upstairs, Adam Wollman lay sleeping. Gretchen stared sightlessly at the screen. *Psychic.* What was Adam dreaming? What exactly did Adam know about her—about anyone who got too close to him? Is that why his parents ran away for three weeks—because he had learned all their secrets?

"Margaret, why don't you tell us how the Psychic Soul Connection has changed *your* life?"

The room grew colder. Gretchen shivered. Adam had said Dana was with them—whoever *they* were. "*Sorcerers.*" Had he used that word because he hadn't wanted to use some other word to describe who they really were?

The women on the TV screen went on and on.

Yesterday, Gretchen would have been laughing. Now she felt sick. Psychics were real; she had seen what they could do. Did that mean black magic was real, too? Did Dana know how to use black magic? Suddenly anything seemed possible. Anything—no matter how absurd or twisted or terrible it sounded.

Gretchen leaned back on the sofa. She was exhausted. It had all been too much, too fast.

Her eyes fluttered closed and the sounds of the rain and the wind and the ocean and the women on television washed over her black thoughts.

The water was as calm and smooth as glass. Gretchen stood on the beach, staring out into the distance. She had never seen anything like it. It was so peaceful. The ocean was like a mirror, reflecting the gray of the sky, stretching out infinitely, as far as the eye could see. . . .

The scene shifted and Gretchen was picking her way across some jagged rocks. She could sense something was wrong; the water was no longer still. The waves were rolling, growing more powerful, hissing and rumbling as they crashed against the shore.

Then she saw her. Dana. She was at the top of the rocks, beckoning with a wide smile on her face. But her eyes were like two dead black stones, like eyes she had seen before somewhere—the eyes of a small boy.

All of a sudden Gretchen lost her footing. The rocks were too slick and too steep and the water was raging all around her. She was slipping, sliding closer and closer to the terrible, frothing foam.

"Dana!" she screamed. "Help! I'll drown!"

But all she heard was Dana's singsong laugh coming from the top of the rocks.

The waves closed around her. The noise was fierce, relentless, a deafening sound that threatened to engulf her completely—

Gretchen bolted upright, gasping for breath. The television set was flickering and raw static was blaring from its speakers. She grabbed the remote control and pressed furiously on the power switch until the television winked off.

Silence and darkness filled the room.

Her breathing was labored, her body drenched

46

in sweat. She leaned back and tried to calm herself. How long had she been asleep? It was only drizzling now; the furious stream of water against the windows had dwindled to a steady, quiet drip. She must have dozed for at least a couple of hours.

Adam! I've been asleep—somebody could have gotten in here. . . .

Instantly she was wide awake. She sprinted into the foyer and stumbled up the spiral staircase, her feet pounding on the wood.

At the end of the long hallway, Adam's door was open. Hadn't she closed it? She couldn't remember—

Please let him be all right . . .

There he lay, his eyes closed, his face at peace.

Gretchen closed the door softly and let out a deep, shuddering breath.

Adam was fine. They would survive the night. Her nightmare was over; the storm had subsided. Todd's warning seemed far away. Soon the sun would rise and she could drive into town.

She padded back down the stairs and glanced at the clock as she headed through the kitchen. Five-fifteen. She tried the phone again; it was still dead. But at least the night sky outside the sitting room had taken on a faint, bluish tint.

All she needed was to relax and collect her thoughts.

Suddenly she had an idea. The Jacuzzi! A clear mental image formed in her head as she pictured herself soaking in hot bubbles, looking out on the ocean while the sun came up.

She smiled. After her bath she would hop in the convertible, and go tell off that idiot hick cop at the police station.

Gretchen slid open one of the glass doors leading out onto the patio. The air was damp and chilly and the breeze ruffled her curls. She wrapped her arms around herself; she was wearing only a T-shirt and shorts, and her feet were bare. The atmosphere had a washed-out, pure feel.

The Jacuzzi sat at the edge of the big white flagstones, covered by a black canopy. Gretchen hadn't even tried it yet. She squinted at it. For some reason it didn't look right. She drew closer. Was there a lump under the cover? It was hard to see in the dark. . . .

Gretchen leaned over and examined the cover closely. There *was* some sort of lump under there, poking up on one side. She hadn't noticed it before. Maybe something had happened to the tub during the storm. Could a branch somehow have got caught under there?

Oh, well. There was only one way to find out. Gretchen gripped the cover with both hands and yanked it away from the tub.

There was something in the water— something bulky and oddly shaped. At first it didn't register. *What on earth—*

Then Gretchen screamed.

The shrill sound pierced the morning, echoing long and loud against the cold walls of the house, sailing out beyond the peninsula and over the ocean.

Todd!

Todd was dead.

His body lay in the Wollmans' Jacuzzi. His head was sticking just above the surface, his eyes open, his glassy pupils fixed on the brightening morning sky. Wet curls were plastered to his head. His hands floated in front of him, drifting, as if they belonged to someone else.

The rest of his body was submerged in the dark water—water that had been darkened by his blood.

Gretchen stumbled backward and tripped over the canopy she had dropped at her feet. Her body smacked against the flagstones. A whimper of fear and pain escaped her lips. But she kept moving, groping across the patio, kicking, struggling desperately to get away from the tub. Her limbs felt heavy; their weight slowed her down, no matter how hard she tried to move.

Just then she heard the faint wail of a siren.

The police! Gretchen pulled herself to her feet and ran back into the house, dashing through the sitting room and into the kitchen. *Todd . . .*

The chandelier in the front hall blinked on and Gretchen heard sneakers on the spiral steps.

"Adam!"

He appeared in the kitchen door, his eyes wide with mute terror. She scooped him up in her arms.

"Adam," she whispered, stroking his hair. "Adam, something terrible has happened . . ."

"Gretchen, we've got to get out of here!" He

49

wiggled out of her grasp and slipped to the floor, grabbing her hand. "You don't get it!" he cried. "This is a setup. They're gonna get you for killing Todd!"

The sirens outside grew louder.

"Wh-what . . . I don't—"

He tugged urgently at her arm. "We don't have any time, Gretchen. We've got to get out of here. Now!"

Gretchen hesitated for a moment. Todd was dead. It was clearly no longer of any importance to stop and think. The opportunity to debate her own actions ended as the police cars skidded to a halt in the gravel out front.

"Come out of the house now!" boomed a gruff male voice out of a loudspeaker.

But by that time, Gretchen and Adam were already halfway down the wooden steps to the beach.

PART II

The fire from the night's ritual had dwindled to a few smoking embers. But the circle around it remained closed, arms intertwined, the energy of seventeen believers focused inward. Even in the torrents of rain, they had kept the fire alive.

"We have offered our first sacrifice," called the High Priest. "Do the spirits accept?"

"The spirits accept," chanted the congregation.

Dawn was breaking in the east. The High Priest's eyes shifted to the small earthen temple at the edge of the clearing. "Bring forth the one who betrayed us."

The masked figures stepped out of the temple, holding the girl between them. Her face was white with fear. She was swathed in a robe of black, her mouth gagged by a tight red rope.

"Tonight we shall offer our second sacrifice."

A soft beating of drums began inside the temple.

"Our altar is stained with the blood of the first," the High Priest cried, his voice trembling. He pointed a long, sinewy finger in the girl's direction. "You thought you could stop this, you foolish child? It has been written! The Trail of Blood will end in blood! And tonight the altar shall be stained with yours—"

"*No!*"

The cry had erupted from behind the temple. It was the Soothsayer's voice.

"The child has escaped!" she shrieked, her disembodied voice permeating every corner of the clearing. "*That* has not been written. He has escaped!"

FIVE

"This way," Adam shouted, pointing toward the woods. "Through there. Hurry!"

Gretchen stumbled hopelessly across the sand. "I'm trying," she panted.

An impenetrable wall of foliage ran along the deserted beach—but Gretchen could see a small opening ahead.

"The path will take us into the forest," Adam called. "Move!"

The early morning sun was now quite bright. Gretchen guessed they had been running on the shoreline for about an hour. But there was no way of telling—she had no watch, and every step she took across the unforgiving sand seemed to take an eternity. Her legs felt as if they were made of lead.

"I need to rest for just two seconds," she gasped when they reached the path.

Adam's eyes darted nervously across the

beach. "I don't think that's a good idea," he said quickly, grabbing her hand. "They know we headed away from town. They'll get here soon. Once we're in the woods, I know how we can lose them."

Gretchen nodded. She didn't trust herself to speak.

"Come on," he urged, tugging her arm.

Once again she took up the flight.

The solid, packed dirt was a relief under her bare feet. They flew into the woods. Whipping branches stung her face and arms. Soon the roar of the ocean faded into silence. The forest grew darker as treetops closed overhead; the path steepened, and the air became dank and moist.

"This path will take us into the mountains." Adam said. The incline had slowed them to a brisk walk. "When we get high enough, we need to cut into the forest. They'll never find us there."

"Are you sure you know where this path goes?"

Adam turned his eyes to her. "I'm sure."

Gretchen knew better than to question those eyes.

By now the path had grown less clearly defined. Thick roots crisscrossed it every few feet, making it look as if it were some grotesque, heavily veined limb twisting through the forest. In a few places, the brush was so dense that the leaves and branches closed across the path, forcing the two of them to hack their way forward with their arms.

Adam paused for a moment in front of her, his eyes scanning the ground. He bent over and picked up a large, heavy stick. "Here," he said, handing it to her. "You're bigger than me. You go first and clear the path."

Gretchen hesitated. "But I don't know where I'm going. What if we get lost?"

"We won't. I'm right behind you." His arched eyebrows were grimly set. He jerked his head forward. "Go on."

It seemed suddenly that Adam was much older than his years—much older than she. He was a bitter old man, and she was a frightened little child.

I have no choice. My life is in his hands.

The realization struck her like a slap—but she couldn't deny its truth.

"Go on," he repeated.

She grabbed the stick and strode past him into the wilderness.

After hiking continuously for what Gretchen judged to be at least two hours, Adam let them rest.

They collapsed at the base of an enormous redwood. Gretchen knew they were deep in the mountains. The smaller vegetation had thinned, then disappeared completely where the redwoods had started. They had long since left the path. Here the forest had an eerie, dreamlike quality: all she could see were huge tree trunks separated by wide expanses of rich, brown soil.

The trunks soared high into the sky, obscuring the sun at great heights, drenching the forest floor in a shadowy half-light.

The only sound was the rapid beating of her own heart.

"Adam," she whispered. "I'm scared."

"Me, too," he said quietly.

"You know what? They're gonna think I kidnapped you."

"I know."

"They're gonna think I murdered Todd—and that I kidnapped you so I would have something to bargain with in case they found me." She swallowed and dug her toes into the earth. "I'm wanted for murder and kidnapping."

"I know," Adam said softly. "I know."

"What are we going to do?"

"We just have to stay calm. We'll figure a way out of this."

Gretchen's jaw tightened. "Dana," she breathed. "Dana did this to me. If we can find her, we'll get the truth."

"Maybe," Adam said. "But Dana's only a small part of it. I don't think this has as much to do with you as it does with me."

"What do you mean?" Gretchen cried. She leaned back against the tree and threw her hands up. "Dana wanted to destroy my life. First she stole my boyfriend. Then she must have gotten tired of him—so she followed me here, killed him, and pinned it on me. She's sick—sicker than anyone could possibly imagine."

"She may be sick, but remember, Gretchen, she's not alone. She's with these people. They're using her to get to me. They wanted to scare you away. They tried with the note, but that didn't work. So they decided to take you out of the picture for good by killing your ex-boyfriend and making it look like you did it."

Gretchen swallowed. How could a seven-year-old boy be saying these things?

"That's crazy, Adam," she said finally. "None of this makes any sense." She held her breath for a second. "I think we should go back to town," she said quickly. She sat up straight and stared into the woods. "I didn't kill Todd—and you can vouch for me. You can be my witness." Her voice rose in pitch. "We can explain everything! We can find Dana . . . it wasn't smart to run. We need to go to the police right now."

Adam didn't respond.

"Adam?" Gretchen turned and looked in his direction.

He was sprawled on the ground and his body was twitching. His eyes were wide open, staring upward, but they had become glossy, dilated.

"Adam! What's wrong?" She rushed over to him and grabbed his arms. He was shaking violently now; his head lolled to one side and his mouth opened and closed spasmodically.

"Answer me!" she shrieked, gripping him tightly. "Answer me, Adam, please."

"Trouble," he mumbled. His voice was toneless, as if he were talking in his sleep.

"What? Wake up, Adam," Gretchen pleaded. "Please wake up."

"Trouble," he repeated dully, his arms writhing in her grasp. "Lacy . . . there's trouble."

"Adam!"

All at once he stopped moving. He blinked a couple of times, then shook his head, his eyebrows knitted in confusion.

"What's going on?" he said, looking up at Gretchen. His face became alarmed. "Stop it. You're hurting me."

Gretchen realized her fingernails were digging into his arms. She let go of him. "Are you okay?"

"I think so," he said uncertainly, sitting up straight. "What happened?"

"You had some kind of seizure or something. Adam—I'm worried. Are you sure you're okay?"

Adam nodded, but his expression seemed far away. "Was I shaking and stuff like that?"

"Yeah, you were. Has this happened before?"

A look of understanding crossed his face. "I black out sometimes. My parents told me about it a while ago. The doctor said it's nothing to worry about."

Gretchen couldn't believe what she was hearing. "How can you say that?"

Adam shrugged. "I feel okay now. It lasted only a few seconds, right?" He paused. "I'm fine."

"But you said something! Do you remember what it was?"

His face was blank.

"You said something about trouble," Gretchen prodded. "You mentioned Lacy's name—"

"I don't remember."

She squeezed his arm again and forced herself to look directly into his eyes. "Think, Adam. Please think hard." Her voice was shaking. "I have to know."

"I-I can't." His fingers kneaded the soil beneath his hands. "Gretchen—it's no use. I won't be able to remember. I never can remember what I say during my blackouts."

"But . . . you said . . ."

He looked at the ground. "I'm sorry."

Gretchen leapt to her feet and began pacing frantically. The soil cut at her aching feet. "Your parents. When this happened before, did they mention if you said anything?"

"No. They didn't want to talk about it. It scared them more than it scared me."

I'll bet it did.

Adam began dusting himself off. "Gretchen, you can't let it get to you. It doesn't matter what I said. There's nothing we can do about it."

"But you said my best friend was in danger! Of course it matters. I have to do something. I have to get in touch. . . ."

Suddenly she realized Adam was staring at her.

"You're *not* going to try to find a phone," he stated.

"I have to, Adam," she whispered. "You can't stop me."

"No, I can't. But the police can. They're gonna be all over the place, looking for you. So are *they*."

"I hope the police find me!" she screamed. "I didn't do anything! If I stay here, *they're* going to get Lacy, and she's going to wind up like Todd. And it's going to be my fault."

"Take it easy, Gretchen." Adam's voice was calm and even. "We don't know anything is going to happen to Lacy. But they're going to get you if you do anything stupid. And if the police get you, I'm done for. There's gonna be nobody around to protect me. By the time they find out the truth about Todd, I'll be dead."

Hot tears formed at the corners of Gretchen's eyes. She fought them back. *I'm not going to cry*, she swore to herself, brushing a hand roughly across her face. "Adam, I'm going to ask you to do a favor for me, okay?" She knelt in front of him. "I want you to stay here. I'm going to go find a phone somewhere—"

"Gretchen! You can't—"

She put her hand gently over his mouth. "Let me finish. I'm going to find a phone somewhere. I'm going to mark my path with Xs in the dirt every few feet so I can find my way back. If I don't find a phone within a couple of hours, I'll turn around."

Adam raised his eyebrows. She took her hand away from his face.

"I don't think it's any later than eleven right now," she went on. "But if I'm not back when it starts to get dark, you leave. Follow the sun west.

That'll take you back to the ocean, and you can find your way to town from there and get the police. Got it?"

"Please, Gretchen," he begged. "Don't do it."

Gretchen stood and picked up the stick Adam had handed to her on the path. "You told me last night that you couldn't look into the future. Is that true?"

"Yes."

"So you don't know if anything's going to happen to me, right?"

Adam's eyes shifted.

"I'll be back as soon as I can." She bent down quickly and hugged him for a second, planting a light kiss on his cheek. "You know what to do if I'm not."

The forest was endless.

On and on it went, down into valleys, up hills, and back down again, always the same—the immense, reddish-brown trunks and black earth stretching infinitely in every direction.

Gretchen diligently marked an X in the ground with her stick every twenty paces. At first the swiftness of her movement, coupled with the intense concentration of her counting, had kept her occupied.

But now she could feel the faint tinglings of panic creeping up her spine—like a slow-rising tide on an empty shore.

How long had she been gone?

Maybe it hadn't been such a good idea to leave Adam behind. If the police had dogs, they could have trailed the two of them through the woods. They would have found Adam by now. She couldn't let herself think about that . . .

The image of Adam squirming on the ground in his strange trance suddenly flashed through her mind. She bent over and savagely cut an X into the dirt, forcing herself to remain focused. Was Lacy already dead? Todd had called; six hours later his body was stuffed in the Wollmans' Jacuzzi. Was Adam's blackout a warning—or just a fuzzy indication that something terrible had already happened to Lacy?

Somehow she had to figure out who *they* were. Adam didn't know himself—or perhaps he did, and just didn't want to let Gretchen know. Did the Wollmans know? It wouldn't be a surprise if they did. They had certainly left a lot of other important things concerning their son unspoken.

Gretchen's pace slowed and her heart fluttered erratically in her chest. Her feet were torn and bloody; her T-shirt was damp with sweat. Each breath became an effort. Hunger and exhaustion settled over her like a thick blanket of fog, blotting out her surroundings. Random images appeared in her mind's eye: the hamburger she had eaten the night before, her bed at home, Todd's face—

Stop it!

She realized suddenly that she had forgotten to count her steps.

In a frenzy she turned and ran, scanning the ground for the last X. Ten, twenty, thirty paces; there was only the same barren soil. *Oh, no . . .*

There! She spotted it out of the corner of her eye, far to her left. But it didn't seem to be in the right spot. She knew she was completely disoriented. She walked over to the X and stood next to it, her head whipping around in agitation. Should she try to find the one before? Maybe she'd better head back. . . .

Her stomach growled and twisted painfully. She had to get back to Adam—then the two of them could scout for food. He was probably starving by now. She would turn around. But first she had to rest, just for a second . . .

Her body slumped to the ground. It was as if someone had cut a puppet's strings. The cool earth felt good against her hot, aching limbs, and she lay motionless, unable to think.

Her eyes closed. Emptiness enveloped her. She knew she had to concentrate on something, but now she couldn't remember what it was. Time flowed past. She struggled to stay awake, but it was of no use.

As she faded, she became aware of a sound.

It was a low kind of buzzing—almost like the wind, but higher in pitch. The sound grew higher and louder until it reached a whining peak, then lowered and abruptly vanished. It was almost like a car rushing past. . . .

A car! Gretchen jerked awake with a start, blinking her eyes. Had she really heard it? The noise had been off to her right, in the direction of a fairly steep incline. She pulled herself to her feet and ran.

Her bloody, filthy toes dug into the ground as she scrambled up the slope. She leaned forward and used her hands to pull her along. The sun grew brighter as she neared the top. Her heart soared. That could mean only one thing.

Please, please, please . . .

When she staggered over the crest of the hill, the most welcome sight she had ever seen greeted her eyes: the sparkling asphalt of a two-lane highway.

Gretchen felt tears on her cheeks as she slid down the steep embankment to the road. She'd made it. Where there were roads, there were people. She would flag someone down—someone who could take her to a phone. She could save Lacy *and* Adam.

She plopped down on the side of the road and waited.

A car would be coming any minute.

Then a thought prickled in the back of her mind.

I'm a fugitive.

She had fled a murder scene; most likely, she was wanted for homicide and kidnapping. In a tiny town like Madison, it was a pretty safe bet that very few people fit that description.

Almost no one.

Adam's words echoed in her ears: ". . . *if the police find you, I'm done for.*"

66

And in a tiny town like Madison, a murder and a kidnapping would be big news. Her description—maybe even her photograph—had probably been broadcast all over the region. "Gretchen Childs: Fugitive." An hysterical laugh escaped her lips. Maybe she had already made it to *America's Most Wanted*.

Suddenly she was no longer eager for a car to appear. Suddenly she was very scared.

A low rumble sounded in the distance.

Panic seized her. Instantly she was on her feet, clawing desperately at the embankment. The noise grew louder every second—but she couldn't get a firm enough grip to hoist herself over the top. Clumps of dirt came off in her hands as she tore at the wall of eroding soil.

She froze and clamped her eyes shut. The roar of the engine filled her ears as the car sped past her.

It was followed by the screech of brakes.

They're dead. That's it. Adam, Lacy—dead.

Gretchen turned and faced the car.

It was a blue sedan—an old four-door that looked at least fifteen years old. The door on the driver's side flew open.

A boy got out. He was tall and blond; Gretchen knew she had seen him before. Then she screamed. It was Zander—the boy who had been with Dana and Todd at the parking lot! And if he had been with Dana, maybe he was with the people who had killed Todd—

"Gretchen!" he yelled, beckoning to her. "Get in! I know you didn't do it. Come on!"

She was unable to move.

"You've got to trust me," he begged. "You may be dead if you don't. Get in."

Six

Gretchen stood staring at Zander with disbelieving eyes. "What are you going to do to me?" she asked.

"*Do* to you?" Zander looked confused. "I'm trying to help you! Do you realize how lucky it is *I* found you? Now come on!"

Gretchen's eyes quickly roved the highway in either direction. She had no alternative but to go with him. Escape was impossible. But her feet remained motionless.

"I-I . . ." she stuttered.

Zander immediately rushed to her side and put his arm around her. She glanced at him out of the corner of her eye as he hustled her across the highway. His face was etched with fright. He looked haggard; his blue eyes were bloodshot and framed by dark circles.

"What's going on?" she whispered.

"I'm not really sure." His voice quivered as he

flung the car door open and shoved her in the passenger side. Then he ran around the front of the car and hopped in, slamming the door shut and firing up the engine. Tires squealed as the car bounced forward.

"Wait!" Gretchen cried. "I have to mark this spot. I can't lose Adam."

Zander slammed on the brakes and looked anxiously behind him. "There are tire marks on the road where I stopped," he said in a rush of words. "We'll be able to find it again. But we should be moving. We'll draw attention to ourselves if we're stopped on a highway."

Gretchen gazed at Zander as the car sped away. His eyes were riveted to the road in front of him. He seemed absolutely petrified.

"I have to get to a phone," she said. "Then I have to come back here and get Adam."

"Is Adam the kid you're baby-sitting?"

"Yes."

"Does he know you're in trouble?"

"What? . . . Of course. He's—" She stopped herself. Something didn't seem right. Why was Zander so frightened? "Why don't you tell me what you know," she said carefully.

He breathed deeply, then let out a long, trembling sigh. "Dana disappeared. She killed Todd. I heard the two of them screaming at each other last night through my window."

"Did you see her do it?"

"No. But I heard them yelling. She was telling him to get out, and he was telling her that she was crazy. They mentioned your name a lot. I couldn't hear everything because of the rain. But then he stopped yelling and the house went dark." He choked on the last words. "A couple of minutes later I heard doors slamming and a car driving away." He opened his mouth as if he were about to say something else, then closed it.

"What? What is it?"

Zander shook his head. "The police are looking all over for you," he said.

"I figured as much."

"But Dana's also a suspect. They're looking for her, too. That's why I came looking for you."

Gretchen was bewildered. "*You* came looking for *me*?"

"Yeah. I figured if I found you before the police did, I could hide you until the police got Dana. But then the more I thought about it, the more I realized that if Dana disappeared, she was probably going after you to kill you, too. So then I figured I had to protect you from her." He laughed bitterly. "It all sounds pretty crazy, doesn't it?"

"No." She felt strangely relieved. It *would* have sounded completely crazy—to anyone but her. "It doesn't sound crazy at all."

Zander ran a hand through his sweaty hair. "I can't believe Dana's a psycho. I mean, I always knew she was weird, but—"

"How did you know to come looking for me out *here*?"

He shrugged. "The news said the cops lost

you at that nature trail on the beach. I figured you headed up to the redwoods. This is the only highway that cuts through the middle of the forest. I was taking a wild guess—and I lucked out."

"The police are going to think the same thing you did."

Zander's eyes darted to the rearview mirror. "Yeah. I've thought of that."

Gretchen's mind whirled. Zander didn't know much. She was no closer to finding out what was *really* going on. Dana had murdered Todd; that was the only certainty. Was Dana on her way to kill Lacy right now?

"We have to get to a phone," she said.

"I know, I know. There's a town about ten miles from here." His voice rose slightly. "It's pretty risky. Do you have to make the call?"

Gretchen stared out the window at the trees rushing past. "Yes. Yes, I do."

Zander said nothing. They drove in silence for a few minutes.

"Did Dana ever mention Adam to you?" Gretchen suddenly asked. "You know, the kid I'm baby-sitting?"

"Not that I can remember. Why?"

"Did you ever notice her hanging out with any weird people?"

"No." His eyes narrowed. "But Todd told me a couple of days ago that he had just found out that Dana was involved in something bad. Really bad. I didn't think anything of it at the time because—well, because Dana's sort of weird, and it wasn't that big a surprise. But he was really upset about it. I guess she had been keeping it a secret from him, and he found out about it by finding some strange stuff under her bed."

"What was it?" Gretchen turned and looked at him. "Did he tell you?"

"He said he found a book that looked really old. It was handwritten in a foreign language. And a white dress with all these weird symbols."

"Anything else?"

"He said that he thought she had become mixed up in some kind of cult or something." Zander nodded in a preoccupied way. "He was really freaked out about it." He paused. "Oh my God, Gretchen—do you think they brainwashed her or something? I thought she killed Todd because she was jealous of you. Maybe *they* made her kill Todd because he discovered she was a member. . . ."

"Anything's possible," she whispered. A painful lump had formed in her throat. She was unable to say any more.

Todd must have known they were going to kidnap Adam. He tried to warn me, and that cost him his life.

A sign appeared in the distance on the right side of the highway: SCENIC REST AREA ONE MILE.

"I'll bet there's a phone there," Zander said. "It'll be safer than going into town."

Gretchen nodded. In the distance the

73

highway curved off to the left. She strained her eyes. There seemed to be something jutting out into the road—a car of some sort, and a flashing light—

"Gretchen, get down!"

Without hesitation she dove into the back of the car. She curled up into a ball, wedging herself between the backseat and the back of the passenger seat. There was a dirty beach towel on the floor next to her. She grabbed it and draped it over herself, suffocating in the stench of old sand and filth.

"Just take it easy," he said. His voice sounded muffled through the towel. She could feel the car slowing down. "There are three cop cars. I'm just going to cruise right by."

"No!" Gretchen cried. "I need to make this call. You make it for me. Call my friend Lacy." She rattled off the number.

"Are you insane? What if they see you?"

"They won't. Just pull in and act natural." She said the ten digits again. "Say it back to me."

"Gretchen, this is so stupid—"

"I don't care!" she shouted. "I have to know if she's okay. Say it back to me!"

Zander reluctantly repeated the number. "Now be quiet," he said. "Don't make a sound and don't move a muscle."

Gretchen felt the car turn off the road and roll to a stop. She heard the harsh crackle of a police radio. Her heart galloped in her chest. Zander slammed the door.

"Howdy." His voice was far away. "What's going on?"

"We've got two fugitives in the area," said a man's voice. "Haven't you heard? It's already big news."

"No, I can't say that I have," Zander replied. Gretchen was amazed at how relaxed he sounded. "I've been driving around all day."

"You notice anything peculiar while you were driving?" asked another voice.

"What do you mean?" asked Zander.

"You didn't see any girls about your age on the side of the road or anything, did you, son?" asked the first voice.

Gretchen bit her lip.

"Naw—I would remember that."

Several men laughed.

"You live around here?" asked the second voice.

"Yeah, in Madison."

"Do the names Dana Hess, Gretchen Childs, Todd Wilde, or Adam Wollman mean anything to you?"

"Nope. Are they from Madison?"

"The girls are from San Francisco," said the first voice.

"Leave it to city girls to come down here and cause trouble," said the second voice.

"Sorry I can't be of more help," said Zander.

"That's okay, son. You let us know if you see anything you think we should know about."

"Sure."

In the darkness under the towel, Gretchen heard the sound of fading footsteps. Voices barked out of the radio.

"You think we're gonna find them today?" said the first voice.

"The Childs girl was headed east into the forest," said the second voice. "She's gonna hit this road eventually."

Gretchen struggled to keep her body from shaking, but it was no use. The policemen were talking about *her*. Until now, she had understood the danger, but it had seemed remote, intangible. That was no longer true. She was cowering inches away from a lifetime in jail. The fetid towel smothered her; she was suddenly overcome with panic. *Escape*, she thought frantically. *I have to get out of here. . . .*

"Say, do you officers know how I can get to Roseberg?" Zander's cheerful voice burst through the silence. "I think I got mixed up somewhere."

One of the cops laughed. "You beach bums from Madison must not make it up into the mountains very much. Roseberg's back that way—the way you came. You passed it about twenty miles ago."

"Oops. Oh well. Thanks a lot."

The car door opened.

"No problem." The officer's voice sounded much closer—footsteps away.

Zander slid into the driver's seat and slammed the door. The engine sputtered to a start. Gretchen felt herself being pushed against

76

the backseat as the car rolled onto the highway and picked up speed.

"Stay down there," Zander said. "I've had enough risks for one day."

"You handled yourself pretty well," Gretchen whispered.

"Really? I was scared out of my mind. I guess I'm a natural con man."

"What about Lacy?"

"Your friend wasn't home. I left a message telling her you were okay."

"Not home!" Gretchen gasped. "Oh, no . . ."

"What's the matter? Why is it so important?"

"It's a long story. I guess I should tell you. At least what I know of it."

"That would help."

"Wait—are you really lost? Why did you ask those cops for directions to Roseberg?"

"So that they wouldn't be suspicious that I was making a sudden U-turn. We've gotta go back and get the kid, right?"

Adam! He was still out there alone in the middle of the woods—scared, hungry, exhausted, desperately waiting for her to return. Unless someone had gotten to him first. . . .

"I should have never left him alone," she said out loud.

"Why did you take him with you in the first place? It just makes you look more guilty."

"See, that's the thing. Adam's involved in this, too. In a way, he's at the center of everything."

"What do you mean? How?"

Gretchen started to speak, but she couldn't find the words. How should she begin? Should she tell him *everything*? Would he believe her? But even as these questions raced through her mind, she knew she had to convince him of the truth. He didn't even know her—yet he had just risked his life for her. She *had* to trust him; she had nobody else.

"Zander, do you believe in things you can't see?"

"What are you talking about?"

"Just answer me. Ghosts, magic, psychic powers—do you believe in that stuff?"

"Uh—not really, no. But what does that have to do—"

"I didn't believe in that stuff, either," she interrupted. "Until I met Adam Wollman."

"Gretchen, you're freaking me out." His voice was shaky. "You're not making any sense."

"Listen. Adam is a psychic. He proved it to me. It would take too long to explain to you now, but you just have to trust me. Yesterday in the parking lot—remember? He knew all that stuff about Todd and Dana. He can learn everything about a person just by *looking* at him."

"I remember." Zander's voice was quiet. "But I thought it was just a coincidence."

"It wasn't. And last night, Adam told me that Dana is with this group of sorcerers who want to kidnap him—the people Todd must have been talking about. He got that just from looking at Dana at the parking lot."

"That can't be right. There has to be some sort of logical explanation."

"I swear to you it's the truth."

"Sorcerers?"

"That's the word he used," she groaned. Her back was beginning to ache from being curled up between the seats. "Two nights ago—the first night I was there—they left a note on the front door step. It said something about a 'Trail of Blood' and how nothing was going to stop them from getting Adam."

"Jeez, Gretchen! Why didn't you call the cops?"

"I did. Todd called me last night, just as the storm was starting." Her voice cracked. "He told me I was in danger, but the cops told me it was probably just a prank." She burst into tears. "It's their fault." Her body shook uncontrollably and she buried her eyes in the towel, racked by convulsive sobs. "It's their fault Todd's dead. . . ."

"No, it's not, Gretchen." Zander's voice was hard. "It's Dana's fault. And she'll pay for what she's done. Believe me."

Gretchen wept.

"What does your friend Lacy have to do with all this?"

"Adam went into some kind of trance when we were running through the woods." She sniffed. "He said that Lacy was in trouble. But when he woke up, he couldn't remember."

Zander didn't respond. "This is bad," he said finally. "It's unreal. I can't even . . ."

Gretchen felt the car slowing down. Her heart began pounding in alarm. "Zander—what's wrong?"

"Nothing. We just passed the skid marks. I'm going to try and find a place where I can hide the car off the road. Then we can go get Adam."

A few seconds later the car swerved sharply to the left, hurling Gretchen against the door. She felt a jolt as it rolled over a short mound. All of a sudden her head slammed against the seat in front of her and the car began bouncing violently.

"Zander!" she screamed. She could feel in the pit of her stomach that they were careening down a steep hill. "Stop!"

The car jolted to a halt.

"You all right?" asked Zander.

"I think so."

"Sorry. I didn't mean to scare you. I didn't think it was going to drop off like that."

Zander opened the door and came around to Gretchen's side of the car, throwing the towel aside and helping her to her feet. She blinked at the forest around her. The car had stopped perilously close to the trunk of a redwood. She glanced back up toward the highway. Two black tire tracks cut across the brown soil to where the car was resting. The hill was even steeper than she had imagined.

"Oh, no," she gasped. "Do you think we'll be able to get the car out?"

Zander shrugged. "We'll worry about that later. Let's find the kid first."

"He's on the other side of the road. It's about a two-hour hike."

He stared at her as if she had lost her mind. "Two-hour hike? Are you serious?"

Gretchen nodded.

"We'll never find him!"

"I marked the path. Let's go." She looked at the sky. Had the sun already begun its descent? The shadows of the trees were slanted across the forest floor. "We have to hurry. I told him to leave if I wasn't back within four hours."

"How long ago was that?"

"I have no way of telling. I don't have a watch. Do you?"

Zander shook his head. He turned and looked at his battered car. The left side was badly dented. "Man," he muttered. "We'll never get out of here."

Gretchen stared into the afternoon sky. With all her might she fought back the hunger, the exhaustion, the panic that hung like a spectre over her shoulder. "Like you said, we'll worry about it later. That doesn't matter now. We just have to get to Adam in time. If we don't, he'll die. That much I'm sure of."

SEVEN

They flew through the redwoods.

It had taken them several minutes to find the final X Gretchen had left on the other side of the road. But once they had found it, the string of Xs was easy to follow—a straight line of evenly spaced markers that sliced across the forest floor.

"We're moving much faster than I did on my way out," Gretchen shouted breathlessly over her shoulder. "It shouldn't take us that long."

The sun was on its way down. The air seemed to have a slightly reddish tint. Bright shafts of light struck Gretchen's eyes in the few places where direct sun penetrated the treetops.

Had she been gone more than four hours?

Gretchen forced herself to breathe evenly as her torn, burning feet glided over the earth. The pain was starting to become unbearable; she was aware that she must have been losing quite a bit of blood. Her head felt light and spacey. At least the ache in her stomach had vanished—but that was probably because if it hadn't, hunger would have overwhelmed her completely.

The line of Xs stretched on into the distance.

And then, without warning, it ended.

Gretchen stopped in her tracks and stared at the ground. *This can't be right . . .*

"Is this the place?" Zander panted, walking up beside her.

"No—we must have—I don't . . ."

"Did you make any turns?"

"No, but . . ." Gretchen's head whirled one way, then another. She could see the last *X* she had left; she could even see the *X* beyond that. The line they formed pointed directly to a tree a few feet in front of her. The soil at the base of the tree trunk was dark in some spots, as if something had been rolling and tearing at the ground. . . .

"There must be some mistake," Gretchen whispered. All at once her legs felt as if they had been turned to jelly. She pitched forward.

"Gretchen!" Zander cried, grabbing her by the shoulders. He led her over to the base of the tree and gently sat her down. "Take it easy. Just sit down for a second." He let her head rest against his arm.

She opened her mouth, but all that came out was a wheezy hiss. For the first time she realized how dry and cracked her lips and tongue were. It was as if every drop of moisture had been wrung from her body. Her head swam.

"Water," she croaked.

Zander's forehead was heavily creased, his eyebrows slanted downward. "You don't look so good." His eyes flickered over her face. "We can't keep on like this. You'll kill yourself. We have to get out of these woods and get you some food and water."

"Adam," she gasped.

Zander shook his head. He ran a hand gently through her hair. "He's gone, Gretchen. He left. There's nothing more we can do for him now."

Gretchen reached behind her and grabbed onto the trunk of the redwood. With every ounce of strength left in her body she pulled herself to her feet.

"What do you think you're doing?" Zander demanded.

"I'll be okay." The words sounded as feathery and insubstantial as the wind. Her throat worked convulsively as she tried to swallow. "I'm fine."

"No, you're not." Zander stood up and put his hands on her shoulders. His eyes hardened. "You're dehydrated and exhausted," he said sharply. "Look at you! You're delirious. If we stay out here much longer, the sun will go down and we'll never find our way out. We're going back to my car. *Now*."

Gretchen wrenched herself free of his grasp and staggered away. "No. Not yet. I swear I'll be okay for a little while longer. We just have to look for him."

"No way. If we—"

"We have to!" He started to say something but she held up her hand. "Look, I told him if we weren't back in time he should go home. Home is west—that way. If we hurry, we can catch up to him. I know we can! I'll mark my path like I did before."

Zander stared at her. "It's suicide. We'll never make it out of here. I'm going back to the car."

Gretchen turned and began walking unsteadily in the direction of the setting sun. "Suit yourself," she called. "I'm going after Adam."

A few seconds later she heard Zander's footsteps behind her.

"I can't believe I let you do this," Zander whispered.

Gretchen stopped and leaned heavily against a tree. The forest was noticeably darker. They had tried following the sun, but for some reason it seemed as if the sun had been slanting off to the right. Now they couldn't tell where it was at all. The purplish twilight around them appeared to come from all directions.

"I don't get it," Gretchen said. Thirst had reduced her voice to a monotone growl. "The redwoods should have ended by now. We should have hit the path."

"I get it," Zander stated. Gretchen could clearly hear the fear in his words. "We don't have any idea where we're going. We're completely lost."

"We need to cut back to the left," she said dully. "He must be to the left."

"He's *gone*, Gretchen!" Zander shouted. "Do you understand that? We're not going to find him. He's *gone*."

"Five more minutes. Then we'll head back."

"Gretchen, we're turning around right now. If we don't, we won't be able to see the marks I cut into the ground. We'll be stuck out here for the night. And there's no way you're going to be able to make it through. . . ."

She stopped listening. Something had caught her eye. Directly in front of her, the forest rose gently, reaching a level summit several hundred feet away. Just over that summit, she could see a tiny patch of clear sky, as if the trees beyond had been removed.

"Look!" she said excitedly, cutting Zander off. "There's a clearing up there." She pointed ahead. "See?"

Zander followed her finger with his eyes. "Yeah, Gretchen, I see," he said sadly. "That doesn't mean a damn thing."

"What are you talking about?" she cried. "Of course it does. It's at the top of a hill, which means we might be able to see above the rest of the forest. We could figure out where we are. If it's a clearing, maybe Adam stopped there to rest."

Zander just shook his head. "Gretchen, you're babbling. These are redwoods," he said softly. "They're some of the tallest trees in the world.

There's no way we'd be able to see above them from up there." His voice grew strained. "And even if it is a clearing, we have more chance of running into Bigfoot up there than we do Adam Wollman. We're turning around this second!"

Gretchen looked at him. Then she turned and bolted up the slope.

"Gretchen! Come back here!"

She could hear his feet scurrying after her. The light grew brighter the closer she got to the top; the sky seemed to open in front of her. She could see now that it *was* a clearing. The trees had obviously been cut away there for some reason. She ignored the pain, the hunger, and the terror. Just a few more steps—

"Stop it!" Zander screamed.

But by then she had reached the top.

She stopped dead in her tracks.

"What the—" she breathed. She sank to her knees, entranced by the unreal vision in front of her. "Zander—look."

He stumbled up beside her. "What . . ."

Just over the crest of the hill, an enormous, perfectly diamond-shaped plateau had been fashioned out of dark, almost black earth. It was at least two hundred feet long. A circle of rough-hewn stones some ten feet across lay at its center, filled to the rim with huge blackened chunks of charred wood. In the right corner stood a primitive-looking hut of mud and bark.

"What is this place?" Gretchen whispered.

Zander didn't answer. Instead he tentatively

stepped out onto the diamond. For some reason, a streak of alarm shot through Gretchen. "Zander—don't!"

"It's okay." He bounced on the balls of his feet a couple of times, then turned to look at her. "Weird," he said, his face wrinkled in confusion. "The ground here feels warm—even through my sneakers. It tingles."

Without thinking, Gretchen joined him. He was right; the ground *did* feel strange against her ragged feet—almost as if it were electrically charged.

"I guess this must be some sort of campground," Zander said, looking around. "Seems like kind of a random place to have it. I mean, it doesn't look as if there are any paths that lead to it or anything." He walked toward the firepit.

The flesh at the back of Gretchen's neck began to crawl. *There's something bad about this place. I can feel it. Something isn't right here—*

"Gretchen, come check this out." Zander kneeled and looked closely at the circle of stones. He seemed absolutely mesmerized. "Look at the carvings on these rocks."

A feeling of icy dread washed over Gretchen as she walked toward him. Why hadn't she listened before and gone back to the car? Adam wasn't here; that much was clear. She bent down next to Zander.

"Look."

Gretchen gasped. Each of the stones was

engraved with hundreds of tiny, intricate letters and symbols. Some of them she recognized: a bird, an axe, the crescent moon, an eye. Others were completely alien—a backward *R*, something that looked like a hand with only three fingers, seven squiggly lines in a row. . . .

"What do you think this is?" she asked.

"I don't know. Look over here." His hand moved to a tiny line of red paint that ran across the top of one of the stones. He followed it with his finger as it twisted through the delicate carvings. Gretchen saw that it stretched from stone to stone, wrapping like a river around the circle until she couldn't see it anymore.

She looked more closely. The line was actually made up of tiny little droplets—individual marks of paint shaped like miniature tears. The color was a deep, rich, blood red. Its effect was hypnotic. *A trail of tears*, she said to herself. *A trail of—*

Gretchen's heart lurched in her chest. She sprung to her feet. "Zander—we've got to get out of here."

His eyes remained glued to the rocks. "But—"

She grabbed his shoulder. "Now!"

Suddenly a loud rattle sounded to her right—followed by an explosion of shattering glass.

Horrified, Gretchen turned in the direction of the noise. It had come from inside the hut. But the open entrance was pitch black; her eyes couldn't penetrate its shadows.

Slowly she became aware that Zander had stood and was inching toward it.

"What are you doing?" she whispered.

He motioned with his hand for her to be quiet. Then without warning he dashed through the door, his body instantly swallowed up by the darkness.

"Zander!"

"You!" She heard him scream. She raced after him.

"Oh my . . ." Gretchen gasped as she stopped in the entrance.

Dana lay writhing on the bare dirt floor of the hut. Her eyes were wide. She was wrapped in a cloak of satiny black material, her hands and feet bound tightly together by thick strips of red rope. Another piece of rope was strung tightly across her mouth, gagging her. Shards of broken glass were scattered all across the floor. The hut was cluttered with goblets, masks, jugs, and drums; on one side of her stood a stone platform stained with dark splotches, on the other a small wooden table under which were stacked two wooden crates.

"Dana!"

Zander grabbed Dana roughly under the armpits and dragged her into the clearing. His fingers worked furiously, untying the gag. Finally she spat the rope out of her mouth.

"I can't believe you found me," she whispered. "I was so scared you were going to leave without finding me. If I hadn't managed to knock that glass over. . . . But it doesn't matter now." She sighed deeply. "I'm saved."

For a moment Zander sat still, gaping at her. Then he drew his arm back and slapped her viciously across the face, knocking her to the ground.

"Saved?" he hissed between clenched teeth. "We ought to kill you right now. You're a cold-blooded murderer!"

"Zander!" Gretchen cried, putting her arm around him. "Take it easy. Relax."

Dana lay facedown, weeping into the dirt—the dirt that felt as warm under Gretchen's feet as if it were alive.

"You're sick," Zander said thickly. Gretchen could feel his body trembling. "You killed Todd—and now you want to kill that kid."

"I didn't kill Todd," Dana wailed. "I would never hurt him. They did it. They want Adam. They killed Todd—"

"Liar!" Zander snapped. "You're nothing but a liar!"

Gretchen grabbed his shoulder, desperately trying to pacify him. "You've got to just calm down, Zander," she said soothingly. "We've found Dana. She's not going anywhere. Now we can get some real answers."

"Gretchen, you believe me, don't you?" Dana pleaded. She rolled onto her back, pinning her arms underneath her. "You know I would never hurt Todd . . ."

"No, I don't know, Dana. Why don't you tell us what happened."

"I promised them I would deliver the child,"

she babbled hysterically. "But they wanted sacrifices to ensure success. They told me I had to give them Todd. I refused, so they—"

"Who are *they*?"

Dana clamped her mouth shut, then opened it slowly. "I-I-it doesn't matter—"

"Dana!" Gretchen shouted.

"You wouldn't believe me if I told you!"

"Try me," Gretchen whispered, shaking her head. "You'd be surprised."

"The Order of the Fiery Dawn." She spat out the words. "Does that mean anything to you?"

"Yes, as a matter of fact, it does. They're a bunch of sick, demented lunatics who believe in black magic, talk about a 'Trail of Blood,' and for some reason, want to hurt Adam Wollman." She glared at Dana. Her lips quivered. "And you're one of them!"

Dana looked shocked. "How do you know about the Trail of Blood?"

Gretchen slumped into the dirt. Exhaustion and burning pain seemed to fill every part of her being. "You left a note on my doorstep, remember? 'The Trail of Blood ends in blood.' Sound familiar?"

"That wasn't me," Dana whispered. "I swear I don't know what you're talking about."

"Lies!" Zander suddenly cut in. "All lies. She's lying about killing Todd. Are you gonna believe her, Gretchen?"

Gretchen was silent for a moment. She glanced around the strange clearing, growing darker with each passing moment as the sunlight faded. "We're not getting anywhere here. First things first. Why did you kill Todd?"

"I didn't!" Dana cried. "They made me call, then I told him to get out, to run away—that they were going to kill him. But he didn't believe me. He said I was crazy."

Zander pounded his fist into the dirt. "He was right!"

Dana looked at Gretchen frightfully. "He said I just wanted him to leave Madison because I was jealous of you—because I couldn't stand the thought of you and him being in the same town for the summer. I begged him. I told him they wanted to get him and Adam Wollman, and that they would probably kill you, too."

Gretchen licked her cracked lips. "What happened next?"

"That's when they showed up. He ran upstairs and tried to warn you. But it was too late. They killed him right then and saved some of his blood to splash on the altar—"

"Stop!" Gretchen put her hands over her ears and squeezed her eyes shut. "That's enough. Please. . . ."

"You don't understand what you're up against, Gretchen," Dana went on. "The Order of the Fiery Dawn has waited eight hundred years for Adam Wollman. Nothing will stop them. They have powers you can't imagine. You can feel it all around you—you can feel it in the ground! Everything they've predicted has come true. And they're certain that if they sacrifice Adam Wollman, every single believer will get *his* power. And if that really happens, if their prophecy of prophecies is fulfilled, they'll unleash themselves—"

"Shut up, Dana." Gretchen stood up and began pacing around the black soil. "So where's Adam?"

"How should *I* know? He's not with you?"

Gretchen whipped her head around. "Don't play games! Of course he isn't. He's with you and your sick friends."

"I'm not one of them anymore, Gretchen. I betrayed them when I told Todd to run away. I realized then that I was mixed up with something so evil. . . ."

"Spare us." Zander's tone was biting, hateful. He stood up and looked at the hut. "If they hadn't threatened Todd, you would have let them kill that kid," he said in a faraway voice. He looked back at Dana. "You probably would have let them kill Gretchen, too."

Dana was silent.

"So is that why you're up here alone, all tied up?" Gretchen asked. "You betrayed them—now they're going to kill you?"

"That's right." Dana's tone was flat and eerily resigned. "There need to be two sacrifices before Adam is offered. Todd was the first. I'm going to be the second. Tonight."

"Is that why you tried to drag Lacy into this? One last chance to find somebody to take your place?"

"Lacy? I don't understand what you're talking about—"

"Dana, I'm sick of this." Gretchen stood over her. "I'm hungry, I'm thirsty, and I'm exhausted. I don't have time for any more lies. Tell me about Lacy or we're leaving."

"Please," she sniffled. "I swear I don't know what you're talking about. I'm not lying—you have to believe me. I was brought here last night during the storm and I've been here ever since. They left me this morning when the sun came up. They're going to kill me tonight. I don't know where Adam is—and I don't know anything about Lacy. That's the truth."

Gretchen glanced at Zander.

"We should get out of here," he said, looking up at the sky. "The sun will be below the horizon soon and it will be too dark to find our way back."

"Take me with you!" Dana begged. "Please. I'm sorry for what I've done. It's my fault that Todd's dead—I know that. It's too late. I'll carry that forever. But I don't want anybody else to die. You have to believe me. I'll help you find Adam. We just have to hope they haven't gotten to him already."

"Why should we trust you?" Gretchen demanded. "How do we know you won't stab us in our backs?"

Dana closed her eyes. "I'm so sorry," she murmured. "How many times can I say it?"

Gretchen stared at her for a minute. Then she

95

bent over and yanked her up roughly. She began untying the rope that bound Dana's hands.

"Gretchen," Zander warned. "I don't know—"

"I can't let her die," Gretchen said. She brushed a tear away quickly. "Nobody else should have to die."

EIGHT

The ocean was close now—very close. The smell
of salt and the roar of the waves filled the air.
Evening sunlight streamed through the trees. The
path grew firmer and more tightly packed as it
twisted downward, finally leveling off and
opening on to the broad expanse of sand.

I made it.

Adam stumbled onto the beach, exhausted.
Hunger tore at his stomach and thirst at his
parched throat. The sun was a great red ball
hanging just above the horizon. It would be so
nice to lie down for a minute, to rest—but he
knew he had to keep moving.

If he didn't get back to Gretchen in time . . .

He had been too scared to sit still when she
had left to make that call. He hadn't wanted her
to go. The woods were big and empty—and too
quiet. But he hadn't felt alone. It was as if

someone had been hiding behind every one of the huge tree trunks: one of *them*.

He'd told her he'd wait. But finally he just couldn't take it anymore. They needed food, water, information. He was going to sneak back home to get supplies and try to find what was happening—if the police had found out who really killed Todd. *He* knew who had done it, but the police would never believe him. He laughed out loud at the thought: a seven-year-old boy telling the cops that his baby-sitter's ex-boyfriend had been murdered by a bunch of people who believed in black magic.

"You've got quite an imagination, kid," they would say.

That's what people always said when he told them things.

Adam sprinted along the shore. He was close to his home now; he recognized the coastline. He had to make sure he wasn't seen. Get in—get the stuff—get out. Every second counted. Soon the woods would be too dark. Then he would never be able to find Gretchen.

At last he rounded a rocky bend and turned on to the strip of beach that ran along the peninsula. He glanced up at his house, perched there on the bluff. The big windows reflected the brilliant blue of the sky. It looked the same as it always did—stark, white, cold. Had he expected it to look any different, now that something terrible had happened there?

Suddenly a thought occurred to him. He

couldn't see through those windows—but someone inside could see *out*. A missing boy on an empty beach would probably stand out pretty clearly if anyone happened to be in the house.

Adam immediately ducked down. His chest heaved. Somehow he had to figure out a way to get up there without being noticed. That definitely meant he couldn't take the wooden staircase.

There was only one choice: he had to climb.

He stared at the rocky bank in front of him. It was probably at least one hundred feet tall. And it was steep—more like a cliff than a hill. He leapt on to it.

At first it wasn't that difficult. He clung tightly to the rocks and pulled himself up as if he were a spider, one hand and one foot at a time. But soon his elbows and knees nicked against the jagged edges. His arms and legs became scratched and smeared with blood. Sweat dripped into his eyes. He forced himself higher. A few times he glanced down into the narrow space between his body and the face of the cliff. For some reason, the ground seemed much farther away than he thought it would.

Now he was only ten feet from the peak.

All at once he froze.

The faint whisper of voices drifted down to him.

". . . the girl?"

"There couldn't be any . . ."

Adam strained to listen, but the rest of it was

lost in the wind. There were at least two men talking, maybe more. Were they the police? He felt his palms get sweaty. He looked down again; there was no turning back.

Slowly, deliberately, he eased his way up across the last little bit of rock and peered over the edge. He was near the right side of the back patio. A thick wall of hedges obscured his vision.

". . . don't think so."

"Bound to. Sooner or . . ."

The voices seemed to be coming from the front of the house. Adam quickly scrambled into the bushes. He could see that a yellow ribbon had been strung around the entire property: POLICE LINE: DO NOT CROSS.

Keeping to the edge of the cliff so he could stay hidden in the bushes, Adam bent over and slowly crept around the house. Several cars were parked in the driveway—a jeep, a station wagon, a sports car. None of them looked like they belonged to the police.

There!

An old man in a flannel shirt and jeans walked across the gravel.

"It'll be dark soon," he called. The other person—or people—was obscured by the left wall of the house. The man opened the door of the jeep, tossed something inside, then slammed the door shut and headed back across the driveway, disappearing behind the wall.

Nobody else appeared. Adam knew he couldn't afford to wait. Somehow he had to get inside the house. But first he had to work his way around to the shrubbery in front so he could get a good look into the eyes of whoever was out there—and learn just who they were.

He got down on his hands and knees and began crawling.

"We should really be going," said a woman's voice. "We don't want to be late."

"We'll stay here till sundown." It was the old man's voice. "If nobody shows up by then, we'll leave."

"What'll we tell the police if they come back?" asked the woman. "That we're concerned citizens?"

"They won't come back tonight," said the man. "Their business is done here for the day. They think he's out in the redwoods somewhere."

"They're probably right."

"Maybe. Maybe not. Our task is to stay here until sunset."

Adam had now positioned himself so that he could see most of the driveway. He was about a dozen feet from the gravel, close to the station wagon. He lay on his stomach and slithered forward to get a better look.

Standing next to the police line that ran across the front of the house were four people: the old man in the flannel shirt, a blond woman who looked to be about thirty years old, and two tall, strong-looking middle-aged men, both of whom had shoulder-length brown hair and short beards. They looked as if they might have been twin brothers.

"But this is futile," said the woman, throwing her hands into the air. "We've been here three hours. He's not coming back."

The old man shook his head. "A little while longer. Then we go to the sacrifice."

Sacrifice? Adam bit his lip to keep from screaming.

These people were sorcerers.

"Your task is complete," said one of the bearded men. "She's right. Anyway, it doesn't matter if he doesn't show. The Soothsayer has alternate plans."

"Oh?" asked the old man. "What are those?"

"If none of us find him, she plans to contact him tonight," said the other.

"And how will she do that?"

The bearded men glanced at each other. "Are you questioning the Soothsayer's power?" asked the first.

The old man suddenly looked frightened. "Of course not," he said quickly. "But why didn't you say anything sooner? We've been wasting our time here."

"The Soothsayer doesn't want to share her secrets with the Outer Circle unless its absolutely necessary," said the other in a flat voice. "You understand, don't you?"

The old man nodded silently.

"Stop it," snapped the woman. "The Outer Circle and the Chosen need to work in harmony right now. It's crucial—now more than ever."

What are they talking about? Adam peered at

them through the bushes. *I have to see their eyes—*

At that moment one of the bearded men began walking toward Adam across the gravel.

Adam held his breath as every muscle in his body tensed for flight. His heart beat so loudly in his chest that he was sure the man could hear it.

But the man stopped when he reached the station wagon. He opened the passenger door, reached in, and pulled out a crumbling leather-bound book. On its cover was a circle of red drops.

Adam stared at it. He had seen books with that same design before—at the mall. He had been telling Gretchen about them yesterday. For some reason, he had always been fascinated by the drawings, even though the text was written in a language he couldn't read. The books seemed to draw him to them like a magnet whenever he saw them. It was strange. He couldn't explain it. They even seemed to tingle in his hands when he held them.

Of course, he hadn't mentioned that part to Gretchen.

The man leaned against the side of the car and began reading. His green eyes were visible just over the tip of the cover.

Adam took a deep, silent breath.

He focused every part of his waning energy on those eyes. And slowly, very slowly, an image began to form . . .

"Tonight the Outer Circle and the Chosen are

one," chanted the High Priest. "For tonight is the Night of Nights."

"Tonight is the Night of Nights," chanted the Chosen.

The Soothsayer's acolyte stood at the entrance of the temple. He gazed in ecstasy at the sacred fire before him. The ceremonial mask hid the smile on his lips. For in only one year's time, it would be the true Night of Nights—the night before the Fiery Dawn.

Every year, for eight hundred years, they had celebrated this same night in this same way—in preparation for the New Age.

Tonight's ceremony marked the final symbolic ritual.

Next year's ceremony would be the one they had been waiting for.

"We have watched the child Adam for six years," called the High Priest. "Next year is his seventh year. It has been written that he is to be sacrificed in his seventh year."

"It has been written," answered the Chosen.

The acolyte thought then of all those generations of believers who had come before him. He thought of the first ones, the ones who had written The Book. They had gone to their deaths knowing they would never see the fulfillment of the Prophecy of Prophecies. But they passed on their legacy of wisdom nonetheless.

He was one of the lucky few to have been born at this time.

Next year the believers would be transformed—

The man's eyes shifted. He snapped the book

shut. A car was coming down the road. Adam watched as the man tossed the book back into the station wagon and walked over to the three others.

"I wonder who this could be?" the man asked.

Adam's entire body was shivering. His breath came in shuddering gasps. The prophecies in that book were about *him*. Is that why he had been drawn to it in the first place—because it predicted his own death?

A white Volkswagen bug rolled through the front gate and came to a stop behind the jeep. A short, pretty girl with bright brown eyes and chin-length brown hair stepped out.

Lacy. Adam instantly recognized her from when he had looked into Gretchen last night. She was Gretchen's best friend. And she was supposed to be in trouble. *He* had told Gretchen that when he had blacked out. . . .

"Hello," she said tentatively.

"Hi," said the woman. "Can I help you?"

"Well, I don't know." She smiled nervously. "I'm a friend of the girl who's taking care of this house and baby-sitting the Wollmans' son."

The four of them glanced at one another.

"Have you *seen* your friend recently?" asked the man who had been reading the book.

"Uh—not since she left San Francisco."

"Have you heard about what happened?" asked the old man in the flannel shirt.

"Well, yeah. I heard there was some kind of accident."

"Sure—if you call murder an accident," said the woman. She sounded angry. "You know, your friend is in a whole lot of trouble."

"Please." Lacy shook her head. "I'm sure Gretchen had nothing to do with it, ma'am. That's why I'm here. Because—" She suddenly stopped herself. "Do you mind if I ask who you are? Are you friends of the Wollmans?"

"Yes—yes, we are, as a matter of fact," said the old man. "And we're very concerned about Adam. You see, your friend took him with her when she—uh—left."

"So you must know Gretchen's mom." Lacy's tone was suspicious.

"Well, we've never met," he said smoothly. "But Mrs. Wollman has mentioned her plenty of times."

Run, Lacy, run! Adam silently pleaded. Never before had he felt so helpless. Why couldn't she see that she was in danger?

"Well, if you know anything about the Childs family at all, you know that none of them would ever be involved in anything like this," Lacy snapped. "Somebody is setting Gretchen up!"

"Look, there's no need to get upset," said the woman in a soothing voice. "We don't mean to accuse your friend of anything. If she was a friend of the Wollmans, I'm sure she had nothing to do with it. It's just that all of us are under a great deal of strain. We're concerned, you see. We're all on the same side here."

106

"Where *is* Mrs. Childs?" asked the man who had been reading the book.

"She's at the police station. We drove down here together. Why?"

"I see. And you just came up here to have a look?"

Lacy didn't answer.

"So Gretchen is still missing, I take it?" he asked.

"That's right," she said.

The man glanced at the three others. "I'll tell you what," he said. "I'm going to the police station right now. I'll give you a ride back down there."

"But I have my own car," she said. "Why would—"

"No," the man interrupted. "You're coming with me."

Lacy's eyes darted from one face to another. Then she began backpeddling slowly toward her car.

"Get her!" the man cried.

In an instant, the other bearded man, the woman, and the old man in the flannel shirt jumped forward and tackled Lacy. She squirmed and kicked furiously—until the man who had been reading the book strode over and cuffed her savagely in the jaw. Her body went limp.

"Throw her in the jeep," he ordered. "Let's get out of here. Now."

The woman looked at him fearfully. "But what about—"

"Don't worry." The man's lips parted in a humorless smile. "We'll bring them to us. We've got a bargaining chip."

Adam stared hopelessly as the cars vanished out the front gates.

NINE

"Tell us about the Trail of Blood," Gretchen said.

"What do you want to know?"

"Everything."

The woods around the crackling fire were pitch black. It was as if the entire universe had shrunk to this one tiny bright spot; nothing existed outside the three of them. Gretchen stretched out in front of the flames. She was more tired now than ever—but at least Dana had provided them with a meal. When Gretchen had untied her at the clearing, Dana had gone back into the hut and reemerged with jugs of fruit and water, a loaf of dense dry bread, and a tinderbox. They had immediately stuffed themselves. But as they were following Zander's path back through the woods, the forest had grown dark. By the time they had reached the spot where Gretchen had left Adam, night had fallen completely. They couldn't see a thing. Gretchen's path of Xs, the path that could take them to Zander's car, was invisible.

They were stuck—stranded until sunrise.

"It started a long, long time ago," Dana began. "Almost eight hundred years, although its origins go back thousands of years before that. But it was eight hundred years ago that a group of people in Scotland formed a secret society called the Order of the Fiery Dawn." She paused. "They weren't ordinary people. They were all supposed to be very . . . powerful. They were sorcerers."

Gretchen shot a look at Zander.

"Anyway, they put together a book of prophecies about things that would happen in the future: wars, battles, assassinations—violent things. They called it the 'Trail of Blood.'"

Gretchen swallowed. "Did anything they predict actually come true?"

"Everything. Everything happened exactly as they said it would."

"But that's what they always say about stuff like that," Zander said impatiently, as if he were trying to convince himself he was right. "It's always a lot of vague mumbo jumbo that can be twisted to fit any situation."

"Not this."

Zander sneered.

"The Book is very specific—it gives names, dates, times. The range is huge. It covers so many things. . . . But everything they predicted, no matter how big or small, is connected. All of it

110

has some direct effect on the future of their secret society. All of it points in some way to the Fiery Dawn."

"What *is* the Fiery Dawn?" Gretchen asked.

Dana stared at the fire for a moment. "It's hard to explain. Since the beginning, every generation of the Order has had one woman who's blessed with certain powers. They call her the Soothsayer. She helps and advises the High Priest. You could say she's a psychic."

A shiver ran down Gretchen's spine. "A psychic?"

"Well, not exactly. She can't predict the future. But she can tell things about a person just by looking at them. And she can look into the past. She knows if something important has just happened, even if she didn't see it."

"Just like Adam," Gretchen said hoarsely.

"Exactly. Just like Adam."

"Is that why they want him?"

"They've been waiting eight hundred years for Adam Wollman. His death fulfills their final prophecy. He's the special child: the Nonbeliever with the Soothsayer's power. They believe that when Adam is sacrificed, his power—the power that only the Soothsayer has possessed up till now—will be transferred to every single believer. *That's* the Fiery Dawn—the beginning of the New Age."

"'The Trail of Blood ends in blood,'" Gretchen whispered.

Dana nodded. "That's it."

"So they're waiting for the day when all these people are suddenly going to have these incredible powers." Gretchen stared at Dana. "They'll be unstoppable!"

"That's right."

"How-how many believers are there?" Zander stammered. "I mean, how many people are we talking about?"

"Thousands, all over the world."

"Thousands!"

"But this is the center. This is where the Chosen have come to live. About half the people who live in Madison are members of the Outer Circle." She shook her head. "You can even get a copy of The Book at the local antique shop—"

"That's impossible!" Zander cried. "I've lived here my whole life! I would know. . . ."

"No, you wouldn't," Dana replied coldly. "The Order is very discreet. Nonbelievers can't see it, even when it's staring them in the face. Take Todd's family. They've been renting that house next to yours every summer for the past twenty years—and they have no idea, either."

Rage suddenly flamed in the pit of Gretchen's stomach. "Is that why you used him?" Her voice was trembling. "Because he lived here and because nonbelievers are so easy to fool?"

"At first—yes," Dana said. She sounded ashamed. "But then I grew to love him. You have to believe me, Gretchen. I've been with the Order my whole life; my parents are members of the Outer Circle. But I changed when I met Todd. He was so

112

different from anyone I had ever met—so good. He made me see how evil they really are. . . ."

"You *changed* a little too late." Zander said bitterly. "Todd's dead. You make me sick. You haven't changed at all. You're still one of them—"

"I'm not!" she screamed. "I'm not!"

"Calm down," Gretchen hissed, her eyes shifting nervously between them. What if she *was* still one of them? But there was no longer any time to worry about that. "It's useless to scream at each other. We've got to concentrate on saving Adam and Lacy."

"Sure, we can concentrate," Zander muttered. "We can concentrate all night long. It's not like we're going anywhere."

Gretchen desperately tried to focus, but her mind kept going in circles and drawing blanks. Zander was right—there was nothing they could do. In a way, everything was still completely unclear. How had she even gotten into this mess?

"You know, Dana, there's one thing you haven't explained to me yet," she said. "Why did you pick *me*?"

"We didn't pick you. It's the only part of this thing that's pure coincidence. It's a total fluke you happened to be Adam's baby-sitter. I didn't even know that you knew the Wollmans. If I had, things may have turned out much differently."

"How's that?"

She shrugged. "I probably would have used *you* to get to Adam instead of Todd."

Gretchen's stomach twisted. At least Todd

would still be alive, she thought numbly as she gazed into the fire. *A total fluke.* For some reason, that horrified her even more than the fulfillment of all the bloody prophecies.

"The second the sun comes up, we're going straight to the cops," Zander stated. He glared at Dana. "You're going to tell them everything."

Dana nodded miserably.

Suddenly a thought occurred to Gretchen. "Dana—when is Adam supposed to be killed?"

"Tomorrow night."

"It's *written* that he's going to be killed tommorrow night, right?"

"That's right."

Gretchen nodded. "That gives us time!"

Dana stared at her blankly.

"Look, the Order of the Fiery Dawn believes in prophecies. Like you said, they've waited eight hundred years. So you can bet they're going to wait another night. They wouldn't kill him *before* tomorrow night—because that would mess up the prophecy. See what I'm getting at?"

Zander sat up. "You're right! When the sun comes up, we'll just go to the cops and show them that clearing. Then we'll round everyone up—"

"It won't work," Dana interrupted harshly. "Listen—everything in that book has come true. Everything. They've harnessed powers you can't begin to understand—powers you can feel."

Gretchen's feet suddenly tingled with the

memory of that strange black earth at the clearing.

"Do you think *we're* going to stop them?" Dana's voice rose an octave. "You can forget it! I know them well enough to know what they can do. They've probably been controlling this whole thing. I bet they let you find me so they could toy with us. I wouldn't be surprised if they knew exactly where we were right now—"

Suddenly she broke off. Her eyes were pinned across the fire to the empty space between Gretchen and Zander. "Oh, no," she gasped.

Gretchen spun around. Far in the distance, deep in the endless black of the night, she could see a tiny, flickering light. Then it disappeared—only to reappear a few seconds later, a little brighter than it had been before.

"Someone's coming," Zander whispered in horror.

The light stopped bobbing for a moment and seemed to shine directly at them. Then it started bobbing again, this time much more wildly.

"We're dead," Dana said softly.

Now Gretchen could hear the sound of pounding footsteps.

"We've got to do something!" Zander muttered. "We've got to run—"

The bright light bore down on them. Gretchen could just barely make out the shape of a small figure as the gap between them closed. . . .

"It's me!" cried a boy's voice.

"Adam!" Gretchen jumped to her feet. The

huge flashlight in his hands winked off and fell to the ground as he dashed into her open arms. She squeezed him as tightly as she possibly could, as if making sure it was really him.

"Where've you been?" she whispered. "How did you find us?"

Adam knelt beside the fire. He looked terrible; even in the uncertain firelight Gretchen could see that his face was dirty and scratched and his shirt was torn. Drops of blood ran down his arms.

"Adam—are you okay?"

He nodded. "I went home." His breathing was labored. "I got scared after you left, so I decided to go home and get some supplies and stuff." He glanced at her. "It was a dumb thing to do. I'm sorry."

"It's okay, Adam," she said, running a hand through his rumpled hair. "It's okay. You're safe now. How did you get all cut up?"

"I had to climb—" he broke off, his eyes roving over Dana and Zander's faces. "What are *they* doing here?" he asked tensely.

"They're with me now, Adam. It's okay."

He stared at each of them for a few seconds, then nodded slowly. "For now, anyways."

"How did you *find* us?" Zander asked incredulously.

He shrugged. "I was on the path. When it got too dark, I turned on the flashlight. I followed the path till I hit the redwoods. Then I just kept going the way Gretchen and I went this morning. I've got a pretty good sense of direction."

Gretchen sighed. "I guess you do. Either that or a whole lot of luck."

"I could see the fire from a long way off. I figured it was you."

"Well, you made it," Gretchen said. "That's all that matters. You got the flashlight and everything. Did you see anything when you were home? Did you get anything to eat?"

"A little. I grabbed some stuff on the way out. I didn't want to stick around." He jerked his head in Dana's direction. "*They* were at the house when I got there."

"Adam! Oh my—"

"Don't worry—they didn't see me," he said quietly. He looked down for a moment, then turned to face Gretchen. "They took Lacy while I was there."

"What?!"

Adam nodded. "There were four of them. I was hiding in the bushes when she drove up. She told them she had driven here with your mom, and that your mom was at the police station."

Gretchen's eyes grew watery. "My mom?" she choked.

Adam nodded. "Yeah. Anyway, one of them asked if Lacy wanted a ride back. I guess she must have figured out then that they were bad, because she tried to get away." He shook his head sadly, averting his eyes. "They grabbed her and knocked her out—then they drove off. There was nothing I could do. I mean, I couldn't let them see me. . . ."

The sound of the crackling fire filled the night. "I know, Adam." A tear fell from Gretchen's cheek. "I know."

"So after that, I ran inside, got some stuff, and ran away as fast as I could so I could get back here and tell you."

"They're going to kill her," Dana said in a faraway voice. "They need a sacrifice for tonight—and now that I'm gone, she's going to be it."

Zander stood up. "We're going to my car right now. Adam, do you feel well enough to keep walking?"

Adam nodded.

"But there's no way," Gretchen said. "We'll get lost."

"No, we won't." He walked over and picked up Adam's flashlight. "All we have to do is find that first X. It's a straight line to the road from there."

Dana shook her head. "I'm telling you, they're—"

"Shut up!" Zander shouted. "I don't want to hear it. We're going to the police."

"He's right, Dana," Gretchen said. "We have to. My mom is there. It isn't that late yet. We can stop them if we're fast enough."

Dana lowered her eyes. "I wish I could be as hopeful."

Zander began throwing handfuls of dirt on the fire. Sparks flew and the flames crackled and dimmed. "Get up, Dana," he snapped. "Give me a hand with this."

Gretchen put her arm around Adam and watched numbly as the two of them reduced the fire to a heap of bright red coals. *Hang on, Lacy. We're on our way.*

The darkness around them was complete. The rhythmic sound of crickets chirping had replaced the sound of the fire.

"Stay right here," Zander said, clicking on the flashlight and directing the intense white beam onto the ground in front of him. "The first *X* is right around here somewhere. . . ." He inched forward.

"Gretchen?" Adam murmured.

"Yes?"

"I learned something tonight. I *can* predict the future."

"What? But . . . I thought—"

"You told me that I said Lacy was going to be in trouble, right? And I saw it—even though I couldn't do anything to stop it. That must be how it works." She could feel him shivering under her arm. "I make predictions when I black out. I can't remember them, but I see them happen later and I can't do anything about it—"

"Take it easy, Adam." She rubbed his shoulder. "Don't worry about that right now—"

"Found it!" Zander yelled. The flashlight was fixed to a spot of earth about forty feet away from the fire. "Let's go."

Gretchen's arm slipped from Adam and she ran to where Zander was standing. Dana was close at her heels. "Come on, Adam!" she called.

There was no response.

Zander whipped the light in Adam's direction.

He was lying on the ground.

"Adam!"

The three of them ran back and stood over him. He writhed and kicked in the dirt. Zander shone the light in his face. His eyes were open, but they had that dilated, unconscious look—the look Gretchen had seen before.

"He's in a trance," she said. "He may say something important—"

"Nonbelievers!" he cried.

Gretchen blinked, unable to comprehend what she had just. The voice that had come out of Adam's mouth had *not* belonged to Adam. It was the voice of an old woman.

"Nonbelievers," the voice repeated.

Dana stepped backward, her eyes white with terror. She pointed a trembling finger at Adam. "That's the Soothsayer's voice!" she cried. "The Soothsayer!"

"Bring the boy to us unharmed," the voice demanded. "You have until midnight. If you do not deliver the boy to us by midnight, your friend's blood will flow."

PART III

"Join hands," called the High Priest.

The Chosen spread their arms and locked fingers, their white robes glowing red from the light of the flames. The fire in their midst roared and leapt higher.

"The Nonbelievers have defiled our sacred ground." His whispery voice was strident, wrathful. "They have stolen what is ours—our food, our bread, our water. They have stolen the one who betrayed us. But they could not prevent the Second Sacrifice. It has been written."

"It has been written," answered the Chosen.

A slow, steady, rhythmic beating of drums began inside the temple. *Boom . . . Boom . . . Boom . . .*

"Bring forth the Second Sacrifice," commanded the High Priest.

The Soothsayer's masked acolytes stepped from the temple door, holding the young girl between them. Her brown eyes shone brightly above the red rope that gagged her mouth.

"The Trail of Blood flows one more night," chanted the High Priest in a singsong voice, staring at the girl.

"The Sacred Fire burns ever bright," answered the Chosen.

A faint, muffled cry could be heard from the girl.

"I've seen enough," said the High Priest disdainfully. "Keep her out of sight until the time comes."

The three of them disappeared into the dark doorway.

Just then the Soothsayer stepped out from behind the temple. She looked into the eyes of the High Priest and smiled. "I have made contact with the Nonbelievers," she said. "They'll be here soon."

The High Priest nodded. Everything was proceeding according to The Book. "The prophecies will be fulfilled," he said. "The Fiery Dawn awaits us."

TEN

"Adam!" Gretchen shook his limp body. His face looked deathly pale under the flashlight. "Adam, wake up!"

At last his legs stirred. His eyelids fluttered, then slowly opened. "What's going on?" he mumbled.

"You went into another trance."

His sleepy eyes widened. "Did I say anything?"

Gretchen glanced at Dana. Nobody said a word.

"Well?"

Zander turned the flashlight away from Adam and aimed it at the pile of smothered coals. "I guess I should try to start this fire up again," he muttered.

"Why?" Adam stood up straight. "I thought we were going to the police. What's going on?" His voice rose. "Tell me!"

"*You* didn't say anything," Dana said. "Somebody else did."

"Who?" Adam sounded scared. "Tell me what happened!"

"Adam," Gretchen began, "I want you to take a deep breath and try to relax, okay? Something very strange—"

"Let me handle this," Dana interrupted. "Adam, the Soothsayer just spoke to us—through you."

"Dana! For God's sake, he just had a seizure. He has no idea what just—"

"It's okay, Gretchen," Adam said grimly. "I know about the Soothsayer."

"How do you know about her?" Dana demanded.

"I saw her helper at my house." Gretchen could hear the venom in Adam's tone. "He was the one who took Lacy. But before he grabbed her, I got a good look at him. In a vision, I saw the ceremony last year. I saw everything. *You* were there!" Adam looked hard at Dana.

Everyone was silent for a moment. Gretchen kept her eyes fixed on Zander's shadowy form. He was desperately trying to restoke the fire. With the exception of the dim red glow of the coals and the light of the flashlight on the ground, the forest had once again become a wall of impregnable, inky blackness.

"All of you are so sure of yourselves," Adam's disembodied voice went on. "You're so sure everything's gonna fall into place. Well, you waited for me up there at my house and you didn't see me—even when I was right in front of you. *I'm* still here. *I'm* still alive!"

"Not for long," Dana whispered.

Zander suddenly reached for the flashlight and stormed over to Dana, grabbing her roughly around the neck. He shoved the light in her face so that the bulb was inches from her eyes. "If you open your mouth one more time, I'm gonna hurt you," he said. His voice was hard. "I mean it."

Gretchen held her breath as Zander glared into Dana's squinting eyes. Finally he pushed her away from him and turned back to the bed of coals.

Despair settled over Gretchen.

What's happening to us? We're all going crazy. We're acting like wild animals. Maybe Dana's right. Maybe they are manipulating us, just when we need to pull togther most—

"So what did the Soothsayer tell you?" Adam asked calmly.

"We have to bring you to the temple by midnight," Dana replied. "If we don't, Lacy's dead."

Zander whipped his head around. "Dana—"

"Enough!" Gretchen barked. "We've got to come up with a plan—now. We're not doing Lacy a bit of good by sitting in the middle of the woods, threatening one another. We need to think."

"Well, we can't go to the police," Zander stated. "That's completely out. We're on our own."

"Why?"

Zander leaned over and blew on the coals. A small flame leapt into a pile of twigs he had carefully erected in the middle. "Because we don't have enough time," he said. He slowly began adding tinder to the tiny fire. "It's probably about nine or nine-thirty right now. It would take us at least two hours to find our way out of these woods and back to my car. And assuming we did find my car in two hours—who's to say we'd be able to get it out of that ditch? Even if we did, even if everything went as fast as possible, we wouldn't get to the police station until midnight at the earliest." He flashed his eyes at Dana. "Something tells me that when your friends give an ultimatum, they stick to it."

"You're right about that," Dana said.

Now the fire was crackling.

"Okay." Gretchen sighed, kneeling beside the flames. "So we can't go to the police. That leaves us one choice. We have to figure out a way to get Lacy out of there."

"Well, that's not an option." Dana sat down next to her. "Gretchen, you've just seen with your own two eyes what they can do. They contacted us through Adam. Don't you understand yet? They have powers. . . ." Her eyes darted anxiously around the fire. "I think we should get out of here," she announced loudly. "If we go there, we'd just be falling into their trap." She bent her head. "I'm sorry for saying this, but our only hope now is to save ourselves."

"Then save yourself," Zander said evenly. "Get out of here. Run away. That would be the natural thing for *you* to do, because you're a coward. But don't waste our time by trying to get us to run with you—because it's not going to happen."

"I-I don't—"

Zander shook his head. "You know, the whole thing makes sense to me now." His voice no longer carried its former bite. It was as if he had given up wasting his energy on Dana. "All you care about is yourself and your own well-being. It's pathetic. You're still just like them. That's why anyone as selfish as you would want to join them." He paused and tossed a stick into the fire, then fixed his eyes on Dana.

"They've convinced themselves that they're better than everyone else," he went on. "It must be nice to feel like that—to feel like you're above other people, that you can do anything you want, that you have all kinds of secrets and powers. I bet it makes you feel strong. Well, *nothing*—no magic or psychic powers or anything like that—is gonna make me think that somebody is better than somebody else. Everybody's the same. That's why I don't think our situation is as hopeless as you make it out to be. If anything, *we've* got an advantage because we haven't fooled ourselves into thinking we're all-powerful."

Gretchen stared at Zander's somber face, glowing and flickering in the firelight. For the first time, she noticed how beautiful it was—

strong, yet amazingly gentle at the same time. She opened her mouth, but a lump had formed in her throat, making it impossible for her to speak. In a space of about thirty seconds, he had abruptly made it seem as if everything might actually work out—as if she might have some chance of seeing her best friend alive again.

It was the nicest thing that had happened to her so far during the whole terrible ordeal.

Dana rubbed her eyes with her hands. "You're right, Zander," she said, sniffing. "You're absolutely right. But I want to change—I want to change so badly, you don't know. I'll stay with you. I already have one death on my hands. I don't think I could live with another."

"Good." Zander took a deep breath and looked around the fire. "So what are we going to do?"

Gretchen cleared her throat. "Somehow we have to sneak in and get Lacy out of there."

"That won't work," Dana said. "I can tell you that right now. There are going to be at least—" She looked up for a minute and counted to herself. "At least twenty-three people there. There's going to be a huge bonfire. It's very bright. It lights up the whole clearing and the woods around it. There's no way anyone could get in there without being seen."

Zander looked at the fire for a few seconds, then raised his eyebrows. "Unless everyone was looking in one direction—the wrong direction."

"What do you mean?" Gretchen asked.

"If someone created some sort of diversion—enough to distract everyone's attention, even for a few seconds—it would be enough for somebody else to sneak behind that hut in the corner."

Dana looked doubtful. "That's where the Soothsayer sits. She'll be back there until they bring Lacy out."

"Lacy's going to be in there?"

Dana nodded. "She'll be bound and gagged. There'll be four other people in there, too—two drummers and the Soothsayer's acolytes. I'm positive the High Priest will keep her in there until he sees Adam."

Zander stroked his chin, lost in thought.

"So I'll be the diversion." Adam's voice rose above the crackling fire.

Gretchen gasped. "No! Adam, I don't think that's what—"

"Why not? It makes the most sense. I'm the one thing that's sure to distract their attention—*everyone's* attention. We just have to figure out the best way to do it."

Zander glanced at Gretchen. "He's got a point."

"Somehow I've got to keep them busy long enough for somebody to untie Lacy," Adam said.

"It'll be hard," Dana whispered. "The second they see you, they're going to want to tie you up, too."

"It might be easier if they don't know how many of us there are," Zander said distantly.

"They'll know by now," Dana said. "I'm sure

they will. They know I'm with Gretchen and Adam—and they probably know you're here, too."

"That's true. But maybe we're thinking about this the wrong way." He leaned forward. "What if we could convince them that you killed us?"

"How on earth—"

Zander's lips curled into a barely perceptible smile. "You show up there with Adam. Tell them that we rescued you—then you killed us when the Soothsayer told us to come. Tell them you want to prove yourself."

"How will *that* help us?" Adam asked.

"Because then they'll think there are only you two. If they aren't expecting to see Gretchen and me, they won't be on guard for us to do anything."

Dana shook her head. "The Soothsayer will know it's a lie the instant she looks at me."

"It doesn't matter," Zander insisted. "It'll be too late by then. All we need is a couple of seconds to get in there and get Lacy out. We *want* the Soothsayer to look at you, so she won't be paying attention to the hut."

"There's no way," Dana said. "The drummers, the acolytes—the temple will be protected. You won't be able to get in there without fighting your way through."

Zander gazed into the flames.

"Is there anything you can think of at the clearing that might help us?" Gretchen asked. "I mean, you got all kinds of stuff out of that hut when we left—food, water, the tinderbox. Maybe there's something already there that we can use against them."

"There are some knives in there, used for sacrifices and things. Is that what you mean?"

"Yeah—exactly." Zander looked up. "If we know where the knives are, we can . . ."

Dana's head was shaking again. "They're sealed in boxes. You'd never be able to get them out in time to do anything with them. They won't do us any good."

"Tell us everything that's in the hut," Gretchen said. "Sometimes things you least expect can be the most helpful."

"Well." Dana's forehead wrinkled. "Let's see—there are cups, plates, jugs of water, um . . . masks, drums . . . knives, candles, fireworks—"

"Fireworks!?" Zander exclaimed.

"Yeah—to celebrate the Fiery Dawn." Dana shrugged. "Makes sense to celebrate with fire, right?"

"Do you know exactly where they're kept?" Zander asked.

"They're in some boxes under the table."

Gretchen looked up. "Those two wooden crates?"

Dana nodded.

"Perfect!" Zander shouted. "Is there a way to get into that hut from the back?"

"Yes, but—" Dana looked uncertain. "There's the Soothsayer's door. . . ."

"What's the matter? Is it locked?"

"I don't know. Nobody's allowed to use it except the Soothsayer."

"It doesn't matter," Zander said impatiently. "We'll break it down if we have to. Here's what I think we should do. Dana—you and Adam walk into the clearing at the corner directly across from the hut. Start talking about how you killed us. That'll distract everyone and hopefully bring out the Soothsayer, too."

Dana stared at him over the fire. "Zander, I—"

"Just let me finish. Gretchen and I will be hiding in the woods behind the hut. While you're keeping them occupied, Gretchen and I will get in through the back door. One of us will set those crates on fire while the other grabs Lacy. By the time we're out of there—*kaboom*! That'll create a big enough distraction so the five of us can get away into the woods. We'll all split up and head in different directions as fast as we can. By the time morning comes we'll be fine—east is the highway and west is the ocean. Got it?"

Everyone was silent.

"Zander—that's completely insane," Dana said finally.

"Maybe," Gretchen said. "But at this point, it's our only hope. I say we do it."

"Me, too," Adam said.

Gretchen looked at Dana.

"How are you going to set the crates on fire?" Dana asked.

"We've got the lighter and those matches from the tinderbox," Zander said. "We empty the

134

lighter fluid over the crates and toss a match on them." He snapped his fingers. "Simple."

Dana closed her eyes. "It'll never work."

"Dana—are you coming or not?" Gretchen demanded.

"Yes." She sighed. "I'm coming."

Zander stood up. "There's no sense in waiting any more." He grabbed Adam's flashlight. "The path I marked will take us there. Let's go."

ELEVEN

The white beam of light danced across the ground.

"There," Zander whispered.

The four of them moved to the deep gash in the soil. "We must be getting close," he said in a low voice. "I don't remember leaving this many marks. . . ."

"Are you sure these are the marks you left?" Dana asked nervously.

"I'm sure. But it seems like we've been walking for hours. I guess we're moving slowly."

Gretchen's eyes had gradually become accustomed to the darkness of the night. She could make out the silhouettes of the redwoods and judge the vague tilt of the ground beneath her. Her eyes scanned the forest.

"Hey—look over there," Dana said, touching Gretchen's arm. "Right in front of us."

Far in the distance Gretchen could see a dim orange luminescence.

"That's it," Dana said. "That's the fire."

Zander flicked off the flashlight. "Then we don't need this anymore. We just follow that light. We'll split up when we get closer."

All at once Gretchen heard a soft thud.

"What was that?" Dana hissed.

Gretchen squinted, trying to make sense out of the formless sea of black and gray. She could see the outlines of Zander's and Dana's bodies—but Adam seemed to have disappeared.

"Somebody's going to die tonight."

Gretchen jerked. It was Adam's voice. It sounded as if it had come from beneath her.

Not again. . . .

Instantly the flashlight was back on. Adam was stretched on his back in the dirt, blinking his eyes. He looked around him fearfully.

"Oh, no," he whispered. "Did I have *another* blackout?"

Gretchen felt ice in her veins, as if all the blood were draining from her body.

"Yeah," Zander said quickly, pulling Adam to his feet. "But it doesn't matter. Are you all right?"

"I guess so." He brushed himself off. "Did— uh—I say anything?"

"It doesn't matter," Zander repeated numbly. "Can you walk?"

"Sure, but—"

"We can't stop right now. We have to go forward." He turned the flashlight off again and began walking away.

Adam tugged at Gretchen's arm. "Tell me

what I said. I want to know. I have a right to know."

"You-you—" She couldn't finish.

"You didn't tell us anything we didn't already know," Dana said quietly. She turned and followed Zander's receding shadow.

"Gretchen," Adam pleaded.

"Dana's right, Adam." She slipped her hand into his. "I know you don't want to hear that, but it's all I can tell you. I'm sorry."

Silence filled the air as the four of them padded swiftly toward the glowing light. The ground became steeper and softer under their feet.

Soon Gretchen could hear a faint, steady thumping. *Boom . . . Boom . . . Boom . . .*

The smell of smoke wafted through the forest, accompanied by a distant, almost inaudible rumble.

Now the thumping was quite loud.

"The ceremonial drums are beating," Dana said. "That means they're preparing for the sacrifice. It must be close to midnight."

The light ahead of them stretched and flickered and grew in intensity above them until it dominated their field of vision; the rumble had become a roar.

Zander stopped in his tracks and crouched down, staring up at the top of the hill. "Here's where we split up," he whispered. "Gretchen and I will go first. Give us about twenty minutes; that'll be enough time for us to position ourselves in a safe place behind the hut." He glanced at Dana. "The hut's off to the right—that means you go left. The second we hear you and Adam in the clearing, we'll go in and get Lacy. That's when you take off. Remember to split up right away. If there's any sign of trouble at all before that, get out of there as fast as you can." He paused and took a breath. "We'll see you again some time tomorrow."

"Good luck," Adam said. He reached over and squeezed Gretchen's hand.

Gretchen nodded. She was too frightened to answer.

"I hope I can earn your forgiveness here tonight," Dana murmured. "For Lacy's sake— and Todd's."

Zander looked at her but said nothing. He put his hand on Gretchen's arm. "Let's go."

Gretchen hesitated for a moment. "Adam—" she began.

"Go on," Adam said. "I'll be okay." He smiled. "Remember what I told you—I can take care of myself."

Gretchen gazed into his shiny black eyes, the eyes that no longer threatened her. *Please make it out of here alive, Adam. Please make it—*

"Come on, Gretchen," Zander gently urged. "It's time."

Fifteen minutes later, Gretchen crawled forward and poked her head around the trunk of a redwood.

The clearing stretched in front of her.

It looked very different from when she had seen it before.

It was alive.

A wild inferno was raging in the circle of stones. A group of figures in white robes stood around it, hand in hand, their faces obscured by cavernous hoods. Gretchen blinked. The blaze was ferocious, volcanic; she could feel the sweltering heat from where she was hiding. How could those people stand to be so close?

"Gretchen, you've just seen with your own two eyes what they can do . . . Don't you understand yet? They have powers. . . ."

Gretchen squeezed her eyes shut and clenched her teeth, chasing Dana's voice out of her mind.

"Well?" Zander whispered. "See anything?"

She forced herself to scan the rest of the clearing. Directly in front of her, some thirty feet away, was the back of the hut. A tiny, ancient, withered woman wrapped in a black shawl leaned against a small wooden door. Her eyes were closed and her face was pained; she looked as if she were asleep and having a bad dream.

Either that or she was in some kind of trance.

To the left of the hut, facing the fire, stood a hunched, cloaked figure leaning against a staff.

Gretchen quickly withdrew her head. "The Soothsayer's there," she whispered, turning to face Zander. "There are a bunch of people around the fire. There's also somebody standing off to the side; I can't tell if it's a man or a woman."

"Do you think it'll be hard to get past the Soothsayer?"

"I don't know. Maybe you should take a look."

The two of them switched places and Zander inched his head around the tree.

"She won't be a problem." He pulled his head back. "Jeez, she looks like she may keel over any second. If she keeps her eyes closed, we can just sneak up and clock her over the head with this." He shook Adam's flashlight.

Gretchen swallowed. Until now she hadn't even considered the possibility of violence—of actually hurting someone. Had that been naive?

"I don't know," she said. "It may be too risky. What if she screams?"

"Well, hopefully she'll get up and go around front when Adam and Dana show up. Then we won't have to deal with it. All we can do now is wait. You've got the lighter, right?"

"Yeah."

"Make sure the plug at the bottom is loose. You don't want to get held up by fumbling with that. We have to be as fast as we possibly can. I'm not going to untie Lacy until we're out in the woods. I'll just pick her up and throw her over my shoulder. She's not big or anything, is she?"

Gretchen shook her head. She pulled the lighter from her pocket and loosened the plug. *This is so crazy . . .*

141

The sound of the bonfire filled her ears. She stared at Zander. He looked neither scared nor excited; his face was as impassive as if it had been carved from stone. But as he gazed back at her, she could see an undefinable sort of sadness around his eyes—as if he felt it was unfair she should have to endure any more.

She stuck the lighter back in her pocket, then reached forward and took his hand. "Zander, I don't know what I would have done if you hadn't been here," she whispered. "I'd probably be dead by now. There was no reason for you to even get involved in any of this. I was ready to give up back there—but what you said changed my mind. I just wanted to thank you . . . before it's too late."

"We'll make it, Gretchen." He leaned forward and kissed her lightly on the lips. "We'll make it. I promise—"

"The child has been delivered!" a wheezy voice cried.

Gretchen froze. Her heart pounded fiercely. *Here we go. . . .*

Zander raised a finger to his mouth to indicate silence. He leaned over and poked his head around the tree. "The Soothsayer's gone," he said, grabbing her arm. "Let's go!"

And then she was dashing around the huge trunk and sprinting toward the clearing.

As she ran, she became acutley aware of her surroundings. Everything unfolded in slow motion. The light of the fire cast grotesque, flickering shadows on the trees outside the clearing. Drums pounded. The cloaked figure had spread his arms and raised his staff; the people encircling the fire were lifting their joined hands into the air. The Soothsayer tottered toward the fire. Gretchen couldn't see Dana and Adam; they must have been standing on the other side of the flames.

The two of them tiptoed the last few steps to the hut and leaned against the back wall. They were to the right of the door. Zander held up a hand. *Wait,* he mouthed.

Gretchen could feel the hot earth twitching under her feet.

"It is the one who betrayed us!" shrieked the wheezy voice.

"Where are the others?"

"I've killed the others," came Dana's faint reply. Gretchen winced. Her voice sounded afraid—unconvincing. "I've come to redeem myself. I've delivered the child."

"So you beg forgiveness? We'll see about that. Bring forth the Second Sacrifice. We'll see if you're worthy of redemption after we've spilled your friend's blood."

The tempo of the drums on the other side of the hut's wall suddenly increased.

Gretchen's mouth fell open. *The Second Sacrifice! That's Lacy—*

She watched in horror as Zander leaned back and hurled himself against the door. It snapped open and his body fell into the darkness—

143

followed by the crash of shattering clay and glass.

The drumming abruptly ceased.

Gretchen held her breath.

"You fool!" screamed an old woman's voice. "You've tried to sabotage us!"

Gretchen felt cold sweat at the back of her neck. It was the voice that had spoken through Adam.

"Bring that Nonbeliever out where we can see him."

There was a rustle and tinkling of debris.

Gretchen crouched behind the wall of the hut and slowly let her breath out. Why hadn't she followed Zander through that door? She'd been paralyzed—unable to move. What was the matter with her? She had just ruined it for all of them. Now they were all dead. . . .

"Dana, what did you hope to accomplish by bringing this boy here?" asked the wheezy voice. "Did you actually think you could prevent the Second Sacrifice?"

"I-I don't know what you're talking about," Dana cried. "I thought he was dead! I swear!"

"You make a poor liar," said the Soothsayer. "Hopefully you'll make a better sacrifice. So where's the girl—the baby-sitter? Is she lurking around here somewhere, too? Is there something you want to tell us, Dana?"

Gretchen closed her eyes. *We're all going to die—*

"She went to the police station hours ago."

Zander's voice boomed across the clearing. "They'll be here any minute. You're finished."

Zander! What in God's name are you—

"Such a courageous young man," said the Soothsayer. "And so optimistic! Your voice is loud and true and strong, unlike your sniveling friend here. I wish I could believe you, but unfortunately, I can't. By the time your friend gets here, we'll be done and gone—and you'll be dead."

Gretchen's mind worked feverishly. Was Zander trying to tell her something? Did he want her to run—to try to get the police? The Soothsayer was right; she'd never make it. She couldn't stand it anymore. She had to peek through that door.

Cautiously, silently, she placed her cheek against the rough thatched wall beside the door frame. The wall felt cold and damp under her skin. Then, with excruciating effort, she forced her head to lean to the left.

The hut was in a shambles. Heaps of broken clay and glass were strewn everywhere. Several masks had fallen to the floor, their leering faces pointing in all directions. A single tall red candle flickered on the stone platform.

No one was inside.

Gretchen shifted her gaze to the front door. Zander was being held just outside by two cloaked men with small drums hanging around their necks. The three of them obscured most of her vision—but she could see the backs of the white robes around the fire beyond.

Where was Lacy?

Her eyes jumped back to the candle. The decision was instantaneous. She leapt into the hut and grabbed it. With her other hand, she fished the lighter out of her pocket and whirled around, sprinkling the fluid over the two wooden crates under the table. She dipped the flame into the drops of liquid. With a soft *whoosh*, the crates caught on fire.

"Look! There's someone in the temple!"

Gretchen bolted out the front door and tackled Zander as hard as she could. . . .

KABOOM!

The tremendous heat and wind from the explosion smothered her the moment she struck the ground. She squeezed her eyes shut, keeping Zander's body pinned beneath her. Tiny bits of searing-hot debris stung her arms and legs.

"The temple!" an anguished voice howled. "The Nonbelievers have destroyed it. . . . "

Gretchen opened her eyes. The clearing was in pandemonium. White-robed figures were running in every direction, while others stood hopelessly around the fire, struggling desperately to join hands and keep the circle together. The Soothsayer was gone. Burning chunks of wood were everywhere. A heap of smoldering ruins stood where the temple had been.

"Zander," she whispered into his ear. "Are you okay?"

"I don't know," he moaned. "My ankle . . . I think I may have twisted it when I broke down that door."

"Can you walk? We have to get out—"

Lacy!

Gretchen suddenly noticed her sprawled on the ground a few feet away from them. She was covered in a tattered black robe, bound and gagged with red rope—exactly the way Dana had been when Gretchen and Zander had found her. She looked bad. Her hair was singed and her face was cut—and her eyes were closed.

Gretchen rolled off Zander. "Lacy, get up!" She scrambled over and knelt beside her. Her body was slack and her eyes remained closed. Gretchen put Lacy's head on her knees and began working at the tight knot in the gag. "C'mon, Lacy," she breathed.

Then she became aware of people standing around her.

"Get up," ordered a gruff male voice.

She looked up. Looming above her were two tall, powerfully built men. Their faces were covered by large wooden masks flecked with jewels. The full, wide lips were carved in a flat line. It was neither a smile nor a frown: it was nothing. The eyes were two black holes.

Gretchen tried to stand, but her shaky legs seemed unable to support her weight. The men reached over and pulled her to her feet, holding her tightly between them. Their grip was like an iron vise; she knew it was unshakable.

"We have the baby-sitter," called one of the men.

The cloaked figure with the staff had been hunched over the scorched ruins of the temple. Gretchen still hadn't seen the figure's face. But upon hearing those words, the figure turned—revealing the wizened face of a decrepit old man. His deeply furrowed skin was a dead chalk white, except for two huge purplish sacks under his dark eyes—eyes that glistened with hatred.

Gretchen's insides turned to water. It was the face of pure evil. It was the face of death.

He stood before Gretchen. "Do you know who I am, child?" he wheezed.

Gretchen struggled to meet his stare, but she felt herself wilting beneath its authority. "No," she whispered.

His cracked lips parted in a toothless smile. "You think I am death."

Gretchen's eyes widened.

"Yes, child," he said, nodding. "I have powers, too."

She opened her mouth, but he raised his hand.

"Silence. You're right. I am your death. But not until you have performed one last function—as a baby-sitter."

"Wh-what are you talking about?"

The old man sighed. "Adam has vanished. He and Dana ran when you destroyed our temple. But you see, I know Adam Wollman—I know

148

him better than his own parents do. I have been watching over him his entire life. And I know that despite his gift, he has a soft spot for people. He would never save himself at the expense of others. Which means that he didn't run too far. He's out there—hiding somewhere close by, watching us."

"You'll never find him," Gretchen said, averting her eyes.

The man smiled again. "You're probably right, child. Some of us chased after him. They're out there looking for him now, but I doubt they'll succeed. He's a clever boy. Which means we have to bring him to us." His eyes narrowed. "More specifically—*you* have to bring him to us."

"How?"

"Simple. Call to him. Tell him you're going to be killed if he doesn't come right away. He'll come—because he'll know it's the truth."

"I won't do it." Gretchen looked him directly in the face. "I'd sooner die than bring Adam back here. Anyway—what do I care? You're going to kill me no matter what."

"You're right about that, child." His eyes burned. "But you *are* going to help us in this way."

"I won't! You can't make me."

"That's where you're wrong. You see, I know a little something about human nature. People always succumb to their fear of death. They always collapse at the last moment if they think there's any chance at all of saving themselves. It's in our blood. So you may let us tie you up and prepare you for the sacrifice—but when that knife is raised above your head, you'll scream his name. I know you will."

TWELVE

The circle of hooded figures around the fire was once again complete. Seventeen people stood hand in hand, heads lowered, chanting softly in a language Gretchen had never heard.

Gretchen stood just outside the circle. She stared into the wall of flame—the flame that she was certain would consume her dead body before the end of the night.

The masked men had not let her go. Their grip had neither changed nor shifted. They stood on either side of her in perfect silence, their bodies as rigid and lifeless as statues.

Zander and Lacy lay at her feet.

Zander's left ankle was broken. It was twisted inward and horribly swollen. Beads of sweat bathed his wrinkled forehead. His eyelids fluttered and his back arched in pain.

At least his suffering will be over soon. . . .

Lacy remained bound and gagged. She still appeared to be unconscious.

The old man walked over and looked contemptuously at the two bodies on the ground. He flashed his eyes at Gretchen. "Prepare yourself for death, child," he said.

I'm not going to call Adam's name, she swore to herself. *I won't let it happen. He can't make me. He can't!*

He turned and shuffled toward the fire, looking around him with annoyance. "Where is the Soothsayer?" he muttered. "Why is she still out there looking for him?" Finally he cleared his throat. "We will commence the ceremony without the Soothsayer," he announced. "She'll come back once we have the boy in our possession."

The circle of figures stopped chanting.

Behind Gretchen there began a slow, pulselike beating of drums. *Boom . . . Boom . . . Boom . . .*

"The Trail of Blood ends in blood," cried the old man.

"The Trail of Blood ends in blood," answered the circle.

Gretchen's heart pounded in her chest.

"We have waited eight hundred years for the Fiery Dawn." His voice was breathy and strained. "Everything in The Book has come to pass. Tonight we offer the Second Sacrifice. Tomorrow night is the Night of Nights. It has been written."

"It has been written," answered the circle.

The tempo of the drums increased.

"The Nonbelievers have defiled our sanctuary.

They have destroyed our temple. Our relics are burned—lost forever. But the prophets wrote of great sadness and turmoil before the Fiery Dawn. It has been written."

"It has been written."

The blood drained from Gretchen's face. *They knew all along what was going to happen. They were expecting it.*

"But with every defeat comes a victory," the old man continued. "For now we have four offerings. Four children in their prime to give to the spirits, in thanks for the Fiery Dawn that awaits us." He turned and waved his staff at Gretchen. "Bring forth the first of the Second Sacrifices."

The masked men stepped forward two paces, dragging Gretchen between them. Her body went limp as her last reserves of hope and strength evaporated.

"Somebody's going to die tonight." Adam's words echoed in her head. *He foresaw all of our deaths. Now he has to stand by and witness them without being able to do anything about it, just like he said he would.*

"Do you have anything to say before your passing, child?" The old man's eyes bored into hers.

"No." She focused all of her concentration on making her voice firm. "No, I don't."

"I see. Very well." He held out a trembling hand.

The masked man on Gretchen's right reached

into his robe and withdrew a glittering dagger. Its pristine silver blade was at least a foot long; its handle was of finely polished, delicately carved ebony.

The old man took it and studied it for a moment, holding it in front of him as if he were admiring its workmanship.

"Your death, child," he said quietly. "Take a good look. The sands in the hourglass are few." He brought it closer to Gretchen's face. "You feel the urge to cry out."

Gretchen bit her lip. *No, no, no . . .*

"All of the sacrifices are to be made with the same blade," he said loudly. "It has been written."

"It has been written," answered the circle of figures.

"Stop!" Adam's voice suddenly cried out from the woods behind them.

No, Adam! Run! Gretchen heard the sound of uneven footsteps, followed by a loud thump.

"This has not been written!" he said.

The old man's jaw fell open and the dagger slipped from his hands. "What have you done?"

The masked men abruptly let go of Gretchen's arms. She whirled around. *Oh my God!*

Standing next to the remains of the temple were Adam and Dana. The Soothsayer's body lay on the ground in front of them, her head turned toward the fire, her eyes open with the same vacant stare Gretchen had seen on Todd's face just two nights ago.

It was the stare of death.

"This has not been written," Adam repeated breathlessly. "Your prophecies were wrong."

"How did this happen?" cried the old man.

"I was hiding in the woods," Dana said. For once her voice was clear and confident. "I saw the Soothsayer find Adam. I ran out and jumped on her. I grabbed her around the neck. I wasn't planning on killing her—but she was so frail. I strangled her. I killed her!"

"But—but that's impossible," stammered the old man. "It couldn't—"

"Look at her!" Dana pointed at the lifeless heap on the ground. "She's dead. The Book says that *she's* supposed to make the final sacrifice. Well, The Book's wrong. There isn't going to be a final sacrifice—and there isn't going to be a Fiery Dawn. The Trail of Blood stops right here!"

"This can't be happening," said the old man, but the fire had gone out of his voice.

"It *is* happening," said Adam. He shook his head. "You're finished. Now that your book has failed you, you have nothing. Your powers don't exist anymore." He glanced down at the ground. "You can feel it. You know it's true."

Gretchen rubbed her feet across the soil. In her terrified state, she hadn't even noticed—but Adam was right. The earth beneath her no longer tingled with a living warmth. It was just plain, ordinary dirt.

The old man sank to his knees. "There must

be some mistake," he whispered. "Some key to the text that we've overlooked for all these generations—"

"Give it up," Dana said. Her voice quaked with anger. "I can't believe I bought into your lies for so long! I've wasted so many years—my whole life."

The men who had been holding Gretchen backed away from her. One of them pulled the mask from his head, revealing a bearded middle-aged face.

"You!" Adam jabbed his finger in the man's direction. "You were at my house this afternoon. I looked into you—I saw you in my vision at the other ceremony!"

The man's face went pale, as if he had been stricken with a terrible illness.

"That's right. I was hiding this afternoon. I saw you take Lacy, just like I said I would. And I saw somebody die tonight, too—just like I said I would. But it wasn't any of us—it was your Soothsayer!"

"They're the ones who killed Todd," Dana said evenly, her eyes also glued to the bearded man. "The Soothsayer's acolytes. They showed up at his house with the Soothsayer—and killed him right in front of me."

Nobody responded. There was nothing more to say.

The great bonfire had dwindled somewhat. The robed figures were no longer holding hands; they had removed their hoods. The broken faces of seventeen ordinary men, women, and children stared sorrowfully at Adam, their silence betraying their defeat.

Adam suddenly whirled around. "Listen!" he said. He turned back, a smile spreading on his face. "Dogs barking! You hear that? You know what that means?"

Gretchen strained to hear, but she was too close to the fire.

"They're getting closer," Adam said. "They'll be here any second!"

Gretchen's ears began to detect a savage barking.

Then, without a word, everyone—all of the robed figures, the drummers, and the men with masks—stampeded out of the clearing into the woods. For a brief moment the air was filled with the baying of dogs and the sound of running feet.

"Go ahead!" Adam yelled. "Run! It's no use!"

The only one of them who remained was the old man.

An instant later the clearing was swarming with German shepherds.

"Freeze!" shouted a strident voice.

Gretchen blinked. Before her mind could process what was happening, a dozen uniformed policemen in bulletproof vests were kneeling in the clearing, their shotguns leveled at her. Dogs were tearing at the ground inches away from her feet, their teeth bared, saliva dripping from their jaws.

"Put your hands over your head!"

Gretchen raised her hands uncomprehendingly into the air.

"No!" Adam's voice was desperate, imploring. "You've got it wrong! They're getting away!"

But the policemen didn't seem to notice. Several of them surrounded her. One of them grabbed her arms and pulled them roughly behind her back, snapping her wrists into handcuffs. The sharp metal bit into her flesh.

Her mind began racing. She tried to think of something to say, something to prove her innocence.

But the only words that came out were: "How did you find us?"

"Easy," snapped the police officer. "We happened to find your friend's car off the road. We did a little investigating, and discovered he lived next door to the boy who was murdered. Seemed like sort of an odd coincidence, so we let our dogs here take a whiff of the seats. They did the rest."

"You've got it wrong," Zander gasped. He was clutching his ankle in agony. "She was trying to save him. *They* did it. The old man—"

"Easy, son." Two officers gently lifted him and carried him to the edge of the clearing. "He's badly hurt," one of them yelled. "We may need to get a chopper in here."

Two other officers bent to remove Lacy's gag and bindings. She had finally regained consciousness. "What's going on?" she asked groggily. "Gretchen? Gretchen—what happened?"

But Gretchen was unable to reply. She had been reduced to a pair of eyes and ears; shock had made any kind of reaction impossible.

"This one's hurt, too," called another officer as Lacy was carried away and gently placed next to Zander. "We're definitely going to need that chopper."

Radios and walkie-talkies crackled as Gretchen was hustled to the opposite edge of the clearing. She looked at Adam. For some reason, his expression was one of absolute horror; he had never looked more frightened. Gretchen gazed at him in confusion. Some policemen tried to drape a blanket over him, but he shook it off. "The old man," he said, licking his lips. His head whipped around frantically. "The High Priest! He's gone!"

"Son?" asked one of the police officers.

"Didn't you see him? The old man kneeling on the ground. He was still here when you got here! He escaped!"

The policemen looked at each other. "Maybe we should send some men into the woods," said one of them.

Just then a fat officer with a wide hat and a gray shirt stepped into the clearing. A hush fell over the rest of the men.

"So here she is," he said. He waddled over to Gretchen and stood in front of her. "I'm Sheriff Peters, Miss Childs. And you're in a whole lot of trouble."

* * *

159

"So let me get this straight one last time." The sheriff sighed and leaned across the table. "We know you're exhausted. We all are. But what you're telling me is that twenty-two people just disappeared a few seconds before we showed up? Just vanished into the woods without a trace? And *these* are the people who are responsible for killing Todd Wilde?"

Gretchen nodded, unable to speak anymore. She hadn't seen Zander, Lacy, Dana, Adam—anyone—since she had been bundled into a helicopter back at the clearing. For the past three hours, she had been sitting in a wooden chair in a tiny windowless room—a room lit by a single dangling bulb. A small, thin cot stood against the wall opposite the door. She had been sitting across a small table from the sheriff and one other man. The clock on the wall read two o'oclock when she had first arrived. Now it read five.

"And the woman whose body was in the clearing was with them, too?" the sheriff asked.

"That's what I've been telling you for the past three hours," Gretchen finally croaked.

The sheriff nodded disappointedly. "So you say. The one the Hess girl killed, right? We've been trying to identify her, but it seems there are no records. She didn't have any identification, and her fingerprints didn't produce a match."

Gretchen stared at him. *And they never will*, she thought.

The sheriff glanced at the other man. The two

of them stood. "Why don't you lie down on that cot and try to get some rest, Miss Childs," the sheriff said. "Right now we've got a lot of questions that need to be answered. We'll be back in a little while."

"But-but they'll—"

The bulb winked off and a heavy metal door slammed behind them.

Gretchen staggered over to the cot and stretched out. The only light in the cell was coming from a small window in the door. Her eyelids fluttered, and the burning ache in her feet and joints began to fade. A flurry of images swept through her mind: Adam, the dead Soothsayer, the old man—

The old man!

Gretchen suddenly gasped. Her heart was pounding. Had she just seen his face in the window at the door? She could have sworn he was standing there, staring at her . . .

I've got to sleep. I'm seeing things. I'm perfectly safe here. I just need to rest. . . .

"Miss Childs?"

Gretchen snapped awake with a start. She was groggy. The bulb was back on and the sheriff was standing over her. "What's going on?" she asked confusedly.

"It's ten o'clock. It's time to go home," the sheriff said gently. "You're mom's waiting for you."

Gretchen sat up quickly. "What happened? D-did you find them?"

The sheriff hesitated. "I'm afraid not, Miss Childs. But we'll—"

"You have to keep looking," she interrupted. "The rest of them are out there somewhere." Her voice rose. Tears started pouring down her cheeks. "You have to keep looking and looking. You can't ever stop!"

The sheriff took her hand and led her through the door. "We won't. But don't you worry about that anymore. It's no longer your concern."

Gretchen staggered into the waiting room. The first people she saw were the Wollmans. They were huddled around Adam. They were sobbing, begging for forgiveness for having left him alone—for having been afraid of his . . . gift. It was obvious they had no idea what their son had just been through.

"Gretchen!"

Before she knew what was happening, she was deep in her mother's embrace. "Oh, Gretchen," she was saying. "Everything's going to be okay. . . ."

Gretchen rested her head on her mother's shoulder. Her eyes wandered through the waiting room. Through the window, she could see their white VW bug in the parking lot. She managed a smile through her tears. Everything *was* going to be okay.

Suddenly a man appeared in the parking lot. He glanced into the window. Gretchen's heart froze. It was the old man!

"Look!" she screamed, wrenching free of her mother's arms and pointing out the window. "There he is!"

Silence filled the waiting room. All eyes were fixed on Gretchen. The parking lot was empty.

It wasn't real. It was just my imagination.

"What is it, Gretchen?" her mom asked.

"I-I thought I saw one of them. I thought . . ."

The sheriff looked at Gretchen's mom. "I think you'd best be getting your daughter home now, Mrs. Childs."

"Yeah," Gretchen whispered. "He's right. I need to go home."

Epilogue

"So you get your cast off tomorrow, huh?" Gretchen asked. "Are you psyched?"

"Yeah." Zander smiled. "Because this cast is the last reminder I have. Once this comes off, I'll never have to think about it again."

Gretchen reached over and squeezed his hand.

It was a beautiful August Saturday afternoon in San Francisco. Zander had come up to see her, as he had every weekend since she had gone back home. Together, they had helped each other to cope with the memories and the nightmares. And during that time, they had become more than just friends.

Today, he had even brought a special treat with him: Adam. It was the first time she had seen him since she had left Madison.

She leaned over and kissed Zander.

"Yuck," Adam said. "Did I come up here just to watch you guys make out?"

Lacy laughed. "Really. I mean—is that any way to behave in public?"

Gretchen smiled. Sitting in this café, just the four of them, everything seemed to fade into the distance. But it had been so hard to smile. Todd was gone, Dana was gone, and everything had changed. She closed her eyes, forcing herself not to think about what she always did, every hour of every day . . .

They're still out there.

The old man stood on the busy street corner, watching.

Four people sat around a table on the opposite corner. They were smiling, laughing. One was a teenage girl with long chestnut curls. One was a blond-haired boy with a cast on his right leg. One was a small girl with short brown hair.

And the last was the child.

At least Dana was paying for her crimes, the old man thought. She would be punished by the law for the death of the Soothsayer. And she would be punished by the Order—in due time.

But these . . .

The chestnut-haired girl reached over and kissed the blond-haired boy.

The old man's heart squeezed with hatred. The August sun was hot. He longed for the cool of night and the peace of the new sanctuary.

The child was so close, and at the same time just beyond his grasp.

But not for long.

The prophecies would yet be fulfilled. . . .

The night trembled to the might of Nantierran artillery blasts, growing faster and faster as the crews settled down into their rhythm. The enemy earthworks erupted in a shower of dust, red-hot ricochets plowing high into the air. Mortars sent shell-bursts tearing down into the castle roofs. Aelis watched, breathing heavily as the fires shone in her eyes.

Able to see the fall of their own shot in the dark, the goblins would crew the guns by night, while human artillerymen would maintain the fire by day. The castle walls would dissolve like sand before the wind.

A presence loomed behind Aelis in the darkness. Death drew Count Retter like a moth unto flame.

"You have waited long, Majesty."

"I wait no more!" The queen stamped at the mud with her hooves. "Varre! How long?"

"One week—perhaps nine days, depending on the temper of their stone."

Aelis stood posed against the gunfire. The flashes outlined her perfect figure against the chill night sky. One week. One week, and Castle Kerbridge would be gone.

"Count Retter—you may plan your assault."

B·O·O·K·S

CAPTAINS OUTRAGEOUS
Roy V. Young

CITY OF THE SORCERERS
Mary H. Herbert

GO QUEST YOUNG MAN
K. B. Bogen

THE HIDDEN WAR
Michael Armstrong

MUS OF KERBRIDGE
Paul Kidd

F.R.E.E.LANCERS
Mel Odom
(Available Summer 1995)

Mus of Kerbridge

Being the tale of a dashing young rodent, his companions, and their adventures.

Paul Kidd

MUS OF KERBRIDGE

First Printing: April 1995
Printed in the United States of America
Library of Congress Catalog Card Number: 94-60835

9 8 7 6 5 4 3 2 1

ISBN: 0-7869-0094-6

TSR, Inc.   TSR Ltd.
201 Sheridan Springs Rd.   120 Church End, Cherry Hinton
Lake Geneva, WI 53147   Cambridge CB1 3LB
United States of America   United Kingdom

For my beloved wife Christine,
who somehow manages to put up with all of this. . . .

Book One
Mouse & Maiden

Chapter One

Mouse!

neaky, sneaky . . . edging through shadows. Clever! Clever to hide so! A little mouse crept across cool, smooth floors, hugging the skirting boards beneath gleaming racks of copper pans. The great, empty kitchen lay quiet; there were no cats, no dogs, and no giants with their stamping feet. With the fall of midnight, only the smaller residents of the household stirred about their busy lives.

The kitchen was a fine place to live—warm and safe; there were mouse nests up in the rafters and under the floorboards near the fire's glow. Food had always been easy to find here, but this mouse roamed farther than his fellows, seeking new things to eat and smell and see. It was dangerous—cats and giants prowled his world like great monsters in the mist—but the mouse reveled in his own cleverness.

Logs shifted in the fireplace, making ashes hiss softly in the dark. Whiskers aquiver, the mouse froze, eyes staring wide. A faint noise from across the room teased him; the mouse's ears fanned out, twitching as he curiously bobbed his head.

Tappy tap, tappy tap . . . Is no danger? Perhaps is eaties! Is it tasty?

Aaaah! The mouse spotted his prey: a fine fat moth pressed against the glass cylinder of a lantern, frantically trying to reach the light. It furiously beat its wings at the glass, falling back exhausted only to try again.

Ha—eaties! The mouse inched forward and pounced on his prize, holding the struggling insect in his paws. Turning his head sideways, he bit with wicked little teeth into the moth's head. Eyes slitted in ecstasy, the mouse nibbled steadily away at his

meal, feeling himself quite the cleverest creature in the world.
Lovely bugs! Fresh meats! Lovely juicy crunchy meats!

WHAM!

The world suddenly turned black; with a squeak of terror the
mouse flung himself sideways, slamming against a hard, cold wall.
He leapt the other way, only to bounce against a slick, shiny barrier.

Trapped! The mouse staggered sideways and fell, his head reel-
ing. *Frighten! Die now! I die. . . .*

The market square of Kerbridge town lay broad and open
beneath a haze of summer dust. Sparrows took baths in gaps
among the cobblestones, while here and there an insect found
energy enough to fly. An orange cat lazed beside a horse trough,
enjoying a golden beam of sun, content to leave the little birds in
peace.

The beer garden stood all but empty; fat purple grapes hung
from the bowers overhead, and shiny green flies cruised up and
down the tables. The air smelt of mown grass and spilled beer and
hot sun on dust. Utterly content, Pin-William lounged in the dappled shade with his broad leather hat tilted down over his eyes.

A gawky human boy appeared at the edge of the garden, a lad
of eleven or twelve years, and quite unremarkable except for the
chipped old milk jug that he cradled in his arms. The boy nervously stepped over to Pin-William and tried to draw the man's
attention.

Pin-William shifted in his seat, and sunlight gleamed from his
neatly polished cloven hooves. The satyr's outlandish costume
hung festooned with ribbons and buttons, buckles, lace, and bows;
from his befeathered hat to his rapier, he had the gaudy panache of
the master of a fair.

For all intents and purposes, the satyr's upper half could pass
for human; a handsome, angular face lay in shadow beneath the
wide brim of the hat, and a fashionable black beard lined his jaw.
The face seemed so beguiling that it took a few moments for the
more startling features to become apparent. The ears beneath the
hat were tall and sharply pointed, and a pair of neat, glossy horns
jutted from two holes in the hat's brow. The hooves, propped so
comfortably upon the table, were polished to a dazzling shine; the

satyr wore no breeches, nor did he need them.

"You have something for me, lad?"

A gleaming brown eye shone beneath the satyr's hat. The boy gave a start, and then hefted his milk jug.

"Sir? I have trapped you what you asked."

"Indeed? Excellent! Pin-William thanks you!" The satyr sat up, and with a flamboyant sweep of his hand, he drew his hat back from his brow. "Show me your catch, my lad! Let's see what your labors have won."

The boy brought the milk jug up onto the table, and Pin-William cocked an eye to peer inside. A fine fat mouse stared up at him in fright. The creature's ribs heaved in and out, and its whiskers quivered with agitation.

"A fine big fellow! Indeed lad, that's just what I wanted. Prithee, where did you find him?"

The boy tossed back a rebellious forelock of hair. "In the castle kitchens, sir. I caught him dining on a moth. I suspect he's the devil that soiled milady's fine pastries yesterday!" The boy seemed pleased with his capture; he brushed at his errant hair once more and tilted the jug to show off his prisoner to its best advantage.

The satyr slyly stroked his mustache, then took the jug and placed it squarely on the table. He reached into his belt and drew forth three bright new copper pennies, twirled them once, and slapped them down into the page boy's palm. Pin-William sardonically tipped his hat, and the lad scampered off to spend his new-found fortune.

Left alone with the mouse, Pin-William sat back and poured himself a mug of droll, expensive wine. He swirled the beast inside its jug and gave a most unpleasant smile.

"Well little thief, let us see what we can make of you."

Frighten! Frighten! All is unhappy—all around is frighten!

Trapped inside the milk jug, the mouse lived in a world of terror, waiting for the predator to strike. The little creature shivered as it stared with glittering black eyes into emptiness.

So cruel! So cruel to play before they kill! To die and never eats—never curl up with nest mates again. Sad sad sad . . .

Pin-William sat back, furiously shaking his head as he cleared the rodent's thoughts from his own mind. The satyr took a quick swallow of wine before looking up at his client.

"Aaah, yes. Quite—disturbing." The mouse's terror still hung over him like the claws of some hideous great cat. "Its mind is extremely small. I shall have to modify the basic agent; the task you intend is quite complex. I cannot force second-level concepts onto a creature this primitive."

Pin-William's client slowly turned from the window. The floorboards shuddered as four hooves shifted in the darkness.

"I did not ask for excuses."

"Excuses?" Pin-William pressed a hand against his heart. "My lord, I made no excuses—merely an assurance! Fear not, sir, I am already on the case!"

The client moved forward, light catching from the silver hilts of rapier and pistol. Tall and gaunt, the man had dressed himself in a cassock of dull black silk. His clothing covered only his human portion; behind his torso, the centaur's afterbody shone dapple-gray. The nobleman's four hooves were planted firmly on the ground, and his tail hung ragged as a corpse's winding-robe. He tilted his narrow, pock-marked face toward the nervous satyr.

"Magus—you are being handsomely paid for your ingenuity." The noble stroked his trailing mustaches with one lace-cuffed hand. "If there is a problem, then 'tis my suggestion that you *solve* it."

Pin-William bridled, then swept his hands out in an extravagant gesture. "My lord! Doubt you Pin-William? Pin-William the sorcerer! Pin-William the scholar! Pin-William the alchemist!" He leapt to his feet, his hands excitedly waving at his impressive store of magical instruments. "Oh, sir—I take no offense, since you are new to these parts, but surely you must have caught some glimmer of my reputation? Pin-William the ingenious! Pin-William the cunning . . ."

"Quite." The nobleman pulled a scented kerchief from his sleeve and waved it thoughtfully beneath his nose. "Since so vast a reputation must have been well earned, then clearly you have already thought of a solution to the problem. . . . "

"Indeed, sir, indeed!" The satyr bowed, sweeping the floor with his hat. "A solution that would *stagger* the minds of lesser folk! For I am Pin-William, who marches to his own music, stepping boldly forth where others choose to . . ."

The nobleman fixed Pin-William with an icy stare, and the satyr faltered. Moving back to the table, Pin-William plucked up a quizzing glass and carefully inspected his captive.

"Using a mouse as an agent is one of my most refreshingly new ideas! Unfortunately, the controlling process is usually performed on larger animals, such as horses and canines; the broader mind framework makes communication far easier." Pin-William struck a pose, holding aloft his quizzing glass like a magic sword. "But will this halt me? No, sir, it shall not! Where common craft fails, Pin-William thrives and prospers!"

Bored, the nobleman gazed out of the window, examining the town walls. The town of Kerbridge sat on the cool green banks of the river Fandin, a broad, brown waterway that wound down the fertile valleys of southern Duncruigh until it reached the capital city. Rich river trade, a university, and a cathedral made the town of Kerbridge important. In all the island kingdom of Duncruigh, there was no finer seat of learning, no taller church spire, and no doughtier citizens. Their baron served as commander of the royal armies on the continent, an appointment Kerbridge citizens thought his due.

Out across the river, work gangs were preparing star-shaped sconces to guard the town's approaches. Old medieval walls were giving way to the science of modern gunnery. Above it all, up on a high outcrop of rock that overlooked town and river alike, stood the baronial castle—worn and gentle beneath its sheath of primroses and moss.

The troubles on the continent were worrisome. The tiny country of Welfland had turfed out its lazy, indolent king and embraced the dangerous tenet of republicanism. Even so, the young ruler of Duncruigh, King Firined, had rallied to the defense of the fledgling democracy. Duncruigh's traditional enemy, Nantierre, had risen to the cause of the exiled Welflandish king and sought to regain him his throne.

Welfland, like Duncruigh, was a maritime nation. If Nantierre gained Welfland, with its fleets, mariners, and shipyards, then Nantierre's dreams of invasion could finally be realized. The thin strip of water separating Duncruigh from the continent would no longer be defense against their enemies.

The country faced invasion, and grim times were ahead. Worst of all, the price of brandy had trebled almost overnight. Pin-William sniffed suspiciously at his last bottle of best *amber-blanc*, sighed, and reached toward an old stone jug of beer; in times of trouble, even the greatest men must make little sacrifices. . . .

The satyr's current client was paying well—extremely well. The task seemed unusual, but harmless. Pin-William adjusted his broad lace falling band collar and straightened the braids of his gaudy coat.

"The mouse shall be properly prepared, sir, never you fear! I shall enter into the creature's mind and bend it to my will. With the maps of the castle that you have provided me, I shall guide the creature into the private quarters of the baronial family, and your prize shall be most swiftly won!"

" 'D's blood, man! You tell me the beast's mind is too small to control!" The nobleman whirled, his long tail flying and his hide rippling with shadow. "Where's the point of having an agent that cannot be coerced to obey?"

"Aaaah, sir—have you no faith in my talents?" The satyr snapped his fingers at the air. "If the mouse's mind is too small, then I shall expand it! The basic spell structures have been defined, but never properly explored. I, Pin-William, shall perfect them!" Pin-William patted the neck of the old brown jug. "He shall be molded unto our needs, never fear. Now, sir—tell me once more of your commission."

The half-horse shifted his hooves, then adjusted his deadly rapier and dagger in their sheaths. "The commission, sir Wizard, is to snare me a lock of the baron's daughter's hair." He looked out the window, hiding his eyes. "A small thing to you, perhaps, but more precious than gold to me." The nobleman scowled and drummed his rear left hoof against the floor. "Though she has spurned me, though she has denied me such a gift—yet I shall have it! I shall carry her favor by my heart when I return to the continent."

The satyr leapt to his feet and boldly clapped his hands.

"Though shot take you and fever wrack you, you'd bear her remembrance with you e'en unto your grave?" He sighed. "Ah, sir! How can I refuse? You touch onto romance, and I cannot deny the lure! Pin-William shall win your goal!" The satyr waved a finger on high. "Ha! By your return from the wars her ladyship's heart will have softened! Verily you shall sweep her off her hooves!"

The nobleman scowled, turning to stare out of the window once more.

"Proceed as you wish. I will meet you in the orchards near the castle at seven of the evening. I shall bring with me a pouch to attach to the creature. It can store the lock inside once it has gathered it for me."

The half-horse hid himself beneath the black shadows of a cape and stalked slowly through the door. Pin-William ushered his guest outside, bowing low. His short, pointed tail stuck out, wagging gleefully behind him as he bent from the waist.

Odd's fish! Such a fuss over a girl! Hooves up on the table and the bases of his horns well scratched, Pin-William pondered the task before him. An odd case; the baron's daughter was a plain little thing by all reports—more of a scholar than a doe-eyed lover. A half-horse of course—a brown-haired bay. But to inspire such love? Clearly the girl ran deeper than he had heard. At least with the baron away on the continent there would be fewer soldiers for the mouse to evade. The good Lord seemed to be smiling on the endeavor!

The day grew hot, and a long, cold drink seemed the best aid to Pin-William's concentration. The magician read for half an hour, covering scraps of paper with half-remembered formulas. The books he had looted from the ruins of his dead master's workrooms were less than useful sometimes; after two years of private practice Pin-William still felt unsure about his chosen art. Were it not for his vast stores of intelligence, bravery, and natural aptitude, he would have been almost afraid of dabbling with such powers. . . .

The hints he sought were enmeshed with the usual boring warnings about curses and responsibilities. The satyr gave a snort as he began to plan his spells. Changing the structure of a mind couldn't be too much a problem: it wasn't as if he would be changing the way the creature *thought*. The emotions flowed from the organs—the spleen, the heart, and the liver. Creative thought came from the immortal soul—a facility that a mere beast surely lacked. The brain acted merely as a storage device, like a sort of cupboard, so it would simply be a matter of opening up some extra drawers and stocking them with a few concepts. In this case, why not simply give the mouse copies of Pin-William's own?

The satyr whistled tunelessly as he laid out his workboard, cleaned it, asperged it, and readied all his tools. Hooves tapping merrily across the floor, he stood back to admire his preparations. Moving briskly, he snatched up the milk jug and dumped his prisoner out onto the desk. The mouse skittered to its feet and looked fearfully around itself, seeking a means of escape.

Its eyes met Pin-William's gaze and froze; the mouse had time for only one terrified jerk of surprise before its mind was held firmly in the satyr's grasp.

Yes . . . no challenge at all. Pin-William gripped the creature's mind inside his claws and gave a silken smile. Down on the desk, the mouse arched its back and gave a dreadful tortured *scream.*

Hurting! Hurting! It burns, it tears, it rips! The mouse's world became an all-consuming haze of pain. The inferno coursed down into his forepaws and blasted up into his skull, tracing its way through every nerve and sinew.

Terrifying images suddenly tore space for themselves inside the mouse's mind. There was now another level to the pain—regret, fear, outrage, injustice. Somehow raising his head, the mouse opened his eyes and looked into the face of his tormentor.

The creature loomed above, boring into him with great, dark eyes. The mouse met him look for look, accusing him, flinging out a question that had never before dwelt in his mind.

Why?

The mouse tumbled backward as he felt the creature blasting through his mind. New concepts flooded in a senseless storm; skills stripped of meaning and rooms without doors.

Oblivion came only slowly. The mouse lay staring at the walls until the room finally began to fade. . . .

I live.

He lay on his side in a nest of wood shavings and floss. Each limb, each strand of fur seemed isolated and alone. The mouse dragged in breath, making the supreme effort to bring his body back under command. He had only just started to succeed when he suddenly stiffened in shock.

I feel. I think! I am alive!

The simple conscious revelation that he *thought* had never occurred to him before. The concept shocked him—it seemed as though he struggled from a dream into a brand-new waking world. His heart pulsed, his lungs drew air; concentrating, the mouse could feel his whole body from snout to tail. The information from his senses was being arranged into strange, unfamiliar patterns. . . . He now remembered a past, and the present jumped into strange new context.

My feet! My poor handsome feet!

The mouse held up his forepaws and stared at them in shock. They were utterly changed, one joint now sticking out at right angles from each paw. They—they didn't seem to *hurt.* Bewildered and frightened, the mouse clenched his new feet; they could now bunch up like little balls. . . .

The mouse looked up to find himself inside a strange square enclosure hemmed in by shiny bars. A small pan of water sat in the middle of his floor, and the mouse gratefully dipped his nose into the cold, refreshing liquid and drank. The bitter taste in his mouth faded, and strength slowly flowed back into his limbs. Whiskers dripping, the mouse sat back and gave a sigh.

Movement caught his eye. There, looking out at him from beyond the bars, sat a handsome mouse. The captive's heart leapt with joy! *Someone to touch, to cling to for comfort!* Wild with delight, the mouse flung himself at the prison bars. Delicate fingers reached out to touch the other mouse; instead of warm fur, his paw pressed up against something cold and smooth, and the mouse recoiled in surprise.

Cold!

Staring in disbelief, he reached out with his ugly new forepaw and watched as the other mouse copied his motion *exactly.* The mouse cautiously touched the hard surface of the mirror, exploring his discovery with a sharp, inventive mind.

His own face; his own eyes. The mouse sat back and stared at himself for the first time in his life. The sharp little face peered back at him with astonishing intelligence, mesmerizing the rodent with its gaze.

How strange—how wonderful. . . .

Up on the balcony, Pin-William watched his prisoner and smiled. A whole new school of magic had been invented in a single afternoon! With the evening winds streaming through his hair, the satyr lounged back to savor a jug of ale, a bacon pie, and life's rewards.

So far it had been a most *gratifying* day!

Chapter Two

Miriam

iriam Jerrick sat beside a table with her embroidered apron skirts fanned out over her forelegs. Her long brown hair spilled in sausage curls, catching the glint and glitter of the setting sun. Although the open doors let river breezes fill the room, the air still seemed oppressive; Miriam's hide twitched as though irritated by a persistent fly.

Perched on a hill among fragrant orange groves, Castle Kerbridge had an air of genteel decay. The castle had been refurbished to make it into a comfy home rather than a forbidding old fortress, and the old arrow slits were now replaced by glazed windows. The outer bailey, ruined in a war many centuries past, now upheld a gorgeous wilderness of wild rose and flowering hawthorn. Though neatly kept and homey, the castle clearly had once seen better days.

Miriam's mother, Baroness Jerrick, sat reading the packet of letters that had just arrived from the continent. Left to her own devices while her mother read, Miriam idly watched the courier eat dinner on the battlements outside. The harpy's hands stretched awkwardly above him at the folds of his mighty wings—none of which seemed to inconvenience him since he gripped his meal in his feet. Despite fangs, claws, and a most *remarkable* bouquet, the fellow's visits were always welcome. Papa's letters were Mama's lifeline.

The baronial family of Kerbridge were half-horses. Miriam stood about a hand higher than a human girl of similar build and nineteen years of age. In beauty, she hovered on the comfortable side of plain; her eyes were lustrous green, and her snub nose had been well dusted with freckles.

Just below the waist, Miriam's resemblance to a human dramatically ended. Her lower body was that of a young bay mare with slender jet-black legs and a hide of rich red-brown. Her shimmering black tail trailed down to the floor, caught at its very top by a bright bunch of silken bows. There were ink stains on her fingers, and a book peeked from the pocket of her apron. Though trim and well-chested, Miriam turned few heads, a failing she greeted with a due sense of relief.

Lady Jerrick interrupted Miriam's flow of thought with a heartfelt, weary sigh. To Miriam's amazement and dismay, her mother hung her head and carelessly dropped her letters to the ground.

"Mother?"

Miriam quickly crossed the room, laying her hand on her mother's arm. "Is Papa all right?"

Lady Jerrick wearily raised her head and rubbed her eyes. "The taxes have been voted. Parliament will not maintain the armies on the continent."

"No!" *God preserve us, what will happen now?* "Surely they can't just abandon them!" Miriam's father and her older brother were both serving with the army!

"*Parliament!*" Lady Jerrick spat the word like some foul oath. "Leymond and his traitors bringing us down from within! They should go to the block, the whole vile brood!"

Shocked, Miriam stamped her back hoof, and the steel shoe struck sparks on the flagstones. Her mother stood, her tail lashing back and forth in hate.

"Damn them to hell!"

Miriam was shattered; of all people in the world, surely her mother could find the easy solution? She had always done so in the past. . . . Miriam edged closer.

"Mother . . . Please? Surely there's money somewhere?"

The baroness breathed hard, mastering herself; finally the woman reached up and straightened out a fold in Miriam's bodice. "The king will try his best, my darling. The crown purse will do what it can, but His Majesty will be overstretched." She swallowed. "Thy father's supplies must be paid for from our own funds."

Miriam's heart went cold; there simply *was* no money! Her

father had bankrupted himself equipping troops for the army. Without supplies, her father's men would starve—or worse, find themselves overrun as powder and shot gave out during battle. Without a Duncruighan army on the continent, Welfland would surely fall, and Queen Aelis of Nantierre would finally have a navy. . . .

Miriam felt a surge of fear; not in five hundred years had invaders come to Duncruigh's shores, and now there was no one to stop them. What could be done? Sell land? Take a ruinous loan from a moneylender? Either option would be the sure death of the family.

Lady Jerrick stood, her tail slashing the air behind her. "I-I just can't see what I can do. I am going into the gardens to think. Please child—I must be alone for a while."

Eyes glazed with bewilderment, Miriam's mother wandered from the room. Miriam stared after her, completely helpless. The money would run out at the end of the season; if an answer could be found, it must be found quickly.

Tail trailing sorrowfully behind her, Miriam paced down to the library, her hoofbeats echoing down empty passageways. Once there had been far more people living here in the castle; Miriam vaguely recalled a childhood when the castle had thronged with life. Laughter had warmed the tired old hallways, and a fire had blazed in every room. Miriam remembered peeking though banisters to watch a great ball, gasping at the color and grandeur of it. She had sat enraptured for hours, tapping little hooves to the music until her mother had finally found her and bustled her away.

No one ever came to visit anymore. Hard times had come, and then father had gone to the wars, hoping to win back a fortune for the family. . . . Suddenly turning aside, Miriam wove through the deserted passageways, coming out into the open air near the ancient ruined chapel in the northern grounds.

So much of the castle lay in disrepair now—so much decayed. The quiet, moss-covered jumbles of cold stone and fallen columns had always been Miriam's refuge. Tall arches reached to the open sky as if to hold aloft the clouds themselves. The stones overflowed with wild fennel, thistle stalks, and rosemary. Slipping between the weeds, her skirts held well out of the way, Miriam stole down into the old chapel's crypt.

The crypt was clean and dry, and breathed an air of tranquil disarray. Spectacular fan vaults sprang up from the floor, framing an altar at the far end of the room. Here, Miriam had made her own special, secret refuge. A chart of the bodily proportions of human and half-horse hung from one wall, and a small shelf held the instruments she used to heal the hurts of small animals. It was here that she had splinted a sparrow's broken wing, and nursed an egret that had swallowed a fishing hook. Miriam loved all living things; her strong gentle hands had a healer's touch.

In her dreams, she saw herself as a lady and a scholar—a hero from an ancient storyland. A strange fantasy, perhaps, but without dreams, what else is there to live for?

There would be no escape today; Miriam sat unhappily on her big old chair, her rump cradled by the seat and her front legs standing unsupported. She stared at the pages of a book, but somehow the words made no sense. Her eyes blinked, unseeing, as her mind worried at the problem before her. Miriam's sharp mind had slowly worked out an unhappy solution—and the girl felt her courage fail.

Hours passed, bringing no escape from her decision. Miriam's whole world became somehow distant and unreal. The last light of the evening sun shone through the window, warming her bowed shoulders as Miriam paced slowly back toward the keep. Long shadows trailed from the fallen columns as she passed them by; her hoofbeats sounded dull and hollow as she reluctantly made her way inside.

She found her mother in the vast, empty dining hall, contemplating a portrait of her husband. The household accounts and deeds lay on the table, and Miriam knew all too well the tale they told. The family could take no more expenses lest it be reduced to utter penury.

Miriam looked up at the portrait. Her father's wise gray eyes were calm and dignified; a sword hung at his side, but a pen was in his hand. He had always been a good father, encouraging his scholarly daughter. Miriam stared at the portrait, her face pale.

"Mother?"

Miriam's voice sounded terrified, even to herself. The smooth brown hide of her flanks twitched fitfully. "We have no fortune, but we—we have a title. . . ." She shivered. "An advantageous marriage. That would bring us money."

Her mother's arms wound around her. Miriam clutched her mother tightly while Lady Jerrick folded the girl against her heart. "Yes, my darling. Indeed it would."

Miriam would do what she could to save Father's men. God knew, it was little enough. Held tight in her mother's arms, Miriam wept for fading dreams.

Pin-William's client waited for him in the shadows of the castle's orange groves. Darkness had thrown its cloak over the warm night, making the air seem close and still, and the night hung heavy with the blood-thick scent of oranges. The half-horse nobleman loomed among the trees, dwarfing the wiry little satyr.

Pin-William absently stroked the butt of his pistol, doffed his hat, and swept down into an elaborate bow.

"My lord! A very good evening to you."

"Magus." The nobleman shifted his hooves in the depths of the shadows. "Our agent is prepared?"

"Indeed, sir. Indeed! It has created a most promising new line of research. Your lordship has the pouch?"

"Of course. I had it of a doll maker in town, and it should fit our creature. I have also brought a map of the castle."

Pin-William carefully took the little green backpack, marveling at the fine workmanship of the straps. Something hard and smooth seemed to be held inside. Pin-William looked inquiringly at his companion, but shadows hid the stallion's face.

"A good luck medallion. Not to imply I lack confidence in your ability, Magus, but . . ."

"Of course, sir! A little extra help is always welcome! When we deal with the fantastic and insubstantial, who can say what works and what does not?"

Pin-William reached into the cage and snatched forth the mouse, leaving it dangling helplessly by the tail.

"Well, my lord, let us begin! We shall sit comfortably here, and I shall keep you informed as to its progress." The satyr sketched an elegant bow. "I would appreciate it, sir, if you would keep an ear cocked lest we be discovered here."

They nestled down in the shadows beneath a gnarled old orange tree, and Pin-William went to work.

Free!

The mouse tumbled down into soft, fragrant grass. Rolling to his feet, he instantly dashed off into the shadows. A wave of sheer joy swept through him as he fled the Tormentor.

I am quick! I am clever! I am free!

Needles of white fire tore suddenly through his brain. Kicking and squealing, the mouse tumbled to a halt. The pain pierced him through and through, convulsing him with agony. He felt strong fingers picking him up by the tail. When he could see again, he found himself dangling far above the ground, held up before the Tormentor's gaze. The huge, wicked eyes bored into him like knives.

Foolish.

Burning claws raked the length of the mouse's spine, making him jerk his feet with fear.

No more! Please don't hurt! Just kill. Kill me and be done. Oh, why are you so cruel?

No. I will not kill. But the pain will be waiting for you whenever you disobey.

I-I will obey. Please don't hurt me. Please?

Wear the backpack and enter the castle. Go.

The pain faded. Helpless in the clutches of a terrible enemy, the mouse rose miserably to his feet and padded off into the orange grove. Behind him the dark eyes of his Tormentor seemed to burn into the mouse's twisty tail.

Tiny pink feet whispered through leaves as the mouse made his way uphill. Finally the trees seemed to end. The mouse sheltered fearfully before an open stretch of roadway. His eyesight failed when he tried to look farther; of the castle gates, he could see nothing but vague, looming shadows.

Sensitive mousy ears read a whole world of sounds into the night. Whiskers twitching, the mouse huddled under a fallen leaf and peered out at a terrifying world.

Go! Why do you wait?

I am frightened.

Coward! Inferior little beast, get moving!

Owls! I shall be eaten by owls. I hear their wings, their hoots, their hunger! The mouse gazed about and wrung tiny paws in fright. *It is all open—nowhere to sneaky sneak. All my cleverness will come to an end in ripping claws and tearing beaks. . . .*

Straight to the castle doors. You will go there now.

NO!

The fire came flooding back overhead, making the little creature squeak with fright.

Do as instructed.

Trembling, the mouse crept out into the open. In terrified little fits and starts, he made his way to the castle drawbridge. Somewhere in the distance, thunder slowly rolled across the air.

A storm brewed, and the night grew oppressively warm. In helmets and buffcoats, the guardsmen felt utterly stifled; a flask of cold ale was more than welcome. The two guards propped their halberds against the castle wall and passed the jug happily back and forth, enjoying a quiet yarn while they drank the rich, cold brew.

Working for half-horses had its good points. They were the noisiest beasts in all creation, and even the baroness couldn't manage to creep up on a soldier unawares. Best of all, the creatures quaffed great quantities of ale, and seemed to expect that everyone else should, too.

One soldier was passing the jug back to his fellow when his eye strayed down to a movement on the cobbles. A mouse padded purposefully across the threshold, wearing a tiny green satchel across its back. The soldier blinked; the mouse raised its head, looked up at him with frightened brown eyes, and then dashed off into the shadows. The other soldier proffered the ale, but the man shook himself and waved the jug away. Enough was clearly enough.

The plod of heavy feet sounded from the courtyard, and the soldiers stashed their beer and stood smartly to attention. The castle sergeant walked ponderously out from the shadows, his matchlock musket at rest across his shoulder. Silver buttons winked on the sleeves of his coat, and wooden cartridges clattered from his bandolier, giving good warning of the old soldier's approach.

The sergeant had lived long in this family's service—a craggy old campaigner with gaunt cheeks and knowing eyes. Flattered to be trusted with the safety of the baron's wife and daughter, he took his responsibility very seriously.

The sergeant stood a moment, taking in the scene, and the nearer halberdier tugged at his helmet in salute. "Sergeant."

The sergeant stroked his beard, coldly eyeing his subordinates. His voice was hoarse from years on the parade ground—a thick brogue that grated uneasily on the ear. "Anythin' to report?"

One soldier briefly thought of the mouse he had seen. "Uh—no, Sergeant. Nothing at all."

The sergeant shrugged; a quiet night then. "The bishop'll be stayin' tonight, so ye can both stand down. Lock up tight and then pass the keys back to me." He stared at the soldier closer to him, sniffing reflectively. "Ye'll walk the rounds tonight, Gareth."

The soldier tilted back his helmet and whined protestingly. "Awww, Sarge. . . ."

" 'Twill teach ye the folly of drinkin' on duty! I told ye to stay spruce for Bishop Kaxter." He shook his head bitterly, fixing the soldiers with his glare. "My life! They took all the good ones and left me with the likes of ye! I catch ye drinking on duty again, boy, and I'll pull your arse up over your ears and use ye as a footstool—*Do ye hear me!*"

"YES SERGEANT!"

"Wonderful! I'm so soddin' glad to hear it!"

Shaking his head, he stalked off into the shadows, his bandolier clattering in the dark.

Chest heaving, the mouse sheltered behind a pile of horse dung in the courtyard. The choking reek of manure would hide his scent from the cat that stalked the grounds.

The way grew difficult, and the mouse felt so very tired. The cobblestones formed an endless field of hills bordered by mighty gutter cliffs. Though he was a far-ranging member of his species, the mouse had never traveled so far in all his life; it was dangerous to be abroad in the open, but fear of the mind-fire drove him on.

Strange! Strange! The world seemed somehow clearer. Causes and effects had become important. The cat would probably not be in the courtyard after all; smoke came from the kitchen chimney, so the cat would be snoozing by the fire. Why had that never occurred to him before?

The thought made him dizzy; the whole castle could be his to explore! Once he discovered all of the patterns, he could move through a world without fear!

Why do you wait?

The mouse almost sobbed. *I am tired! The way is long and I am small!*

Rest then. But not long.

The mouse squeezed his eyes shut. One of the strongest of his new feelings was toward the Tormentor; a sort of *sick* feeling. The mouse thought how good it would be to see the Tormentor torn to pieces by a cat. The image gave him pleasure, and that made him afraid. It was wrong to wish a cat death on anybody.

The courtyard seemed clear as far as his short vision could tell; that was what made cats and owls so terribly dangerous. The mouse sat on his haunches, stretching high to gain a better view. His ears raised up to read the sounds. His path seemed clear of predators and giants. The mouse made one last scan, searching the air for scent of an enemy.

Nothing. Good!

You are rested.

Yes yes! Don't hurt me! I am doing just as you say!

The mouse gave a hop and a jump, then twittered up along the gutter and slipped beneath the castle doors.

Miriam sat opposite her mother at the dinner table on a long, low chair with all four hooves folded up beneath her. Her sleek brown body seemed quite at ease, but appearances fooled no one tonight. Miriam had scarcely even picked at her food. Over a whole evening, she had eaten no more than a human.

Miriam played with her long-handled fork while the dinner conversation ebbed around her. The five house servants were arrayed at the table's lower salt, and even though they had two visitors tonight, the table still felt conspicuously empty. Miriam's

father, brother, their manservants, and the stablemen had gone off
to the wars.

Their visitors tonight were quiet; the harpy courier sat down
with the servants, who seemed somewhat fearful of the creature.
The second guest sat at Miriam's elbow—the bishop of Kerbridge.
A fat, jaunty human with steel-gray hair and the rough red cheeks
of a country squire, he sensed the gloom on the air and tried his
best to dispel it.

On Miriam, it seemed a wasted effort. The girl stared down
into a hundred dismal futures, watching herself bartered off to save
her father's life. . . .

The servants rose and bid the gentry goodnight, but the girl
hardly even registered the fact. Miriam reached for her wine, and
her hand visibly shook. Her mother watched gravely, and then
stretched quietly out across the table.

"Art thou all right, child? Please try to eat something."

Her mother used the familiar "thou" reserved for closest family
and friends. Miriam hung her head, her face hidden by the cascade
of her long, soft hair. "Nay, Mama. I've no appetite tonight.
Prithee—may I be excused?"

Her mother leaned forward unhappily. "Dost thou wish to
speak with me some more on this matter?"

"Nay, Mama. I trust thee. Do what is best for the family."

"Go then. But I am there for thee if thou needs me."

Miriam rose, bowed once to her mother, and then curtsied
deeply to the bishop. The man reached out to engulf Miriam's
white fingers with his own enormous shaggy fist.

"You are a good daughter, Miriam. Sleep well, my child, and
worry not. We are all in God's hands."

Miriam bowed her head. "Thank you, Your Grace. Goodnight."

Tail drooping, Miriam clopped out of the room, her dainty
hooves echoing in the empty hall. Dame Jerrick looked after her
for a long, long time.

The bishop sadly shook his head. "A fine girl, Your Ladyship.
You are very lucky."

"Yes. Yes I am." Lady Jerrick sighed unhappily and looked up at
the portrait of her husband that hung from the wall above. "I married for love, Your Grace. I had always treasured the hope that
Miriam would be able to do the same." The baroness pushed aside
her own plate, her food barely touched. Her gray eyes were infinitely

sad. "I had wanted so much for my little scholar. . . . Can we at least save her the indignity of marrying beneath her station?"

"We shall try, madam. We shall try."

"A mouse!"

A giant! The mouse spurted down the castle hallway, and a scullery maid's boot smashed down a whisker's-breadth behind him. Were it not for his lightning speed, he would have been mashed flatter than a penny.

A tapestry hung inviting folds down to the floor. The mouse dashed beneath the cloth, doubled back, and suddenly fetched up against the foot of a hollow metal giant.

Something pounded viciously into the floor beside him; the maid kicked at the tapestry, smashing her feet against the wainscotting in an attempt to pulp him flat. Heart pounding, the mouse squirmed into a gap in the metal giant's heel.

Stuck.

Stuck!

The backpack! The horrid satchel had caught on the sharp edges of the hollow giant's foot. The mouse tore at the straps with his strange new forepaws, tugging loose one cord after another. The backpack spilled free, and the mouse slithered into hiding as the maid's voice thundered in his ears.

"You 'orrible little thing! Thievin' vermin!"

Inside the hollow giant were rough wooden bones; the mouse climbed up and up and up, until he had reached his final refuge inside the creature's head. Outside his hiding place, the whole world shook and trembled to a monster's wrath. The mouse squeezed his eyes shut and covered them with his tiny hands in fright.

"Lud, girl! What are you doing? You'll have that armor down around our ears in a moment."

A new voice; the angry blows instantly stopped.

"A mouse, Mistress! A filthy mouse!"

"Stop it, Millie! Leave the poor wee thing alone."

The new voice rang soft and sweet; the mouse opened his eyes in wonder, peering out through a slot at his rescuer.

A female four-legger had interceded for him, facing down the other monster. The mouse's enemy quailed, and then came back to the offensive.

"Madam—where one mouse escapes, ten more breed!"

The four-legger female looked flushed and upset as she put a hand over her eyes.

"Leave it be! Why must everyone kill and hurt? Does no one take simple pleasure in life and beauty anymore?" The girl turned away, her long hair hiding her face, but the mouse saw the tears brimming in her eyes.

For the first time in his conscious life, someone had shown him a kindness. The mouse peered from the visor of the old suit of armor, wishing he could do something for the woman in return. The first monster retreated, leaving the lovely four-legger alone. She brushed the back of her hand across her eyes, sighed wearily, and paced slowly off down the corridor with her head bowed in thought.

The mouse leaned from hiding and watched the giant go, savoring the beautiful summer scent of her hair. His heart soared in wonder; *kindness*—someone had helped him! This hard, cruel world had not turned totally against him. . . .

Follow her. The Tormentor's voice; the mouse jerked his whiskers in alarm.

Why?

Do as you're told. The girl is to be followed.

The mouse fought for breath, suddenly frightened for the girl. He would not let the Tormentor hurt her!

Why? Tell me why!

For an answer, fire blasted through the mouse's mind. He squeaked, tumbling down through the armored suit to crash against the ground. Pain twisted through him, pinning him senseless with agony.

You will do as I say because you have no choice. You are a *tool,* nothing more. Next time you question me, I shall increase the pain slowly until you *beg* to die.

The mouse clenched his tiny hands, shivering with rage.

I wish I could bite you! I wish stoats would pierce you with sharp, sharp teeth! I wish you to scream while you die!

The emotion was sharp, powerful, and utterly hopeless.

Hate? Why, you *hate* me—I feel it! So you can actually hate? The enemy mind probed, but the mouse shook it angrily away, much to the Tormentor's puzzlement.

I cannot read you. How odd! The Tormentor gave up his questioning with a snort. **Your hatred is futile. Go fetch your backpack and hurry after the girl. Move swiftly.**

Ears drooping, the mouse climbed painfully from the suit of armor, pulled on the heavy backpack, and then padded down the hall.

Pin-William sat up, shaking himself. The satyr distastefully worked at his mouth and then reached for his wineskin, his face set into a frown as he spared a glance to the heavens. Clouds were gathering to the north, blowing ragged scraps across the face of the full moon. The air hung still and heavy, pressing breathlessly close.

A huge shape stirred among the shadows as the black-clad nobleman loomed closer. "Well?"

Pin-William snorted. "Hateful little beast. It fights me, my lord. It fights me! But what is the willpower of a lesser creature when contested against mine own?"

"Quite." The half-horse's tone dripped with irony. "Nevertheless, he performs his tasks."

"Indeed, sirrah! Indeed! He well realizes the consequences of disobedience."

"How far has the creature penetrated, magician? How much longer must I wait?"

"It is heading toward the family apartments, my lord, on the proper path to reach the family chapel."

The nobleman's eyes glittered avidly in the moonlight. "And the satchel! Does it still bear the satchel?"

Taken aback by the intensity of the nobleman's manner, the satyr faltered, one hand going to his curving horns.

"Well—yes, sir. Yes, of course."

His patron leaned back and hissed with glorious anticipation. "Excellent! I have some special instructions once the creature has reached the chapel."

"But, my lord! I have told you my concentration must remain . . ."

The nobleman leaned forward, his face cruelly outlined in shadow. "*Do it.*"

"Cer-Certainly, my lord. It shall be as you command."

Pin-William gave his client a nervous glance, then firmly pulled his hat down over his eyes once more. Clearing his mind, he reestablished the link with his agent.

Miriam walked wearily through the small chapel outside the family apartments. Essentially unused, the chapel was an anachronism—harmless but depressing, like the holy symbols carved over every window. Once, perhaps, the family had been important enough to fear *fiendish* assault. These days, the chapel served simply as a status symbol; a foolish, empty gesture that always made Miriam feel slightly sad.

The girl opened up her bedroom door, sank onto her bed, and sat staring despondently about her refuge. She had so little to show for nineteen years of life: a few books, combs, and knickknacks, a half-finished monograph on the local wildlife. Miriam idly flicked through the pages of her own work, gazing dully at her drawings of field mice and sparrows, shadow cats and tiny, fawnlike pegasi. Miriam turned page after page, sighing tragically. There were notes on structures of wing, on diet and mating habits—all probably of interest to no one but herself.

A light knocking sounded at the door, accompanied by the music of a tinkling tray. Miriam drew open the door to discover Jane, her mother's half-horse maid, waiting outside. The girl's broad, honest face was wrung with sympathy. Hitching up her skirts in a small curtsy, the maid examined Miriam and then clucked unhappily.

"Oh, child—your face looks so long!" Jane stooped and hefted a wooden tray that held a glass decanter and a single goblet. " 'Er ladyship asked me to bring you a tot. She says how it might 'elp you sleep the better."

Miriam could hardly think, her mind whirled so. Spirits? She had never drunk spirits. "I . . . Yes, thank you. Perhaps it will, I don't know." Miriam put her hand to her brow, feeling helplessly confused. "Thank you, Jane. Just leave it here. I-I shall be all right."

Jane gently put the tray on the bedside table, then stood with one leg hovering uncertainly above the ground.

"Mirie? Is there anything you'd like to talk about, love?"

Miriam kept her back turned and her face well hidden. "No, thank you, Jane. I really just need to be alone."

Jane curtsied once more and softly closed the door, leaving Miriam to her thoughts. The maid walked down the corridor toward the servant quarters, missing the furtive little movements behind a tapestry as she passed.

Alone in her room, Miriam glumly undressed for bed. She awkwardly pulled the stays of her bodice and tugged off her gown and petticoats. Miriam wiped her hooves carefully and then sat herself in bed. Every half-horse combed her own tail unless she had a sweetheart to do it for her. It was a uniquely personal task—both through custom and practice. A stranger accidentally pulling on a centaur's tail could trigger a ferocious kick.

Miriam combed out the knots and snarls caused by a day's wear and tear, then brushed the flowing hair until it gleamed. Next came the currycomb and body brush; grooming before bed was a painful bore, but it helped to keep the sheets clean. By the time she reached her top half, Miriam felt weary of the whole business. She set to work with her hairbrush, then looked into her mirror, locking gazes with her own sad eyes.

Freckles! Cursed freckles! Miriam leaned forward, tweaking her nose. There were more of them all over her cleavage as well! She tugged open her nightdress and bit her lip unhappily; her breasts were like a damned farmgirl's—great unsightly puddings of things. With solid flanks and long, strong hands, she looked exactly what she was: a quiet country girl. No chance of ever catching a handsome suitor's eye.

Miriam thought about what it would be like to enter a cold, loveless marriage; to have some hateful man spend himself on her. The girl shivered as the fantasy became more graphic, and Miriam suddenly found herself backed against her bedroom wall.

It was the price she had to pay for the wealth and privilege, but . . . her life had not been so very rich, nor her wealth so very great. Any shopkeeper's daughter might live as well. To have her body bartered off like so much meat at the market . . .

Miriam sobbed for breath, and her eyes alighted on the decanter Jane had left behind. With trembling hands, she quickly poured a glass, took a deep breath, and choked the vile stuff down. Gagging, she somehow managed to finish the whole cup, only to collapse in an agonized fit of coughing.

Blood raced to her cheeks and nose, bringing them a cherry glow. Brushing aside her hair, Miriam poured herself another draft, and this time it went down easier. She sat miserably in bed, feeling the liquor do its work while depression settled over her like iron chains. She spared herself one last glance in the mirror; her eyes were puffy from crying, and her cheeks were blotched and red.

Hideous. Who in hell's name cares?

Miriam crawled miserably into bed. Emotional exhaustion and brandy did their work quickly; with one long, slim leg trailing out of the covers, Miriam slept like a stone.

Chapter Three

Shadow Claws

he only sound in the hall came from the pitter-patter of tiny little feet. Head bowed and legs burning, the mouse plodded steadily up the wainscotting of a staircase. His Tormentor had praised him, had promised him rest at the top of the stairs, and so the creature staggered onward in a haze of pain.

A strange, quiet room stood at the summit of the stairs. The mouse slid down onto the chill flagstones and looked warily around. It felt cool and restful here, and the air swirled with the scents of old incense and sleeping stone. The mouse sat up on his haunches, his clever ears lifted, but he sensed no movement. He might almost be alone in the world. . . .

The girl. See if the girl is in her room. Go down the corridor and check behind the second door.

Rest! You promised me rest! I am tired, I cannot think, and my tongue is swollen.

The reply took a moment in coming.

Soon. First check on the girl, and then you may recover your strength here in the chapel.

Wearily dragging his tail, the mouse moved on. He raised his nose as he passed a tall stone block; whiskers quivering eagerly, the mouse halted and pawed at the lace altar cloth.

Water! There's water here! Oh, please, let me stop to drink.

Move on. Remember the mind-fire.

Reluctantly, the mouse turned away. Beneath most doorways in the castle there were gaps easily passable by a mouse, and from one of these leaked the yellow glow of candlelight. Hugging the wall, the mouse crept forward to peer beneath the door, his tail twisting and curling curiously. He could smell her! Oh, that wonderful memory; the scent of *kindness*.

Is she there?

Yes. Sh-She is there. The mouse felt his chest tighten. *Don't hurt her, I beg you!*

Indeed? How *quaint*. Fear not, Sir Mouse, we'll not hurt your lady fair. You may rest now. Go back and have your drink while I confer with my colleague.

The alien mind slithered to the rear of his consciousness. The mouse shivered, then peered again under the door. There she lay— the four-legged giant who had saved him. She was clearly asleep, stretched out on a bed far above.

They must not make him hurt her! He would not obey, even if the mind-fire pierced him and killed him.

Even if it tore him to pieces.

His first real decision; the mouse stopped shivering and straightened his back. The Tormentor's power held him only as far as fear could. The mouse had discovered courage.

He walked slowly back into the dark, sweet-smelling chapel, heading for the rough white altar cloth. The scent of water drifted from above; a drink was but a climb away.

Wait!

The mouse chittered angrily. *What now?*

Take off your pack and open it.

Water! Please, I thirst. Have you no pity?

This will take but a moment, and then you may drink. Quick now!

The mouse hissed with frustration, then struggled to remove his little green backpack. Finally the wretched thing came free and clunked to the ground.

Open it, quickly!

The mouse plucked at the cloth with his little hands, not comprehending.

Fool! Pull at the cords *thus* and *so*.

A clear image came into his bright, cunning mind. *Ah! A novel concept—how very clever.* The mouse pulled at the knot, carefully observing the way the strings were tied. The pouch fell open, and something shiny showed within. The mouse poked his nose curiously into the backpack, but then recoiled. Something felt . . . wrong.

There is an object inside. Remove it.

The mouse chittered in distaste, but he had little choice. He lifted up the satchel and shook it, and with a loud 'clink' a small red bottle rolled across the floor. Corked and sealed with wax, it nevertheless exhaled an air of dread.

Break it.

The mouse extended a cautious paw. The vial was smooth and hard. *How?*

It's quite fragile. Roll it to a wall and kick it into the stones.

The mouse looked about. *What if I roll it down the stairs?*

No. It must be broken inside the chapel.

The mouse nudged the bottle. It rolled easily, and some sort of strange fluid sloshed inside. Nose screwed up in disgust, the mouse pressed his rear paws up against the bottle and braced his forefeet in a crack. With one almighty kick, the bottle flew through the air to smash against the wall. The mouse fastidiously shook itself before turning around to examine the results.

A foul green stain spattered the stones where the vial had broken open. The mouse instinctively backed away, his eyes staring in alarm. *What is it? What have you made me do?*

But for once, there was no answer.

Pin-William opened his eyes and drew a quick breath, tilting back his leather hat. "It has been done as you directed, my lord. The mouse has broken your vial."

Wrapped in shadow, the nobleman lifted his empty gaze and smiled darkly. The blob of devil spit had not been costly to the half-horse warlock. His soul had long been in pawn, and his master still delighted in seeing his servant prosper.

Pin-William felt a sudden chill. He laid one hand on the butt of his pistol; the hammer lay half-cocked and the priming seemed firm.

The nobleman saw the action and grinned, his voice swirling like ashes in the wind. "*Nerves, O Magus?* Now, when we are so close?" The half-horse posed against the skyline, lightning gleaming in his eyes. "You disappoint me, satyr. Your *cowardice* may yet cost me my prize."

The magician bridled, stepping boldly forward. "Cowardice! *I?*" Pin-William gulped like a fish out of water. "My Lord, you wrong me! Have I not pursued this task with dogged will, dazzling ingenuity? Oh, sir, you wound me!"

The noble unsuccessfully motioned for silence, but the satyr seemed willing to go on. Suddenly the half-horse held up his hand, staring intently toward the road.

"*Hist!* Be quiet, fool! Look there!"

Pin-William halted his monologue and whirled in alarm.

"What . . . ?"

The noble lunged forward; his dagger blade rammed into the satyr's back, sinking to the hilt. The centaur grinned as he clutched his prey and screwed the weapon home. Pin-William struggled, shuddered once, and then lay still. Breathing hard, the noble pushed the corpse aside.

The death had felt most . . . *uplifting*. The half-horse shivered with delight as he relived the exquisite pleasure of steel sinking into living flesh.

Now the girl! The half-horse felt a thrill of anticipation; girls were always the most delicious prey. This one was a soft, gentle, little thing by reputation. He had never seen her, but he could picture her most clearly. He imagined the terror he would bring to her, the pure mindless horror of her final moments, her agony as she bled and screamed and died. . . .

A hired assassin, he lived only to kill. Gold would line his pockets when the night was done, but his greatest rewards were more . . . *immaterial*.

He breathed raggedly as he walked over to the clearing that he had prepared hours before. The noble looked around himself with a morbid shiver of satisfaction. The crooked shadows of the tree branches loomed like the claws of some insane beast; even the insects had taken flight, leaving the orchard still and quiet. He crossed to the center of his diagram and closed the circle behind him with the point of his sword. Secure within his protective web, he began the summonation, whispering prayers to dark, soulless powers.

The centaur tossed his bloody dagger to the ground, his voice hissing like a graveyard wind.

"With this act of treachery, I do consecrate." The candles flared high, and the half-horse's face shone skull-like in the evil light. "From my mind I conjure fear, I call forth hate, I summon power."

His voice fell to a hoarse whisper. "Come to me, my creature, my *love*. Slay and be joyful."

The shadows formed into obscene clots that pulsed like pustules on some plague-ridden child.

The noble's voice breathlessly beguiled. "*Come. . . .*"

Something filthy spurted up out of the dark; the shape swelled and bloated, then erupted into nightmare as the creature boiled forth. A twisted, insane thing, the fiend writhed and gibbered as it leered hungrily down at its creator. It was the stuff of sheer insanity—part corpse, part beast, part shadow. Tentacles and claws shivered with lust as the creature howled in the darkness.

The nobleman shivered before it, swaying helplessly before the child of his own crippled soul. He had slain all the good inside himself, bringing to life his foul, unspoken fears. The nobleman sobbed, staring in horror at his own eyes rolling crazily in the beast's sockets. He trembled in ecstasy before the creature—loving it, hating it, desiring it, *fearing* it.

The noble laughed hysterically, his creature capering before him in the wind. "Kill her, my sweet! *Take* her—use her—rend her perfect flesh and send her screaming down into oblivion! *Destroy her.*"

The creature swelled with lust, rearing up in triumph as lightning sheeted through the sky. Turning, it slithered into the night, hungry for fulfillment, and the nobleman laughed as he watched it go.

The fiend scuttled forward on mismatched legs, claws and pincers striking sparks from the cobblestones. Its form, ragged as a month-old corpse, gave forth a charnel reek of disease and corruption. The creature reached the castle moat and drove on without pause, poisoning the waters as it passed. With powerful thrusts of its leprous tail, it surged to the castle wall. Sheer, smooth stone was no barrier; grinning and giggling, the creature slithered smoothly up the battlements.

Souls! The fiend could smell them all around it—the souls of the living, pulsing with life. The scent sharpened the creature's hunger, honing its anticipation for the kill. A girl; a soft, lovely girl. How they squealed when taken! How they screamed as the living flesh was stripped from their bones! Her blood would be hot and wet, her flesh sweet. The monster panted, thrilling to the hunt.

One day it would be free! Free of the mewling half-man who

had given it form and life. Unshackled, the fiend would wallow in gore and human filth, bringing mindless terror wherever it chose to go. . . . But tonight, it was bound. The creature heaved itself over the edge of the wall and slithered down into the castle courtyard.

A figure stood silhouetted in a doorway, peering upward at the stormy sky. Plumed and helmeted, the castle guard trod out into the courtyard to make his rounds. The man winced as dry lightning sheeted through the air, throwing fantastic shadows across the courtyard walls.

One of the shadows whirled—a shape of such insanity that the guard staggered back in disbelief.

With blinding speed, the fiend scythed its claws toward its prey. The guard ducked under the first cruel slash, then drove the point of his halberd at the creature. The blade skittered harmlessly aside; only silvered weapons, fire, or sorcery could pierce a fiend's leprous hide.

The creature lashed out and trapped its victim in a web of sucker-pads and paws. Disease and rot began to spread where the monster touched bare flesh. The fiend savored the smell of the man's soul a moment more, and then *bit*. Blood fountained up into the air, spraying stains across the courtyard walls.

A scream sounded from behind. A half-horse woman stood in the open doorway, shrieking as the monster dropped its toy. It lurched forward, stretching out with gore-spattered claws, and the woman instantly turned and fled.

Disappointed, the fiend looked back at its first kill of the night and licked its chops. A good beginning, but now the alarm would be given; there was no more time for stealth. The fiend slithered onward through the night to claim its prey. . . .

Splashing happily in the chapel font, the mouse washed his fur in the cold, clear water. Fatigue had drained away, and with it went the last vestiges of the Tormentor's presence. The sick pressure of the alien mind had gone.

Free! The mouse dipped into the water, his tail moving slowly behind him as he swam. Really free! Free to go home, free to think, to discover who he was and what he could do. A whole unknown world to explore! Life would be very strange; he saw things so differently now.

He dragged himself up out of the old stone font and shook himself briskly dry. The mouse vigorously scratched at his ear with one hind leg; one last shake of the fur and he was done. The mouse fearlessly walked over the edge of the altar, head downmost, calmly climbing down the tablecloth to the ground.

He stood on the smooth, cold flagstones, pondering his next move. Food would be nice, and then sleep. Surely he could find a space nearby that would be safe and warm. . . .

Fur suddenly stiffened, ears lifting as he sensed thunder on the air. The mouse shuddered; he feared storms—the noise and violence battered him into a quivering wreck. It would be best to find shelter before . . .

No! The mouse suddenly had to fight for breath, cold fear clamping his chest. Something dangerous was near! Claws and teeth, blood and death! The mouse looked around in panic, wildly seeking his enemy, but saw nothing, heard nothing, smelt . . . *something.*

A vile, stinking mist rose from the broken glass vial, spreading out across the floor. The mouse backed away from it as a sick, numbing terror filled him from whiskers to tail. Danger came! Something wild with clicking claws and pointed teeth. Something evil coming for . . . *the girl!*

With a sob of shock, the mouse raced from the room. He must warn the kind lady! Death was coming, and they must flee and hide!

The green mist spilled out across the floor, defiling the holy ground. Lightning flashed, and the mouse ran on.

Chest heaving raggedly, he struggled underneath the girl's bedroom door. The lady giant lay fast asleep on the bed high above, with one long leg trailing to the floor. Throwing caution to the wind, he scampered up the giant's leg and raced atop the bed.

He stood on the haunches of a giant. . . . The size of the creature was simply *staggering.* For as long as he could remember, giants had lurched through his life—huge, clumsy, and dangerous. He had fed from their unwanted castoffs and hidden from their jealous rage, but never before had he really considered one of the creatures. Perched on the giant's rump, he stared down the length of her and caught his breath in awe.

Her flesh felt warm and pleasant beneath his feet. The mouse determinedly made his way along the giant's flanks, clambered up onto her shoulder, then peered down in wonder at the girl's sleeping face.

How to warn her? The mouse scuttled down onto the pillow and stared at the sleeping giant's face. With little pitter-pats of his forepaws the mouse prodded at her cheek, hoping she would awaken. The giantess snorted and simply ground her face against the pillow, and so the mouse tried again. Abandoning caution, he tugged at the corners of the woman's eyes, trying to force them open. The girl stirred and frowned, screwing her eyelids firmly shut.

In an agony of distress, the mouse skittered backward and forward across the pillow. He could feel danger coming closer with every breath. The mouse climbed her hair, then desperately twittered in her ear.

"Wake up! Wake up!"

The strange sound of his own voice startled him. The mouse froze, then worked his mouth and felt words tumbling out onto his tongue. His voice piped small and high, quivering with emotion. "Awake, Lady, please awake!"

The giant slept on, and the mouse felt a surge of desperation as he skittered back and forth.

"Please! Oh, it will kill you! Please wake up! It is coming for you—flee and hide!" He suddenly knew what he had to do. He took a firm grip in the girl's hair and nuzzled her soft, warm skin. "Forgive me. . . ." He nipped her ear, sinking sharp little teeth into her flesh.

"EEEARGH!"

With a squeal of pain and outrage, Miriam catapulted out of bed. Her hand flew up to her ear, clutching at something small and warm.

"*Ouch!* Damnation—what was that?"

Confused and blinking, Miriam shook her head, trying to make the world jump into focus. Part of her mind registered a muffled little voice squeaking in her ear.

"Don't hurt me! I am sorry! I had to wake you! Please don't hurt me, kind lady."

Miriam absentmindedly combed a wriggling lump out of her hair. She drew a ragged breath, feeling her heart pound. Her head swam as she tried to make sense of the images around her.

Bed. Brandy. Lightning.

Oh, lightning! Was that all? Miriam relaxed, the whole world suddenly jumping into context. She straightened her back and heaved a grateful sigh. Why did her ear hurt?

Something soft stirred in the palm of her hand. Miriam frowned and carefully opened up her fingers. A mouse stared up at her with glittering black eyes.

Miriam's eyes widened; *a mouse!*

"Please, kind lady, please don't hurt a mouse!"

Miriam's jaw dropped, and she heard herself whimper. The mouse looked up at her and wrung its tiny paws.

"Flee, run, hide! It is coming!" The mouse chittered in panic. "Oh, it is coming, and it will kill you! Teeth and claws and blood and death! *Run!*"

The girl fought for breath, feeling light-headed as the mouse tugged frantically at her fingers with tiny, perfect hands. The creature was weeping with distress.

"Oh, Lady, you saved me when the two-legger would have squished me flat! Now I help you. You must believe me! A wicked thing comes to tear and kill. He comes for *you!* Flee with me—run and hide!"

A piercing scream ripped through the evening gloom. Miriam scrambled out of bed, the mouse carefully cradled in her hands, and stood uncertainly in the middle of the chamber. She heard the sound of a door splintering, and a sudden icy breeze bit through the air.

Something was coming! She could feel it!

"Down the stairs! Run, quickly!"

Miriam needed no further urging; hair streaming, she raced out into the corridor. Her hooves skidded as she took the corner and lunged into the family chapel, only to rear backward in alarm.

The floor ran ankle-deep with a foul green mist. Miriam gasped as the slick, greasy fog caressed her hooves. She skittered aside in panic, rearing and plunging back toward the altar. She glanced up to gauge the distance to the stairs, and felt her strength fade with shock. Miriam whimpered and backed away as she looked into the eyes of death.

The fiend pulled itself into the room, slithering easily across the desecrated ground. It reared up into the air, fangs gleaming hungrily as it blocked both exits with its moldering bulk.

Miriam stared helplessly at the apparition, and her hands

numbly dropped the little mouse onto the altar. Eyes rolling madly, the girl shrank back against the wall.

The creature sighed in anticipation, its claws and tentacles opening to take her. Slithering forward like a massive slug, the creature passed the altar, then gave a puzzled frown.

A sudden stench of burning filled the air, and the beast's nostrils flared. It snarled and whirled, eyes questing.

The mouse backed across the altar; he had deliberately shoved a candle against the monster's hide. The trembling mouse perched on the edge of the old stone font, staring up at the monster with glittering, intelligent eyes.

The fiend slowly raised a tentacle and gave a leprous smile.

"No!" the girl sobbed.

The giggling horror craned its neck to see her more clearly. *Aaaah! The mouse's death would cause her pain?*
Die then!

The tentacle lashed down toward the mouse, streaking through the air with blinding speed. The mouse instantly sped aside; the fiend's claw smacked straight down into the font of holy water.

The creature gave a gurgling howl of pain and staggered back, trying to scrape the searing water from its scales. Miriam snatched up the mouse and bolted from the door. Sparks flew from her hooves as she pounded down the stairway and out into the castle yard, pursued by the monster's chilling screams.

Holy ground! She had to reach holy ground; it was her only chance! The night lit up in fury as Miriam galloped frantically through the weeds.

The fiend raged behind her, smashing columns as it pursued her through the ruins. Claws and tentacles gouged weeds and flowers as the nightmare-creature screamed with hate.

Hanging on for dear life, the mouse clung in Miriam's hair and peered fearfully over her shoulder. "It's gaining!"

Miriam took a jump over a fallen column, knocking the breath out of her small passenger. She stumbled and fell heavily, grazing her knees. Miriam glanced behind and saw the sickening shape of the fiend outlined against the sky.

"*It—it doesn't tire!*" Miriam's voice shook with hysteria. She staggered to her feet and sprinted on, dodging through a wilderness of fallen stone.

The mouse's hands dug tightly into her long hair. "Leave me,

Lady! Drop me here, and I shall try to bite him as he passes. I-It might stop to hunt me. . . ."

The fiend screeched close behind them.

Her hooves slipping on the mossy stones, Miriam ran on through the darkness, fear giving her greater speed. "Th-Thou canst hurt it!" Miriam drove through tall sprigs of fennel, and the scent of crushed aniseed stung sharp on the air. She held the mouse tight lest it do something foolish.

The ruined chapel! Starkly lit by lightning flash, the arches lifted into the empty sky ahead. Miriam sobbed with relief and plowed onward, toward safety.

Something exploded from the weeds beside her. Miriam screamed and leapt aside as claws tore great streams of hair from her tail. Miriam slipped sideways down a grassy slope, the monster snapping at her hooves. She crashed against a column, jumped away from dripping jaws, and lunged into the ancient crypt. She slammed the portal shut with her rear hooves before collapsing hard against the wall. Weeping in terror, she stared out into the night.

Safe! She was safe!

Miriam's head swam with giddy disbelief.

"Mouse! O mouse! We're safe" Her voice sounded brittle, and she caught a tittering laugh before it began. "It-It can't come in here! It's hallowed ground here, you see? It's still hallowed. . . ."

The door splintered into fragments. Miriam shrieked, rearing clumsily away as the fiend erupted through the doorway. The creature snapped toward her, its claws reaching out to rip and tear, and Miriam cringed against a wall, eyes closed as she waited helplessly to die.

A long moment passed while Miriam's flesh crawled in expectation, and a small part of her wondered why it should take so long. Would it let her die quickly, or . . .

The mouse began tugging at her hair, trying to gain her attention. "Look, pretty lady! *Look!* The beastie stops!"

Mewling unhappily, the fiend wavered at the threshold. It surged forward, only to whimper in frustration and withdraw back into the weeds.

The mouse capered happily on Miriam's shoulder. "See? We are clever, we are quick! Flashing hooves and twisty ways!" Tiny feet danced as the mouse twittered in glee. "Pretty lady took us where the beastie cannot go!"

Shouts sounded from the dark outside, and Miriam felt a surge of hope as she heard the voices of the castle guards. Her voice cracking, she screamed for help.

"HERE! OVER HERE! HELP ME!"

The fiend hissed venomously as footsteps pounded close. It snaked behind itself with a tentacle, probing the rubble. The limb suddenly flashed forward, and a vast chunk of rock hurtled through the air. With a squeak of alarm, Miriam ducked, the wind of the rock's passage jerking at her hair. The rock smashed against the wall behind her and exploded into wicked shards. Miriam crouched behind the altar.

"Preee-sent!"

The monster whirled in sudden panic as a voice bellowed out from close behind it.

"Give fire!"

Muskets cracked, and three holes blasted through the fiend's carapace. The creature screamed and whirled in agony, its wounds running with blue fire. Howling in rage, the monster surged toward its enemies and opened its jaws.

A man strode forth and opened out his arms, blocking the fiend's attack. The bishop!—and still dressed for dinner! A fourth shot rang out, and a silver bullet crashed into the monster's skull. The foul body reared in astonishment, already stiffening as life fled its grasp. It crashed into weeds, collapsing into ashes as the rain began to fall.

"O mouse! O mouse, look!"

Miriam staggered to her feet, weeping in relief as she saw the monster die. She gratefully reached toward the mouse upon her shoulder, only to probe empty air. Confused, Miriam stepped backward in alarm.

"Mouse?"

Suddenly she saw him. A small brown body lay among the shards of rock and rubble, with a trickle of blood soaking through its fur. The girl gave a cry of fright and swept the tiny creature up into her arms.

The assassin shrieked from the center of his carefully drawn symbol, shaking his fist at the heavens. His fiend was dead! Destroyed until he could rebuild it from his nightmares! How? How could it have failed? His reputation lay in ruins. A master sorcerer, a king among assassins, and he couldn't even slay some filly of a girl!

The girl was to have *died!* Her loss would have ended the only hopes her family might have had of raising funds for the baron's troops. In one fell swoop the Duncruighan army could have been destroyed—but now the plan was ruined!

The sorcerer panted, staring at the castle walls in hate. All was not yet lost: his patrons would know a way. There might still be time to . . .

A loud *click* sounded from the shadows behind him. The half-horse whirled, staring as a pistol shot stabbed toward his eyes. The assassin's head snapped back, his lifeless eyes still filled with disbelief as he crashed back onto the ground.

Pistol smoke drifted in the empty orange grove. Lurching drunkenly on cloven hooves, a shadow staggered from the trees and disappeared into the night.

Rain lashed against the windows as Miriam huddled in her mother's arms. Lady Jerrick stroked her daughter's hair, not daring to speak. Death had come close to claiming her child tonight, and the baroness needed comfort even more than her daughter did. She clutched Miriam tightly, rocking the girl gently back and forth as though she were a baby.

A polite knock sounded at the door, and the baroness hesitantly cleared her throat. "Come!"

Wet through to the bone, his coat hanging open, the sergeant of the castle guard stood dripping at the threshold.

"Yer Ladyship? The bishop's found a body and a summonation site over in the orchards. The rain has washed most of the signs away, but we're looking for whoever did the fellow in." The guardsman rubbed at his cheek, water dripping from the elbow of his sodden coat.

The man's silver buttons had gone. Miriam stared at the sight for a puzzled moment, and then looked up into the sergeant's eyes.

The man plucked at his coat and smiled. "Anything'll do in a pinch. The critter got more out of 'em than I ever did!"

Miriam reached out to take the man's old, callused hand.

"Thank you for tonight, Sergeant. Thank you *all*."

Her voice was small, but her face had filled with a most remarkable calm. She held him with her wonderful green eyes, and the soldier's craggy face blushed red.

"Aaah—that's all right, Damsel. 'Tis I that should be apologizin' to ye. With the baron gone, I should have kept a watch so tight that nary a *mouse* could have slipped by. . . ."

Miriam suddenly sat up and bit her lip. She drew her blanket about her shoulders and brushed back a straggling lock of hair. "Mother? I-I might go to bed now. My head throbs—the night is catching up on me."

Lady Jerrick edged forward, one hand touching her daughter's cheek. "Wouldst sleep with me tonight, darling? Thou can if thou wishes."

Miriam seemed in an agony of indecision. "I—thank thee, no. I shall be best left alone."

"I love thee, Daughter."

"I love thee, Mama."

Miriam hunched her shoulders down into her blanket and left the room, watched by her two guardians. She could feel their eyes on her long after she had left the room.

Once properly out of sight, Miriam began to hurry. She quietly drew open her bedroom door and carefully dropped the bolt behind her. Mincing delicately across the carpet, she crept over to her open bedside drawers and she peered in at the cozy nest she had made among her underwear.

The tiny mouse lay sleeping peacefully, his chest moving slowly as he breathed. One of his front legs wore a delicate little splint; dislodged by the breeze of the fiend-hurled rock, the mouse had fallen heavily to the ground. Miriam had tended the little soul as best she could. She had been fretting about the mouse's welfare ever since.

He seemed so very small to have done so much. . . .

The mouse stirred and awakened. Folding her legs beneath herself, Miriam knelt down and leaned closer. The mouse looked up at her with adoring eyes.

"Kind lady . . ."

Miriam stroked the silky fur along the mouse's back.

"Shhh! Soft now. How dost thou feel?"

"Tired. My foot hurts. The beast is truly dead?"

"Yes, my brave mouse—it is truly dead."

The little mouse closed his eyes. "You saved mouse once more. I thank you, sweet lady."

"Thou hast saved my life too, little friend."

The mouse's eyes flickered open. "Friend?" The mouse seemed dazed. He found the concept nestled in his mind and felt a surge of joy. "You-You would like mouse for a friend?"

"My truest friend." She reached down and carefully kissed him on the ears, and he sighed and nestled deeper into his bed. The pain in his foot faded clean away.

"*Friend* . . . feels nice. . . ."

"Sleep now, my friend. Sleep and be happy."

Sleep. . . .

The mouse closed his eyes in contentment. Gently blowing out the candles, Miriam crept into bed.

There would be much to talk about upon the morrow.

Chapter Four

White Rose

he long bright hall shone with silken banners that curled and lofted in the breeze. Each flag bore the symbol of a pure white rose—the badge of the queen of Nantierre. Sprays of blossoms brightened the air with sweet perfume, while armored guardsmen stood stiffly at intervals along the walls. The guards glowered silently at the crowds of courtiers that milled and bleated nervously at the far end of the room.

A beautiful young half-horse posed regally upon the throne. Soft curls of golden hair cascaded down over pale shoulders, and her luscious equine hindbody shone dazzling white. The diamonds that sparkled from her brow were shamed by the wildfire of her eyes.

Queen Aelis of Nantierre tossed back her sleeves and sneered down at her cowering minister of war. "*Coward!*" Her voice was sweet poison, pure and deadly with rage. The quaking, balding human minister suddenly developed a stammer.

"Your M-M-Majesty! There's n-nothing else we can do! We m-must consolidate our current possessions, ready to withdraw to winter quarters. To overextend this late in the season . . ."

"ENOUGH!" Aelis hurled a vase against the wall, narrowly missing the court alchemist; the courtiers flinched at the sound of shattering glass. "You pursue war as though it were some stately *game!* You have the bloodlust of a heifer! I WILL NOT HAVE IT!" One silver-shod hoof clashed against the floor, scarring the wood-work. "I have ordered you to take the towns of Beckenraude and Lael. *Ordered it!* Why must my plans always be hamstrung by *fools!*"

"M-M-M-M-Majesty!"

"You are a coward, sir! A *coward!* Never once have you been on the field of battle! Never once have you heard a shot fired in anger!" The queen sidled toward the quivering minister, her hooves prancing with the need to kick and kill. "INSECT!"

"I . . ."

Aelis gave a shriek of rage, shattering a filigree table with her foot. "*Out!* Out of my sight! You are dismissed!" She clenched her fists in hate. "Go cower on your estates. Be thankful I do not see fit to take your worthless head!"

The minister turned tail and scuttled hastily from the room, fleeing for his life.

The queen slowly mastered herself, then curtly signed for the court astrologer. Wings and clawed hands held high above her head, the old harpy tercel trod forward, her voice creaking out between her long, carnivorous fangs.

"Are you sure this is a wise decision, Majesty? The portents for continued action . . ."

Aelis whirled angrily, but the harpy calmly stood her ground. The old bird scratched at her own scrawny throat with a rasp of claws. "He must be replaced then. The Viscomte De Bergenon . . . ?"

"Be quiet old hag!" Aelis's silken tail slashed the air behind her; she poured herself a glass of wine, ignoring the servants standing near to hand. "There'll be no more mewling fools to destroy my careful plans!" Aelis angrily sipped at her wine, then signed to her seneschal. "You! Summon the court armorer—and have the Royal Guard prepare to march!"

The harpy waddled forward in alarm, her talons clattering against the floor. "Majesty! What do you intend? A replacement . . ."

Aelis's satin skirts swept across the floor as she descended from the dais. "I am taking command myself! I let you sway me once with your tales as to the 'role of a queen.' I have had enough! I rule in *war* as well as in *peace.* I shall stand at the head of my army as befits a prince."

A fat, grizzled old satyr sped into the room and made a clumsy bow.

Aelis fixed the armorer with a steely glare. "Armor. Sword.

Pistols. Field pieces, not parade. Are they ready?"

The satyr stared up at his queen with worshipful eyes. "Enchanted, blued, engraved, and polished, Your Majesty. I have never made finer."

"Bring them to my chambers then. You shall see me decked out in your handiwork."

"Majesty!" The old harpy floundered forward with her talons gouging at the floors. "Majesty, no! This is no task for a mere queen! The portents . . ."

"*Silence!*" Aelis angrily stripped off her jewelry, scowling at her aged adviser. "Portents be damned! Your liver is as pale as the rest of them! I'll show you how a *queen* lives and dies!" Aelis stormed off to her apartments, servants trailing like foam spreading in her wake.

Outside the palace walls, a hundred heralds called the guards to arms. Before the eyes of an astonished populace, the young half-horse hurtled aside her scepter and girded on her sword.

The queen of Nantierre would go to war.

Chapter Five

Visitors

hem . . . page four—"

"No—don't say the page numbers Mus. They're just for reference."

"Oh—sorry. Uh . . .

"Drink to me only with thine eyes,
And I will pledge with mine;
Or leave a kiss but in the cup,
And I'll not look for wine. . . ."

Perched comfortably in the cup of Miriam's hand, the mouse carefully spelled out the words on the pages of the book before him. His nose nodded up and down as he read, whiskers bobbing with the verse. He broke off, and looked up into Miriam's face, seeking approval. "Is that right?"

The girl sat with her chin propped in her other hand, and her eyes shone. "O Mus! That's *lovely!* I would never have believed it. How canst thou learn so fast?" Miriam was utterly fascinated. Her thumb gently stroked down the mouse's back, making Mus arch with pleasure.

The mouse was visibly pleased with himself. "I'm doing well? I am clever?"

"Thou furry egotist! Yes—very clever indeed."

They lay in dappled shade by the riverbank, beneath a great gnarled willow tree. Bright sun shone down on the grass, and wild oats nodded in the heat, murmuring softly as the river breeze caressed its hand across them. The mouse sat in comfort, enjoying himself. A curtain of willow leaves screened their little refuge from the heat, trailing down into the river to make wavering ripples in the current.

Mus was with his friend, and all seemed well with the world.

Over the past few weeks his world had been filled with wonder; learning, laughing, and healing had changed him, and the Tormentor seemed a bad dream, best forgotten. The *fiend* had faded into half-remembered terror. Only the pair of little pistolettos lying by Miriam's side were an indication of how deeply her life had changed.

The mouse served as a diligent self-appointed bodyguard, keeping constant watch with sharp ears and clever eyes. One of the sergeant's men would also be close by, ever watchful lest an assassin come near. So far the guard had remained tactfully out of view.

Miriam had dressed simply in one of her pretty country gowns, and wore a great straw hat to protect herself from the sun. As usual, her shawl lay forgotten beside her on the grass. Her elegant tail switched from time to time, but even the flies seemed to have fallen beneath the river's drowsy spell.

For his part, the mouse felt in fine form today. The sun shone warmly off his handsome pelt, and his whiskers were well brushed. Mus wore a tiny strand of blue silk ribbon about his neck, tied up in a neat little bow. His sharp little face shone with curiosity as he drank in his astonishing new world.

"Reading . . ." Mus looked up at the girl with his strange, wise eyes; he suddenly seemed ill at ease. "I don't think I am actually learning this *reading,* Miriam. Truly—I think I might have always known, but am only now remembering. . . ."

The half-horse raised her friend up to eye level and thoughtfully stroked his skinny tail. "Hmm. Methinks it is the mark of this *Tormentor* of thine. He seems to have given thee rather more than he originally did intend."

Mus slumped, looking miserable. "It—It's not my own doing, then? All that I am is merely a reflection of *him.*"

"No, my friend—for thou art *good,* and that quality is from within thyself." Her stroking hands gave comfort. "Thou art brave and thou art clever. Thou art also my friend. My own dear *Mus.*"

The mouse looked up gratefully. "I thank thee for the name, Miriam. I feel more of a—a *person* for it."

"*Mus*—the ancient word for *mouse.* A dignified title—I'm glad it pleases thee."

Sitting up on his haunches, the mouse waved one tiny paw in theatrical self-importance. "Sire Mus, lord of all the lands from thy bedroom floor to the kitchen parlor." He bowed humbly. "Forever at the service of his lady fair."

Miriam gaily acknowledged the bow. "Thou hast been reading my silly storybooks again—I can see the signs."

Mus changed position, favoring his right foreleg. "Thou left one open on thy table last evening when thou went for dinner. A most interesting tale." The mouse leaned eagerly forward. "A play, I think. A *centurion* was in rebellion against his emperor for the love of the emperor's bride! There was a great war! How romantic! How dashing! How thrilling. . . ."

". . . how silly. Yes, I know the one thou means. '*Eagles Fallen*' or some such, is it not?" Miriam suddenly grinned, her freckled nose wrinkling. "Thou hast enjoyed it, eh? Two hearts fighting a whole world to find their perfect love! Empires in turmoil, loyal comrades and foul traitors!" The girl grew louder as the plot fired her imagination. "The evil emperor is cast down, the crown is won, the lovers at last united!" She faltered and grew bitter. "At least plays can have happy endings." Miriam hung her head, feeling misery pluck at her with cool fingers. "How foolish to think that life might be like a fairy tale."

Her melancholy moods came in fits and starts, and even Mus had trouble rousing her from them. Mus groomed his fur and tactfully left his friend to her thoughts. He worked at his pelt with a tiny comb made from a grass burr, brushing his handsome pelt to a shine. Miriam roused from her reverie enough to notice her friend still favored his right arm.

"How's thy leg, my friend? Does it still pain thee?"

"Mmm?" The mouse shook himself back into the real world, then carefully stretched out his right arm. "It hurts me, but I'll exercise later." The mouse shrugged. "I shall try writing again tonight. I can't form the letters so well with my right hand as with my left. Is that bad?"

"Nay, mouse—I'm still astonished thou canst write at all!" Miriam gave Mus's injured leg one last careful inspection. "We should soak it in warm water tonight. It shall give you an excuse to be outrageously pampered once again."

The mouse sat up eagerly. "A bath! Wilt thou make it a real bath once more?"

Miriam tried to scold, but spoiled it all by wrinkling her freckled nose. "Mus! Thou art the most hedonistic creature on earth! I've already had a bath this week. Mother shall think me a water nymph! Boiling up bath water turns the whole house upside-down."

The mouse pleaded pettishly. "Please? It feels so warm and nice, and thou laughs so prettily!"

"No—I'd best not. But we shall give thee a bath in a bowl if thou wishes."

Mus looked at her sideways. "With the nice herb in the water? *Please?*"

"Thou primp and dandy! I've never seen a creature take such pride in its appearance!" Miriam shook her head indulgently. "Balsam of aloe-vera for a mouse!" She sighed. "Oh, very well."

Mus beamed happily. "A bath! And a game? Dost thou wish to play chess or cards tonight? Or dost thy mother want thee downstairs?"

By tactful agreement, Mus's existence remained a secret between himself and Miriam. Somehow it just seemed wise; Mother would have shown the poor creature off to the whole county, and Mus would have been very unhappy. It seemed best to allow the mouse to discover himself piece by piece, without the burden of fame.

Miriam thought about games. "We'll play games tonight, after I have come up from dinner. But then we really should study—I have a lesson at university on Monday with Professor Titus."

"What subject?"

"Conversational languages. My Nantierran accent still grates upon the ear." Miriam made a face.

Mus considered. "I'd like to come with thee if I might. I would like to learn this other language. I find the concept intriguing."

Miriam stroked the mouse and lay back to peer up through the tree boughs above. "I shall carry thee in my apron pocket, and thou canst listen to the lesson. I don't think thou wilt understand much, but I can try to teach thee later. 'Tis a beautiful language—so much softer than our own. So . . . *romantic.*"

"Romance . . ." The mouse sighed. "Will we ever know love, Miriam?" Mus's voice filled with melancholy. "I'm lonely, Miriam. Thou art life and light and beauty, but I would dearly like a mate—and that shall never be."

"Mus—darling, what's wrong?"

The mouse looked up at her with deep, mournful eyes. "In all the world there is but one of me. Not mouse, not man."

"No, Mus, there are other mice!"

"I am not a mouse, Miriam. I don't know what I am, but I'm not what I once was."

"I-I'm sorry, Mus. . . ." Miriam scooped the mouse up into her hands. Mus kept his face hidden and let his voice fall to a whisper.

"I tried—didst thou know that? I tried to seek out other mice. I watched them from a distance. They . . . they were *animals,* and I was not." He scrubbed furiously at his eyes. "They ran from me. They knew I was alien."

He tearfully clasped Miriam's finger. "I love thee, Miriam. Thou art all I have in the world."

The girl pressed the little creature to her cheek.

"Don't cry, Mus. Don't cry. I love thee. Thou'rt not alone."

The mouse miserably rubbed his nose against her face. Miriam forced her voice to be bright and gay. "We'll find thee good friends when thou wishes—whenever thou feels that the time is right. There is no need to be lonely—'tis a magical world!"

Mus gave a tearful little sniff, but ceased his weeping. Miriam propped the mouse on top of her breast and leaned back on the tree, gazing moodily out across the river.

"Aah, Mus. Love—life's sweet balm. Sweet pleasures, true love and soaring joy. A mate would be a fine thing. . . ."

The mouse snuffled unhappily. "A little sex would not go amiss either."

Miriam cleared her throat in embarrassment. "Hmm. Well as to that, I'm sure I wouldn't know."

Mus despondently waved his hand. "I *mourn.* I shall never know the experience again."

"I might never take pleasure in it myself, my friend. I may '*discover life*' all too soon."

Her tiny companion winced. "I feel crawly whenever thou hast mentioned this marriage thou'rt being forced into. I beg thee not to go through with it! Thou wilt pine away and die!"

"There is little I can do about it, my darling. If I would save my father and brother, they must have money."

"But what about *thee!*" The mouse was beside himself with despair. "Thou'lt wither like a wildflower left to shrivel in the sun. I can't let thee to do this terrible thing!" Mus stroked his whiskers, his brow furrowed. "I'll not allow it! I shall read some books on money and discover how it can be made. How much didst thou need?"

"Thousands of marks, brave mouse. Thousands. You'll not find money in a book."

"I'm clever! I can find a way!"

"O Mus . . ."

The mouse leaned back on a grass stalk and dreamt majestic dreams. He would find out about money—what it was for, and where it might be found—and then Miriam would be free. Mus wanted only happiness for Miriam—she meant everything to him.

A faint noise caught his attention, and the mouse turned his questing nose toward the bushes.

"Someone comes. I hear hoofbeats. I smell a four-legged giant. The guard has not seen him."

Miriam stood, hiding her pistols beneath her outer skirt. Hat tilted back and eyes narrowed, she quietly awaited her unwanted visitor.

A face appeared above the riverside bushes—a dark, brooding man with haughty eyes. His close-bearded face swam coolly in the shadows of his broad black hat.

As he drew closer, the sheer scale of the man filled Miriam with a thrill of fear. A half-horse—tall, austere, and powerful; his upper body sat atop a vast, majestic stallion's form. His equine body shone blacker than the depths of hell, chased with highlights of rippling blue, and massive muscles slid beneath his hide. A wicked scar marred one of his glossy flanks, giving him an air of savagery.

His clothes were dark and unadorned with lace, seeming all the more perfect for their sheer simplicity. He moved along the pathway with utter arrogance, as if the whole riverside were too dull even to contemplate. Miriam shivered slightly as she looked at the stranger's hands and imagined what so huge a man could do to her. . . .

He lifted aside her curtain of willow leaves, and eyed Miriam in disdain. "You, girl! Do you work at the castle?"

The swine thought her a mere servant! Cold anger flooded through Miriam, and her tail slashed through the air. Her face frozen in distaste, Miriam primly answered. "Sir, indeed I do live at the castle." She haughtily flicked her eyes over the man's pristine, perfect clothing. "I was not informed, sir, that we were expecting a *chimney sweep* today."

"Chimney sweep?" The man's deep voice rang with the accent of some strange foreign place.

Miriam pawed the tree roots with her hooves. "Sooth, sir, you have the manners of one." Miriam straightened her back, and the stranger placed his fists on his waist, his tail lifting high behind him.

"Do you know whom you are talking to, girl?"

Miriam disdainfully lowered her long lashes. "Sadly sir, I do not. A *gentleman* would have introduced himself." Miriam smoothed an imaginary wrinkle from her skirt, waiting.

The stranger's rear hoof stabbed at the ground, gouging the earth as he controlled himself. He removed his hat and made a calculating bow.

"Torscha Retter of Lørnbørg, emissary for the Republic of Welfland." His voice rang deep and smooth, clipped short by a foul temper.

Miriam dropped into a serene curtsy, her tone deliberately cool. "Damsel Miriam Jerrick of Kerbridge, sirrah. I stand at your service." She straightened once more, and tried to wither him with her eyes. "You are a long way from Welfland, sir." Her tone implied that it was perhaps high time that he returned.

If Retter felt taken aback at discovering his companion's identity, he refused to show it. His eyes flicked over Miriam's plain dress, her hat and freckles, and the pet mouse perched upon her shoulder.

"I see that this is indeed the path to the castle." The man solemnly replaced his hat. 'Good day, Damsel. I am sorry to have disturbed your *busy* routine."

Miriam's mouth dropped open in outrage, but the man had the supreme insolence to completely lose interest in her. He swept past Miriam, leaving her gaping helplessly in rage. The girl squealed in anger, stamping with her hooves.

"My goodness! Wasn't he tall!" Mus blinked owlishly after the departing stallion.

Snorting with ill humor, Miriam stomped off down the river with the mouse perched gaily in her hand.

That evening, Miriam dressed carefully in her only decent gown while Mus bustled about her waist, busily adjusting the set of ribbons, laces, and bows. He achieved very little, but it seemed heartless to hinder him. Finally satisfied with his handiwork, Mus leapt nimbly across to the mantelpiece and sat back to admire.

" 'Tis good to see thee in thy finery!" The mouse was enormously pleased as he inspected his friend from his perch upon the mantel. Miriam turned to view herself side-on in the mirror and smoothed her skirts.

"Mmm—'twill do, I suppose."

"Why hast thou taken the trouble?"

Miriam frowned into the mirror. "Visitors. That cur we met at the riverbank is staying on with us, along with a pair of gentlemen from the army."

Mus hopped in front of the mirror, taking the opportunity to peer into the glass and vainly preen himself. "Why hast thy mother invited them to stay here?"

"Hmph! They have all recently come from the continent. Mother is hoping they have news about Father. For *my* part, I can wait to hear the tales from Mother." The girl irritably snatched up her ivory fan. "I'll attend dinner for Mama's sake, but I shall be damned if I will speak with *that man*."

She primped her hair into place and then turned to go. "I shan't be long, so we can still have our game. Shall I take some books off the shelves for thee?"

Mus casually waved one hand. "Nay—no need to bother. There are things to do and things to see! Have thee a good dinner—and uh—if there should be cake . . ."

Miriam's face lit up in a knowing smile. "I shall bring thee the crumbs, never fear!" Her tail trailing regally behind her, Miriam trotted from the room.

As soon as the door had closed, Mus scampered over to the sideboard and disappeared into the hollow wall. He took his sneaky ways into the visitors' quarters, eager to spy out their baggage and see what treasures he could find.

Miriam floated through the dining-room doors in a swirl of lace. She swept over to her mother, crossed her front hooves, and dipped down into a curtsy.

"Mother—good evening to thee."

"Daughter! So here you are at last." Lady Jerrick tugged her guests eagerly forward, her eyes sparkling. "Gentlemen—I present my daughter, Damsel Miriam Jerrick. Miriam—I have the honor to introduce Baron Vardvere, major general of his majesty's army;

and these are his companions, Citizen Torscha Retter of Welfland, and Sir William Merle."

Miriam curtsied once more. "Baron, Sir William, you are most welcome, sirs."

The baron made a bass, rumbling reply.

William Merle stepped forward with a look of absolute amazement on his face. "Twuly an honor, ma'am."

Eh? Miriam blinked, then rose and examined their guests. Baron Vardvere she had met several times before, being an old friend of her mother's. A human, he was perhaps fifty years of age, with a face dominated by a bristling gray mustache. His clothes were of a conservative cut, well patched along the sleeves.

Retter and his companion were both half-horses. Retter's massive bulk and stiff pose dominated the entire gathering. By contrast Sir William Merle seemed nothing but a carefree cavalier. The chestnut stallion had an easy, cheerful face framed by long blond lovelocks. He seemed quite hypnotized by Miriam, and his eyes made desperate attempts to avoid staring at her cleavage.

Miriam's mother waved offhandedly toward the dining table, where Jane was just lighting the candles. "Dinner will be served shortly, gentlemen. You must be famished after so long a journey." She smiled at her daughter, excitement brimming in her eyes. "Miriam? These gentlemen have just come from the continent where they served on thy father's staff. Citizen Retter is special emissary from the senate of Welfland to the king and parliament of Duncruigh. They—they have much news of thy father!"

Aah—thus Mother's excitement; the news must be good. Miriam turned eagerly to the gentlemen. "Sirs, I must hear more! Tell me, how is my father?"

She had expected the old baron to answer, but instead it was Retter who turned to speak, his tone grave and formal. "Your father is well, but very tired, Damsel. The campaign this season has been hard, and we are pressed back inch by bloody inch. General Jerrick was injured in a skirmish about a month ago. . . ."

"Injured!"

"Nothing serious. The baron is now much recovered. There is no need to be frightened."

His last remark was made with a patronizing air that instantly brought ice to Miriam's eyes. She proudly turned her back on Retter and faced Baron Vardvere. "My lord, we are some distance from the capital. It was most kind of you to come and see us. You have our deepest gratitude."

The mustache quivered into life. "*Hmm-haw*. Lord Jerrick asked that we might visit you, though of course, *mmm* we would not dare intrude. . . ."

"Fa, sir! We're overjoyed to have you!" Miriam's voice shone bright and earnest, and the baron smiled behind the curtain of his mustache. "You'll be attending the opening of parliament in two weeks' time?"

"*Hemmm-hmm*. Indeed, Damsel. Indeed. With your permission, *mmm* we shall recover here before moving on to the capital. Good rest and pleasant company would be a boon beyond price."

"And *pleasant* company is always welcome here, sir." Miriam gave Retter a meaningful sideways glance.

Lady Jerrick and the baron bent their heads together in talk, leaving the younger folk to mingle. Miriam deliberately distanced herself from Retter, and Sir William Merle pressed eagerly forward, his eyes gleaming. "A pweasure to meet you at wast, Damsel! Your father speaks much of his '*wittle scholar*'. I almost feel I know you."

She smiled for him, her fan flirting coyly. "Then I shall have to whittle away your advantage over me, sir, and get to know you." She cocked her head thoughtfully. "You're one of these gallant gentlemen who deliver orders in the field. My father has written much about your courage, sir."

"Your father is too kind. In twuth, we do wittle enough."

Miriam snorted, dismissing the false modesty. "Fie, sir! You are too coy. In any case, tell me of the military situation. I would be grateful for your opinion."

Merle thirstily accepted a glass of wine from maidservant Jane, then gave a predatory grin. "We smite them, miwady! Smite them! Your father is cunning. Queen Aewis curses his name nightwy before she wetires—or so wumor has it."

Miriam smirked, fanning herself. "He would be pleased to hear it, cavalier, though I fear you speak in jest." Her eyes suddenly became more penetrating. "But come, sir, how goes the war in truth? I hear Queen Aelis has appeared at the head of her own troops, and that Nantierran morale now soars to the clouds." She fixed the nobleman with a cool, calculating gaze. "How goes the siege of Lael? Will the fortress hold?"

Merle blinked in surprise, quite unprepared to be questioned so. "I—ah—that is, who can say? The citadel is well supplied, but it will not be rewieved. Du Montmarle's army bwocks our woad to the city . . . "

A rich voice disdainfully cut across Sir William's words. "A lady is hardly interested in such topics, Willy! Prithee don't *bore* the girl with things she doesn't understand."

Miriam slammed her fan shut with a *snap*, whirling to rake Retter with an angry glare. "A *gentleman* would not presume to dictate what I do or do not find interesting!" Her eyes narrowed. "When I do not understand what is being said, I assure you I will say so."

Retter snorted, somewhat put out. "As you say, madam. I had forgotten your conceit. It is not an unusual trait in one so young, so privileged, and so inexperienced."

Miriam's mother caught part of Retter's last remark. Miriam reared back, ready for an angry retort, but Lady Jerrick foiled her by stepping physically between her daughter and their guest.

"Well, gentlemen—I fear I have been ignoring you most cruelly! Please forgive the slight." Lady Jerrick's fan moved slyly back and forth as she looked from her daughter to the arrogant Mister Retter. "I trust you gentlemen will see fit to appease my daughter's curiosity. Miriam studies politics, of course–don't you, my dear?"

Trying hard for her mother's sake, Miriam drew a slow breath and controlled herself. "Yes. Ah, yes indeed." She tried to put on a gay smile for Sir William. "I must confess that the awful Queen Aelis is something of a hero of mine. I admire her courage, her independent spirit. . . ."

Retter muttered something in the tongue of Nantierre; Miriam looked at him levelly, answering him in the same language. "*Surely not, sir. I would imagine she knows her parentage better than that!*"

"Miriam, come help me at the table for a moment, would you?" Lady Jerrick curtly extended her hand to her daughter and drew the girl aside. She spoke to Miriam sotto voce as she casually scrutinized a vase of flowers. "Very well, young lady, what's set thee off tonight?"

Miriam glared over her shoulder at the imposing Mister Retter. "That man, Mother! Ooh, he makes my blood boil! He is a pompous, arrogant boor. He deserves a good quashing!"

"Well be sure that it is not *thou* that provides it. He is a guest in our house, a friend of thy father's and an emissary from Welfland. I'll tolerate no further insolence from thee."

The filly sighed, brow furrowed. "Yes, Mama. I shall try."

"Good girl. Now speak to the guests—and *do* try to be pleasant."

Happily ensconced on Retter's bed, Mus kept himself royally entertained. The guest rooms were crowded with baggage of all shapes and forms—a wealth of things to open and explore. The mouse shamelessly poked through private correspondence, avidly reading papers and official documents—anything that came to paw.

Sitting on his rump in the middle of an impressive parchment, Mus spelled out the letters and rubbed his hands with glee.

COMMISSION:

The People of the Free Republic of Welfland do hereby grant their servant CITIZEN TORSCHA RETTER the post of special emissary to the King and Parliament of our trusted and cherished ally, the nation of DUNCRUIGH.

Citizen Retter is hereby empowered to represent the case of the Republic to our ally. The Citizen will regain his current military rank once he chooses to abandon this civil commission.

God guide his thoughts.

The scroll ended with a silly picture of a chain being broken. Mus looked at it curiously for a moment, and then decided to turn another page. Burrowing beneath the stiff paper, Mus heaved the great, ungainly letter over on its side. Climbing up to a better vantage point on top of Retter's pillow, the mouse sat down to read the next document in the pile.

The handwriting was *terrible*.

Montremarte Palace
August 9th, Anno 1641
My treacherous son,

Know that your mother is dead. Dead from grief and sorrow at the savage blow you have dealt her. Almost to the last she still pleaded for you. Such is a mother's love. She could never believe how utterly her only son had betrayed her, or the degradation to which you could fall.

I write to you from mine own halls, at mine own desk. King's troops are once more in possession of the Southern Marches, and your peasant rabble have fled. The king comes unto his own again.

This foul disease of "republicanism" shall be seared and cauterized like the pustule it is. Our land shall be purified. It is God's will.

I curse you with each outgoing breath. You have slain your mother as surely as if you had stabbed a dagger through her heart. I cast you out! I reject and revile you—you are no longer my son.

Look not for mercy should we meet upon the field. I know you not.

> *Gerhard Retter, Count of Southmarch,*
> *General of His Most Pious Majesty's*
> *Army of Welfland.*

Well! Mus sat back on his haunches and smoothed his whiskers. How exciting; a real live mystery! There was far more to this *Retter* fellow than at first had seemed.

And Retter owned a sword—a real sword! The weapon of a gentleman, the arm of a hero; every adventurer needed a sword! Mus's fancy began to run away with itself. He saw himself with a glittering blade in hand, a fair young lady mouse sheltered behind him as he held the foe at bay. *Swick, swack!* A thrust through the eye and the evil cat was gone. . . .

Suddenly the door handle began to turn. Mus looked left and right, then leapt swiftly down into the clothes trunk. The mouse burrowed beneath a shirt, hiding just in time as a giant entered through the doorway.

Bother! Just when the night was becoming fun! Muttering irritably, Mus sat down to wait for the intruder to tire and depart, impatiently folding his paws. *Go away, drat you! Why of all the confounded nuisances . . .*

With a squawk, Mus suddenly felt papers, shirts, and britches thundering down on him. The chest lid closed with a *bang,* pushing him deep into the smothering layers of fabric. Someone had locked him in! Mus struggled out from under the folds of clothes and blinked in fright.

Trapped! Trapped again! The mouse collapsed in a hopeless heap of misery. *Oh, no—whatever shall Miriam say?*

Dinner became both interesting and uncomfortable. Retter sat elegantly at Miriam's side, letting the tableside conversation pass him by as though it were quite beneath him.

By contrast, William Merle was absolutely charming. Vivacious, engaging, and with a sly and lively wit, the gallant gentleman soon won Miriam's affection. He delighted Miriam and her mother with tales of derring-do.

Miriam cunningly drew out Baron Vardvere and his talkative young aide, enticing them into telling more of their adventures. Sir William laughingly described his best hat being snatched from his head by an enemy harpy; the creature had been trying its best to relieve him of both his life and his dispatches. William laughed at memories of the danger, lamenting only the loss of his hat.

"A handsome beast of a thing with a great white pwume." He ruefully shook his head. "Wretched creature probabwy gave it to his wife, who feathered her damned nest with it."

Miriam laughed, winning a grateful smile from Sir William. Her eyes wandered around the table and suddenly came to rest on Retter. The huge black stallion sat brooding privately, and something prompted Miriam to bait the fellow. Idly twirling her glass, she watched her prey over the rim.

"Lud, Citizen, but we prideful nobility are boring you!" Miriam fanned herself. "Surely our emissary from Welfland's senate has some adventurous tales to tell?" Her green eyes were wide and innocent. "Some breathtaking tales of derring-do in the back benches perhaps? Or stirring accounts of bills passed and motions proposed?"

Retter turned his cool blue eyes upon her, frowned, and then looked distastefully away. "I am sorry, *Damsel,* but I must refuse. The journey has fatigued me more than I had thought." He turned and bowed to Lady Jerrick. "With your kind permission, madam, I shall take the airs upon your battlements and then retire."

Back stiff and tail held high, Retter stalked from the room. Miriam smirked triumphantly and took a sip from her wineglass until she suddenly met her mother's unforgiving eyes. Lady Jerrick scowled and quickly folded her fan.

"General, there is a rather good port in the decanter, should you care to indulge." Her tone hardened. "Miriam! A word outside, if thou please!"

Miriam quailed and hastily put down her glass; tail drooping behind her, she apprehensively shuffled out to the corridor. Her mother joined her a moment later and firmly closed the door.

"There is nothing so unbecoming in a young lady as rudeness—but when rudeness becomes *insult,* it is unforgivable. I shall not tolerate such behavior from thee!"

Miriam felt her cheeks burn with sudden rage. "Mama! That's not fair! You saw him! You heard him! He just sits there, so superior to us all—when he is *nothing!*"

"Be quiet!" Her mother's gray eyes raked her with contempt. "I had thought thee nearly a woman, yet all I see now is a thoughtless, petty child! Hast thou stopped to think what sort of man thou hast insulted? What he is or does? Hast it even occurred to thee that he might not find war a subject for mirth and casual stories? That he might have seen too much of it?" She shook her head, then folded her arms. "Go to thy room. Thou'rt dismissed!"

Miriam felt tears of rage come to her eyes. "But *why?* What have I done wrong? That unspeakable cur has been deriding me all night! I will not have myself slighted by some arrogant leveling *citizen!*"

"ENOUGH!"

Miriam jerked back as if slapped; she backed away, her mother bearing down with sparks flashing from her hooves.

"Thou'rt too full of thyself tonight, young lady! *Go to thy room!*—And pray God to grant thee wits by morning. Thou'st shamed me in front of my guests. Now get thee gone!"

Miriam's cheeks burned, and her eyes welled with tears of outrage and confusion. Racked by the injustice of it all, the girl fled to her room.

The moon hung high over the valley, turning the river into a band of restless silver. Retter leaned on the cold stone battlements and gazed toward the sparkling lights of Kerbridge town. Hooves scuffed on the stones behind him as Willy Merle came to the walls. He switched his tail, then gazed across the ruined outer bailey.

"A beautiful pwace. Peaceful. It is good to find peace again."

Silence. Merle indicated the tumbled stones below them.

"This house has seen better days, what? No wonder the general always seemed short of gold."

"They have enough to live in luxury."

Willy shrugged. Thinking of the girl, he suddenly smiled,

propping his chin on his hand. "My goodness, what a fiwwy! She's spirited, that's for certain. I'd fear to match wits with that one—I feel certain I'd receive a fair pounding."

"She values herself highly—I'd agree on that."

"God's bwood so she should! I could lose myself in those eyes forever. . . . "

In poor humor, Retter regarded his friend. "She is hardly a breathtaking beauty."

"An angel!" William put his hands to his heart. "A woman worth fighting for! I swear off dainty court maids forever. Oh, those bosoms!" William thumped his forehead against the crenelations. "That backside! You see what the country air can do for you? Lord above!"

Retter irritably folded his arms, brooding off across the courtyard. "You will find much the same on any farmer's daughter. And the farmer's daughter will at least have the virtue of having worked to earn her place."

William sighed and turned to confront his friend. "Torscha! Whatever has gotten into you? I swear, I've never seen you wike it. You've been baiting that poor girl all night!"

"She is proud, pampered, and useless. Why should I bother to like her?"

"You wrong her! I thought her quite charming."

Retter took off his hat and combed his fingers through his long black hair. "I saw a whole nation brought to its knees by an indolent, wealthy, lazy nobility." The words were sharp and bitter. "Now I see other lands cursed by the same disease."

Sir William straightened. His voice grew quiet, and his lisp disappeared. "I am a nobleman. I thought us friends. . . ."

Retter wearily rubbed his eyes. "O Willy! That is not what I meant. . . ."

"You are unfair, Torscha. Lady Miriam strikes me as a most excellent sort. I hardly blame her for raking your black arse over the coals. Indeed, I think I like her all the more for it—your behavior has been disgraceful!" Willy straightened his immaculate goatee. "Good night to you, Torscha. I trust you will be in better spirits tomorrow."

The nobleman retired back indoors, leaving Torscha Retter to his troubled thoughts. The huge black half-horse stared moodily out across the river, then turned and wandered back into his rooms. His pixie manservant sat by the door, polishing the half-horse's brutal suit of jet-black armor. Retter tipped his hat onto the bed and gave a sigh.

"Good evening, Gus."

"Ho, Colonel. The luggage has arrived, and I haff laid out your—UT!"

"What is it, Gus?"

"A maus! A filthy maus! Ugh!"

Eep! Mus blinked dazedly as his prison lid was lifted. Strong fingers snatched him up by the tail, and the mouse found himself dangling with his feet splayed helplessly wide.

His mouth dropped open as he met his captor's eyes.

The creature that held him had the slit-pupils of a cat. Above the giant's angular face there sprouted a pair of delicate, feathery antennae—just like those of an enormous moth—and great, gauzy wings jutted from below his shoulder blades. A pixie! Mus blinked in amazement as the creature's feelers stood stiff with disgust.

"Filthy creature! Uch! I shall throw it to the cat!"

Cat! Mus drew in a breath to plead for his life, but a strong voice cut in before he had the chance.

"Aaah! Wait just a moment, Gus. I feel I know this fellow from somewhere. See—he has a collar."

Mus found himself hanging before a darkly handsome, bearded face; Retter's blue eyes sparkled with amusement.

"Well, little fellow—we meet again! I fear you are not really supposed to be abroad." He frowned, peering into his clothes chest. "I trust you didn't befoul those shirts, my furry friend, or I shall have harsh words for your mistress in the morning."

Mus felt half of a mind to bite the rude fellow! *Soil your shirts, indeed! What do you think I am? The nerve, the unmitigated gall, the . . .*

"A handsome little chap, aren't you? No wonder the Damsel takes such pleasure in you."

Eh?

"Yes—truly a dashing rodent. The collar is quite your color."

Mus puffed himself up, fluffing out his fur; at least the fellow had taste!

"Very well, Gus! Would you be so kind as to deliver our diminutive guest to Damsel Miriam Jerrick." Retter solemnly placed Mus into the Pixie's hands. "My compliments to her, and she-can rest assured her pet has been most pleasant company."

Citizen Retter watched as the mouse was borne through his door. To his immense surprise, the tiny creature seemed to wave him good-bye. The stallion twitched in puzzlement, took one step forward, and then resolutely turned away.

The hour grew late, and it was clearly time for bed.

Chapter Six

Retter

he town of Kerbridge gaily gathered for Sunday morning church. Streets thronged with crowds all decked out in their Sunday best: humans, half-horses, satyrs—even a pixie or two that had come to town for Sunday market. The great bells rang gaily up in the steeple, and the vast cathedral doors yawned open wide.

Miriam eased her long body down from the family carriage, pausing to gaze out across the busy streets. Her mother waited impatiently, and so Miriam quickly moved down to her side. Baron Vardvere, Sir William Merle, and Colonel Retter stood beside their own carriage, awaiting the ladies. They doffed their hats as one, bowing formally to the Jerrick women; Miriam and her mother curtsied gracefully in return. Smiling in welcome, Lady Jerrick took the old general's arm, and on her other side she snared Sir Willy Merle. The two gentlemen were led off to meet some of the town worthies, leaving Miriam standing face to face with the immaculate Mister Retter.

Miriam looked for rescue, but there was no escape; Retter dutifully extended his arm, and Miriam had no choice but to accept it. Retter stood stiff and proud, towering over her like a god of blackened steel; a strange man, with pain and anger hidden like a reef in his eyes. Miriam suddenly found herself meeting his gaze. The girl flushed, then angrily looked away.

They halted by the steps while Miriam tried to find her tongue. Her cheeks burned red with embarrassment; Miriam was not used to apologies.

"Sir? My-my behavior last night was rude, and it was also . . .

ill informed. I ask forgiveness if I caused you offense."

Retter remained silent, staring down with drawn brows.

When no response seemed forthcoming, Miriam irritably stamped her hoof. "*Sir!* I am apologizing to you! At least you could have the manners to accept my offering with grace!"

The huge stallion sighed, and his face filled with an uncomfortable expression. His voice grew very soft, as though he hardly cared whether he was heard or not. "Forgive me, madam. I was not rejecting your apology—merely pondering whether it was necessary. As I recall, you taunted me for not having tales of derring-do to tell. Indeed, I have none. My war has entirely lacked amusement. Homes burned, a land laid waste, and always our liberty threatening to vanish like smoke on the wind. . . ."

His shimmering black hide twitched fitfully, highlighting the cruel scar on his flanks. "My military adventures make a very poor story. I have been caught in ugly riots, seen men beaten to death by enraged mobs. My one skirmish ended in complete disaster— General Scheller's staff was attacked from the air by harpies. I shot one, hacked down another, and found myself lying in a ditch. There was a gash opened up clean along my side. I never knew I had so much blood in me."

He met Miriam's eyes, seeming sad and far away. "Not tales with which to amuse ladies over dinner. My accounts of back-room politics might be more entertaining. There at least we create, rather than destroy."

Miriam stood wide eyed and attentive, feeling privileged to have gained an insight into this strange, lonely man. Retter kept the world at bay with a fence of irony, defiantly rejecting a universe that had hurt and disillusioned him.

Miriam's voice grew hoarse.

"I would be honored to hear you speak of your part in your government, sir. Pray—do not think badly of me. I am not an idiot filly who thinks war some gallant adventure. As a healer, I cringe at the thought of every wound suffered. As a woman, I mourn the loss of every mother's son."

Retter looked into Miriam's face, suddenly interested. "Healer?"

"Yes, sir." Miriam could not find it in herself to look away, and stood gazing up into his eyes. "I am a student of physic. I think you yourself, sir, are in sore need of healing. Your spirit bears ragged wounds. I . . . please, don't let them fester."

Retter looked at her for a long moment more, then frowned and turned away. "Nonsense. I have no time for such silliness."

Their small contact had been broken. The old, hateful Retter had returned; he watched as the townsfolk doffed their hats to the nobility and gave a sour scowl.

"The first family of the community." He sadly shook his head. "The power at your fingertips, and what have you done to deserve it?"

The girl's eyes narrowed. "Sir, my *power* as you call it is nonexistent. My family is deferred to, *Colonel,* but in return, we use our influence to guard and guide our people. We are theirs as much as they are ours. We intercede and fight for them day after day, world without end!"

The stallion's smooth brow arched in surprise. "But your family is all but penniless!"

Miriam's anger flared. Her tail lashed the air behind her. "Who should know that better than I? Yes, I would like a fine wardrobe of clothes. I would like a lavish house and jewels and parties—but penury is what I have, and it must satisfy me." She contemptuously raked her eyes over Retter. "Power? Well, sir, we earn what we have. My father is a general through merit, not through birthright. I flatter myself into believing he is a good one, but his empty purse will be his undoing. To stave off that day, sir, I must now sell myself into loveless marriage—so there's your *power* and *privilege.*"

The last words were scornful and bitter. Miriam turned her back on the huge foreigner and simply walked away. She mechanically stalked on past the cathedral doors, afraid to look aside in case someone saw the tears lurking in her eyes. Miriam made her way to the family pew, flicked out her tail, and sank down on her usual cushion.

Something stirred inside her apron pocket, and a tiny bewhiskered face peeked out. Mus saw that Miriam was crying, and swiftly clambered up her dress. Miriam silently gathered the mouse up against her cheek, wetting his fur with her tears. Mus nuzzled her in silence, wondering what to say.

"Look, Miriam! Dost thou see the shafts of light shining in the air like glittery bars? How beautiful."

Miriam nodded miserably; Mus rubbed his nose and tried

again. "How tall this place is! How peaceful! I don't feel quite so small beside thee now. We are all small in this place."

Snuffling, the girl kissed the mouse on his furry head, then busied herself with a handkerchief. "O Mus, thou tries so hard. Thou'rt a true friend." She gave him a watery smile, her eyes red and weepy. "See? I am recovered. But we must get thee back into my pocket before the others arrive."

A sudden presence loomed above, and Miriam quickly hid the little rodent in her hand. Miriam looked up to discover her mother's dark, forbidding gaze.

"Young lady, thou hast abandoned our guests! I pray thou hast an explanation."

Miriam felt utterly wretched. "I-I am sorry, Mama. I was upset—I thought it best not to shame thee in public."

"My own daughter weeping like a baby for all to see!" The baroness stamped her rear hoof in disdain. "And prithee, tell me what has thee bawling this time?"

The girl's face flushed deeper. "Th-that's not fair, Mama! Can't I have feelings without it being an attack on thee?"

"Not when thou hast them in public! *Oooh,* thou art becoming a petulant child."

Miriam straightened her back. "Mother. I tried to apologize to Colonel Retter for my behavior last night, and the wretch decided to tax me further! Since he saw fit to abuse my company, I felt it best to deprive him of it." She defiantly met her mother's eye. "I was in the *right.* I thought it the best way to preserve harmony."

Lady Jerrick shifted stance, then sighed in frustration. "Truly Miriam, I cannot understand thy mood this past day gone! So thou'st just *decided* not to get along with Colonel Retter? That's the long and the short of it, eh? Well I must say I'm most disappointed. I had expected more politeness toward a guest."

Miriam clenched her fists. "No, Mama! It is not like that at all! I tried! I really tried! I almost liked him for a moment, and then he . . . Mama?"

Miriam's mother wore a long-suffering expression. "Miriam, *what* is that thou'rt holding in thy hand?"

Eep! Mus's tail had trailed out from behind Miriam's fingers. It quickly slithered out of sight as Mus snatched the offending member back, but far too late; Miriam coughed nervously.

"That? Uh—why nothing, Mother!" Her eyes widened as she

looked past her mother's shoulder. "Oh, look! Squire Sheppard and his sons have come to town. . . ."

"Miriam! Thou'rt as transparent as a window! What art thou hiding?"

Miriam hunched her shoulders in defeat and opened her hand. Mus impudently sat up on his haunches to gain a better view of Lady Jerrick. Miriam's mother blinked in surprise, disturbed by the mouse's penetrating gaze. The baroness sighed and covered her eyes; her voice sounded infinitely tired. "What is that filthy creature doing here? Lord's sake, Miriam, hast thou no idea of how a lady behaves?"

Filthy? Mus drew in an indignant breath, and Miriam firmly clamped his muzzle shut. "O Mama! He's not filthy, and I know perfectly well how to behave. The poor little fellow hasn't hurt anyone. . . ."

"Ooooh, thou'rt a difficult child! I have half a mind to take my hairbrush to thy backside, young lady! We shall have words later today, my girl—mark you well!"

Lady Jerrick swept off to collect her guests, leaving her unruly daughter to her own devices. Mus angrily struggled up out of Miriam's grasp.

"Filthy! Me? Why that dropsied old nag!"

"Hush, Mus."

"Hairbrush indeed! If she touches one hair of your hide—if she *dares* lay a hand to thee, I'll make her regret it! I shall empty my commode into her chocolate and put spiders in her bed. I'll show *her* filthy!" The mouse folded his arms and snorted through his whiskers. "One precious hair of thy hide—I swear it."

Mus delved down into Miriam's apron and came back with his comb. Vain as ever, he tried to smooth his bristling fur back down. "Filthy? *Huh!*" And with that, the mouse grumpily retired into Miriam's apron pocket.

Safely back at Castle Kerbridge, Miriam and the family guests settled down for Sunday lunch. Bishop Kaxter had invited himself to the meal—no doubt keen to cast an eye over Dame Jerrick's other visitors. His great, burly figure trundled like a juggernaut back and forth across the Jerricks' hall, dragging Sir Willy Merle in his wake like a toy horse on a string. Over a vast jug of the bishop's wine, the guests examined the stuffed heads of wild boar, manticores, and chimeras, most of which the bishop had shot himself.

The rough old cleric smiled as Miriam walked into the hall, and he immediately took the girl under his arm. "Greetings, my dear! I trust the service bored you as much as I? So it seemed by your expression in any case!"

"Miriam!" Lady Jerrick turned to angrily scold her daughter, only to be halted by the bishop's belly laugh.

"Lud, madam! Surely you'll not offend my intelligence by claiming the service interested you? Why I remember preaching to you at this little one's age, and watching your hooves twitch back and forth for a whole hour—a most annoying habit by the way. I only saw you do it once or twice today."

Lady Jerrick snorted, refusing to be mollified; she returned just in time to catch sight of her daughter surreptitiously dropping cake crumbs into her apron pocket. The baroness firmly set her glass down on the table and folded up her arms.

"Right, young lady! I want a few words with thee!"

Miriam froze, darting an embarrassed glance at their four guests. "Uh—what about, Mama?"

"Thou knows full well, Miss! Come!"

The girl firmly planted all four hooves and calmly stood her ground. She pitched her voice low so as not to be heard by the nearby gentlemen.

"Mother, please. Another time."

Lady Jerrick's eyes widened. "I say *now*, my fine filly!"

"Please, Mama!" Miriam glanced at the menfolk in embarrassment. "You shame me!"

Miriam's mother bristled, her tail held high as she bore down on her rebellious daughter. The menfolk surreptitiously retreated into a far corner, pretending to be absorbed in their conversation.

"How dare thou take that tone with me! Thou'rt an ungrateful rebellious *child,* and I shall not stand for thy nonsense! A girl who is approaching her marriage . . ."

"*Child!*"

". . . who is approaching her marriage must start to behave like a *woman.*"

Miriam's temper snapped, and her hooves danced with rage. "I *am* behaving like a woman! 'Tis thou who art behaving childishly! Thou'st been harrying me all day! *I will not be treated like a foal!*"

"Ha! A grown woman does not use her pocket as a zoo! When I think that in our town's cathedral, in front of mine own guests, thou'st seen fit to keep with thee a filthy, diseased, revolting *mouse,* my pelt quite stands on end. Thou and thy pets have gone too far this time. . . ."

"ENOUGH!" A high-pitched voice cut through the tirade. "*That,* madam, is the final straw!"

All eyes gaped as a tiny figure struggled out of Miriam's apron pocket. The mouse angrily shook out his fur, his small face bristling with fury.

There was a *crash* as Sir William's wineglass hit the floor.

The mouse climbed out onto the table and shook one tiny finger at Lady Jerrick. "Madam—you are most insulting! You have shamed this girl before your guests. Have you no sense of decency? My ears burn in embarrassment for her!" The mouse paced back and forth, staring upward at Lady Jerrick's ashen face. "As for my being '*filthy, diseased and revolting,*' I can only say that I will suffer no more insult! I am far cleaner than you by the *smell* of it, and my health is quite fine, thank you." His tail thrashed emphatically.

The baroness made a strangled sound, looking pale.

The mouse swept the crowd of giants with his angry gaze. "I am not a pet! Damsel Miriam has been kind enough to become my friend, and I am as much a guest here as the rest of you! I had as much right to go to church as anyone else. Damsel Miriam was kind enough to offer me transportation in her pocket. If you begrudge the girl her kind heart, then I pity you all. As it is, I seem to be the only one here who truly appreciates her."

Tail held high, Mus proudly twittered across the table to Miriam. "Couldst thou take me home now, my lady? I'll not force the presence of such a *revolting creature* upon these high and mighty folk a moment longer."

Silence reigned absolute. Miriam swept Mus up off the table and looked around at the dumbfounded gathering.

"Pl-please excuse us. I shall be back to explain shortly. I prithee patience." She made a quick curtsy and fled the room, the mouse safely cradled in one small hand.

All eyes stared after Miriam as she disappeared through the door. The stunned silence was suddenly shattered by a loud guffaw from Bishop Kaxter. The rest of the group whirled to find the Bishop laughing with delight, thoroughly enjoying himself. He poured a glass of wine, stuffed it into Lady Jerrick's hand, and steered her firmly over to a chair.

"Here, my dear—have a drink! It shan't make life any easier, but it does make the jokes rosier." Supremely unconcerned, he raised his glass to the assembly.

"Cheers!"

Chapter Seven

A Mouse of Kerbridge

n the golden light of sunset, the evening meal looked rather promising. Decanters of rich amber wine stood waiting by the table, and the delicious smell of roasting meat wafted through the kitchen doors. There would be a goodly crowd for a change. A seventh place had been hastily arranged; a collection of thimbles and buttons, with a folded kerchief for a chair.

One by one, the guests gathered; Torscha Retter, dark and immaculate as ever, lending an air of dignity to the occasion; Sir William Merle and the bishop, both enjoying their lives to the full. Lady Jerrick and General Vardvere entered very quietly, the general trying his best to soothe the baroness's nerves. The group remained standing in speechless discomfort as a clock ticked loudly in the hall.

The final dinner guests arrived; Miriam's hooves could be heard coming slowly down the corridor. The young filly walked into the dining hall, looking bright and dainty in her one and only evening dress. Perched upon her shoulder sat the diminutive guest of honor. Decked out in a neat white collar, Mus wore a cavalier's hat and plume taken from a tiny doll. Miriam placed the mouse gently upon the table; he looked up at her, winked and smiled, then pattered purposefully across the table to sit on his haunches before the baroness.

Miriam bowed gravely. "Mother, may I present my companion, Mus of Kerbridge. Mus—Lady Barbara Jerrick, Baroness."

The mouse swept his hat off with a flourish as his tiny little voice piped through the air. "An honor and privilege to meet you, my lady. Your daughter speaks of you often. I pray you will forgive my rude outburst of an hour ago. I-I spoke from anger, and I never meant to offend."

Lady Jerrick crawled with embarrassment. "Why-why of course, my dear fellow. Pray, I hope *you* will forgive *me* for the grave insults I dealt you. I-I spoke in ignorance."

The mouse beamed up at her. "Lud, madam! Forgiven and forgotten. I hope we can be friends."

Lady Jerrick smiled nervously, and then suddenly broke into a relieved grin. "I should be *honored!*" She graciously turned to indicate her other guests.

"Well, Mus—allow me to introduce Major General Baron August Vardvere."

The tiny mouse bowed elegantly once more. "An *honor,* my lord! I have read your '*Dissertation of Tactical Vogues*' and found it quite fascinating."

"*Harrumph!* You've read it?" The old baron blinked in surprise. "*Hemmm*—fascinating y' say? Well, I'm flattered to hear it!" The great shaggy mustache quivered with a grin. "I'll have to give you some of my other books, then!"

"Oh—oh, it would be an honor, sir!"

Lady Jerrick moved the mouse on toward the bishop.

"Bishop Kaxter of Kerbridge See."

"A pleasure to meet you, Your Grace."

The bishop enthusiastically shook the rodent's paw. "A privilege to meet *you,* sir! Your friend Miriam has clearly been busy schooling you. You amaze me, sir! I must try to monopolize you later today for a chat."

The mouse grinned happily, pleased as Punch. "I shall look forward to it, Your Grace."

The baroness indicated the next guest. "Sir William Merle—Mus of Kerbridge."

Sir William theatrically swept off his hat in reply to the mouse's bow, positively bubbling with joy. "Greetings, sir mouse! An unexpected pweasure, but a greatly appreciated one!"

"Delighted to make your acquaintance, my lord."

Only one guest remained. Lady Jerrick motioned to Torscha Retter. "And of course, Mus, I am informed that you have already informally met our distinguished visitor, Citizen Retter."

Retter bowed with enormous dignity, and Mus replied in kind.

"An honor to make your acquaintance, sir. Your mission touches on those dearest to me—I wish you every success at parliament."

Retter gravely inclined his head. "Thank you, sir—I shall endeavor to do my best."

The introductions having been successfully concluded, Lady Jerrick clapped her hands. "Well! Let us eat then. There is much to talk about, it seems."

Everyone sat down to dinner. Mus nestled politely on the kerchief provided him, laying aside his fine new hat and sitting between Miriam and her mother. Jane served the dinner, staring in numb amazement at the mouse.

Mus had no cutlery, but no one really minded his eating with his hands. His manners were perfect, and his conversation delightful; the mouse told the gathering of his three full weeks of conscious life. The mouse had been reading, studying, and observing, always discovering more and more about his strange new world.

Lady Jerrick still seemed utterly stunned; caught up in a discussion with Mus about the difficulties of rose gardening, the baroness soon became as captivated by him as the rest of them. Miriam bubbled over with pride and joy as Mus became the life and soul of the party. He ended up locked in conversation with the indomitable Citizen Retter, somehow turning the discussion toward poetry. Retter's face animated with sudden passion as he carefully explained the techniques of rhyme and meter, juxtaposition and allusion. He showed an astonishingly deep knowledge of so flippant a subject, his eyes glowing as he wove a poem before the enraptured little mouse; a wondrously sensual love poem, all strands of gossamer hair and the caress of skin on skin. Miriam found herself listening carefully, her meal forgotten as the man's deep smooth voice held her spellbound. His clear blue eyes met Miriam's, and he suddenly stumbled on his words.

Miriam hastily looked away and vaguely heard her mother complimenting Retter on his poem " . . . most unusual piece. I don't believe I am familiar with it."

Retter cleared his throat, becoming all stiffness and dignity once more. "Ah—no, madam, it is one of mine own. I-I don't quite know why I chose to recite that particular verse."

Miriam looked up quickly and felt a shock as she found Retter's eyes still upon her; she blinked in surprise, trying to find her tongue. "I—that is . . . you never said you were a poet."

Retter looked disdainfully away, and Miriam once again felt a flash of dislike as the man dismissed the subject. "I am not a poet, madam—otherwise I would have chosen to tell you that I was. I turned my back on such foolishness long ago."

He returned to his meal, leaving Miriam to glare at him in cold antipathy.

Mus perched up on the edge of the parlor table, his tail switching slyly back and forth. One hand stroked his whiskers as he watched Retter's eyes. He would gain no clues from Retter. Mus twirled his whiskers, then tapped his tail against his rack of playing cards. "I discard this one."

He looked across to his partner, Miriam, smiling craftily as she pulled out his indicated card. Willy blinked, snatched up the discard and instantly laid down his hand.

"Ha! Knight, Page, Ten, and Nine of Wands. My trick!" Willy sat back, enormously pleased with himself; he seemed quite shocked when Mus crowed and made a dizzy little dance.

"Ha! Not so, not so!" He indicated two more of his own cards, which were duly plucked out of his special rack and laid upon the table. "Queen and Eight of Wands! I bracket and absorb. Six points to us!"

Miriam clapped gleefully as the score was recorded. Retter frowned in irritation at his partner, William Merle, but the cavalier could only shrug and roll his eyes.

They sat upon the balcony under a spray of jasmine flowers, warmed by the cheery yellow glow of candlelight. In these last few days of summer, the weather seemed determined to leave everyone with kindly memories. The night was warm and clear, and the stars shone in a cloudless sky.

Three more hands were played, and Mus won them all without so much as ruffling his fur. With cool dignity, Retter folded his cards and placed them carefully back down upon the table. Mus gave a cheer and leapt up onto Miriam's ample bosom. The girl laughed as the mouse nestled in her cleavage. Lounging on his back, one elbow propped on either breast, the little mouse kicked up his heels and smiled. "An excellent game gentlemen! An excellent game! You are exciting opponents."

Retter brushed at his mustache and then neatly folded his hands. "A thumb-sized shyster! I bow to you, sir, and to your talented partner—the two of you have trounced us, fair and square." He narrowly eyed Sir William. "Although there is something to be said for partners who throw away aces. . . ."

For his part, Sir William seemed to have greatly enjoyed being beaten. He grinned affably across the table at one and all. "I can feel no shame at wosing to opponents of such surprising skill—or of such dazzling beauty." He gallantly raised his glass to Miriam and drank. Flushing at having received such a surprising compliment, Miriam reached for her fan. Unable to see Mus, she could feel him sprawled comfortably between her breasts. She reached down and evicted him just in time, as Lady Jerrick's voice chimed in from behind.

"Faith! Are you young people still corrupting our poor guest?"

Retter wryly brushed his handsome beard. "I fear, madam, that it is more a case of *our* being corrupted by our furry friend. Six games and I have yet to win a trick! If there were money wagered, Mus would be able to buy and sell us all."

Once again on his favorite perch, Mus pattered across Miriam's shoulder, pricking up his ears.

"Money? Wager? Whatever do you mean?"

Miriam quickly tried to intervene, but it was too late.

Happy to increase the rodent's stock of information, Retter made a swift reply. "A wager? Well you see, we often play these games for money. You bet a sum of money . . ."

Miriam hurriedly leapt in. "Mus! Mother has some cake for you."

Lady Jerrick rocked back on her hooves in surprise; not having been born stupid, she played along with her daughter's lead. "Ah, yes, Mus, we are just gathering for evening supper. Would you care to join us?"

Mus sat up, suddenly attentive at the mention of food.

"Oh, thank you, my lady! I should be ever so pleased. You are too kind."

Miriam scooped Mus up off her shoulder and deposited him in her mother's hand. "Mother—why don't you take Mus out to the parlor?"

The baroness blanched slightly as the warm, furry body settled in her hands. "Well I—ah . . ." She swallowed, and then saw the mouse looking up at her with trusting, innocent eyes. Her face softened, and she instantly forgot her aversion to rodents. Lady Jerrick bore

Mus from the room; the last thing anyone heard of them was Mus excitedly praising the baroness's soft auburn hair, and Lady Jerrick's warm laugh as she replied.

Miriam spared a last glance after her mother, and then quietly turned to face the two stallions. Her face shone pale behind the delicate kiss of freckles on her cheeks. "Gentlemen. I-I must ask a favor of you both. Mus . . . cares very much for me. It might be best not to raise his hopes about . . . about money." Miriam looked out over the balcony railings at the stars. "He is too innocent to understand the difference between romance and reality." She hung her head in misery. "He-he believes in miracles. Perhaps it's why I love him so."

Miriam despondently walked from the balcony, leaving the two stallions alone. William Merle downed the contents of his glass, looked after Miriam's retreating tail and swore.

" 'D's blood, I feel so damned helpwess! To-to see a *pearl* like that hurled before swine. . . ." He angrily threw the contents of his glass out into the night.

Retter coolly poured himself more wine. "Well, my friend—it seems more rides on our mission than we'd supposed."

Willy angrily slapped his hat against his withers. "A budget for the army would save that girl from making a terrible sacrifice! She deserves better. Far better."

Retter irritably scuffed his hooves. "The *army* might appreciate my efforts, too. Why don't *you* make the girl an offer if you like her so well?"

William whirled. "You know damned well why I can't! My fortune is gone. If it weren't for the army, I'd be ruined!"

"So you do like her?"

"Of course I bloody wike her! And if you had a whisker of sense, you would too! Perhaps it's time you thought of someone other than the honorable Torscha Retter and his vale of misery!"

Merle's hooves clattered angrily against the floor as he trotted back inside. Torscha Retter silently finished his drink before following him; his head hung bowed in thought, and his eyes were troubled.

The next morning, Miriam awoke to a strange, repetitive noise outside her window. The noise had hovered at the edge of her muzzy mind for some time, and all efforts to ignore it proved futile. Finally Miriam hurled aside the covers, tugged on a dress, and irritably threw open her shutters.

Leaning far out over the windowsill, her ample breasts in dire danger of falling from her dress, Miriam scowled out into the cold. The wretched noise grew louder, full of the sound of snapping twigs and breaking wood. Chopping kindling at this hour? Absurd! The girl rolled up her sleeves and headed for the garden, ready to give the culprit a good piece of her mind.

Despite the cold of the dawn, it promised to be a fine, hot day. Miriam walked briskly through the kitchen hedge and wound her way into the ruins. The noise became louder as she neared its source, and Miriam gradually slowed her steps. She cautiously approached the old garden wall and finally spied the source of the commotion.

Colonel Retter! Miriam stared in shock as the huge black stallion rampaged about the weeds. Retter ran wild, rearing and bucking like a mad thing, lashing out with his rear hooves to shatter old dead trees. Sweat sheened his jet black hide and matted his flying hair—Miriam smelled the sting of it and felt her muscles twitch. Retter's face was twisted with rage, and Miriam fancied she could hear him hissing under his breath.

"You *killed her! You! It was you!*"

He was mad! Miriam drew back, feeling a surge of fear as she saw the ferocious power of the man. Muscles bunched and surged as his great black legs tore at the turf. Miriam swung fearfully away, then suddenly found herself face to face with Sir William Merle.

"Good morning, Wady. I am sorry your rest was disturbed." For once, William Merle seemed conspicuously under-dressed, clearly having just risen from his bed. He saw the alarm in Miriam's eyes and laid a reassuring hand on her arm.

"He . . . he's not truly dangerous, my wady. Not to us. But Torscha gets these dark moods from time to time and is best left alone." He sought her eye. "Pwease don't think harshly of him. It is my fault. I-I taxed him too hard about something last night. I expect he stayed up all night hounding himself."

Miriam shivered as she heard Retter rearing and bucking on the far side of the wall.

"*Terrifying* . . . what could set such anger in a man?"

William winced, looking evasive. "I fear, madam, I should not be the one to say. But . . . I said some foolish things. About him being uncaring about other people."

Miriam raised a sardonic eyebrow. "Foolish? Indeed?"

"Yes, miwady. Torscha cares very much—perhaps too much." He looked toward the garden wall. "We must go. He'd be mortified if he thought we knew. Let us go inside. I fear it is remarkabwy chilly."

Arm in arm, they walked to the house. Fresh out of bed, Willy looked delightfully disheveled. Though rumpled and half asleep, he still tried his best to be gallant; Miriam laughed.

"Oh, Sir William, you look very much how I feel!"

The cavalier rubbed at his eyes, yawning hugely. "Aah—ah yes, I see what you mean. That little rodent's fault, I'm afraid. There I was, all set to turn in when the little devil came prancing through the back of the mantelpiece and asked me to describe what a ship was like! Then he had the extreme rudeness to trounce me at chess."

As they reached the kitchen door, Miriam stopped and looked back toward Colonel Retter. "Sir William—is there anything that we can do for him?"

"No, Lady. He fights himself. It is best not to intervene."

Arms linked, the two half-horses walked into the kitchen and escaped the cold. Behind them, the sound of Torscha's private war went on.

The next day dawned without the benefit of Colonel Retter's noisy early morning activity. When next they met, Miriam noted no sign of the raging beast that so frightened her in the orchard; nevertheless, Miriam found herself watching his eyes, anxiously wondering whether the beast still lay within.

Long days passed in relative peace. Retter and Willy were often in Miriam's company; in this respect they served as bodyguards, replacing the sergeant and his ever-attentive men.

One hot midday, Miriam found herself walking along beside the moat, flanked on either side by her gentlemen companions. Sir William was enjoying himself hugely; the towering stone walls of the castle, the quiet moat with its water lilies and clean white swans—it all seemed just too picturesque.

Willy sighed in absolute contentment as the river breeze moved through his hair. "Wud, madam! My heart will dwell here forever. Your home positivwy casts a spell on me!"

Miriam smiled for him, her green eyes sparkling. "Oh, Willy! We're going to have to keep you here permanently. I swear neither I nor this moldering old house have ever reaped such compliments as you shower on us. You quite make me forget how plain and ordinary we are."

"Plain and ordinary!" The blond cavalier reared in astonishment, scandalized by Miriam's self-derogation. "Madam! Enough of such talk! You—you wound me every time you downplay yourself. I think I have never admired a woman for her wit and intellect until I met you. That such simple beauty—I—er, that is to say . . ." Embarrassed by his own outburst, William turned and waved a hand toward the moat. "Torscha—have you ever seen anything so wuvwy?"

The towering black half-horse looked at his friend with sardonically hooded eyes. "You mean the castle?"

"Uh—of course I mean the castle!"

Retter ran his eyes over the old medieval walls, the shallow moat with its water birds and weeds, then glanced at the trees that grew beside the waterline; finally he shrugged.

"Romance is always a self-deception. The castle? It is insecure. The trees should be cleared away to make fire lanes, the walls should be replaced with revetments. The moat should stay. . . ."

Miriam felt a flash of anger. "Is that all life is to you! Practicalities? I don't know whether to laugh at you or feel sorry for you! Where we see cool trees and calm waters, you see only fortifications and fields of fire!"

Unperturbed, Retter looked down at her from on high. "That is the castle's function, madam. It is a fortress, and your penchant for picturesque settings has made it a bad one."

Miriam stood with one black leg half raised in threat. "It is a *home,* sir! If you want fortresses, I suggest you go down and look at the town. The new earthworks there should be quite hideous enough to thrill even *your* ugly soul."

"Clean and efficient. I have no complaints about them."

Sir William swiftly came to intervene. "Truwy, Torscha, you must rediscover your sense of romance one of these days. I asked you whether you thought the castle was *beautiful.*"

The black stallion folded his arms and scowled derisively at the aging walls. "No, sir, I do not find it beautiful. I dislike this beauty of yours because it poses a *threat;* right now we need function, not frippery."

Miriam's temper blazed. Fists bunched, she turned to confront the rude, arrogant pig who insulted her home. "And *I,* sir? Sir Willy did not ask but meant to. Am *I* beautiful?"

Retter folded up his arms, and finally the admission was dragged out of him. "Yes, madam. Since you force the issue. You are indeed beautiful."

"And therefore *useless?*" Miriam's hooves danced with rage, and her face choked red with anger.

Retter swished his tail and snapped back at her in contempt. "Since you would have it so, *yes!* Yes, you are useless! Unable to even look after yourself, you tie up men in protecting you—men who could better be used elsewhere!"

Miriam gave an incoherent squeal of rage. Rearing backward, she snatched a tiny pistol out from her skirt. Before the horrified Sir William could stop her, she had cocked it, leveled the piece and fired. The bullet split a sapling fully sixty feet away. Retter's wide eyes traveled from the smoking pistol to the target as Miriam grimly sheathed her gun.

"And *that,* sir, is how helpless I am! Since you feel you are better used elsewhere, please take your protection and *go.*"

Tail held high and back proud, Miriam trotted proudly back along the pathway. When she moved properly out of earshot, William furiously whirled on his companion, his hooves clawing up the soil. "Why must you do that? She has never been anything but kind to us. If you ever, *ever* insult her again, you shall have me to answer to! "

Retter blinked, amazed at his own loss of temper. "I-I'm sorry. Truly I am. That was stupid of me. . . ."

"It is not *me* that you owe an apology to, sir! I suggest you go and attend to *that* matter at once—but you may end up with one of those pistol balls lodged in your stupid head!"

Retter flicked his tail. "I . . . yes, of course." His dignity settled back into place again. "Please forgive me, Willy."

The black stallion departed; William stood alone beside the moat, his hide twitching as he stared into the murky waters.

Retter found Miriam in the library, sitting cold, aloof, and in no mood for company. She saw the stallion as he came through the door, slammed her book shut and hefted it like a hammer in her hand. "*Out!* I shall not say it again. You have insulted me for the last time, sir. I will not suffer more."

Retter bowed deeply, and with great dignity. "Madam, please hear me out. I apologize most profoundly for my behavior just now. My loss of temper, the insults I delivered—I deeply regret them. I spoke in foul temper and poor taste, neither of which I can forgive myself for."

Miriam blinked in confusion. *Eh?*

The Colonel straightened and caught her eye. "I ask your forgiveness, madam. My own preoccupations most rudely governed me. I am entirely at fault, and can say only that it shall never *ever* happen again."

The girl was quite dumbfounded. "I—uh—I accept your apology, sir." What else could she do? Retter had completely confessed his wrongs; it must have taken some courage to have sought her out.

Retter placed his hat back upon his head. "I, of course, withdraw my remarks—except for declaring you to be beautiful. A man would have to be stupid to think otherwise."

"Yet I am not useless?"

"In general, madam, my opinion on the functionality of beauty remains unchanged. In your case, I make an exception." The stallion looked out of the window. "I would ask a favor of you, my lady. Our friend Mus—I wish to prepare a gift for him, but I wish to consult with you about it beforehand. If you will tolerate my company, I wonder if we perhaps might talk about it later."

Surprised, Miriam felt quite unsure what she should say. "Very well, Colonel. I should be interested to hear your ideas."

"I shall look forward to seeing you later, madam."

"And I you, Colonel." Miriam shook her head in wonder at herself. "If only to show you the error of your contempt for beauty and romance."

A week later, on a warm and sunny afternoon, Mus and Miriam accompanied Retter on a walk below the castle walls. They strolled through the orange orchard, past streams and willow trees, until they came to a pond beside a deserted mill.

The millpond lay in perfect, dreaming peace. Afternoon sunlight slanted through the trees while ferns trailed green fingers down to caress the darkened water. It was a place of fallen logs and smooth round stones, of soft shadows and fragrant moss. The tranquil water scarcely even stirred beneath the breeze.

Colonel Retter and Miriam made their way down between the trees. Tall, straight and strong, with his tail held proudly high, Retter radiated an aura of cool dignity as he walked at Miriam's side. His thick, muscular legs surged powerfully over the pathway.

Mus balanced on Retter's broad shoulders, wheedling and coaxing. "Oh, *please*, Colonel! Why must I wait? *Please?*"

The huge half-horse's eyes were hooded, and his face quite unconcerned. "Because anticipation is a fine thing. The more we think about what we can't have, the more we want it. The more we think about what we *might* have, the better we treasure it." Retter eyed the mouse and gave a smile. "Besides—I must teach you about this present before I let you run off with it."

The mouse groaned in frustration, his voice twittering as he wrung his hat between his hands. "Oh, can you not give me a hint? Is it big? Is it small?—Oh, Miriam, make him say something!"

Miriam cocked her head prettily, looking down her freckled nose in mock annoyance. "Nay, thou childish creature, I shall not! Thou canst jolly well grit thy teeth and learn patience."

The two half-horses moved side by side, picking their way between moldering, moss-covered logs. The air grew rich with the scents of rotting leaves and swirling water. Suddenly realizing where they were, Mus opened his eyes wide; his ears rose as he turned to Miriam and spoke in a hushed whisper.

"Will we visit the *dragon?*"

The girl edged closer to Retter's shoulder to see Mus eye to eye. "Wouldst thou like to?"

The mouse stared out across the water. "I fear it—but it's so *beautiful*. Oh, let us go and see it."

Miriam looked up into Retter's face, her brows arching mysteriously. "Well, Colonel—shall we confront Mus's dragon?"

Caught by her challenging green eyes, the tall man could only nod in agreement. The filly hitched up her apron-skirts and knelt beside the pond, waiting for Retter to join her. She drew a long, deep breath, and then tucked a straying wisp of hair behind her ear. "A beautiful place, is it not?"

Retter looked about himself with mild interest. "It has a certain . . . peace about it."

"*Peace* but not beauty? Ah well. I usually find that the two go hand in hand, but I am somewhat reclusive. Let us see whether we can conjure up some company for you, Colonel." Miriam gracefully pulled up one of her sleeves. Leaning forward across the water, she began to slap her hand against the surface. Stately ripples drifted out across the pond while Miriam gazed down into the pool. "Mus found him injured, so I healed him. He lurks here beneath the waters—Mus's dragon."

"Mus's *dragon?*"

"Sssh—here he comes."

Something stirred beneath the waters, and Retter felt Mus take a firm grip in his hair. With his own breath hushed, the colonel leaned out across the water.

Gold glinted in the depths as a huge carp rose to the surface. The great monster of a fish was perhaps as long as Retter's tail, clad in great flat scales of gleaming bronze. Pale saucer-eyes peered in a grave, unblinking stare at the surface folk. His fins cruised in slow, unhurried patterns as he drifted quietly up into the light.

Mus gasped in awe and stared widely. "The *dragon* . . ."

Retter blinked in wonder. "Faith! A dragon indeed. What a monster!"

Mus's voice dropped to a bare whisper. "He could swallow me at a gulp."

"Hold tight, then. I'll not let you fall."

The creature gazed up at his audience while Torscha and Mus stared back in rapt fascination. Quite unconcerned, Miriam reached under the water and rubbed the fish beneath his bewhiskered chin.

"There was a hook through his mouth, poor thing. I took it out and cleaned the wound." She chuckled indulgently. "He likes us to visit from time to time."

Retter never let his gaze wander from the carp. "He let you take out the hook—just like that?"

"Oh, yes. It took a while to coax him into trusting us, but once he knew us well enough, he let me cure him." Miriam searched in her apron with her other hand and came out with a piece of bread, dropping it into the water near the fish's head. With all due solemnity, the carp rose to the surface and sucked the food into his mouth, then sank back down into the deeps and swam away. The last that they saw of him was a ponderous swirl of water and a glint of hidden gold.

The half-horses sat together in silence, enjoying the tranquillity of the water and the whisper of the ferns. It seemed no real surprise when a high, sweet voice rose above the gentle murmur of the stream.

"There is a lady sweet and kind,
Was ne'er a face so pleased my mind;
I did but see her passing by,
And yet I love her till I die.

Her gesture, motion, and her smiles,
Her wit, her voice my heart beguiles,
Beguiles my heart I know not why,
And yet I love her till I die.

Cupid is winged and doth range;
Her country so my love doth change,
But change she earth, or change she sky,
Yet I will love her till I die.

Oh, I shall love her till I die. . . ."

The voice trailed sweetly off, leaving the listeners to sigh with delight. Miriam looked up to see Mus's bright eyes upon her. "My lovely Mus! What made thee sing?"

The mouse seemed suddenly shy. "I-I saw thee standing there, the dragon at thy feet and kindness in thine eyes. . . . Thou'rt love itself. Art not angry?"

"O Mus—thou gentle soul. I thank thee."

Retter's face seemed lost and lonely as he gazed from Miriam to the mouse.

"You are fortunate, madam, to own a heart so totally. . . ."

He looked out across the pond at some strange and distant scene, then finally winced and closed his eyes, turning his face away from the tranquil waters. There was a long uncomfortable silence, suddenly broken as Retter surged to his hooves.

"Shall-shall we give our friend his present? As a discoverer of dragons, he seems to have need of it."

Retter coolly brushed off his great black legs. Mus stirred on Miriam's shoulder and vigorously scratched his ear with one hind foot. The motion brought Miriam back into the real world. Shaking herself, she led the way over to the edge of the shadowed glade. Mus jumped down onto a tree stump, where he sat twitching with impatience while Retter busied himself with a small wooden box.

Beside himself with excitement, Mus hopped up and down on his little pink feet, hoping for a better view. Retter noticed the motion and turned a calculating eye upon the jittering mouse. Under the baleful pressure of the colonel's gaze, Mus subsided.

Retter looked at Mus for a long moment with his darkly thrilling eyes. "Well, sir! Damsel Jerrick informs me you wish to style yourself a *gentleman*. What say you to that?"

Taken by surprise, Mus sat back and stroked his whiskers. He drew his brow into a frown. "Colonel Retter? Miriam has taught me much, and she claims I am good at heart." He seemed embarrassed to be talking so, but Retter listened with grave attention and so Mus spoke on. "I-I read, sir. I love to hear stories. Now, it seems that the qualities that the storybooks praise are courage, honesty, a love of justice, a gentle nature, and devotion to duty. Miriam says that these are the traits of a true gentleman. I would very much like to have those qualities, so yes—I would dearly love to be a gentleman."

Retter regarded the mouse with considerable respect. "Why—well said, Sir Mouse! Well said! There are many who could learn from you." He opened the small box and poked about inside. "In any case—there is something no gentleman should be without. Indeed, I fear you may need it more than most." Retter withdrew a glittering object from the box and gravely proffered it to the mouse. "A gift, Mus. Please accept it with my compliments."

It was a tiny, perfect sword.

Mus gasped and reached out to clutch the hilt. Fashioned from a ground-down needle, with a cup-guard made of a brass sequin, it balanced superbly in his hand. Mus sat up on his haunches, his eyes shining as he beheld his wondrous present.

"It's *perfect!* Oh, how can I ever thank you enough, sir?"

As cool and suave as always, Retter graciously bowed.

Sitting atop the tree stump with his hat tilted jauntily across his eyes, Mus began to prance back and forth on his hind legs while waving his tiny sword.

After watching the mouse for a moment, Retter moved thoughtfully aside. The eyes that alighted upon Miriam's face were . . . troubled. "My lady, may I speak frankly with you?"

Miriam blinked. "Uh—very well, sir. My ears attend you."

Retter paced uncomfortably up and down before her, his back stiff as polished ebony. The sun traced rippling blue highlights on his flanks as he walked. "Madam, I-I fear I owe you an apology. For no good reason I have behaved very poorly toward you—behavior I now deeply regret." He ceased pacing and stood, one hoof half raised in uncertainty. The air of dignity about the man was breath-taking.

"I ask you to forgive me, my lady. Can we perhaps forget our foolishness and start again? I would be honored to count you a friend. You have my respect, Lady. I pray that one day, I might perhaps earn yours."

Oh, my . . . Miriam blinked while her heart fluttered like a sparrow in her breast. Matching Retter's stately dignity, Miriam bowed her head. "You are a most gracious gentleman, sir. A-a peace offering from you is neither deserved nor expected. I accept your apology, and pray you will accept mine." She raised her gaze to Retter's and looked uncertainly into those strange blue eyes. "As to friendship—who can say? If we start afresh, who knows what might grow?"

Retter bowed to her. "Indeed, madam. Who can say?" He straightened, his face suddenly inscrutable. "I thank you for your patience. And now—if you will forgive me, I shall monopolize our friend Mus for a while."

Tail held proudly high, Retter trotted to his tiny student. "Ha! Now, sir, basic fencing! We shall start with footwork."

Miriam sank to all four knees by the stream and smiled.

Summer had finally faded into autumn, and rain lay fresh on the castle's cobblestones. Major General Vardvere's coach stood ready in the courtyard, horses nodding in the cold. The wind rose and fell fitfully between the trees as if unsure quite what to do with itself.

Miriam walked arm in arm with Torscha Retter, looking small and delicate beside the majestic stallion. The girl lagged her steps, slowing their progress through the castle ruins. She felt loathe to finish this particular walk—for it meant the end of something precious. When they returned to the courtyard, Retter must go.

Everyone was leaving, and Miriam felt lost and empty.

The tall stalks of fennel were crowned with glistening drops of rain. Miriam and Retter reached the ruins of the old castle chapel, then stood listening to the breeze. The ruins smelled of fresh rain and damp earth, wet grass and wild parsley.

The wind tugged gently at her hair as Miriam spoke into the silence. "This is where it all happened. I fled here with the fiend on my tail—here to the old crypt." She indicated the door to her private refuge. "The ground is still sanctified, and the creature could not follow." Her gaze wandered to a patch of dead grass nearby—a weird, twisted blight among the green young stalks around it. "It died there—shot down by the guards. The grass won't grow. Why won't it grow?"

Retter's hand gripped her chin, forcibly turning her face from the grass. "It's over. Don't carry it with you, my lady." His hand lingered on her chin, and then gently dropped away; Miriam could still feel the warmth where they had touched.

Retter looked at her with those strange, deep eyes of his. "I must leave today. But there are things to be said. Mus has asked that I tell you more about myself. He says it would make friendship between us easier."

Miriam smiled wistfully. "He is wise, for all his innocence."

"The best kind of wisdom, then. Wisdom of the heart."

They stood in silence while the tall, powerful man collected his thoughts. With sad dignity, Torscha finally began to speak. "Know then I am Torscha Retter, eldest son of Count Gerhard Retter of Lørnbørg, Lord of the Southmarches of Welfland."

Standing stiff and tall as ever, he avoided Miriam's wise green eyes, looking instead out across the peaceful hills of Duncruigh. "You must understand the passion of our revolution, the *justice* that there seemed to be in it! Years of famine; years in which the nobility grew ever wealthier while the commoners starved. How I grew to despise my own people—the arrogant, hedonistic nobility! How I envy you Duncruighans your rigid sense of duty.

"As the people's poverty grew, there were many . . . incidents. There were bread riots; grain prices had soared, and poor people in town were starving. Associates of my father were deliberately forcing prices up by hoarding grain in my father's warehouses. I confronted my father, but he cursed me for a fool and bid me hold my tongue."

Torscha closed his eyes. "It wasn't a *decision*, you understand. There was no deliberation, no soul-searching. I-I walked into town in a dream. I remember telling the mayor what had happened, and how the grain might be had. Some people gathered—angry people—and we all just walked off to fetch the grain. There was *power* in that moment."

The huge stallion's eyes grew cold. "My father sent soldiers out to stop the looting. It was orderly looting, the town council taking the sacks out onto carts while the crowd cheered them on. The soldiers simply—simply rode into the crowd, slashing with their swords. Laying open faces, hooking out eyes. . . ."

His voice trailed off. He swallowed.

Miriam gently touched his arm. "And?"

"So . . . so I shot down their officers, and the soldiers fled. The crowd caught a few of them. Killed them, of course." He swallowed. "Anyway—that was the beginning. It wasn't really planned. The king sent soldiers to secure the towns, but a militia had already formed and was determined to resist. The king toppled, and the old order fell with him. We modeled a parliament based somewhat on your own, and tried to rule ourselves. Those nobles who chose the side of the people have abandoned their titles, and do whatever they can. Many of us were trained to lead, and we have served our cause well."

Miriam stood spellbound. "And the rest of your family, sir?"

Retter straightened his back. "My mother is dead; a broken family proved too great for her to bear. My father has sworn to slay me. He now pays court to the Bitch-Queen of Nantierre, helping foreigners invade his own homeland.

"One day I shall kill him."

Silence reigned for a moment as Retter looked at the broken ruins all around them. He smoothed his beard, his hands controlled and steady.

"Life has not been good, my lady. My lands are in the invader's hands, and my fortune has vanished in the winds of war. I own nothing but my duty and a sword." He turned to hold Miriam's eyes with his own. "I have never cursed my poverty until now."

Miriam stared up at him with newfound wonder. Suddenly she began to understand the man.

"If you are successful in your mission . . ."

"Then you are saved—yes. To come on this mission, I've had to abandon my friends in a time of direst need. We are losing this war. We need every sword. But . . . I have been to Duncruigh's court before, and I know the king and several men of influence. I was clearly the best man for the task."

"It would seem, sir, we both have our duties to perform."

"Yes. Yes we do."

They walked through to the courtyard where the carriage stood waiting. The baron, Sir William Merle, and Lady Jerrick stood making their farewells. Mus perched on the carriage door, gravely shaking the old baron's finger. The group looked up as Miriam and Retter joined them.

Miriam curtsied once to Sir William, and then more deeply to the baron. "Sirs, it pains me to see you leave. You have been most welcome guests."

Sir William pressed gallantly forward, his boyish face lighting up in a smile. "The pweasure has been all ours, my lady! To have had your sweet company after a year of hardship has been like a waking dream."

"Good-bye Willy. God keep you. You are a kind and gallant man—I shall miss you." She proffered a hand, and William brushed her fingers with a kiss. His voice fell to a whisper.

"Faith, madam—I believe I shall miss you too."

O Willy . . .

Mus scampered along the edge of the coach door, his tail twisting merrily behind him. "Never fear, sir! We shall see you in two weeks when we come to the capital." The mouse skipped and capered on his precarious perch. "Miriam said she would take me with her when she goes. Isn't it exciting?"

Miriam forced a laugh and extended a forefinger so that Mus could climb up onto her hand. The menfolk climbed into the carriage; Gus the pixie doffed his hat and flicked his whip, and the carriage lurched on its way.

Miriam stood in silence, her hands clasped in front of her as she watched them leave. She remained staring down the road long after the coach had disappeared from view.

Chapter Eight

The Walls of Lael

IRE!"

The gun captains stepped forward, linstocks whirling in graceful arcs as the men touched off their guns. Each siege cannon roared and slammed back onto its trail, and massive round shot hurtled toward the fortress wall. The gun crews cheered as rock shards splintered from the battlements. Down in the trenches, gunners scrambled to block the firing apertures with huge gabions—wicker baskets packed with earth—as the enemy returned fire. A shot plowed through the siege battery, and a wounded horse shrieked and fell, its hooves drumming in a mass of its own gore.

Queen Aelis shied away in distaste as an aide put the poor beast out of its misery. Her cruel blue eyes stayed riveted on the fortress wall.

"Will it stand?"

Looking like a bizarre species of beetle in his heavy siege armor, the army's engineer stooped over a huge brass perspective glass. His metal suit creaked beneath an encrusted skin of rust and grime.

"Mmmph. Give me another week and you could have your breach. I would still prefer a more cautious assault."

The queen hissed ill-temperedly, and her perfect face flushed with sudden rage. "*That* is why this war has taken so long. The attack will go on as planned. With Lael in our hands, the way will be open for a lightning thrust into the Welflandish heartlands. We shall hear no more talk of winter quarters!"

Aelis was *magnificent*—as cruel and proud and beautiful as the finest sword. In buffcoat, casque, and breastplate, she looked every inch the warrior-queen. Aelis's lithe, proud body shimmered purest white, and her tail streamed out behind her like a silken cloud.

The queen had descended upon the armies like the furies unleashed. She had stormed through the officer corps, toppling the incompetent, timid, and unsure, and replacing them with better men. The queen had astonished everybody by the uncanny brilliance with which she worked. In a twinkling of an eye talented captains had found themselves in charge of whole regiments, or blustery old colonels had been sent packing in disgrace. In doing so Aelis had won the adoration of the common soldiers; she was their talisman, their good fortune, their white fury. Like an avenging angel, she had set their minds ablaze with dreams of glory.

Aelis looked up at the fortress city of Lael, the last obstacle standing in her way. Her fists were planted defiantly on her hips as though she could cause the walls to crumble through sheer force of will.

Lael was the largest, most modern fortress in the world. Mighty star-shaped earthworks formed layer after layer of impenetrable barriers. For two years it had withstood siege and storm, shrugging off its attackers as though they were summer gnats; army after army had dashed itself against the unforgiving walls. Crushed in open battle, General Jerrick had dashed back into the protection of his fortifications, snuggling down like an old badger in its burrow.

Aelis studied the walls through her own small perspective glass, her front hoof pawing at the ground.

"The saps are still undiscovered?"

"Yes, Majesty." The engineer shambled over to point at a fortress map spread out across the top of a drum. "Explosives have been placed beneath the damaged section of wall, the flanking ravelins and the edge of the ditch. The enemy'll not yet have brought his troops and cannon to the fore since the breach will clearly not be viable for at least another week. And they are right!" The old engineer angrily slammed his hand against his tassets and pointed an accusing finger at his queen. "Siege warfare is an exacting science! Your aggressive tactics could destroy the army! Patience and planning, move and countermove. There are rules, madam, rules devised by wiser heads than yours!"

The queen laughed scornfully, the sound clear and pure on the morning air. "Faith, sir! You give me more pleasure than the rest of my staff put together. I am not deaf to your opinions—I simply feel them outdated. We shall lance us this boil and then forget it. There is work for our swords elsewhere. I intend to sack this city and slight the walls."

"But, Majesty! Our winter quarters . . ."

"Will be in the *capital!* I am aware of the fact that the dikes will flood within the month. That only makes speed all the more imperative." She turned to survey the walls once more.

"The troops are massed behind the rise for the attack. Our mastery of the air will grant us surprise, since our presence cannot yet be known. When the mines explode, we shall attack, relying on shock to silence the enemy guns. Our siege mortars will shell the enemy rear while our harpies storm the walls from above and invade the galleries. We shall smash this accursed city as a hoof crushes a skull!"

Aelis turned to face her generals. "I shall lead the assault myself, in the wave behind the forlorn hope. Alert the guard."

A croak of alarm came instantly from behind as a flurry of skirts and feathers clawed its way toward the queen.

"No, Majesty! The portents! You must not!" The royal astrologer battled her way forward, swirling her pinions in dismay. "Fortresses loom strongly in your horoscope—I fear for your safety! I saw a white rose being choked by a wildflower. . . ."

Aelis stripped off her gloves and drew her brow into an irritable scowl. "Dizzy old hag! What now?"

"Majesty, I beg you—this is a task for a subordinate. Tatravelle or Orielle can go in your stead. . . ."

The queen tossed back her magnificent hair, her blue eyes scornful. "No! I shall lead the assault in person because I wish it! End discussion."

She spared one of her generals a glance. Looming vast and evil in his full suit of armor, the half-horse met her gaze with cold blue eyes. Within the shadows of his open visor, his face seemed driven by an icy cruelty. "General Retter, your half-horse regiments will accompany the second wave. Once we have cracked the defenses, you will pursue and massacre the defenders. Let none escape."

The huge stallion's muscles bunched and twitched. "Majesty. It shall be as you command. No quarter."

"Go."

The other soldiers edged away as Count Gerhard Retter passed.

Encased in blackened armor, his hide as dark as his tortured soul, he seemed the very presence of death itself. Retter pursued the war with the insane, passionless cruelty of a true fanatic, and few would dare oppose him.

Aelis stood, buckling on her helm. She jerked down the pivoted fall and locked the three bars of her visor into place. "Set the fuses. We attack in a quarter of an hour."

The queen galloped off to battle with her adoring bodyguards close on her tail. A delicious thrill of anticipation shivered through her. It was time to write a new page in history; Aelis would storm Lael the impregnable, or die in the attempt.

Whatever happens, the world will remember Aelis of Nantierre forever!

Aelis threw back her head and laughed for the sheer joy of it. Her tail swirling behind her, she dashed off down the hillside, more intensely alive than she had ever felt before.

Far beneath the fortress walls, teams of scaly gnomes touched fire to fuses and then fled for their lives. Inside the tunnels, towering stacks of powder barrels lay rank by rank beneath the battlements. The fuses sputtered, caught, and then stabbed flame straight down into the dark.

Outside in the open air, the ground heaved like a massive ocean swell. Suddenly the fortress walls ripped themselves apart; debris thundered upward as the earthworks slumped and sagged. Four mines, placed with care and planning, had opened the way.

"FOR GOD, THE QUEEN, AND NANTIERRE!"

With a fanatical howl the assault troops flooded down into the fortress ditch. Behind them the air boiled as a thousand harpies surged up into the air, their wings making a numbing storm of sound. Mortars belched from the rear and fat bombshells wobbled overhead, their fuses leaving trails of smoke as they plunged toward the enemy.

"AELIS! AELIS!"

A wave of Nantierran infantry stormed forward to the breach. Behind their infantry the half-horses cascaded down into the ditch, muskets held high as their hooves skidded for purchase on the soil.

Guns thundered from the fortress walls; a cannon shot plowed into the ranks, leaving a charnel horror of smashed and butchered men. The next ranks poured across the shattered ruins of their comrades, their war cries howling above the din of musket fire and shells. A great wave of flesh and steel surged across the ditch toward the shattered battlements beyond.

The harpies dipped and wheeled as they dropped grenades onto the defenders, blasting enemy gunners and hurtling bodies down into the ditch. Blunderbusses barked from the battlements as the defending troops returned fire, and flier after flier whirled down to bloody destruction. Squads of Nantierran harpies landed on the walls to fight a bitter contest for the gun galleries.

Duncruighan infantry formed hasty ranks at the crest of the breach. Brutal volleys tried to throw back the weight of flesh and iron hurled against the walls, and the attack faltered as the battle hid itself beneath a churning fog of powder smoke.

The queen fought her way to the fore of her picked body of half-horse guardsmen. She reared back on her hind hooves with the wind streaming through her golden hair.

"Guards! *Forward over the bodies!*"

"AEEELISSSS!"

Shrieking like wild men, the armored half-horses flung themselves into the breach. The white rose charged into the smoke bringing slaughter in its wake. Caught up in the glorious madness, Aelis shrieked with ecstasy and charged with her men, her legs surging with power as she raged up the sliding debris.

Smoke whipped by with blurring speed. Muskets crashed overhead; men screamed as a cannon smashed whole files into bloody fragments. Bolts of light and shadow flickered as the royal sorcerers blasted their enemy with magic, matched by a storm of half-horse pistol fire. The defenders wavered and fell back before the savage four-legged foe.

"*Onward! Onward for Nantierre!*"

The queen thrilled to the insanity raging through her. Something jerked through Aelis's flowing hair, and the slap of the bullet stung her neck.

The queen reached level ground—the crest of the wall! A figure loomed up out of the fog in front of her, yelling maniacally as it charged her with a leveled pike. She caught the haft on her glittering sword, then skinned her point down into her enemy. The pikeman gave a gurgling scream, his blood spurting out to drench the queen's sword hand as he fell. She leapt over the body and thundered on, howling out for joy.

"*Onward! Onward!*"

Great four-legged shapes stormed through the fog, engaging
the human infantry. They trampled the smaller creatures underfoot
in a frenzy of rage. The mists swirled, lit by gun flashes and magic.

On! On! Plunging through the melee, Aelis leveled her pistols
and fired. Musket volleys tore across the Royal Guard, and still the
half-horses clove forward! The royal standard bearer reeled backward and crashed onto the ground, his hooves kicking out in
agony. The queen galloped by, snatching up the falling flag as she
charged toward the last remaining knot of enemy. A mustachioed
officer leveled a pistol at her and pulled the trigger, the ball
splashing from her breastplate in a shower of molten lead. Hooves
thundering across the stone, the queen speared the silver lance-
head of her banner through her enemy. She tugged the bloodied
staff free as she passed, her victim's agonized screams ringing in
her ears. The rest of the enemy scattered as the royal guardsmen
burst among them and scythed them down with axe and sword.

"AELIS! AELIS! AELIS!"

The air shook with the sound of her name shouted by thousands of adoring throats. Nantierran banners topped the rise, and
in a single great wave her troops began pouring down into the
town. Aelis stood at the center of the captured breach, her bloodied sword in her hand and her banner at her side. She reared and
screamed in triumph, shivering with the sheer sexual joy of con-
quest. Surrounded by the shattered bodies of the dead, her golden
hair streaming in the wind, the girl shouted for the wondrous
glory of it.

She was Aelis of Nantierre, and she was queen!

Chapter Nine

Wildflower

all half-timbered buildings loomed over the city street, gaudy shop signs proclaiming all manner of strange wares. Beneath the eaves, the streets boiled with riotous confusion; any number of weird creatures rubbed shoulders out on the roadway, all bustling about on their own private affairs. The shadowed street rang to the cries of street vendors and pamphleteers, merchants, prostitutes, and beggars. Together they made up the pulsing lifeblood of a city.

A heavy coach-and-four shouldered through the churning seas of people like some great unlikely man-of-war. Skipping nimbly aside, a harlequin-figure received a faceful of mud from the carriage wheels. The satyr shook his fist after the retreating coach, posing in magnificent defiance until the coach had faded back into the crowd.

A lithe brown stoat sat perched upon the satyr's shoulder, peering at the chaotic streets with wicked eyes. The stoat flowed down from his high perch toward a tiny cage that hung from the satyr's belt. A mouse sat in the tiny prison, staring out at the world through lost and hopeless eyes.

Pin-William suddenly noticed his captive staring at him and irritably slapped the cage, sending the little mouse skittering aside. "Whatta you looking at?"

The dirty, disheveled satyr was but a shadow of his former self. He had eaten no breakfast, and the cheap gin that he had drunk the night before had given him a foul headache. The satyr viciously struck the cage once more and then bobbed down to glare at his captive. The stoat affectionately rubbed against the satyr's beard.

The mouse crowded away from them as far as the tiny cage

would let her.

Pin-Wiliams's eyes shone cruel and hard. "You useless morsel of garbage! You'd best not fail me tonight, else I'll crisp the flesh off your back and let Snatch have the bones!"

The stoat bared his wicked fangs and licked his chops, looking eagerly from master to mouse. The little mouse whimpered timidly with fright.

"I-I'm sorry! I try! Don't—don't hurt me again. . . ."

"You're not the first mouse I've had. One more failure—*one more*—and I'll let Snatch have you! I *so* like to watch Snatch at play." The satyr stroked the stoat, and the creature arched affectionately under his hand. "Oh, I'm sure Snatch will have a lovely time. He might even decide not to kill you."

The satyr leaned closer. "Not all at once. . . ."

The little field mouse wept helplessly, wringing her tiny, perfect hands. "I-I try! Please master, most things are just too difficult to carry!" The mouse crept forward, pleading. "I w-wanted to open the door for you, but the key was too heavy. . . ."

"Useless vermin!" Pin-William scratched at his patchy beard. "The *next* house we rob, you'll do it properly or you'll pay!"

Times had been hard since fleeing Kerbridge. Although Pin-William had managed to pursue his experiments in animal transformation, other magic now eluded him. It seemed as if creating his animal servants had wrung him dry of all his powers, leaving him an empty husk.

He bitterly cursed the wretched field mouse. How he hated her! So frail, so pretty, so *useless*. On a whimsy, Pin-William had lavished his magic upon her to create a tiny little lady, and the spell had somehow overtaxed his strength.

Gone, but not gone forever! Soon he would make a lucky strike! With money he could again become the dapper creature that had made strong men gasp in envy and women sigh with anticipation. Though stabbed in the back and evicted from his home, he was still unbowed! Dusting off his jacket, the satyr tilted his hat on a defiant angle and gazed out across the street like a conquering hero.

Down on the ground, Snatch the stoat coiled evilly about the mouse's cage and smiled. "He will tire of you one day. Ssssoon he will realize he needs only *me*." The stoat stretched languidly. "Will I kill you quick—or ssslow?" Snatch casually lay back on one elbow. The mouse simply sat staring at him with great sad eyes, and Snatch felt a flash of annoyance.

"He will give you to me! I *will* have you!" The stoat hissed in sudden anger, his fangs gleaming.

A small, defiant voice cut across his tirade.

"You *coward*. I despise you—you and your master. Your souls are sick and dying." The little mouse shivered slightly, hunching deeper into the wood shavings on the bottom of her cage.

Snatch rammed his snout up against the bars. He hissed and spat with fury, but the mouse simply watched him with her deep, dark eyes. Finally Snatch backed away and retreated to his master's shoulder. Grabbing hold of the cage once more, Pin-William stalked grandly off down the street, ready to plan another night of thievery.

Decked out in collar, hat, and sword, Mus peered excitedly from the carriage window at the city streets. His whiskers quivered as he breathlessly watched the incredible scene outside. Lady Jerrick laughed to see the mouse so pleased, and tickled Mus's tail for attention.

"Thou likest the city then, Mus? It makes quite a change from quiet little Kerbridge."

"Oh, it's *wonderful!*" The mouse leapt down from the windowsill to perch in the baroness's lap. "How exciting! Thank thee so much for letting me come with thee."

The maidservant Jane sat opposite Miriam, and the two younger women were goggling unashamedly out of the windows. Miriam rose up and craned her neck as they passed a tavern door.

"Saucy fellow! Didst see that, Jane? That man with the ferret shook his fist at us!"

Jane's simple country face blushed red with outrage. "That ain't all, ma'am! I blush to think o' what he was callin' us just now! I'm half of a mind to ask the sergeant to jump off and punch his nose!"

Lady Jerrick chuckled indulgently. "This is not the country, Jane! You must expect such things. With so many people crushed shoulder to shoulder you must learn to turn a blind eye from time to time."

The carriage grumbled to a halt. From up on the driver's seat there came a loud cry of "*Give way there!*" The city's traffic had halted them more than once today; Miriam was fast losing her enchantment with travel.

"It must be a very friendly place!" Mus sat back upon the windowsill, peering out under the curtains. "Just think of so many people all wanting to live close to each other!"

"Oh, Mus, they're not here for fun!"

The mouse blinked his eyes in surprise.

"Really? Well what about that one? Now she *does* look friendly!"

Miriam and Jane looked out of the window to see a trollop calling beguilingly to passersby. Miriam's cheeks blazed red as she grabbed the mouse and tugged him swiftly off his perch.

"Hey!" Mus squawked in indignation.

"Never mind *that* one Mus. She—er—she's trying to sell something."

"Oooh, I see," said the mouse, who didn't really see at all. "Well at least she seems to be having a good time."

"Er—*quite.*" Lady Jerrick intervened to change the subject. "Don't take Miriam too seriously, Mus. Cities are a different kind of living. I was born here, you know."

Mus sat up on his haunches and closed his eyes.

"*All about is hustle—the wainscotting of a world. Here kings are mice and mice are kings, all order o'er turned.*" The mouse doffed his hat. "Pleoniades, Act Four, Scene Three."

Her Ladyship appeared suitably impressed. "My clever Mus! Thou seemst to have quite a memory."

"Oh, nay, Lady! I remember everything I read, just as thou dost."

Mus climbed up Miriam's hair to sit perched happily atop her head, and the girl indulged the little wretch with good humor. By now she had grown used to her unique position as the mouse's personal stage.

Mus waved his hands excitedly as he spoke. "So much to see! So much to do! What shall we do first?"

Miriam peeled the mouse off her scalp and held him dangling up before her nose. "We have told thee a dozen times before, small nuisance!" She cupped Mus in her hand. "We shall go to the theater and see some of thy favorite plays. We shall see the sights, visit the concert halls, *and* attend court. But first we shall be going to a seamstress. I'm afraid I am not really outfitted to be seen in high society." Miriam sighed. "And I shall need a ball dress. . . ."

"Yes! A white one, a white one!" Mus danced about excitedly in

Miriam's palm, his tail shivering behind him. "Oh—just like in the storybooks. Thou'lt look so beautiful!"

The girl rolled her eyes. "Very well—a white one just for thee." She stroked the mouse's nose. "Just like in the storybooks. Thou'rt right. It will look lovely!"

The clatter of the coach's dray team echoed off the walls of nearby houses. Clashing hooves and ringing traces made a brave sound as they swerved into a new street.

Mus sighed. "The royal court . . ." He closed his eyes happily. "And the king! Will I really see the king?"

Lady Jerrick laughed. "Indeed, though we'll have to be careful lest *he* sees *thee*."

He hardly heard her. Mus was in rapture. "Oh—and a court ball! And parties! And all the fine lords and ladies . . . how wonderful!"

Miriam bit her lip and looked down at her hooves.

"Yes—all the most polished, most accomplished members of the nobility." She hunched her shoulders. "I shall be a wildflower among roses."

Mus struck a pose with his paw against his breast. "I am clever. I shall help thee! I have read all thy mother's books on etiquette and dance. It will be simple to advise thee."

Lady Jerrick raised her eyebrows and sighed. "We shall all do our best. At least we have friends here. General Vardvere, Sir Merle, and our good Colonel Retter."

"Oh, it shall be so good to see them all again!" Mus twittered with glee. "The colonel is so wise, and Sir Willy is such fun!"

The carriage rumbled onward into the shadowed streets. Miriam looked quietly out of the window, lost in her own thoughts.

The human noble lounged in his chair and propped his feet up on the inlaid table. Tall, sparse, and dark, Leymond cut an elegant figure in any drawing room, and his reputation as a swordsman and politician made his presence all the more attractive. Fashionably red heeled and obscenely comfortable, he sat drinking hot chocolate as though he had not a care in the world.

He was quite aware that he was being scrutinized. The nobleman lazily rolled his head to view his companion; she stood posed against the window, light streaming in from behind her, and he smiled at this unconscious piece of theater. Here was a woman to be savored like the finest wine—to be sipped slowly and rolled across the tongue. Anything less could never do her true justice.

Like any perfect weapon, the woman held an exquisite, deadly beauty. The moist pout of her bee-stung lips and the wanton glitter of her eyes trapped her victims as a lily traps a fly. Her entire body formed an irresistible erotic promise. She chose her lovers at whim, and few could refuse her.

Few would dare; Lady Jessica Perwryth was a dangerous woman, and her chosen weapons were exultation and despair.

Jessica felt Leymond's eyes caress her, and smiled the sardonic smile that she reserved for him alone. Their alliance was old, satisfying and profitable, and forever spiced with unfulfilled desire. The nobleman stood and ran his hands across the warm hide of her back, inhaling the sharp scent of her musk, feeling her rump arch and flex invitingly beneath his touch.

A half-horse. Such a pity. The human noble sighed wistfully and turned his mind to business.

The woman spoke, her voice breathing softly in his ear.

"Our little country filly has come to town." She lowered her eyelids as she looked sideways at Leymond. "*You* remember—our beloved general's little bumpkin."

The nobleman plucked a quizzing glass from his lapel and thoughtfully polished up the lens.

"Aaaah, yes! How convenient of her. We are still requested to draw her fangs; or perhaps *guard her tail* might be more appropriate?"

Jessica pursed her perfect lips in thought. "Killing her is no longer quite so easy. The girl has quite a little entourage, including that deliciously huge brute of an emissary from Welfland. Killing her might prove . . ."

Sir Rodger Leymond looked pained, and his quizzing glass drooped. "Oh, Jessica! You always think with your claws. Why toss in your hand when the game's the thing!"

"So long as you win."

"Of course." Leymond tapped his quizzing glass against his chin. "I do so hate to lose. . . ."

There was a pause while the nobleman sipped his chocolate.

"Besides which, a death is not necessary. Not yet. It would look rather too suspicious. His Majesty grows curious, and we mustn't give him reason to suspect us." The quizzing glass waggled from side to side. "No no no no. This can all be done simply. She seeks an advantageous marriage? Then let us make sure her marriage is to *our* advantage!"

"*Yes!* Yes indeed!" The half-horse tossed back her hair, keeping eyes squeezed closed as she savored a truly dastardly idea. She held her hand poised, stilling Leymond's tongue.

"Oh, yes! O Rodger! The most malicious thought!"

Leymond reached for his chocolate; Jessica's ideas, like the woman herself, were well worth enjoying to the full.

"O Rodger . . . by all reports this girl has a certain innocent allure. Now just think—to whom would such a woman appeal? If I arrange a match, he will be most grateful to us both. . . ."

The nobleman gave Jessica a reproachful look. "Oh, Jessie! What a perfectly *ghastly* thought."

"Quite grisly, don't you agree? I confess I find the irony too tempting to pass by."

Leymond bowed pleasantly. "Then I shall bask in your pleasure—as always."

"As always, dear Rodger. I *do* hope this poor girl doesn't end up broken quite as quickly as all the others. We want our associate entertained at least until the end of this season's parliament."

Leymond took Jessica's hand and kissed it, savoring the moment. "Truly you are the most delicious of women."

Jessica simpered, mocking him with her eyes. "Why Rodger, surely you always knew *that?*"

The lofty hall rang to the kiss of steel on steel and echoed with clattering hooves. The plain wooden floor was scuffed and scarred from years of sad abuse; wax and polish could not make up for the damage caused by iron shoes.

Two stallions faced one another at swordpoint, blades glittering. The swords touched and parted, circled and clashed as each man fought to drive his weapon home.

Mus watched attentively from his perch on the mantelpiece, keen to pick up the finer points of swordplay. He scampered up and down along the sideboard, keeping abreast of the two warriors as they struggled back and forth. The little creature shouted advice impartially to both combatants; since his voice was drowned out by the sounds of the fight, neither contestant took any notice of him. Mus was having so much fun that he never even noticed the snub.

"Ho, Willy, that's it! Extend! Extend!"

He skittered back the other way along the sideboard as Retter retreated.

"Broken time, Colonel! Broken time!" The mouse slapped his forehead in distress. "No, you lummox! Don't just . . . argh!" Retter's attack failed, and Willy had him on the run once more. Sir William pressed home his advantage with a fury, squandering his energy on attack after attack. Retter met them one after another, falling slowly back. The huge black stallion moved with blinding skill, remaining calm and unruffled. Suddenly he seemed to stumble on the wooden floor; Retter's point wavered, and Willy gave a "*HA!*" of triumph, lunging wildly for the kill. To his surprise, Retter reared up onto his hind hooves. Torscha's blade whipped up over Willy's own to land firmly upon William's extended forearm; a perfect "stop-hit."

"*Damn you, sir!*" Willy tore his fencing mask off and flung it aside, dripping with sweat. "I could have sworn that I had you!"

"Good match, Willy! Good match!" Retter grimaced and peeled back the cuffs of his padded fencing jacket. "That'll be enough for me today! My cursed wrist is stiff as a board. That's all that I need!" He turned to the mouse on the mantelpiece. "Did you enjoy the match, Mus?"

"Oh, indeed, sir!" Mus stood on three feet, using one hand to gesture excitably. "I'd thought Sir William had you well and truly beaten!"

"And so did Sir Willy!" Retter flanks heaved, both pairs of lungs laboring to restore his breath. "Why so aggressive today, Willy? You're usually the slyest bladesman I know!"

No answer came; the smaller half-horse stood facing in the opposite direction and began an attack sequence, fencing against empty air. Mus noticed the foul-tempered expression on the man's face and edged closer to him.

"Willy?"

Retter reached for a towel and mopped at his neck.

"Too much energy, my friend? You seem to have an excess of spleen today!"

Still no answer; Sir William stamped and shouted, hurling himself into a lunge. Retter reclined against the mantel and passed a biscuit crumb to Mus.

"He's been like this ever since you arrived, Mus. How odd."

"Yes, Colonel. 'Tis most unlike him. I cannot think what might be the cause of it."

"Mmmm—quite." Retter frowned. "Ah well—it's better that he works off his humors here than out on the street."

With one hind leg, Mus idly scratched at his ear. "Yes, I suppose so." The mouse sat down and sighed. "Do you suppose Miriam will be back soon? How long does it take to have a dress made?"

Torscha stretched, his broad shoulders cracking. "Lord, what a question! Let a woman into a dressmakers and you might lose her forever!"

Mus was disappointed. "Oh. I had *so* wanted to tell her of things that I saw in the garden."

"Well, why not tell me? Let's go out to the park, and I shall show you the statues. We can walk back by the houses of parliament."

The mouse scoffed his food and jumped up onto Retter's shoulder. His mount turned, reached for hat and cane, and glanced toward Willy Merle. "Willy? We're about to take the airs. Do you wish to come?"

Willy ignored them. Retter shrugged and took Mus from the room. Behind him, the stamp of hooves rang loud upon the air. His teeth bared, Sir William fought with an opponent only he could see.

Miriam emerged from the dressmakers feeling as though she had just been fed through a wringer. The bill for a single dress trailed from one hand, and the girl moved down the street with dazed little motions of her hooves.

The price of all this clothing is going to be staggering! Fourteen gold marks? Lord help me—the cost will cripple us! Miriam's face suddenly grew glum. *It all makes good sense; it is an investment. When the meat goes to the market, a little garnish helps bring a higher price. . . .*

A loud feminine squeal of alarm sounded from behind her, and

Miriam reacted like a true paranoid. In a flash she had jumped aside, pistols drawn and hooves prancing as she tried to decide whether to fight or flee.

A lady stood in the road; a little satyr—slim, dark, and ethereally beautiful. Petite brown horns arched above her brows, and cloven hooves just peeked out from beneath her skirts. She had a small pet, and the satyr wept as she desperately tried to rescue it from the claws of a savage alley cat. Blood ran freely down her right arm, trailing off her fingers to splash on the ground. Her pet screamed as the cat raked it with its claws. The tiny dragon writhed and fought, squealing in its pain.

Snarling like a troll, Miriam charged across the road, and the cat took one look at her hooves and fled. The satyr scooped up the little serpent and wept. Her voice was high and sweet, touched with a burring, singsong accent.

"O Opal! O ma puir wee thing!"

Miriam delved into her apron for a kerchief and gently took the girl's injured arm. "I'll look at him in a moment. Come, let me see your hand."

The satyr gasped as Miriam deftly wrapped up her hand. Miriam was more concerned with quickly stopping the flow of blood than with being gentle. She took the little satyr under her arm and led her toward a nearby coffeehouse.

"*Miriam!* Art thou all right?"

Lady Jerrick raced toward her daughter, the ever-present sergeant panting hard behind her. The sergeant looked somewhat uncomfortable in his civilian clothes. The bag across his shoulders clearly contained at least three pairs of loaded pistols. The baroness cantered over to her daughter's side, saw the blood running down the little satyr's arm and blanched. "O you poor dear!"

The satyr girl gulped and looked sick. "Nay! I-I'm all right, thank ye. I'm fine—trooly."

Miriam would hear no such thing; blood soaked through the satyr's makeshift bandage to drip down her fingers once more. She guided her patient over to a chair and quickly set to work.

The young satyr had a beauty that was utterly entrancing, even through her tears. Her thin, elfin face held a delicate allure, and her tilted eyes were filled with mischief. The girl's pointed ears and tiny horns made her seem all the more exotic. If she were not in such distress, Miriam would have been quite jealous.

Miriam sponged clean the gashes in the satyr's arm. She looked up to find the girl's grave brown eyes upon her. The girl sat watching her with gratitude and wonder. "You-you're vurry kind." Her accent drifted like an ancient song. "I most profoundly thank ye."

Miriam pushed a straying lock of hair, wrung out her cloth, and smiled. "My pleasure. You quite stopped my heart! How's your little friend feeling?"

The girl's pet cringed against her breast, shivering pathetically as she tried to calm it with her free hand. Miriam dabbed gently at the girl's arm with brandy, cleaning out the jagged cuts. "My name is Miriam Jerrick—Damsel Miriam Jerrick of Kerbridge. The lady hounding the serving girls over there is my mother, Baroness Barbara Jerrick."

"I'm so pleased to meet you." The faun seemed utterly bewildered. "I am—*ouch!*—I am Damsel Frielle Delaunsy of Janis Isle." She winced as Miriam went to work on her thumb. "And-this is *Opal.*

Opal was a tiny hedge dragon, a delicate little creature half serpent and half insect; a flat strip of a creature as long, from forked tongue to pointed tail, as Miriam's forearm. Opal's body ran in segments like a long, thin beetle, the facets of its armor shimmering a rich, royal blue. A narrow, wedge-shaped head came equipped with long antennae, wicked little fangs, and frightened eyes. The creature's delicate butterfly wings had torn, and they hung in sad shreds from the dragon's back.

Hedge dragons were rare. The timid, graceful creatures were most at home in faerie woods—places where sensible mortals would never venture. Miriam found Opal watching her with intelligent golden eyes; she reached out her hand and let the little dragon sniff at her fingers.

"She's *beautiful.* Oh, Frielle—wherever did you find her?"

" 'Tis more a matter of her findin' me." Frielle ran slim fingers along the dragon's spine. "Is she much hurt?"

"Well, she'll not fly for a while; not until winter when she sheds her wings and grows new ones."

"Do they do that? How odd!" Frielle was fascinated. "Now how is it that you're knowin' that?"

Miriam smiled. "I study. These little chaps are much like pixies. They shed and regrow twice a year. This little one will shed her skin, too. That's how they grow."

"Oh! Well he—er—*she* has only been with me for a month. I've not seen her do that."

"She's gorgeous! You say Opal found you?"

The little satyr nodded sadly as she inspected her carefully bandaged hand. "There I was, just sittin' in the garden feeling tired and weepy—it had not been a good time for me. I had been up cryin' all night." Frielle's face was sad, and Miriam found herself liking the girl more and more as she lovingly stroked the dragon. "Eventually I just nodded off. When I awoke, there she was! Sittin' atop ma cleavage without so much as a how'd ye do! Fast asleep 'n all. She's jus' stayed with me ever since. We rather seem to get on together."

Miriam ran her soft fingertips down the dragon's nose. "I think I know someone Opal would get along with very well. How's your hand now?"

Frielle kept her fingers stiff as she turned her hand this way and that. The satyr gritted her teeth.

"It hurts. Blast and bedamn it! With a court ball on in a fortnight's time, too!"

"You're going to the ball? Why how splendid! At least I shall know *someone* there."

Sudden recognition dawned in Frielle's face. "Curse me for a twit! *Jerrick!* Of course!" The satyr's eyes became more appraising. "You'll be the flower of the countryside we have all been hearin' about. Sir Willy Merle's done you good publicity."

"You know Willy?" Miriam was overjoyed to hear Willy's name mentioned.

"Well, of course! Everybody knows Sir Willy; he loses more money with better grace than any other gambler at court. A very silly boy, but one can't help loving him." Frielle suddenly gave Miriam a sly look. "We wondered what could have held him captive up in the country when all the parties were down here. And when he finally arrives, all he can talk about is this sweet young country lass. . . ."

"Oh, my!" Miriam blushed hotly and looked hastily away.

Frielle grinned, then wisely turned her attention to another topic. "So Miriam—have you just arrived in the city?"

"Yes!" Miriam casually tried to cool off her cheeks with the backs of her hands. "Only yester evening."

"Well, we should link forces. We can be outsiders together,

eh?"

The half-horse girl looked puzzled; Frielle leaned her cheek on her good hand, sighed, and elaborated.

"We are likely to be shunned, m' dear. We're both country bumpkins come to town on the hay wagon. Faith! I come from farther away than you. The Channel Islands. I was at court all last season an' still they turn their backs on me! We can cling together for support, eh?"

"I should be *delighted*." Miriam's face glowed with relief. "I'd despaired of meeting anyone. This whole trip was beginning to look like a disaster."

Frielle struggled to her hooves, and Opal settled about her neck like some strange jeweled collar.

"Well, I really should be gettin' home now. I'm so dreadfully late! Aunt Kala will be beside herself with worry."

Miriam surged up onto all four feet. "Will you be all right? Should we walk you home?"

Frielle simply stared. "Well . . . thank you. If-if it's no trouble."

"Of course not!" Miriam smiled and took her by the arm. "No trouble at all."

Chapter Ten

Illusions

R ESIGN!"

"SIT DOWN!"

"IS THE HONORABLE MEMBER A COMPLETE MUTTON-HEAD?"

Parliament's galleries were full of angry, shouting men; opinions were divided as to whether it was best to bellow at the speaker's chair, the delegate at the center of the floor, or simply at each other. The result was pure uproar.

Down on the floor the speaker banged his staff in a futile effort to restore sanity.

"ORDER! ORDER!"

"SIT DOWN!"

"NO FOREIGN WARS!"

"RESIGN! RESIGN!"

Torscha Retter kept his hands firmly over his ears. He grimaced at Baron Vardvere, but the old gentleman seemed utterly helpless; the baron's efforts to open debate on military finances had been futile. A sizeable clique seemed determined to see all such discussion shelved. The entire voice of the opposition was orchestrated by one man; a tall, elegant individual clad in a magnificent suit of pearl-gray silk. He casually caught the speaker's eye and raised one finger.

"The chair recognizes—QUIET!—The chair recognizes the honorable member for Seapoint, Sir Rodger Leymond."

Aaah! The famous Leymond. Retter folded his arms and regarded his foe across a churning sea of faces. Leymond raised his hands for silence, and the chaos slowly died.

"Mister Speaker, honorable members, distinguished visitors . . ."

The man spoke with perfect control, and Retter's hoof stamped in unconscious challenge.

"There's no need for such undignified uproar! There simply *is* no debate! The tax bills for the next year have already been passed. This house gave its decision—its *final* decision—before our last recess three months ago."

"Hear Hear!"

"TRAITOR!"

"SIT DOWN!"

The house dissolved into absolute uproar. Something less than half of the parliament stood violently opposed to Leymond. Retter bore the storm for a few minutes and then took matters into his own hands.

"SILENCE!"

The parade-ground voice roared out above the chaos, and all noise stopped in sudden shock. The huge black half-horse stormed forward onto the floor, and Torscha's voice rang with power as he addressed the assembly.

"Honorable members! The Welfland question is *not* finished. It is not a thing that can be shelved, covered over, or forgotten! There are eight thousand reasons why this cannot be done!" He stood with his hooves firmly planted and flung out an accusing hand at the assembly. "Eight thousand, gentlemen! The number of Duncruighan troops that you have abandoned on foreign soil! Eight thousand men who cannot be fed, and who cannot even come home, since your foolish budget has left them without the means!"

Leymond leapt to his feet, bristling with fury. "By what right do *you* speak before this house?"

Retter withered him with a glance. "By right of eight thousand voices raised in anger. By commission of my parliament, and through my love of God. Sit you down, sir. *I* have the floor."

A murmur of agreement rolled around the galleries, and Leymond flung himself back down into his seat. Ignoring him, Retter paced to the center of the hall.

"Sirs, you have a moral obligation to those men. The vote of this house sent them where they are now, and they have served their king and parliament with valor. Whether you support the war effort or no, those men are the responsibility of this assembly! They are not toys to be brushed aside when you tire of the game. They are honorable, godly men!"

Retter took a breath. "In four days, this parliament will undertake a one-day recess. I propose that a member of this house should offer the motion that this day be used for the debate of the Welfland issue. One day of your time, gentlemen! Just one day! Surely those eight thousand men deserve that much courtesy!

"I have outstayed my welcome. Mister Speaker, I thank you for your indulgence." And with that, Retter took his leave. He nursed a stabbing headache while the tumult grew behind him.

Outside of the parliament house, General Vardvere found Torscha walking moodily through the rose gardens. The wiry old general, mustache abristle, marched stiffly over to confront him.

"*Hem!* Bless me, sir! I never knew you had it in you! Never!" Vardvere shook his gray head in astonishment. "*Hemmm-haw.* Quite amazin'. Your special session is on, my boy! Four days' time; the mornin' after that demned palace ball, though how we are all going to remember to wake up in time is anybody's guess."

He clapped Retter on the shoulder, suddenly beside himself with delight.

"You've done it me boy! We're all but saved!"

She found him lying on the divan, stretched out like a wounded knight. Torscha's skull burned, and the headache flooded his body like a sea of pain. He lay in helpless agony until Miriam knelt on all four knees at his side.

"The general said you were unwell." She laid one smooth hand on his brow. "I've brought something for the headache; here, drink this."

She lifted a cup into view, and Torscha drank, choking slightly at the taste. He finished the entire dose, then felt the cup being taken from his hands.

"How do you feel?"

"It's . . . it's just a headache."

"Just a headache." Miriam's hands traced smoothly down Retter's spine. Her thumbs pressed in against his shoulder blades, and Torscha arched his back in pleasure as Miriam clucked her tongue.

"It hurts there?"

"*Yes! Aaah!*"

"Lie flat then."

Strong hands began to knead the muscles of Retter's back. The stallion groaned with relief, then suddenly tried to struggle to his feet.

"I-I can't! There's only four days until the vote. . . ."

"Be silent and lie still!"

Retter did as he was told and lay down flat, eyes blinking as the woman took him under her control.

God she has strong hands for a woman! Lovely!

Miriam began to speak as she worked. "The whole town is abuzz with your speech at Parliament. I quite burst with pride when Frielle told me what you had done."

"Truly?"

Miriam cocked her head, thinking over the question as though it had great weight. "Yes—yes truly. I felt proud." She frowned as she worked on the stiff muscles of Retter's broad shoulders. "Lud, man, you're as stiff as old teak! Do you get headaches often?"

"Mmmmph. Yes. Ever since the war."

Her voice raked him with possessive scorn. "You're as thick as two stout planks! You must learn to rest properly!"

Torscha mumbled into the couch. "Too much to do . . . Can only relax when I'm with you." It became harder to concentrate; Torscha sank deep into the couch, slipping gradually into sleep. Miriam raised an eyebrow, only half paying attention to his words as she worked at his scapula. "Really? Why's that?"

". . . sun on daisies."

She smiled, not really hearing the reply but aware that he had said something nice. This was the first time she had ever held Retter at her mercy. His hide felt smooth and warm beneath her hands, his muscles thick and strong. Torscha had the most extraordinary smell, a bit like new-baked bread. Miriam inhaled it contentedly as she unknotted the muscles at his spine. She finished off by rubbing at the root of Retter's tail, and he hardly stirred.

"Do you feel any better, Torscha?"

His reply was a sleepy whisper.

". . . *always did like freckles . . .*"

Miriam took a blanket and gently covered up the sleeping giant. Retter's face seemed like that of a peaceful little boy. As she stood Miriam patted his solid rump. "Good night, sweet prince. Sleep thee well."

Clumping on quiet hooves, she left the room.

Frielle waited for her in the sitting room. The little faun stood whooping with laughter in one corner of the chamber, her skirts hitched up to display her furry shins. She giggled as two little creatures dodged and weaved about her feet.

Opal crouched behind Frielle's left hoof, waving her tail from side to side, then suddenly leapt away from the furry bullet that streaked across the floor. Frielle dropped her skirts and laughed as Mus pursued Opal back and forth across the rug. The dragon sprang into the air; Mus surprised everyone by catapulting from a chair back and snatching Opal's tail.

"Tag!"

Miriam boggled. "Mus!"

All eyes turned to her; the little mouse waved cheerfully, one hand resting on Opal's carapace. "Good evening to thee, Miriam! Is Colonel Retter recovered?"

"Yes—quite. Ah, Mus . . . I take it thou'st met Frielle?"

The satyr swept across the floor to take Miriam's hands. "Why surely, Miriam! We've been havin' a lovely time. Your friend Mus strode up bold as brass and asked to be introduced." Frielle turned to stare at Mus in fascination. "He's delightful! O Miriam, how lucky you are! He's quite made me forget what gloom is!"

Miriam's cheeks blushed. "I-I wasn't keeping secrets from you. Mus has to decide who he . . ."

"No no no, I quite understand!" Frielle's wide brown eyes were filled with laughter. "We've been havin' a lovely little talk, he an' I. Seems he an' Opal have taken a real fancy to one another."

Miriam took her friend by the hand and sat to watch Mus and Opal play. The two little creatures separated and began to groom themselves as the women approached. They were of a good size for one another. Opal was far larger—Mus could easily ride on her back—but they seemed to make fine playmates. Miriam bobbed down on her forelegs to meet Mus nose to nose.

"So Mus; a new pair of friends?"

With all due seriousness, Mus sat up on his haunches and replied. "I am most pleased to make their acquaintance." He looked up into Miriam's wise green eyes. "Thou-thou'rt not angry?"

She caressed him with a smile. "Nay, my friend, why should I be angry? Thou knowest best what is good for thee."

The mouse spun and danced with glee. "I am so pleased. Frielle has so much to tell me. And look, Miriam; a real dragon! And she smells of magic!"

Frielle radiated sheer delight. "Opal is most pleased to meet you, I'm sure."

The dragon looked at Mus with intelligent golden eyes. She blinked, and then went back to preening her sapphire scales.

Miriam, Mus and Frielle sat down to chatter while the mouse combed out his fur. Suddenly the evening had taken on a life of its own.

"Oh, Colonel, how lovely!" Miriam stared at the tickets in her hand, quite beside herself with delight. "I thought I should go *mad* with boredom, and then you rescue me!"

Another day of dress fittings had dragged by, and the evening had promised to be dull, but then this! Miriam bubbled with joy as Retter bowed smoothly from the waist.

"Your pleasure is mine, madam. I'd suspected that a week of dress shops and our own tedious company might have taxed you. Our friend Mus has conducted a merciless campaign on your behalf—I don't think a moment has passed when the little devil has not casually mentioned how worn you look of late."

"It was the truth!" The mouse sat perched on the edge of the parlor's harpsichord, where until a moment ago he had been deep in conversation with Willy Merle. "Sir, you wound me! I have done nothing but try to look after a friend's best interests."

"I'm sorry, Mus. I am aware of what you have been doing." Retter fixed the mouse with one cool blue eye. "*All* of what you have been doing. I have left a coin on the doorstep of the bakery across the road. Next time you wish a cream cake, be so kind as to ask us first!"

The mouse sank down into his fur and grumbled. "I only took a nibble. I was bored. Everyone goes off to dress shops and parliament without me."

"Well, we now have tickets to the playhouse. Would you care to come along?"

Mus's ears stood stiff with wonder. "To the theater? Oh, please!

I have read so many plays. I should dearly love to see one!"

Sir William began examining the huge printed tickets.

"Six tickets? Miriam, Lady Jerrick, you, myself . . . surely we are not taking the sergeant?"

The black stallion idly straightened the lace of his immaculate cuffs. "I felt Madame and Mademoiselle Delauncy should accompany us. Miriam? Does that meet with your approval?"

Indeed it did!

"It's settled then! Tonight we see *Troiselle and Pervante*." Retter brushed at his black mustache. "I'm sure the diversion will do us all a world of good."

The group broke up to prepare for the theater, and Miriam found herself walking side by side with Torscha Retter. They paced slowly down the corridor that led to the bedroom suites, both wrapped in their private thoughts. It was a comfortable, companionable silence. Their hooves echoed down the empty halls.

Baron Vardvere's home had the appearance of a fortress. Denied a woman's gentle influence, the general's military ardor had been allowed full rein. Decorations consisted of weapons and armor, flags and hunting trophies, and the only spots of color were the occasional paintings of battle scenes. Miriam's mother had astounded and dismayed the old gentleman by ruthlessly evicting this rubbish from the living areas; more comfortable furnishings had been found lurking in the attic, and these had been dusted off and hauled back into the light. The parlor and sitting rooms were now free of the military theme, and the baron had confessed himself pleased with the results.

Miriam stood by one of the corridor's bull's-eye windows. Night had fallen, and a star was just peeking through the clouds. Down in the street below there came a clatter of hooves as a solitary carriage rumbled by. Torscha stood beside her; she could feel him without having to turn and see. Miriam gazed down into the streets, aware of his warmth against her hide.

"We slipped away from the sergeant today and went to see the markets."

"I know."

"Yes . . ." Miriam turned and looked up into Retter's face. "You're not angry."

The great stallion gazed at her with eyes of shining blue.

"You enjoyed yourself. That is . . . important to me."

A sudden flush spread from beneath Miriam's freckles. She felt her heart twist within her breast.

"Truly?" Miriam looked up at him in wonder. For some reason she suddenly remembered the beautiful scent and feel of him beneath her hands. . . .

"Truly." Retter shifted his attention and fixed his eyes on empty space. "You will look dazzling tonight. I shall be pleased to see you in your new evening gown."

"I . . . thank you. And thank you for purchasing the tickets. It was a kind thought."

"You're most welcome. It is opening night for the play, and everyone who is anyone will be there. We can introduce you into society; it will ease your task of finding a husband."

Miriam felt like she had just been slapped. "You-you wish to make it easier for me to-to find a husband?"

"I wish you success and joy in whatever you choose."

Miriam backed away from him in confusion, her hooves skittering on the wooden floors.

"I-I thought . . ." What *had* she thought? Miriam wasn't sure. *God help her!* She felt something inside herself shrivel in agony. "Torscha. I . . ."

Miriam turned her back and felt her self-possession coldly return. "Thank you for the kind thought, Colonel. I shall dress now. I would hate to fail your expectations."

The stallion blinked. "No. Miriam, that's not what I meant!"

"And what, sir, did you mean?"

"Only . . . only that your happiness is my first and only wish."

"To which ends you want to see me married off as painlessly as possible."

Retter suddenly hurtled down his hat in frustration.

"*Stop it!* Why are you always so quick to find fault? Must *everything* be an attack against you?"

"*Me?*" Miriam was outraged. "Why you presumptuous cart horse! Don't you tell *me* how to behave!"

"Spoiled brat! You need some damned good lessons!"

"Don't you shout at me, sir!"

"I will speak however I damned well please!" Retter pranced in fury. " 'Tis high time someone taught you that respect and love are to be earned, not expected!"

"Love? *You* speak of love!" Miriam threw her hands open in

mock amazement. "I've seen more romantic creatures lying belly-up on the bottom of ponds!"

The stallion stood nose to nose with the girl, bellowing at the top of his voice. "You wouldn't know love if it bit you on the arse part!"

"*Ha! Ha!*" Miriam whooped in triumph. "Now we get down to it!"

Retter was stunned. "Down to what?"

"Don't you look at me so innocently *Colonel Retter!* You were the one to bring up my arse!"

"I did nothing of the sort!"

"Indeed you did, sir! Now we see what has been lurking at the back of your mind!" Miriam's tail hoisted invitingly high; she was too incensed to notice.

Retter stamped in fury, his own tail slashing at the walls. "You keep your arse out of this! I want nothing to do with the wretched thing!"

The filly squawked in outrage. "So now I'm ugly?"

Retter was shoveling sand uphill. "What?"

"I'm ugly! You said my rump was ugly!"

"I-I said nothing of the sort!" Retter desperately tried to defend himself. "It's a beautiful rump!"

Miriam stared; Retter tried to unwedge his hoof from his mouth. "*No!* Not that I'd ever want to . . . Not that *I* find it attractive!"

The girl gave a squeal of fury. "Well, I shall just take it out of your damned sight then!" She stormed off down the corridor. Retter started to follow her.

"You! You know why I want to help you find a husband? Because you're going to need all the help you can get!"

"OH, REALLY!"

"YES, REALLY!"

"WELL I CAN DO WITHOUT YOURS!"

SLAM! Miriam's door banged shut, and Retter raved in the corridor. Why do women always have to get the last damned word?

Damned jennet! By heaven she deserves a good swat on that precious backside of hers! Why I'd like to . . .

Yipe!

Retter felt an embarrassing *presence* beneath himself. The

argument had excited rather more than just a foul temper. The stallion skipped off, hiding in his room before anyone caught sight of him.

The theater was magnificent; crowded, bright and gay, the hall glittered with costumes and laughter and the stalls were alive with nodding heads and shimmering finery. Excitement rose as the stage illusionists began to exercise their craft; strange pastel beetles hopped across the heads of the audience, chittering in fury as they battled each other up and down the hall.

It was going to be a wonderful performance.

Up above the main body of noise, Miriam's party sat in General Vardvere's reserved box. Lady Jerrick, the general, and Frielle's Aunt Kala were deep in conversation, enjoying some silly piece of bandiage from Willy Merle.

Frielle ended up caught between Retter and Miriam; it was an uncomfortable experience. Miriam had entrenched herself behind the glacis of her fine new evening gown. Retter sat with arms folded and brows lowered. Trapped between the two of them, Frielle felt like a city under siege. Dressed in a shimmering confection of apricot satin, with a cleavage line that could raise the dead and halt small wars, Frielle felt somewhat lost and abandoned. The exquisite little satyr cleared her throat and tried to break the ice between her friends.

"Look you, Miriam! Do y' see the box just across from us? I do believe that is the infamous Sir Leymond. He controls parliament's anti-war movement. He has a perfectly terrifying reputation as a duelist. The tall half-horse stallion beside him is Sir Walter. . . ."

Miriam flicked cold eyes over in the indicated direction.

"Is he married?" Her voice was brusque.

"Er-no. . . ."

"Right, best tell the colonel. That's another one he can pencil in on my stud list."

Retter shot Miriam a poisonous look. "I shall check his pedigree. Madam Miriam wants to throw herself at only the very best."

Miriam refused even to look at him. "Well, who knows? Perhaps the fellow might be quite pleasant. That would make a nice change."

Frielle winced; this gay banter had started during the coach ride from Baron Vardvere's townhouse and had been gaining momentum ever since. Frielle frantically fanned herself.

"Oh, lookee there! I do believe that is Lord . . ."

Miriam leaned over the balcony. "Is he a half-horse?"

The little satyr looked pained. "Er—yes, as a matter of fact."

Miriam speared a venomous glance at Retter. "Too old. The colonel wants me to be happy—we must find a more *virile* partner. We can't have me being denied anything, now can we?"

"You're the one who harps on about sex—not me!"

Mercy! Frielle's ears burned red.

With a blast of sound, the opening overture boomed out across the theater as servants ran to snuff the lights. *Saved!* Frielle breathed out a sigh of relief and fanned herself, grateful for a moment's breathing space.

Opal stirred on the satyr's knee, straining forward to stare at a point on the ground near the door. In the darkness of the theater, Frielle could not imagine what held her fascination so. She leaned forward to whisper to the little creature. "What is it, eh?"

The dragon began burrowing frantically down into her lap. Frielle shrugged and sat back to watch the play. Behind her, a fat white Persian cat crept from a neighboring booth and quietly began to prowl.

The curtains drew aside and the play began.

For his part, Mus was being royally entertained. He sat at the edge of the theater box peering down at the stage, curling his tail in ecstasy.

Wonderful! Oh, how beautiful! The stage shimmered with light as the illusionists set the scene. Empty floorboards suddenly came alive with grass and summer flowers. A great castle loomed on a hill in the far distance. Birds looped out over the audience to twist and chitter through the galleries. Mus laughed with the rest as a female robin berated her husband noisily before sweeping off into the rafters.

Enter a pair of fat, sleek ravens. The temperature had taken a sharp drop, and the audience shivered; the stage magicians were true masters of their craft.

One raven ruffled his feathers, his voice a graveyard croak that chilled the blood. "*I have flown o'er the south.*"

"*And I the east did fly. All through the cluttered ruck of spring. What morsels didst thou spy?*"

A laugh swirled like ashes in the wind as the ravens described the sweet tidbits to be found at a nearby battle. Act One led into Act Two, and Mus sat enthralled, drinking in the play. He caught his breath as Pervante staggered from the battlefield. He quailed as the good knight lay helpless under the evil eyes of the ravens. Mus sighed in relief when sweet Troiselle, daughter of Pervante's enemy, set the ravens to flight and tended to the fallen hero.

Concentrating on the action below him, Mus slowly became aware of a constant source of annoyance from behind.

Miriam's voice grumbled petulantly in the darkness. "Keep your eyes on the stage!"

Retter's voice was childishly irritable. "Then stop looking at me!"

Their "stage whispers" were becoming louder and louder; Mus wearily rubbed his eyes.

Surely they can't still be at it?

The play moved on; Pervante languished in a dungeon, certain Troiselle had betrayed him into captivity.

"*That perfect love should hold a viper's sting? So the closer I do hold it, the deeper strikes its barb. . . .*"

Retter snorted. "Better he forget it altogether."

"Hmph! I wouldn't expect *you* to understand what he's going through."

"*That face so sweet should hide a serpent's tongue. . . .*"

"The sooner you're married off the better. At least then someone might take a switch to that rump of yours!"

"Stop bringing my rump into this! Lud, sir, you are obsessed!"

Retter angrily folded his arms; a retort evaded him. Miriam sneered as sweet Troiselle wept bitterly upon her balcony.

"*And I, poor fool, hath thrown love away with both my hands. And in its place, where love once dwelt, there now is duty's bitter pill.*"

Miriam seethed. Her tail swished angrily behind her seat as she fussed and fumed.

The scenery shifted upon the stage, and the theater became suddenly warm and mellow. Miriam's gaze drifted to one of the elaborate private boxes across the hall; Leymond's box. To Miriam's immense surprise, a pouting witch of a woman sat staring intently back at her. Tall, haughty and erotically beautiful, she leaned over to a companion—a great, fat, bloated half-horse stallion. The fellow stirred, and the woman directed his attention across to Miriam. He stared avidly, nearly rising from his seat; the girl pulled back into the shadows and swiftly hid behind her fan.

Miriam's eyes flicked across to Mus. The little rodent was some distance away at the corner of the box, sitting with his nose poking through a gap in the ornamental fretwork.

Miriam smiled, feeling the tension drain out of her. Dear Mus! The girl leaned forward to ask him what he thought of the performance, and suddenly she spied the cat gathering itself for a pounce behind the mouse.

"MUS!"

Who-what where! Mus whirled around as he heard his name shouted, looked up and saw the cat. The mouse hurled himself toward the safety of the giants. *Miriam will save me!*

"Mus! Look out!"

Mus skittered to a halt, and the cat crashed down in front of him. Her leap had been foiled, but she now stood between Mus and his friends.

The world dripped into slow motion; Miriam surged up onto her feet, her mouth open in a gasp of shock. The cat had turned around, her evil eyes ablaze with hunger. Mus wildly flailed around for some means of escape and squealed in fright.

Throw something!

A shape pushed itself into Mus's mind. He frantically snatched it up and flung it through the air. His fur crackled, the floor rocked, and a stench of burning hair blasted back into his face. Mus kept his eyes closed, expecting to feel claws rip though his back. Long moments passed as the little creature trembled in fright; finally a soft hand scooped him up and held him tightly.

"Mus? Thou-thou'rt unharmed?"

Miriam. Of course it is Miriam. She sounded frightened. Mus tightly clutched her with his paws.

"W-Where's the cat?"

"The cat's gone. Quickly, let's get you home."

The rest of the Jerrick-Delauncy party hastily followed as

Miriam raced from the theater. An uproar from the theater's outraged patrons welled up behind them as they ran.

"How is he?"

The entire sum of Mus's friends sat cradling cold cups of coffee in the general's parlor. They looked up as Miriam crept into the room and poured herself a glass of wine. Her face shone pale beneath its mask of freckles.

"He's sleeping. I made him drink something. He just cried himself off to sleep."

Frielle looked up. "Does he know what he did?"

"No. He says he threw something that he found in his head."

The satyr shuddered. "God help him."

Retter paced, his hands clasped behind his back. "Sorcery; it was sorcery. On a small scale, but deadly enough. I've seen it on the battlefield. Perhaps Mus's magical origins have given him powers that we never suspected."

Frielle raised a hand to her throat. "Could he—could he *kill* us? If we frightened him?"

Retter shook his head. "No. It's not in Mus's nature to hurt."

"He came close to doin' a good job on the cat."

Miriam swayed on her hooves, her eyes closed shut. "But he didn't hurt it! Mus never wanted to hurt anything! Not ever. Now he's frightened of what he might do." She leaned against a wall and hung her head; soft brown hair cascaded down over her shoulders. "Torscha, what are we going to do for him?"

"Willy knows of a sorcerer. Tomorrow he can take Mus for an examination." The stallion came and took her by the elbow. Miriam leaned gratefully into him as Retter gently folded her beneath his arm. "Madam, you'll make yourself ill if you worry so. Come—we shall see you into bed as well." He looked to Frielle. "Lady, could you fetch the maidservant and ask her to come?"

"Surely, Colonel."

Miriam's hooves wavered as she made her way toward her rooms, and Retter kept a comforting arm about her shoulders.

"Don't fret, Lady. We'll consult with a sorcerer. A magician can tell us a fuller story." Retter tried to cheer his companion up. "Our mouse has sharp teeth. He may not be as dependent on us as first we thought."

"He's frightened!"

"Sssh—I know. I'll take care of everything with the magus. There's nothing to be done now. Rest and be easy."

Miriam halted just outside of her bedroom door and quivered with fatigue.

"Sir, I . . ." She stopped and tried again. "Torscha, we were acting foolishly tonight. Can we at least call a truce?"

"Please, Lady. Let there be peace between us. We both have our duties to do."

Miriam swallowed. "Friends?"

"Friends."

"Good." Miriam laid a hand on the doorknob. "Sleep well, Torscha."

The stallion looked at her with strangely deep eyes. "Good night, Miriam. Good rest."

Retter paced slowly down the hall, his hoofbeats echoing in the empty corridor. Miriam made as if to say more, but the stallion had already gone. She wearily entered her room and shut the door.

Chapter Eleven

A Fine Pickle

he sorcerer's workshop seemed typical of its kind; a wide, dusty room littered with weird and wonderful paraphernalia. A stuffed crocodile swung from the rafters with its face permanently frozen in an expression of absolute astonishment. The small tree growing out on the balcony grew dozens of eyes the size of lemons, which stared at passersby in obvious curiosity.

Mus peered through a fat, round bottle, and on the far side his observers saw his face swell out to enormous size. The mouse pattered about the sorcerer's workbench while the magician irritably flicked through his source books.

Willy Merle edged closer, trying to peer into the sorcerer's book, but the peek told him nothing; the pages seemed to be smothered in chicken tracks and hieroglyphics.

The sorcerer muttered to himself and flipped the pages, avidly devouring paragraphs. He threw up one finger, forestalling Willy before he could annoy him with a question, then whirled to face the mouse. "You, sir! You say you threw something from your head?"

Mus stretched himself up on all four tippy-toes, his eyes shining deep and black.

"Yes, sir wizard. As I said, I was in peril! A defense just . . . fell into my head!" Mus seemed apologetic. "It has never happened before."

Willy trotted forward. "What . . . ?"

The sorcerer whipped about to scold him. "Sir! I must ask you to hold still! I am a professional, and I give professional consultations. You shall have my verdict once I have completed my examination."

Coattails flying, the sorcerer leapt to Mus's side, and one long bony finger pointed straight at the mouse's nose.

"Close your eyes. Concentrate! Can you feel the place where the power came from? Can you remember the feeling of that moment?"

Mus stared cross-eyed at the fingertip quivering before his whiskers. "I-I think so. . . ."

"Yes or no!"

"Yes . . . sort of."

"Good!" The sorcerer unceremoniously picked Mus up, turned him around, and sat him facing a candlestick.

"Very well, Sir Mouse. Find that place, grab what you find, and hurl it at the candle. Come now, don't be coy!"

Mus closed his eyes and rooted around in the back of his mind. He could *almost* feel something; a slithering sensation hiding in a rear drawer of his thoughts.

"Come come! I'm waiting!"

Mus pulled and tugged, finally feeling something rise up inside. A tingling started down his tail, filtering along his spine toward his nose. As it passed, Mus gave something between a push and a vast, almighty shove. . . .

Piff!

Power crackled through his fur, then sped away in instantaneous release. Mus gasped and swiftly opened his eyes. The candle was alight!

Mus sat up and capered with glee. "Look, Willy, look! I can do magic!"

Sir William seemed slightly disappointed. "Oh." He tipped his hat back on his head. "But last night it was stronger. . . ."

The sorcerer looked down his nose at the half-horse. "Can *you* light candles from a distance?"

"Er- Well, no. . . ."

The sorcerer turned away and bent down to cosset Mus. "Excellent, my dear fellow! Just take a rest for a moment."

Mus looked eagerly up at the magus. "Did I do well?"

"Please, *do* wait until I have finished my examination."

The sorcerer produced a steel ruler and measured Mus from tail tip to whiskers, and the mouse then found himself deposited on a scale and weighed. The sorcerer finally went back to his books and folded up his arms.

"Ha! There's another place, isn't there! A second well to draw from. Look! Look deep and see what you can find!"

Mus had climbed atop a smooth, clean skull. Secure on this macabre perch he hunkered down and shut his eyes, trying to seek the place the sorcerer had spoken of.

"Uh—I can't *feel* anything. . . . . What should I be searching for?"

"Nothing. If it were there, you would sense it." The sorcerer stroked his long nose for a moment and then threw himself into a chair. "I have the solution. Attend well the both of you! Wisdom is priceless!"

Willy and Mus were all ears, but the fellow took his own sweet time. Finally he regarded the mouse across steepled fingertips.

"Mus, you were a common house mouse, but you can claim to be such no longer. Your homoncule—the pattern that controls your body and your mind—has been irrevocably changed. Were you to have children, they would breed true to your own type; that is the nature of the spell." The magician idly took Mus into his hand. "The changes that have been made to you are based on the pattern of a man. You will age in much the speed and way as a man. The interesting point is the shaping of your intellect. Your mind has been prefurnished with a number of concepts (by no means comprehensive) that have helped fill out the void left by the expansion of your faculties. The creation of a being such as yourself has been essayed in the past, but it is not a popular experiment. The mana—the magical aptitude, as it were—is sucked out of the creator and drawn into the creature." The sorcerer suddenly stopped and tapped his nose. "No, not a good explanation. Let us say that in creating a being such as yourself, a magician would commence the slow wane of his own powers. On the other hand, your own powers will slowly increase.

"You have sorcerous powers, Mus. Fire and heat come from the element light—the creative principle. What interests me is the lack of the balancing principle—shadow. You should have a commensurate ability to create cold and darkness; this comes from the negative emotions—hate, fear, self-pity. . . . I conclude that you are an innocent, and thus such elements are not strong enough within you to draw upon."

The human sat back and opened his hands. "Questions?"

Willy stroked his blond mustaches. "How . . ."

Mus burst out excitedly. "I'll be a sorcerer then? Just like in the stories?"

The magus gave an elegant nod. "Indeed you shall, though perhaps only on a scale commensurate to your size. Perhaps not. In fact, I should be pleased to instruct you on focusing and shielding techniques. I confess that you intrigue me."

Willy shifted his hooves. "How . . ."

The mouse cut across Sir William once again. "When will I know the extent of my powers?"

"Why, never. That is the nature of such things."

Sir William cleared his throat. "When . . ."

Mus bounced up and down on his macabre perch. "May I start instruction soon?"

The sorcerer inclined his head. "I have no pressing engagements. Tomorrow afternoon should suffice for a preliminary lesson."

Willy leaned forward. "Are there . . ."

The mouse took a pace toward the sorcerer. "Sir, are there other intelligent animals like myself? I should dearly like . . . That is, if there were a mouse or two . . ."

"Intelligent animals? Why, yes. I believe there's a talking gannet down on the mud flats; one of my colleagues as a matter of fact. An unfortunate accident, that."

Sir William sighed and tried one last time. "Look! Can we . . ."

The sorcerer stood, dusting off his spindly thighs. "I am sorry, Sir William, but I simply cannot chat with you all day! I have other pressing matters to attend to." He picked up Mus and handed him to the half-horse. "Mus, I shall expect to see you tomorrow at noon. Be prepared, sir! I am a hard taskmaster! A nonpareil!" He bowed. "Sirs, I bid you good day."

And with that, they found themselves propelled out the door. They stood on the street under the pale autumn sun, where Mus sighed in relief. "Well, at least I'm not sick! Isn't it exciting, Willy! I'll be able to do magic! I could even be a hero, just like in the stories!"

Willy glowered at the sorcerer's door and snorted in frustration. "Well, Mus, we shall see. We must get you trained a little—just so that you're not a danger. . . ."

Mus twittered irritably. "Really, Willy! We just arranged all that! You know your problem? You talk too much. You should take more time to think!" Mus brushed at his whiskers. "Now come along, we're all supposed to be attending a garden party at Lady Futheringay's this afternoon. You'll never be ready in time if you keep dawdling."

Glowering darkly, Willy jammed Mus deep into his pocket and stomped off down the street.

It hardly seemed the best of days for a garden party. The autumn sunlight had a pale, fragile quality about it that seemed to promise rain.

Miriam bowed low to her host and hostess, hooves crossing as she curtsied. In the brittle sunlight her pale blue gown shimmered like an island stream. "My Lord and Lady Futheringay, an honor to meet you."

Miriam's soft, sweet voice was low and demure. Lord Futheringay pulled at his collar as he caught an eyeful of Miriam's staggering decolletage.

"Charmed." The human's eyes bugged as he stared at Miriam's swell of cleavage. "Quite . . . quite charmed."

Lady Futheringay was stout, short, and decked out in an absurd amount of finery. She briskly ushered Miriam out onto the lawns and closeted herself with Lady Jerrick. Nervously clutching Willy's arm, Miriam allowed herself to be escorted out onto the field of combat.

The Futheringays's mansion stood beside the riverbanks just outside the city walls. It was a place of wide open lawns and closed geometric gardens where fat, gaudy peacocks waddled across the grass. The lawns were a sea of color through which full-skirted ladies cruised back and forth while gentlemen posed gallantly before their fellows. Below the gardens, the river led its long, slow way toward Kerbridge, and Miriam glanced at the waters and heaved a longing sigh.

A suave young human lordling and his lady of the day swaggered across the lawn toward Sir William.

"Lud, Willy! So here y' are at last, fashionably late as usual. . . ."

Willy laughingly gave bow. "In such sweet company, one tends to woose track of time. Sir Arthur Kelson—may I present Damsel Miriam Jerrick."

Miriam curtsied once more, and Sir Arthur smiled. "Charming!" The quizzing glass came to his eye and his gaze fell on her cleavage. "Indeed. . . ." He shook himself and turned to his own lady. "I have the honor of presenting Lady Teresa Haubrey."

The girl gave a sour little curtsy of her own; a small, thin girl with a waistline that most women would kill for, her face was elegant and pale. She sniffed the airs, clearly unimpressed by Miriam.

Men being what they are, Willy and his friend Arthur noticed nothing; they began to discuss horse racing while the women eyed each other with growing hostility. Lady Teresa looked Miriam up and down then elegantly splayed her fan.

"So, my dear! And how do you find civilization?"

Miriam settled herself evenly on all four hooves. "I find it interesting enough, Lady Teresa. I'd not yet venture to say whether I prefer the country to the city."

The human girl waved airily. "Well the arcadian airs seem to have done you good; but then they always *did* breed such nice cart horses out in Kerbridge. . . ."

Miriam's mouth flopped open. *Did I hear that?* She gathered herself to make a furious reply when a musical little voice cut in from behind her.

"Why, Teresa! How pleasant to be seein' you again! And you came with a *man*—how novel of you."

Frielle floated across the lawn, a vision in white lace. Her impish face shone full of innocent charm.

Sir Willy bowed to the two ladies. "Frielle, Miriam; if you could excuse me for a moment? I spy some—er—business associates. I really must go and confer." He fished Mus out of his pocket and furtively passed him to the little satyr. "Madam? Would you be so kind?" He leaned closer and whispered sotto voce. "And keep the wittle wretch quiet!"

Frielle accepted custody of the rodent. "Quite so." For want of a better place, she popped Mus into her sleeve while a fat peacock stalked regally by. The bird shook out its tail feathers, looked at Miriam, and sniffed with disdain.

Frielle took Miriam by the arm and led her down into the gardens. The satyr still wore gloves to conceal the vicious cat scratches on her hands.

"We must be careful, you an' I. They'll look for excuses not to like us. The best defense is to be quick on thy hooves and hit anyone who slights ye."

The half-horse gratefully gripped Frielle's small hand. "We both know why I'm here, but what about thee? What dost thou want here, my friend?"

Frielle sighed, looking sad. "Refuge; the channel isles are in Nantierran hands now. There's no home to return to; they even locked Papa in his own dungeons. Aunt Kala took me in when I fled the occupation."

"Fled?"

"Aye! In a wee boat no bigger'n thy skirts. I never want to see the ocean again!"

A muffled little voice wafted up from Frielle's sleeve. The girl lifted up her arm and asked Mus to repeat himself.

Mus tried again. "I said that this place seems more than a touch unfriendly! You should stay with us out in the country for a while. I'm sure Lady Barbara would agree."

"Why thank you, Mus!"

". . . But not before we've seen what the king looks like!"

Frielle laughed and tickled the mouse through the fabric. "Well, we'll see what we can do to appease you."

They walked about the gardens together, making the best of the watery sunshine as they mingled with the crowds. Miriam had never been very good at names. Fortunately Mus never forgot anything; he made an admirable secretary.

Lady Jerrick approached, hanging on the arm of a preposterously bulbous stallion—a great waddling pudding of a man with a shiny red face and enormous stubby hands. His whole ungainly bulk had been stuffed into the most expensive clothing that Miriam had ever seen. With a dappled hide and multiple chins, the stallion seemed a most unlovely sight.

Miriam had glimpsed him before; he was the man from the theater—the one that had looked at her with such appalling hunger. Miriam instinctively backed away as her mother drew near.

Lady Jerrick positively beamed. "Miriam, dear! May I introduce Lord Albermarle Pumbleby. He has been very keen to meet you." Miriam's mother's eyes shone with encouragement; obviously

Lord Pumbleby had made quite an impression upon her.

Miriam hesitated and then dropped into a curtsy. "My lord, it is a pleasure to make your acquaintance."

The swollen stallion bowed ponderously. His voice bubbled low and crafty, thickened by his pouting lips.

"The p-pleasure is all mine, Lady. All mine . . ."

Miriam quickly straightened, suddenly regretting her dress's plunging neckline. It seemed clear that Pumbleby liked what he saw.

"Well, my dear! I see that Mademoiselle Delauncy has been doing her best to make you welcome. Would you care to meet some of the gentlemen from our p-parliament?"

Pumbleby! So that was where she had heard the name before; Lord Pumbleby held a seat in parliament. Miriam cleared her throat and tried to speak.

"Sir, I'm not sure that I should abandon . . ."

Barbara Jerrick scoffed. "Nay, don't be silly! Frielle and I shall have a wonderful time. You've always been fascinated by politics. Now is your chance to see it firsthand!"

Pumbleby extended one massive forearm. It felt thick and spongy, but powerful muscles ran beneath the fat. Miriam had little choice but to allow herself to be led away.

Lady Jerrick watched her daughter go and positively bubbled with excitement.

"Look, Frielle! I do believe that he's taken a fancy to her!"

The faun shuffled her hooves unhappily. "Indeed, ma'am. You could be right in sayin'."

"Oh, my dear, don't you know who that was? Lord Pumbleby is one of the wealthiest men in the country! He could be the answer to all our prayers!"

A muffled mutter wafted up from Frielle's sleeve.

"I don't like him. He looks like a greedy cat."

Lady Jerrick bent down to scold the mouse. "Don't be silly! He's perfectly charming. A large bulk hides a large heart."

Mus seemed disturbed. "Perhaps." He sighed. "Frielle—I'm very tired. Do you have a cloak hung up anywhere? I'd like to snuggle up in a nice quiet pocket and go to sleep."

Frielle smiled. "Very well, Sir Mouse, I think we can find you somewhere for a nap."

The women walked on through the garden toward the great

house. Behind them an angry sparrow swooped down among the peacocks and set them to flight.

Alone at last, Mus cautiously peeked from the pocket of Frielle's hanging cloak. The cloakroom lay still and quiet, and he could hear no movement in the house. The sun had redoubled in strength, and musicians were playing for crowds upon the lawn.

The tedium had been quite unbearable! Being trapped up Frielle's sleeve listening to empty-headed chatter had been slowly driving Mus to distraction. A devilish prick of mischief hung in the air. Mus wanted to explore; after all, he was a sorcerer now! Surely there would be no harm if he took a wee wander on his own?

The mouse stealthily clambered down Frielle's fur-lined cloak. Mus planted his hat firmly on his head and then pattered off across a plush Harabian carpet. He crossed floors and negotiated potted plants, discovering a whole wondrous world of sights and smells. Finally he looked into a great dining room. The mouse rubbed his paws with greed and instantly scampered up the tablecloth.

Food! Yes, just the spot! Food, and then a bit of exploration. He could be back in Frielle's cloak before anyone knew he had gone.

The mouse slithered up over the table's edge and found himself on the threshold of a whole universe of delight.

It smelled *beautiful!*

Mus wandered between aisles of pure heaven; little glazed cakes sat on platters while mighty cheeses towered overhead. There were cold meats and candied nuts and bottle after bottle of cool amber wine. The corks had been drawn from the bottles to let the wine breathe, and a sharp, delicious smell hung in the air.

It actually smelled rather interesting. How had Miriam described wine? A nice drink that made you feel happy and gay? That sounded rather fun! Mus stretched himself beside a bottle, his whiskers questing as he stroked the cool, smooth glass.

Someone blundered through the doorway. Mus swiftly dodged beneath a stuffed swan and peered out between the feathers. A servant with a tray of pastries entered the room and set them down at the far end of the table.

Mus watched the man carefully. He was a human; a strange fellow

with a deep black skin. Mus had never seen anything like him
quite before—what a wonderful color! The servant looked
furtively about the room, assuring himself he was alone, then
sidled over toward the bottles of wine. The servant poured himself
a drink, then slowly wafted the glass beneath his nose. With an
expression of supreme pleasure, he took a slow sip and rolled it
sensually across his tongue.

"Samuel!"

Lady Futheringay strode into the room like a silken juggernaut.
The servant hid his wine beneath the tail of the roasted swan and
quickly started polishing spoons.

"Yes, ma'am?"

"Samuel, has the oyster basket been prepared?"

"I'm attending to it now, madam. The cook is grinding the
ice."

"Well, see that you do!" Lady Futheringay chased the man away
from the room. "Now do hurry on! Bartholomew has been run off
his feet looking for you."

The dark-skinned servant hurried to the kitchens, and Mus
found himself alone in the dining hall.

The mouse peeked out from beneath his feathery refuge, then
scampered up a drumstick and out onto the tail. He lowered himself down above the wine glass, leaned out over the wine, and
sniffed back and forth with the air of an utter connoisseur.
Whiskers quivering, he dipped his nose to take a drink.

Rather interesting; Mus took a second sip, and his eyes brightened. In fact—he liked it a lot!

The little mouse stuck his nose back into the glass and drank
for all he was worth.

"So, my dear, how do you find the company?"

Pumbleby still had a firm hold of Miriam's arm; she loathed
the feel of his body being so close, and the warmth of his flanks
seemed somehow repellent.

They stood together at the edge of a garden bower, watching
the beau-sabreurs and courtesans walk by. Miriam uncomfortably
looked for an answer that would not offend.

"Sooth, sir, I confess I'm not used to such games."

Pumbleby smiled indulgently. "Ah yes, of course. Well these games become quite b-boring after a while, but they are the prelude to better amusements later on." He glanced sideways at Miriam, and his watery eyes had a glimmer that made the filly shrink aside.

"I-I don't quite follow your meaning, sir."

"No?" Pumbleby gave an oily, predatory smile. "How many of these folk will sleep in their own beds tonight? The best games are played after dark. . . ."

Miriam shivered, then firmly removed herself from Pumbleby's arm.

"I wouldn't know, sir! Nor do I intend to find out quite yet."

"Dear me!" Pumbleby gave her an evaluative look, his interest suddenly aroused. "Don't tell me evenings in the country are spent in silent prayer and meditation!"

"No, sir! But neither have my evenings been spent on—on what you seem to suggest!"

The hunger intensified in Pumbleby's eyes, and his moist mouth began to gleam. "Truly?" He gave a shuddersome sigh. "Oh, Damsel—you are as great a treasure as I have been told. . . . Forgive me if I have offended you." He licked his lips. "I should not like to think that I have chased you away through my virtue of frankness." He sidled closer.

Miriam desperately sought escape. "No, sir, but if you will excuse me I must . . ."

A huge black presence loomed suddenly at her elbow, and Miriam looked gratefully up to discover Retter standing at her side.

"Ah, here you are at last, Miriam! Our hostess has been asking for you. She wishes to consult with us both over a private matter." Retter turned to Pumbleby and bowed.

"My Lord Pumbleby."

"*Citizen* Retter." Pumbleby took few pains to conceal his distaste. Retter said nothing more to him, but took Miriam by the arm and covered her retreat.

Miriam gratefully squeezed his arm. "Thank you Torscha. Your appearance was timely."

The black stallion brushed at his smooth beard. "A gentleman should always know when a lady needs rescuing."

"This lady appreciates the presence of a true gentleman. Kicking

Pumbleby would not have won me friends here. If he touches me once more, I shall scream!"

"Touched you?" Retter's voice grew suddenly hard, and he halted in his tracks. "Madam, if he did offer insult . . ."

Miriam hastened to tug the stallion onward. "No! Nothing overt; but I shall keep clear of him, despite my mother's wishes."

Retter subsided, brooding to himself as they walked up toward the house. Miriam was soothed by the warm smell of him. They paced side by side in complete harmony with the wind mingling their tails.

Two servants carried a burning potted plant out onto the lawns. Miriam watched the sight with vague distraction as she clung to Retter's arm.

"Where's Willy? And where have *you* been hiding, my friend?"

Torscha's hooves flashed in the sun. "I've been shuttered up in back rooms rallying support for our holy cause." He made a face. "Drawing-room politics. I fear I am not very good at it. My time as a soldier has quite ruined my sense of tact."

"Well, you need Sir Willy's talents. Where is he?"

Retter seemed puzzled. "But . . . he escorted you to the party."

"He noticed some business associates and went to . . ."

"No!" Torscha looked positively sick. "God, I'll kill him! I swear I'll kill him! Did you see where he went?"

Miriam was puzzled and alarmed. "No . . . Torscha whatever is wrong?"

"Gambling!"

"Gambling?"

"The damned idiot!" Torscha pranced sideways in alarm. "He's ruined himself thrice over! I thought he might have given it up since meeting . . ."

Frielle came racing down the path in panic. She spied Torscha and Miriam and ran toward them, her skirts hitched up to show off her shaggy shins.

"Miriam! Colonel! Do either of you have Mus?" She was almost sobbing in distress as she put a hand up to her horns. "I've lost him! O Lord help me, I've lost him! He'll get trodden on an' killed!" She jittered up and down in a fine state of panic.

Torscha gently prized her hands away from her forehead and held her still. "Hush! Just tell me slowly. Now where did you lose him?"

"He-He was in the pocket of my cloak, in the cloakroom. I left him there while he had a nap, and now he's gone!"

Miriam tugged urgently at Retter's sleeve.

"Torscha?"

"Shhh!" Retter was trying to talk to Frielle. "How long ago did you leave him?"

"Well—about two hours back. . . ."

Miriam stamped her hoof. "Torscha! Look!"

Torscha and Frielle turned to look. Two harassed-looking servants were dragging yet more potted plants out into the open air. Each plant was scorched or burned. . . .

"Mus!"

Retter took the women by the hand and trotted up toward the house.

"God help us! What's that little pyromaniac up to now!"

Whee! Mus wove gaily down a corridor, dragging his tail untidily behind him. The little creature hiccoughed, swayed, and somehow tangled up his feet. He came to a passage junction and spied three potted plants on a table by the wall.

"*Pow!*"

The nearest plant exploded in a shower of ash. The heat of the tiny fireball vaporized wood, leaf, and stalk, then set fire to both the wallpaper and the rug. Mus whooped with laughter as he twittered down the hall.

His voice crowed drunkenly down the passageway.

"Wheee, magic Mus! Take that you-you cat!"

Peeow! Blam!

The other two plants followed suit. This was easy. Boy, no one had better mess with him again! *Peeow*—instant fricassee!

"An' no one'd better speak to Miriam nasty either," the mouse solemnly informed the skirting board. "Pow!"

He giggled and lurched against the wall.

Oops!

His mouth seemed dry; Mus blasted the top from a wine bottle and danced gleefully beneath a shower of foam. He drenched himself from tail to whiskers and then somehow fell over on his rump.

Time for a little sleep, perhaps. Just a quick snooze, and then maybe another drinkie. Mus wove past a pair of servants as they battled flaming ferns, and found his way into a dish of croutons they'd left lying on the floor. The mouse snuggled deep into his fine new nest and gave a contented sigh.

Wine was fun! But he did wish Miriam could be here. . . .

"Mus Mus Mus Mus!" Frielle awkwardly peered beneath a divan, her hooped skirts riding up to give any passing watcher an intriguing eyeful. Being a hairy legged satyr, she was wearing no bloomers.

"Ha!" Miriam started dragging one of the overstuffed divans away from one wall. Frielle eagerly looked up.

"Ye've found him?!"

Miriam grunted. "Nay, but I have found his hat. The rest of him can't be far."

A throat cleared noisily behind them. Both women gave a guilty jump and whirled about. They discovered a puzzled black servant standing in the doorway.

"May I assist you ladies?"

"No! No thank you. We had but dropped an earring. We've recovered it now."

The servant bowed graciously. "Excellent. Dinner is about to be served, miladies."

"Wait!" Frielle skipped forward in alarm. "Would your mistress be keepin' cats?"

"No, madam. Her Ladyship will not tolerate cats. . . ."

Both women heaved great sighs of relief.

". . . They would fight with her terriers."

Miriam looked quite sick. "Terriers!"

Dinner guests began to promenade into the room. Frielle and Miriam dodged out from behind the drapes and linked up with their escorts just outside of the doors.

The dining hall shone like a fairyland. A vast crystal chandelier glittered down upon a dazzling sea of costumes. The ladies' evening dresses were matched by the magnificent cassocks of the men. Silk and satin, diamonds and lace all shimmered as the crowd gathered about the dining table.

The gentlemen began to seat their ladies. Miriam evaded

Pumbleby and allowed Retter to attend her. She settled onto a padded bench, leaning close to whisper in his ear. "Any sign of the little wretch?"

"Nay, not a hair! Our hostess tells me that some eight or nine of her prize roses are now reduced to cinders! I'll have harsh words for that little fellow! This magic nonsense has gone to his head!"

Miriam's hide twitched; God rot that little rodent, worrying everyone like this! By heaven she would have a thing or two to say to that wayward little furball. If anything ever happened to him . . . Miriam's mind jerked away from the thought. He-he must be all right. He was probably off with the fairies again, out watching the stars and stuffing his face. Yes—nothing to worry about. . . .

Miriam nervously picked at her nails.

Lady Jerrick sat beside Lord Pumbleby, deep in conversation. Miriam's mother laughed gaily at one of Pumbleby's witticisms. Miriam did not like the signs; her mother and that lustful beast were socializing far too well.

First course arrived; chestnut soup. It was one of Miriam's favorite dishes. Mus or no Mus, she felt hungry. Miriam tore into her dinner with a will. "Will you take croutons, ma'am?"

A servant stood beside Miriam with a great basket full of fresh-baked dumplings. The girl reached tongs into the bowl, dug beneath the surface, and came up with three croutons and a dangling little mouse.

MUS!

The mouse blinked at her, threw back his head and crowed.

"*Miriam!* Oh, Miriam, it's been fun!"

EEP!

Heads began to turn; Miriam snatched the creature in her hand and leapt instantly to her feet. Retter hurriedly dabbed at his mouth and followed as she stumbled out of the room. Miriam dodged into a sitting room, opened up the palm of her hand and scowled down at Mus.

"Right, thou little idiot! Just what dost thou mean by . . ."

Mus gave a hiccough and looked up with addled little eyes. Miriam blinked; the mouse was thoroughly pickled!

"*Hic!*"

"*Mus!* Thou'st been drinking!"

The befuddled little rodent tried to preserve his dignity. "I have been shampling wine." He lurched and fell. "Oops! Shorry."

Retter didn't know whether to be angry or relieved. He touched Miriam on the arm.

"Miriam, I should tell Willy and Frielle that we've found him." He scowled down at the rodent. "You try to sober him up or something. I'll be back anon."

"Hurry back!"

Retter hastened from the room, and Miriam turned to confront the inebriated rodent.

"How did this happen? What hast thou been up to?"

Mus played the innocent. "Jus' a few drinkies!" He smiled in pleasure. "It feels very nice! Can I have another drink? I'm ver' thirsty."

"Thou most certainly cannot! Why, Mus of Kerbridge, I'm quite ashamed of thee! Pickled to the whiskers, that's what thou art!"

The mouse hung his head. "*Hic!*"

"Yes—thou might look contrite now. What of Lady Futheringay's fine potted plants? Ooooh, thou hast really done it this time!"

The door suddenly burst open.

"Aah, Miriam my d-dear! Is everything all right?"

Pumbleby! Miriam desperately sought somewhere to hide Mus, and for want of a better place she stuffed him down her cleavage. "Why, Lord Pumbleby! How—how sweet of you to be troubled. I simply felt a trice unwell. I am almost recovered."

Mus burrowed downward, happily lost inside a sea of warmth. Miriam jiggled as Lord Pumbleby rumbled closer.

"I was worried about you, my dear. Your sudden departure . . . Are you *sure* you feel quite well? You appear a trifle pained."

Miriam was suffering. A hopelessly ticklish person, she jiggled as her furry friend rubbed himself against her breasts. The mouse rummaged around trying to make himself comfortable.

"Why, m-my lord, I am QUITE all right." She danced in agitation as Mus decided to lick salt from her skin. Lord Pumbleby edged forward, running his eyes over Miriam's toothsome body.

"I do believe your eyes are watering!"

"No! No please, my lord. I just need a mo-mo-MOMENT to recover my composure!" The girl screwed her eyes shut; one rear hoof twitched and kicked. "Please—if you could be so kind? I-I really must just rest by my-myself!"

Pumbleby seemed loathe to leave, and his eyes gleamed with hidden lust. "Madam, it pains me to see you in such distress. Perhaps I can call upon you at another time. After I have asked your mother, of course. . . ."

"What? Uh, well, I don't really . . ." Mus's tail slithered across Miriam's skin. "Yes! Ah—Mother will know the best time! Now please, sir, I must have peace for a while."

"Certainly, ma'am. Please forgive the intrusion." He breathed in the smell of her and shivered. "I shall look forward to seeing more of you anon. . . ."

Pumbleby bowed awkwardly and took his leave. Miriam's hand instantly dived between her breasts and fished out the little rodent. He hung from his tail, feet splayed wide and eyes blinking.

"Whazzup?"

"Drunken little sot!"

The mouse pouted miserably. "Aaaaw, now thou art mad. I love thee, Miriam. Don' be angry." The mouse rubbed affectionately against Miriam's thumb and looked up at her with adoring, bleary eyes. "Love thee . . ." He nuzzled her happily, his eyes closed. " 'M tired. Sleepy time. Can I sleep down thy front? Smells nice. . . ."

"Thou most certainly cannot!" Miriam spied a tall urn on the mantelpiece; slippery walls were just the thing to stop him from wandering away. She dropped her kerchief in the vase to make a bed.

"Come, sweet prince. Time for a little rest then."

"Mmmm—lovely . . ."

"Be quiet, and I'll be back soon, hear? Don't make a sound."

The mouse's eyes were closed. "A'right."

"Good night, then."

Mus stretched his head up toward her. "Kiss?"

Miriam raised her friend to her lips and lightly kissed his forehead. The mouse smiled and allowed himself to be lowered down into the vase.

"O Mus . . . whatever am I to do with thee?"

Miriam quietly walked out of the room and went back to her dinner.

Nice feelings had given way to a horrible whirling sensation. Mus held tight to his bed and wished it would stop spinning.

Time dragged slowly past, and Mus felt worse and worse. The mouse could only whimper and hold tightly to the walls. Voices buzzed at the back of Mus's head. Alone with his misery inside the vase, Mus tried to listen to what the voices said. A breathy female voice finally caught and held Mus's attention.

". . . told you she was what you were looking for."

"Quite delicious!" The answering male voice hung thick and heavy. "Your judgment, as always, is superb."

"In politics as well as affairs of the flesh?"

The male voice seemed edgy. "Perhaps . . . I want p-proof; something to show you are who you pretend to be."

The female voice dripped sweet promise. "And you shall have it, sir. You shall have it."

Mus leaned his head against the cool porcelain walls of his prison and gave a groan as someone noisily opened up a door. His ears registered a brand new voice.

". . . say you want proof? Here it is—my carte blanche."

"I can't read that! You know I cannot read that silly t-tongue!"

"It declares the bearer to be Queen Aelis's trusted servant." The new voice rang loud and powerful, and Mus tried to burrow underneath his bed. "It empowers him to speak with the queen's voice. Any promises made by the bearer will be upheld by the queen to the best of her ability. The rose seal is the private sigil of the queen herself." There was a sound of paper changing hands. "I think that should be proof enough."

"Yes." The thick, stuttering male voice seemed relieved. "Well then, Rodger—shall we consider the d-deal closed?"

"Yes indeed. Welcome to the fold! Fear not; Aelis will long remember those who made her victory possible."

Hooves and feet finally clumped out the door. Peace at last! Mus gratefully curled up in the bottom of the urn and tried to sleep.

Please let the whirling stop!

Chapter Twelve

Moth In A Bottle

"Oooh, I wish I were dead!"

"Yes—paying for it now, aren't we? Hold still. . . ." Miriam gently dabbed Mus's forehead with a cool cloth, and the rodent winced beneath her touch.

"I'm dying! Oh, Miriam, no one told me! It hurts!" Mus felt utterly wretched. His fur stuck out in all directions, his whiskers were snarled, and even his tail looked limp and unhappy. Mus suffered under the claws of a raging hangover, wailing and trying to hide beneath his tiny paws.

"Lift up thy head now, Mus. Just drink this down for me."

Mus choked down a thimbleful of revolting medicine. Oh, God, it tasted like soap and vinegar! Miriam stood over him until the mouse had swallowed the vile stuff.

"That's a boy. We'll soon have the twinkle back in thy tail." Mus whimpered and Miriam took pity on him as she gently stroked his fur. "Is it really so bad?"

The mouse almost cried. "Terrible. Oh, I've never felt so sick! O Miriam—I love thee, and now thou must hate me. I've behaved like a fool."

"Ssssh—thou weren't to know." She stroked his nose. "Poor dear Mus."

"Did—did I really burn Lady Futheringay's plants?"

"I'm afraid so."

Mus winced. "Oh, how could I do it? The poor lady."

Miriam's hands were gentle. "Dost thou see now why drunkenness is a bad idea? I tried to protect thee."

"I'm an ungrateful, foolish wretch!" Mus wailed unhappily and tried to hide his eyes. "Now Torscha will never speak to me again. He is so controlled and dignified, and I've been so *stupid*. . . ."

Speak of the devil; Torscha entered the room with Willy close on his tail. Willy had already partaken of Miriam's headache cure, and he too looked somewhat the worse for wear; his eyes were those of a dying man.

Retter knelt by Miriam's bedside so he could meet Mus eye to eye upon her dressing table. "So, Mus."

Mus cringed; Retter drew a long, slow breath.

"I shall say nothing about the evils of drink. Your head is clearly telling you better than I ever could. But we must have an understanding." Cool blue eyes bore down upon the rodent. Mus quailed as Retter drove on. "You have an unusual gift, Mus. Sorcery is a talent that only a special few are blessed enough to have. I am very disappointed in the way you have chosen to use it. You have gained in power, but you have not gained in responsibility."

Sir Willy sniffed from the sidelines. "Oh, God—don't harp away so! You sound wike a bloody church warden."

Miriam turned derisive eyes on the suffering cavalier. "Thus speaks the walking dead. You and Mus can commiserate about your troubles together. Mus, look and beware; this is what happens to thee when thou hast led a dissolute life."

Mus subsided down into his bed. "Oooooh, I thought I was caught in a nightmare! The world spun, my head reeled, and the jokes had all gone sour. What is a carte blanche?"

Miriam carefully replaced Mus's head cloth with a fresh cool one. "Why, a carte blanche is an official document. Some powerful person issues a writ that confers the bearer part of his or her authority. 'Tis a Nantierran phrase."

"Oh, yes, he said it was written in Nantierran." Mus pressed a hand to his muzzle. "Ohhh, my head. . . ."

Miriam had stopped moving all of a sudden. "What was written in Nantierran, Mus?"

"The carte blanche of course! The one from Queen Aelis."

Retter immediately erupted up onto his hooves. "*Who?* Who had it, Mus? Oh, my God!"

Mus clapped his hands over his ears and turned a fine shade of green. Miriam sat by his side and took him in her hand. "Who, Mus? Who had a carte blanche from Queen Aelis? Can't you see what it means?"

Mus suddenly stiffened. "Oh, my . . . I'm sorry. My head is sorely addled." He screwed his eyes shut. "I-I couldn't see them—I was in a jug—but there were three. Some of them were four-leggers. Two of them were showing the paper to the third man." Mus's audience waited breathlessly for him to continue.

Willy tried to prod the mouse onward. "Well—do you remember more?"

Mus rubbed his eyes. "Hush, Willy. I never forget anything! Be still and let me think. Oooh, my head hurts so!" Mus combed his fingers through his whiskers. "There was a lady who talked to the first man . . . and then I heard the second man, the one with the paper. I believe that they called him Rodger."

Retter let out a hiss of ecstasy. "Rodger?"

"Yes, a man with a beautiful smooth voice. He works for Queen Aelis. Rather proud of it, in point of fact."

"Sir Rodger Leymond! It has to be!" Retter forgot Mus's agony and stamped his hooves for joy. "Leymond in Aelis's pay! Of course! We can finish him at last!"

Sir Willy also seemed a trifle green about the gills. He leaned weakly against the door and waved his hand.

"We-We don't know that, Torscha."

"Ah, but we shall!" Retter bent down to grin at Mus. "Mus, we shall have to investigate further! You may have found us a valuable key."

Mus covered his eyes and wished that Torscha would go away.

A black shape fluttered up onto the rooftops just as the last dregs of sunset drained off into night. Far below, lamp lighters scurried about the streets while the last few tradesmen wandered home. It was the most pleasant time of the city evening.

The rooftop stalker folded his wings and opened up his pocket. "Herr Mouse? You are all right?"

"Terrible" The mouse struggled up out of Gus the pixie's pocket. "I don't think I like flying at all."

"Iss wonderful feeling once you get used to it! We shall go flying again sometime, yes? I show you very good time."

"Uh, quite." Mus was impatient to move on with his task. "Is the chimney cold? There's no smoke?"

"Nay, Herr Mouse. Cold as a witch's bum." The pixie popped Mus into a pillbox attached to a long piece of twine. "You are ready? Then down we go!" The pixie carefully lowered the box down the chimney until he felt a double tug on the line. Gus hauled the empty box back up onto the roof and then called softly down the flue.

"Good luck, Herr Mouse! I wait for your signal!"

Mus settled his beautiful hat firmly on his head and cautiously looked around. He had ventured into the enemy's lair, and his life was in danger.

The sleek little mouse sat in the fireplace of Sir Rodger Leymond's drawing room. There was a desk covered in pens and papers, and an old clock ticked away noisily in one corner. Apart from the mouse, the rooms seemed utterly deserted.

Leymond was unlikely to keep his secret papers in his desk, but Mus had devised a delightful plan for discovering their whereabouts. He was Mus! He was clever!

Spying! Really spying! Mus stroked his whiskers and thought devious thoughts, then pattered across the floor on crafty little feet. He slipped out into the corridor, concealing himself between an elephant's-foot umbrella stand and a pair of riding boots.

A knock came from the door that led to the street. Down the passageway came the thud of feet as a servant scuttled past. He opened the door and stared in puzzlement at the black-cloaked figure on the threshold.

"Madam? May I help you?"

The voice that answered was touched with a lilting foreign accent. A lady's voice.

"Indeed you may 'elp. I desire that you should pass this letter to your master." A slender white hand proffered an envelope and withdrew.

The servant clutched the letter and blinked. "Madam? That is all?"

Miriam's accent was perfect; almost Duncruighan, but not quite. "Indeed. I bid you a good night."

And with that, she swirled herself into the night. The servant looked at the letter for a moment, then carefully retired inside. He approached a lighted sitting room and knocked upon the post.

"Come!"

The servant silently passed the letter to a tall, imposing human man. Leymond; it had to be Leymond. He stood sparse and haughty, with the dark eyes of a killer. The servant departed, and Leymond moved back inside his room. Mus twittered merrily along the skirting board and quietly peeked around the door.

Mus skulked craftily beneath the curtains while Leymond opened up his mail. The envelope contained a letter and a small brass button from one of Retter's coats. Leymond carefully read the letter, stroking his mustache all the while.

" 'Retain this token, and pass it to the messenger who presents you with its twin.' How absurd!"

Leymond's face grew puzzled, and he ended up tapping the envelope against his teeth. "Who? Why now? What is she brewing?" He tossed the letter onto the desk. "Ah, well."

Mus watched and grew impatient. Drat you, sir! Put your letter away like a nice traitor and show me where you keep your secret papers! Mus combed his whiskers and glowered up at the nobleman. Finally Leymond finished reading, sat up and crossed over to his bookshelf. From the middle shelf, he plucked a thick Bible, the center of which had been hollowed out to form a clever storage space. Leymond dropped his letter and the button into place and closed the book. He dusted off his hands, doused the lights, and swiftly marched out of the room.

Leymond had an appointment with Retter in half an hour. The traitor would be gone for the evening. Mus leapt upon Leymond's chair and thence up to the desk, then pointed a finger at one of the candles.

"Pow!"

The candle instantly puffed aflame, and the mouse twirled his tail in glee. Now Mus needed only open up the window and signal Gus with a bobbing light. They would be in and out before Leymond's chair had even cooled! Mus fussed about opening the curtains and sat back to regard his work with pride.

Something slithered down the drawing-room chimney. Mus blinked in amazement as a pillbox landed softly on the floor. A tiny figure timidly nosed out into the light and sat blinking at the edges of the room. A mouse. A dainty female mouse with a face all filled with sadness. Mus sat stock-still and felt his breath catch in his throat.

Such eyes. . . . She had eyes like great starlit pools of darkness. Mus could have drowned in their infinite sorrow. Her fragile, wasted beauty almost made Mus cry out in alarm. There was a backpack on her shoulders! Mus straightened in astonishment, taking his hat into his hand. The female mouse gasped as she saw him, then cringed aside to flee. Mus felt the grip of terror; she mustn't go!

"Lady, wait!"

She jerked as if bitten, and then prepared to run. Mus almost sobbed in fright.

"Please! I beg you!"

She quivered in shock. Slowly she turned around, drawn in spite of herself, and their eyes met with a strange shock of recognition.The female mouse shrank fearfully away. "Who? What are you?"

Mus crept forward and made an awestruck little bow. "I am Mus of Kerbridge. I . . . I am at your service."

She swayed, and Mus darted forward as she almost swooned and fell. He held her in his arms as she trembled against his fur. At last she opened her lovely eyes, and doubt gave way to wonder.

"Real?" Her sweet voice quavered as her starlit eyes held Mus in their spell. One fine hand reached out to touch Mus's fur. "He said there was another. That there was one before Snatch and I!" Her breath grew ragged with panic. "Run! Oh, run, don't let him take you!"

The female mouse suddenly stiffened in shock and pain; her eyes unfocused as she spoke to midair. "No, master, I'm looking! I try—I really try—*Please!*" Her pleading eyes fixed on Mus. "*Help me!*"

A black, sinister presence slithered down into the fireplace. He paused and sniffed, raking at the carpet with his claws. "Ssssso—a tasty morsel?" The monster gazed at Mus, licked his fangs, and snapped his fingers at the lady mouse. "Out, vermin! Leave me to my prey!"

"No, Snatch! *Please!*"

A stoat! Long and deadly, the creature loomed like a giant above the mice. The lady mouse jerked and writhed in pain, helplessly staggering toward the fireplace. She gave Mus one last pleading glance, then fled into the dark.

"Prey! Ssssoft, ssweet prey! I will kill you, little moussse."

The stoat edged closer, expecting Mus's fear. To his shock, Mus simply stood his ground. The mouse reached back into the far corner of his mind and felt power settle into his grasp.

"Die, mouse!"

Mus stabbed a bolt of flame through the air. The stoat

screamed, and a blue shimmer sprang up between him and the fireball. Mus's bolt howled off the shimmering shield and smashed into the bookshelf, filling the room with a shower of dancing sparks. He gulped in astonishment. His bolt had skipped off! What was happening?

The bookcase caught alight with a sudden roar of flame. The stoat looked around and seemed amazed to find himself all in one piece. He screamed in rage and whirled toward the mouse.

No hero would ever turn and flee from a monstrous beast. Dwarfed by the massive stoat, Mus stood with his hat and plume on his head, and his needle sword firmly in his grasp. The little creature flourished his blade and stamped forward in a mighty lunge.

"En guarde!"

A needlepoint jabbed the stoat in the knee, and the creature gave a squeal of fright. He backed away, bared his fangs, and gathered for another pounce.

Mus settled his grip and extended in carte; he knew just how the attack would come, and was already moving as the stoat hurtled forward. Mus swayed gracefully sideways and let the monster's fangs howl past him. Shock jarred his arm and the stoat reeled aside with blood running from his hide.

"MUS!"

The window shattered, jagged glass exploding out onto the carpet as Gus the pixie leapt into the room. Mus looked about, but the stoat had fled into the dark.

"Gus! The Bible! Save the Bible!"

Mus sped to the fireplace; pillbox, stoat, and string had gone. He heard hooves running across the roofs as the Tormentor disappeared.

Gus! Gus could fly after them! He had to find the lady mouse; Mus tore back into the blazing study. The pixie had stuffed Leymond's secret papers down his jacket. He pounced on the mouse and gripped him tightly in one fist.

"Quick, Mus! Before the servants come!" The pixie took a running leap and flung himself out the second-story window. Gus swooped down onto the cobblestones and touched ground running, speeding swiftly off into the streets.

Mus tugged at Gus's sleeve. "No, Gus! Please! Go after them!" His voice was lost in the tumult of the fire. Mus fought to break free, but he was helpless. Gus fled down the alleyways and left the blazing house behind.

Somewhere far off in the night, a lady mouse wept inside her cage.

Mus sat on the edge of the table, listlessly staring into space. Behind him his friends were reading through the looted papers and chattering excitably.

"Carte blanche, messages, lists of names . . . " Retter leaned back in his chair and closed his eyes; for the first time in days he seemed truly relaxed. "We can bring him down. We'll need further proof—but at last we have a chance!"

Miriam turned to Mus with her eyes all shining full of triumph. "O Mus, thou'rt so clever! A spy, a thief, a hero! An enemy vanquished. . . ." Her voice trailed off. Mus sat staring off into the distance, not hearing a word that she said. Her face still flushed with excitement, Miriam leaned closer. "Mus?"

The mouse closed his eyes and let his voice drift quietly away. "She never even told me her name. . . ."

Miriam's face fell, and she reached out to touch her little friend. "We'll find her, Mus. Together."

Mus slowly shook his head. "No, she's gone. The city has swallowed her whole." He sighed and covered up his eyes. "If only thou could have seen her! Soft as dew on flowers. Trapped by an evil she could not begin to understand. He is killing her, Miriam. Every day she dies a little more."

"I-I'm sorry, Mus."

"I want to go back to the sorcerer for another lesson. I must know why my spell failed. Next time I'll be ready."

"I shall take thee, Mus."

Eyes still closed, Mus nuzzled her hand. "Thy problems come first. *Always*. We shall bring down Leymond and save thy father's troops; and when all is done, I shall ask thee to help me find this Pin-William."

Mus shivered. "And when we do—I will destroy him."

Chapter Thirteen
Lace and Steel

n the cloudless night, the royal palace blazed like a jewel amidst the soft cloth of its gardens. Light poured from the windows, spreading out past solemn ranks of torch-bearing pages, while the courtyard seemed filled by rank after rank of carriages. Proud horses pawed at the ground and snorted, their breath steaming on the chill night air.

Gallantly assisted by Torscha Retter, Miriam alighted from her coach. She spread out her magnificent ball gown and looked wonderingly about her.

Tonight Miriam seemed simply breathtaking. Her hair had been delicately curled into soft rolls and ringlets, trailing down across her ivory skin. The new ball gown swirled about her front hooves like an airy cloud. Miriam's cheery red hide was brushed to a glow; her tail lay bound with a bunch of silken roses, the soft stream of hair trailing down almost to the cobbles. She balanced human and horse in quiet, feminine beauty, and the stars were shamed by the gleam of her frightened eyes.

Miriam's small hands trembled slightly in Retter's grasp, and her weight shifted onto her rear hooves as she unconsciously prepared to turn and run. Retter tightened his grip, his strength flowing down into the girl's arms, and Miriam ceased her trembling. With surprising gentleness, Torscha reached out to draw Miriam's cloak up over her bare shoulders.

"Just stay quietly with me for a moment. There's no rush to enter."

Miriam breathed in the chill night air. She felt quite sick.

"I-I'm sorry." Miriam shivered. "I just can't . . ."

"Shhh—I understand. It's only a building, and the people inside are no better than thee. Indeed, thou'rt worth ten of any of them." Retter firmly held Miriam's arm, and the filly clutched to him for support. She mastered herself after long, slow minutes of courageous effort.

"I must thank thee, sir. Thou hast been most kind. Thou'rt a dear, dear friend."

The black stallion looked at her with his strange, deep eyes, and Miriam fondly ran her gaze over him. Retter stood huge and handsome at her side. Plain cloth and crisp new lace belied the complexity of the man beneath. His sword was exquisitely formed, and its grips well worn with use; beneath his lace collar there sparkled a steel gorget.

He noticed her stare, and Miriam looked hastily away, fixing her attention on the broad parade of steps before the palace. "Are Mother and the baron already here?"

"I see the general's carriage. Mus and Willy must have been here for a while."

"God help us, who knows what strife those two will get themselves into. I'm glad they delight in each other so." Miriam somehow managed a smile. "I don't think Willy has found a troublemaker of his own ilk in years. Mus simply adores him."

They stood in silence, both looking up at the palace doors. Retter finally gave Miriam's arm a squeeze. "Shall we go in?"

Miriam steeled herself and nodded; arm in arm they ascended the stairs.

"*Ladies and Gentlemen! Pray take your places for the imperial pavane!*"

The crowd bustled with excitement as dancing partners sought one another out. Half-horses hastened to fill the far end of the ballroom; by keeping their dancing separate they would avoid collisions with smaller, more delicate races.

The nobility of Duncruigh had gathered for the gala event of the year. The air hummed to the sound of laughter and gossip, and hard minds moved behind a sea of waving fans as ladies assessed their competition.

The crowd was stunning, an incredible riot of lavish costume. Every color imaginable was present in the form of silk and satin, velvet cloth and precious gems. Brocade and fur, smooth hide and tantalizing flesh made an ever-changing pattern of delight as the merrymakers flocked the hall. From their stand next to the musicians, the court illusionists wove charm after charm. Fantastic beasts and will-o'-the-wisps sprang into life to chase one another through the air above.

In the drawing rooms, the rattle of dice sounded above the cheers of the gambling crowds. Leymond lounged against the door frame, quizzing glass elegantly raised as he stared out across the promenade.

"M'dear? *Do* have a look at who has just arrived."

Lady Jessica was holding court, surrounded by her usual throng of four-legged admirers. She stood clad in a taut sheath of silk that lovingly hugged every luscious curve of her torso. Jessica brushed aside her twittering sycophants as though they were bothersome gnats. Her tail held high—granting her audience the barest glimpse of what they sought—she swirled over to Leymond's side.

"Yes, Rodger? There was something I can offer you? Or did you wish to make an offer to me?" Her smile sung sweet, mocking promises. Leymond grinned at her fondly, and then casually indicated the far side of the ballroom.

"Yes, my love. You will note that our foreign friend has arrived in all his martial splendor."

"Oh? How delicious!" Jessica moistened her lips and spied the huge stallion dancing out on the floor. Powerful, black, and forbidding, he cut a swath through the flotsam of mewling courtiers.

A flush spread across Jessica's ivory throat.

"Mmmmm—quite a morsel. But he's on the arm of that wretched bumpkin from Kerbridge! The chesty little idiot looks like she's going to faint clean away from fright."

"Hmmmm, well small harm in that."

Jessica thoughtfully waved her fan. "Lud, no, Rodger, but look at the way she stares at him! It positively makes my stomach churn."

Leymond tapped his chin with his quizzing glass. "Jessica darling, is Herr Retter to your taste?"

The woman smiled; she hungrily regarded Retter through hooded eyes. "Well, I shall have to taste him and see."

"Good! If you could prize him away from the company of that little cornflower, perhaps you might provide him with an evening's diversion."

Jessica smiled craftily. "Leading to . . . ?"

"A scene of some sort; I'm sure that you can engineer something. A duel would be nice. We really can't let him appear at parliament tomorrow. He's becoming tiresome."

Jessica's nostrils flared as she regarded her prey.

"Yes—easy enough. But not before . . ."

"Not before you've had your own entertainment. I quite understand."

The woman regarded him through lowered lashes.

"Why, Rodger—you know me so well!"

"Enjoy your evening, Jessica. *Enjoy*."

Miriam had taken the last two dances with friends—one with Torscha and one with Willy—when from the corner of her eye she spied her mother arrowing toward her, towing Lord Pumbleby in her wake. Whirling around, Miriam grabbed Retter and propelled him out onto the dance floor.

"Come! I can't let you idle all night." Miriam's voice brimmed over with feigned frivolity. "I do find the imperial pavane so marvelously stately, don't you?"

Retter allowed himself to be drawn out onto the boards. The music began, and the dancers gracefully bowed. His arm about her shoulders, Torscha held Miriam deliciously close as they paced out the elegant steps of the pavane. Their bodies swayed and stepped in perfect harmony.

Torscha bent his mouth close to Miriam's ear and raised his brows. "Miriam, thou canst not avoid thy mother's guest all night. She'll be most put out."

They gracefully whirled and reversed direction; pressing herself back against Torscha's chest, Miriam whispered in reply. "Faith! I have no wish to annoy Mother. I-I suppose I must stick to my purpose. But that *Pumbleby* is not to be borne. He's visited thrice this week; he stares at me as if he sees right through my dress!"

Retter's arms were comforting. "I don't like you to be near him."

"Can you see any way to rescue me?"

"Yes; if I succeed tomorrow, then you can tell him to go to hell."

Miriam sighed; there lay the key to it all. Hooves prancing and flashing, Miriam took Torscha's hands up over her shoulders as she led the way into the second round.

"Where's Mus gotten to?"

Retter's breath hung warm within her hair. "He and Willy are watching the experts play cards. I charged Mus with keeping Willy out of the game. I imagine our little friend is scoffing at the tactics being used." He swayed into a turn, his timing smooth and perfect. "Lud! If I had the money I'd stake the rodent myself!"

Miriam gave a rueful smile. "And here's thee with money that thou dare not touch! How much did thy parliament give thee to purchase arms? Four thousand, was it not?"

"If the money were mine, pray be sure I would hazard it."

Miriam kept looking over her shoulder at the crowd near the doors. Her scowl deepened as she whirled into a stately promenade. "That woman!"

Retter blinked in confusion. "Thy pardon?"

"That wretched creature from the theater. She hasn't taken her eyes off thee all night!"

"Truly?" Retter turned to look, but Miriam firmly tugged him around.

"Yes, *truly*." Miriam's eyes were hurt. "She looks at thee as if she wanted to *devour* thee!"

"Thou'rt imagining things."

"Indeed? Well, keep thee away from her. She's a woman and therefore not to be trusted."

Retter laughed as they spun and bowed; the music had ended. "I'll take thy advice, then. I respect thy good opinion too much to risk being *devoured*."

They linked arms and turned to leave the dance floor. Miriam froze as she saw her mother waiting on the sidelines with Pumbleby. Retter resolutely led Miriam across in their direction. "Come. It seems we must both attend to our duties. I have backroom politics to bestir, and thou hast an admirer to suffer. . . ."

Miriam disconsolately shuffled off into her mother's clutches; Retter watched her go, feeling strangely uncomfortable. The thought of Miriam in the company of a prospective husband left

Torscha feeling sad and empty. He stared after her for long minutes, stamping fitfully with his hooves.

A sensual caress of fingertips suddenly rippled down his spine. In his disturbed state, the touch sent a thrilling shiver chasing through his hide. Retter whirled in confusion and found himself looking into a pair of deep, dilated eyes.

Her face was a perfect oval, and her lips were full and moist. They were parted as though in breathless anticipation, and her long hair fell to half conceal a taunting, hungry gaze. The half-horse mare had an equine body shaded a subtle smoky gray, and her tail arched high in invitation as she rubbed at Retter's side. Her voice came straight from an erotic dream; soft and breathy, it caressed along the nerves like an exploring hand. "It pains me to see you standing so forlorn. May I lighten your evening, Colonel Retter?"

Retter straightened his shoulders and backed away from her touch. "I fear you have the advantage of me, madam."

The woman laughed; a clear, feminine sound like the dance of tiny bells. "Oh, Colonel, please forgive me! I've admired you so long from afar that I'd quite forgotten we are not yet introduced." Her fan slowly spread itself wide. "You must think me forward. Well—that I am. I am Lady Jessica Perwryth." She held his eyes in appeal. "I am *bored,* Colonel! *Do* take pity on me. . . ."

Retter bowed, preserving his vaunted dignity; unfortunately this brought his face closer to Jessica's bosom. His nostrils flared helplessly as he drank in the rich, seductive scent of her skin. "Madam, I-I'm pleased to make your acquaintance." He cleared his throat uncomfortably, and his eyes automatically sought Miriam in the crowd. Lady Jessica noticed the direction of his gaze and gave a smile.

"Proud, stubborn. . . . She has a certain country charm. But true pleasure should be sophisticated, don't you agree?"

Retter scowled, unsure whether Miriam had just been insulted. "Madam, I do not know what you mean."

"Oh, come now, Colonel. I'm sure a man as *experienced* as yourself knows how to appreciate the finer things in life. Why quaff cider when you can have champagne?"

The huge stallion drew himself up straight. "I regret that you are mistaken, madam. I desire neither cider nor champagne tonight. I fear I must bid you a good evening."

"It will be a *very* good evening, Colonel. Have no fear."

Retter stalked off through the throng of lesser mortals like a

god of blackened steel. Jessica grinned and looked around to meet
the eyes of the anguished country lass. She saw the girl whirl away,
her fists bunching, and Jessica's mocking laughter raked the air
with scorn.

Oh, wonderful! It was just too, too perfect!

It was all going to be *so* easy. Retter clearly yearned for the lass.
The fool stallion would be like putty in her hands.

The half-horse Lord Algion was the finest swordsman in the
capital, almost as good as Leymond. Jessica had kept him hanging
on in anticipation of her favors, and now seemed to be the time to
use him.

His Majesty King Firined the First of Duncruigh had lost yet
again. He coolly threw in his cards as Leymond raked in the scattered pile of golden coins. Sir Rodger Leymond seemed rather
pleased with his win.

"Lud, Sire, this doesn't seem to be your night!"

The king eased back onto his elbow and eyed his enemy with
absolute neutrality. "Faith, Leymond, you're the deftest gamesman
I've ever seen. I only play with you in the hope of one day seein'
you receive your just desserts."

The king's voice was touched with a lazy, affected drawl. The
young man sat at the center of the room, dressed in a studied,
rakehelly elegance. King Firined the First, implacable enemy of
Nantierre, waved a scented kerchief underneath his nose and gazed
out at the swirling crowds of his admirers.

Hovering unhappily outside the edge of the throng, Sir
William Merle watched the fall of cards like a drunkard scenting
wine. His chestnut hide twitched fitfully and his weight shifted
back and forth from hoof to hoof.

Mus stirred inside Willy's breast pocket, tugging at his signal-
thread, and the stallion retreated to the shadows to speak into his
coat.

"Yes, old chap? You wanted something?"

The faint little voice rang rich with disgust. "They play like
idiots! Can't any of them remember the deck? They all act as if
they've forgotten which cards have been played and which
haven't!"

"Oh, Mus! There are seventy-eight cards in the pack, and it might be cycled through two or three times in a game. How can anyone wemember who played what?"

"*I* can! I remember everything."

"Oh, bosh!"

"Don't be silly, Willy. The cards currently on the bottom of their discard pile are the Page of Wands, the Page of Pentacles, the Seven of Pentacles, the Ten of Swords . . ."

"Really?" Merle was quite incredulous.

"Really. Go and check."

Frowning, Willy shouldered his way through to the card table, where the king caught sight of him and smiled.

"Willy! Why, Willy, where have you been? Skulkin' in the shadows and avoidin' us? We couldn't wait for you. Are you sittin' in next game?"

Sir William bowed elaborately, pantomiming regret.

"Lud, no, Your Majesty! I have sworn on my mother's grave that I have pwayed my wast."

"Aaah, that country lass you've been keepin' company with has reformed you!"

To the ladies' amusement, Willy actually blushed. "Nay, sir!"

The king smiled sorrowfully. "No funds again? Really, Willy, you *must* be more careful. You keep miraculously appearin' with fortunes and then losin' 'em!"

Sir William laughed ruefully and gave a sigh. Across the table, Leymond idly stretched himself. Sir Rodger never refused a bet; his love of gambling was as wild and reckless as his passion for swords. Dueling or gaming, he loved to bet all upon a toss of chance.

Leymond looked at William with calculating eyes.

"We shall play for *real* stakes later, Sir William. There's nothing quite like the thrill of hazarding all on the whim of the deck, don't you agree?"

Willy licked his lips. "Such—such things are behind me now, sir."

"Indeed? A pity; I had so looked forward to finding an opponent with a love of risk. His Majesty plays a more cautious game than our type of man."

"So I see." Willy idly picked up the discard deck and thumbed through the bottom-most cards. Page of Wands, Page of Pentacles, Seven of Pentacles, Ten of Swords . . . Willy's breath hissed in surprise.

Oh, my God!

Willy tried to hide his excitement. "Well, sir, I might just take you up on your offer later on in the evening. . . ."

A steely hand descended onto his shoulder, and Retter's cool voice boomed in from behind. "Pray excuse us, Your Majesty. Sir William has urgent business elsewhere."

The king nodded in approval. "I believe he has. Off you go and attend to it, Willy."

William was propelled out of the room and into a parlor. Retter closed the door behind them and glowered down at his young friend.

"Watch, Willy, but don't play. I should not have to remind you what happens when you play."

William clattered forward, his hooves skittering and eyes bright. "No, Torscha! Listen, this time there's an angle! I could bweed Leymond dwy! Mus?" He eagerly opened up his pocket. "Mus old fellow, come out here and talk to the Colonel." After a struggle of motion in William's pocket, Mus's handsome little face appeared.

"Good evening, Colonel! I trust you're enjoying yourself?"

"Perfectly well, thank you. Do you approve of the ball?"

The mouse looked back toward the door in awe. "The king! I've been in the same room as the *king!* He seems ever so nice. I do wish that he were wearing his crown, though. Why isn't he wearing it, do you think?"

Retter brushed at his beard and kept his face perfectly serious. "I expect that he only wears it at ceremonies, Mus. It must be terribly heavy."

"Ahhh—yes, of course." The mouse pondered these words of wisdom.

Willy fairly danced in excitement. "Never mind that! Look you, Mus can remember cards! He can memorize the sequence of a whole deck, can't you Mus?"

Retter extended a hand and the mouse climbed up into his palm. The little fellow energetically scratched his ear with one elegant, spindly foot.

"Better! Oh, so good to feel the air on one's fur! Willy's been keeping licorice allsorts in that pocket! I smell like a piece of furry candy."

Willy was about to explode. "Mus, tell him! Tell him about the cards!"

Retter's darkly handsome face was lit by curiosity. "Mus, can you really remember so well?"

The mouse seemed puzzled. "Why should I forget anything that I've seen? I don't understand."

"Well—the order of cards in a pack and such."

Mus looked up in bewilderment. "But Torscha, it's just like reading! I would never forget something that I've seen." He seemed hurt. "Just because I'm small doesn't mean that I'm stupid."

"No, no, Mus! I meant no insult. I was not implying that you lacked something that we had, but rather that you had something that we lacked. None of us could lay claim to such a memory."

Retter settled his massive rear body on the bench. "Thou reads a lot of plays. Hast thou read *The Laurel Bearer* by Walter Nandson?"

The mouse sat up on his haunches, waving his hands excitedly as he spoke. "Of course! A beguiling main character. Proud, honorable, at odds with his own nature. He reminded me somewhat of yourself."

Torscha blanched. "Er—quite. In any case, can you quote me the last speech of Act Three?"

Willy Merle leaned breathlessly forward. The little rodent closed his eyes and smiled, his chisel teeth gleaming. Mus composed himself and then drew on an air of tragedy.

"Ahem:
If this be love, then I shall have none of it.
This sad affliction twists a man into a mewling, weeping thing.
A tragic debilitation that ere produced more sighs than joy."

"Incredible!" Torscha shook his head in disbelief. "And you've read it but once?"

The mouse idly toyed with his fingers. "Well—yes. Once is enough. I told thee I was clever!"

Willy leapt forward and fairly crowed in triumph.

"You see? Incredible! Leymond can never refuse a bet. With Mus to advise me, I could win! I know it!"

Mus turned patiently to Sir William. "O Willy, don't be silly. Unless I were the one playing, you'd surely make a botch of it. There's more to cards than remembering a lot of boring numbers. I could beat any one of those ninnies in there at any game they choose to play." Mus brushed at his fur. "I will not play for you; you'd only lose money. You are one of my closest friends in the whole world, Willy, and it's in your best interests that I refuse."

Willy hung his head in shame. "I-I suppose you're right. I'm sorry. It's just the cards. . . ."

Torscha laid a hand on Willy's shoulder. "I know. Come along, we'll go out and mingle. Frielle was looking a little lonely. Perhaps we can cheer her up, eh?"

William bowed his head in resignation. Mus bundled himself into Retter's pocket and pulled open the buttonhole to afford himself a decent view.

"Are you comfortable, Mus?"

"Fairly so."

"Well, let us go then."

Trying hard to maintain an air of calm, Miriam painfully endured Pumbleby's attempts to be witty and engaging. Her goodwill gradually abraded away as the huge, sweaty nobleman pressed his attentions ever closer.

In a purple satin doublet, Pumbleby looked like an overripe plum stuffed too tight into its skin. They danced out in the main ballroom, and Lord Pumbleby's clammy hands held Miriam far too close as they paced through the steps of another pavane. Pumbleby took the opportunity to whisper thickly in Miriam's ear.

"Lud, me dear! You b-b-become more beautiful with each passing day!"

Oh, God . . . "Why, Lord Pumbleby, how . . . how sweet of you to say it. But I am really *quite* plain, and content enough to be so."

"No, my d-dear! You mustn't say it! Your charms are . . . considerable." Miriam could feel his eyes slide across her cleavage and belly to rest upon her silky rear. He licked his fleshy lips in hunger. "Quite considerable."

Miriam shivered involuntarily. Pumbleby slid his hand down Miriam's back, his clammy fingers digging possessively into her hide. The feel of his flesh pressed against her own was utterly loathsome; Miriam frantically pulled away from him. The stately flow of the dance broke in confusion as she skittered backward in alarm.

"Sorry! Oh, forgive me!"

She fought her way to the sidelines, feeling quite sick, and leaned against a wall for support. Her skin crawled at the memory of Pumbleby's touch.

A gentle feminine hand laid itself on her shoulder, and she caught the distinctive tang of Frielle's perfume.

"Miriam! Are you all right, darlin'?"

Miriam kept her face turned toward the wall. "I . . . Yes!" She choked on her own words. "I'm fine!"

A sudden blunder of movement came from behind as Lord Pumbleby struggled from the dance. "D-D-Damsel Jerrick! Whatever is the matter?"

Frielle shielded Miriam with an arm about her shoulders. "Lord Pumbleby, please excuse us. Poor Miriam is quite faint. We'll just be sittin' ourselves down for a moment. I have some smelling salts on me."

The bloated half-horse tried to press forward. "I shall accompany you!"

"No! No, my lord! We'll be fine. I'll return her to you in due course, have no fear."

Disappointed, Pumbleby edged close; he ran his eyes over Miriam's trembling body.

"Well, Miriam. I await your return with . . . *anticipation.*"

Steering Miriam firmly by the elbow, Frielle led her friend aside into one of the many sitting rooms. Shut off from the music and the buzz of the crowd, Miriam visibly wilted. Hitching up her skirts, Frielle fished out a pocket flask and passed it over to her. "Whiskey. Brings the roses to your knees. Last of Papa's own brew." She sighed. "Some Nantierran owns the stills now."

Miriam knocked back a mouthful without so much as a blink. Frielle thoughtfully pursed her lips, then took her own turn at the bottle. They sat together in silence for a while, each thinking her own private thoughts.

Frielle rose and quietly clopped over to the mirror that stood against one wall. Finally she spoke into the quiet, her musical voice hushed and gentle. "I'm an heiress; did you know that? A real live heiress. Last of my line should Papa perish in the prison they've stuck him in." Her mind edged away from the thought. "I had me someone once. Someone of my own." She sighed miserably. "I was hurt, Miriam. Hurt so my soul bled white."

Frielle seemed suddenly embarrassed and quickly turned away

from the mirror. "Aaaw, I don't know what I'm tryin' to say. Are you all right, love?"

The half-horse concealed her face behind the soft curtain of her hair. "I *hate* him! He's a bastard and I hate him!"

"What happened, love? Can ye say?"

Miriam's knuckles whitened about her fan. "He's so *sure.* In his mind he's mounting me already. The way he touches me makes me feel *sick!* When I compare that *animal* to-to . . ."

"To whom, darlin'?"

Miriam swallowed. "Torsch—Colonel Retter might win tomorrow! Then I'd be free! I could have whomever I want."

Frielle cupped Miriam's chin in her cool fingers, forcing her to lock eyes. "And just exactly who do you want?" Frielle sat down beside her and passed the whiskey flask. "It may be none o' my business, Miriam, but I'm your friend, and I'm an islander, so I'll stick me hoof in anyway. You love someone else; so go to him an' be damned!"

Miriam jerked, then looked up with wild, startled eyes.

"Love? *No!* I-I'm not in love with anybody. . . ."

"Drink! The whiskey'll put sense into ye! Stone-cold sober you're as blind as a bat. Fer 'tis as plain as the freckles on your nose that you're quite hopelessly in love!"

Miriam stared in disbelief; her lips pursed in a little **O** of surprise, and her face blanked in an expression of wonder. "*Torscha?*"

Frielle raised her flask in salute. "Aaaaah, that's more like it! See, you do get there eventually!"

Miriam leapt up onto all four hooves, absently knocking over her chair. The girl blinked, dragged in a breath, and came suddenly alive. "My God! He needs me tomorrow! He has to know!" Miriam's hooves jittered. She tried to make a break for the door, but the little satyr barred her way.

"Hush! Sit!" Her folded fan pointed straight at Miriam's nose. "You're not rushin' off half-cocked. You stay here until y've thought this through!" The faun shook her head scoldingly. "The thought of it! Now then, girlie, since our sights are set on M'sieur Retter, we must think. Firstly, what about your money problem? Toss it?"

Miriam swayed. "Torscha will win tomorrow! I trust him. Mama—Mama will understand."

"Good; just as long as you think of it all now."

"Pumbleby. I must talk to him." The half-horse ground her fan between her hands. "Lud! The lustful toad needs a good skinning. It will be a pleasure to give him a good piece of my mind!"

"That's a girl! So I suppose . . ."

There was a sudden knock at the door, and Lord Pumbleby's thick voice drifted through from the other side.

"Miriam, my dear, are you recovered?"

Miriam held up a hand to prevent Frielle from answering.

"No—let him in. As long as he's here, I might as well take the opportunity to speak with him." Miriam rose, rolling back her sleeves. "Thank you, Frielle. You're a good friend."

"Ha! Sure 'n you always knew it!"

The little satyr unlocked the door, which fairly burst open as Pumbleby surged into the room. The haughty satyr lady blocked his charge. Primly gathering up her skirts, Frielle pushed past him and disappeared in a frothing wake of lace.

Miriam stood alone against her foe. Pumbleby waddled forward, his fat flanks heaving as he moved to Miriam's side.

"You appear refreshed."

He tried to press close, but Miriam deliberately kept her distance. She was no longer trying to be pleasant, and the change in attitude surprised him.

"I am well recovered, Lord Pumbleby. I think perhaps it is time that you and I had a little talk."

The fat lord lost his ingratiating smile. He turned and locked the door, pocketing the key, then licked his puffy lips and fixed Miriam beneath his hungry eyes.

"Yes, my dear. Perhaps it is high time indeed . . ."

Lady Jessica Perwryth paced slowly into the deserted library. She stood posed against the firelight, highlights tracing golden fingers across her luscious flanks. Jessica looked back over one perfect shoulder, her eyes taunting. "Well, Colonel? Are you coming in?"

A glass ewer of iced punch stood on a small table by the door, and Jessica playfully ran her finger around the rim. Retter entered and stood by the closed door, his face arrogant and impatient, sharp and strong; Jessica felt a thrilling rush of anticipation as Retter folded his arms and scowled.

"Now, madam, perhaps you would care to tell me this information that you feel will be so important tomorrow?"

The exquisite woman swished her tail. "Fa, Colonel! Can't we just enjoy the quiet? I do so love a moment's peace. Surely I am not *so* unbearable?" Jessica breathed heavily, her smoldering eyes full of promise. She brushed past Retter, trailing soft fingertips along his hide.

"Mmmmm, Colonel! You are a *handsome* man! I find those effeminate courtiers quite sickening, don't you?" She sighed. "A real soldier. A *hero!*" Her wandering hands stroked their way up to the hard, taut muscles of Retter's backside.

With an agile stamp of his hooves, Torscha sidestepped away. "Lady Perwryth, is there any purpose to all this nonsense, or may I rejoin my companions?"

"Ooooo now, Colonel! Always so hasty." Jessica looked pained. "I hope you are not always so hasty to finish things." She ran her fingers teasingly along his spine; Torscha irritably reached around and snatched her hands.

"Stop that!"

Catching Jessica's wrists only brought her closer; she pressed against him, looking up into his face with wanton eyes. "Why, stop what, Colonel?"

"*That,* madam. I fear I shall have to go."

The woman radiated disappointment, then wilted unhappily. "Oh, Colonel. Dear me, I had *so* wanted to get to know you better. Well, perhaps I had best tell you your precious information." She nestled back against him. "Bend down then; I shall have to whisper."

Retter sighed impatiently and bent closer; Jessica stood on the tips of her hooves and wound her arms about his neck, her breath drifting hot against his flesh. Torscha found his nose nuzzling Jessica's throat. He breathed in the scent, his pulse now hammering in his breast.

Jessica nipped his ear. "Aaah! *That's* better, Colonel! *Much* better!" She clutched at him, purring lustfully. "Touch me, Colonel! Hold me!"

"M-Madam! You are being forward!"

"Don't be a fool! I *want* you, Colonel, and I intend to have you. We are alone, and you are a beautiful, *virile* man. There are no commitments, no problems; just here and now. Just you and I, Colonel."

She pressed forward to kiss him, but Retter jerked back, fighting her hypnotic scent. Jessica scolded him as she pulled open her stays. "Colonel, you can't pretend you don't want me!"

"I do not want you!"

Jessica had backed her victim against the wall and began to press herself against his skin. "You want me—I can feel it. Or . . . you want *someone.*"

"No!"

"Aaaaah, the country girl! Our tasty little morsel from Kerbridge!" The woman's eyes gave a predatory gleam. "You want her, don't you?"

"No! I . . ."

"My! You *love* her!" Her voice cut like steel; Jessica's hooks had gouged home, and now she twisted them. "You'll never have her. She is marked for another. She will marry, and you will be left *alone.*"

Torscha fought for breath, and Jessica rubbed against him.

"Would you like to have her, Colonel? To feel her beneath you?" Jessica felt her own pulse hammering in her throat as she prepared to take her prey. "You want her? You want your lovely Miriam? Well, tonight she can be *yours.*" Her hands clutched at him. "I can be whatever you want me to be! Take me like you'd take her!" She pressed his hand to her breast. "Take me, Colonel! Mount your sweet Miriam. I can be her for you, Colonel.

"I can be *her.*"

Pumbleby narrowed his eyes, casting his mask of pleasantry aside. "So, my dear. You think you can p-play the coy lady, eh?"

Miriam stood surrounded by the sweeping skirts of her dress as she raked him with her cold, proud eyes. "Kindly unlock the door. I think you should leave."

Pumbleby chuckled cruelly, his red eyes gleaming. "Oh, perfect! Tall, straight, and haughty–regal as a queen! " He rubbed his huge hands together. "No, my dear, it is not that simple. And no, I am not leaving *quite* yet."

Miriam glanced down beneath his swaying belly, her eyes suddenly growing wide. She reeled backward, sickened by the sight, and Pumbleby laughed aloud.

"Frightened! I *knew* you would be frightened!" He shuddered in hunger. "You are mine, my little bird. All mine. If you want my wealth to save your wretched father, then you must first p-pay; and that payment begins *tonight*."

Miriam snarled and thrust her hands beneath her skirts, reaching for her pistols. She froze in fright as a sharp dagger's edge flicked against her throat.

Pumbleby smiled. "No, my dear, we shall have no truck with your little toy guns. I *dare* you to scream!" His head twitched, and a bubble of spittle appeared in the corner of his mouth. "Do you think I wouldn't kill you? Why not! You are mine! Mine to break or use as I choose."

Miriam shook. "You-You can't get away with this!"

"But I can, my dear. I can! You dare tell no one. And remember—I am not a well man. I will kill you unless you please me." He drew in a shuddering breath. "Now drop the pistols. *Carefully!* I wouldn't want to slip and rip open that perfect throat."

Terrifyingly aware of the blade at her neck, Miriam carefully drew out her pistols and cast them aside.

Pumbleby's head twitched once more, and his breathing became ragged. The razor-sharp steel caressed her cheek. "And now, my dear—turn around and take a nice firm grip on the mantelpiece."

Miriam's eyes flicked left and right in panic, but came back to the steel at her throat. She trembled, then turned her back on her enemy and laid her hands on the mantelpiece.

"That's right! There's no need for this to be unpleasant." Pumbleby swallowed as the muscles of Miriam's hindquarters bunched and tightened. His eyes never left her backside.

Miriam tensed. *Just a little bit closer, you bastard!*

"Oh, you are so beautiful! So perfectly unspoiled. . . ." Pumbleby stepped closer as he prepared to heave his bulk up onto her. "Now, let us to business. . . ."

"RYAAAAAH!"

Hooves flashed as Miriam lashed out with an explosive double kick. Steel-shod hooves cracked into Pumbleby's sagging flesh. The girl shrieked in rage and kicked again, this time feeling the ghastly snap of shattering bone.

Pumbleby reeled back in agony. Miriam leapt over the fallen body, her tail streaming out behind her as she fled. The girl's front hooves crashed into the door, splintering the flimsy wood, and

Miriam burst out into the corridor. Frielle and Willy stared in shock as Miriam galloped down the halls leaving bloody hoofprints in her wake.

"Torscha! Where's Torscha?"

Willy blundered forward. "Miriam, what's wrong?"

"Torscha!" Miriam rammed William aside and fought for breath in great, ragged sobs. "Where is he?"

"The library—Miriam, wait!"

Miriam galloped off down the corridor, smashing an ivory table as she ran. Her friends blinked, and then tore off in pursuit as fast as their hooves could carry them.

Mus sat inside Retter's pocket with his ears standing tall in disbelief. The colonel couldn't! He wouldn't! Not now that he knew he loved Miriam. . . .

Jessica pressed herself up against her chosen victim. "I can be your Miriam for you!"

Torscha coldly prized the woman's arms free, and Lady Perwryth blinked in disbelief.

"You want me! You-you can't refuse me!" Jessica paled in outrage. "No one can refuse *me!* Look at yourself!"

The stallion sadly shook his head. "Yes, madam. My body wants you, but my heart is its master. I thank you for opening my eyes. You are quite right: I love her. Nor shall I ever betray her." He grabbed Jessica's arms and held her firmly distant. "If you will excuse me, madam, I must declare myself to her. You may look for your entertainment elsewhere."

The door suddenly burst open.

"Torscha! Help me, I . . ."

Torscha's and Jessica's heads whirled; Miriam Jerrick stood squarely in the doorway, and her face drained white as she took in the scene.

"Torscha . . . ?"

There Torscha stood, with another woman in his arms. Miriam's world suddenly collapsed about her. Retter shoved Lady Jessica aside, and his eyes went wide with shock.

"No! Miriam, it's not . . ."

With an incoherent scream of rage, Miriam snatched up the

ewer of punch and hurled a great sheet of slush at the other
woman. Drowned and frozen, Jessica squealed in outrage, and then
in fright as the porcelain jug whirled toward her nose. She ducked
aside just in time. The pitcher shattered against the far wall, and
Miriam charged in after it. Jessica dashed out the door as if all the
hounds of hell were snapping at her heels.

Miriam returned to the doorway and stood staring at Torscha
with wounded eyes. "I needed you, you *bastard!*" She whirled and
left him, too proud to cry until she had won the far end of the corridor.

Mus scrabbled up out of Torscha's pocket and tugged at the
man's mustache. Retter stood like a man who had just been shot.
"Torscha? Torscha!"

No answer. *Damn!*

Willy came clattering in the door, looking more lost each
instant. Mus pranced and waved from Retter's coat. "Willy! *Oi!*
Willy—quick, take me to Miriam!"

The young cavalier reached out to take the mouse, when
Torscha suddenly came back to life. He wildly seized Willy's arms.
"Willy, I didn't! I-I did the right thing! I love her! I couldn't
betray her!"

"Torscha, just what the hell is going on?"

Mus had clambered up onto William's shoulders. "Willy—
now! Come along. I must find Miriam and tell her!" The mouse
pointed a tiny authoritarian finger at Torscha. "*You.* Stay put! I
will go set Miriam straight, and then you both have some talking
to do. She'll listen to me."

Mus irritably swatted at William's neck with his tail. "Don't
stand there gawking! *Move!*"

Willy whirled and raced back out into the corridor.

"Mus, for pity's sake, pwease tell me what is going on!"

"Disaster! But I can fix it—now hurry!"

Chapter Fourteen
Final Play

esolated, Miriam listlessly slumped in one of the small parlors while Lady Jerrick and Frielle tried their best to calm her. Miriam was utterly inconsolable, barely even paying attention as Mus paced back and forth in anguish.

"Oh, why did I leave thee alone? It's all my fault!"

Miriam's hand stirred. She apathetically reached out to stroke her loyal little friend. "O mouse of my heart—it was no one's fault, least of all thine."

"I would have sheared Pumbleby's damned head off! Never thou doubt it!"

"My brave Mus. At least *thou* art dependable." Miriam rested her head in her hand, looking quite sick. "I've never felt such a fool. I would have laid my heart at his feet. *All I wanted was for him to love me. . . .*"

Lady Jerrick reeled, her mind still overrun with visions of the near-rape of her daughter. She blinked as she heard her daughter speak of love. "Y-Your heart? Give it to whom, darling? I don't understand. . . ."

Mus paced theatrically up and down the table. "Torscha Retter of course! She loves him, and he loves her!"

"Ha!" Miriam hardly had the energy to be scornful. "He loves me, does he? That's why he was about to mount that slut from the court."

"No, no! You didn't see!" The mouse danced with anxiety. "Please, Miriam—he loves you! I was there! I *heard!* Torscha refused her. She used mating scent on him, but he refused her for love of you! You burst in just as he was throwing her off."

Miriam's voice grew bitter. "Oh, indeed?"

"Yes! Miriam, what's wrong?"

"There's no need to lie for him, Mus." Miriam looked away. "Hasn't he even enough spine to come here and concoct his own falsehoods?"

Mus's jaw hung open. "Lie?"

"Don't invent excuses for him, Mus. 'Tis loyal of thee, but I know him for what he is now."

The mouse stared up at her with wounded eyes.

"Thou-Thou'st never called me a liar before. I could never lie to thee. I love thee"

"Ha! As Torscha loves me?"

On the verge of tears, the heartbroken little mouse backed away. His whole world had crumbled. "We shall prove it to thee. We shall prove we love thee. Love doesn't lie." Mus crept over to Frielle. "Please, my lady—could you take me to Colonel Retter. I think I know what to do."

Frielle carefully carried Mus from the room. Lady Jerrick hung her head in shame. "How could thee? That little creature worships the ground thou walkest on."

Miriam remained sulking in silence.

Her mother fought her own battle with her conscience. "Miriam—thine own pain does not give thee the right to hurt others. If thou must affix blame, blame thy mother. I encouraged Pumbleby. I forced him upon thee."

Miriam nestled close. "No. No one could know what sort of man he was. There's no blame."

They sat together in silence for a long while. A clock ticked loudly on the mantelpiece, but neither woman kept track of the time.

Sir William Merle suddenly clattered into the room with a drawn sword in his hand. He was closely followed by the Jerricks' castle sergeant and an imposing female harpy from the Royal Guard. "Still no sign of him, my lady. Pumbleby has definitely fled. His coach has gone." The wiry young stallion tightly gripped his sword. "God's blood! I 'll rip out that devil's heart for this!"

"Thank you, Willy." Miriam shuddered. "You're a good protector. A good friend."

Willy seemed abashed. "Thank you, my lady."

"Willy, have you seen Mus?" Lady Jerrick wiped stale tears

back from her eyes. "He has Frielle carrying him about in full view
of everybody. He's most upset. I fear he may not be thinking quite
straight."

"No!" The young stallion was shocked. "But-but everyone will
see him! Why is he doing this?"

Miriam suddenly jerked upright, her face flushed with shame.
"*Mus!* Oh, Mus, my darling, what did I say?" She frantically
sought Willy's eyes. "Oh, God, what have I done?"

"Lady?"

"Willy! I-I love him! I love them both!" She leapt to her
hooves. "Where is he?"

The evening's events were passing William by. "Where is
who?"

"*Torscha!* Quick! Where is he?"

"I can't say, Miriam. He was in a terrible state when last I saw
him. . . . "

"Oh, no!" Miriam cried, suddenly all a-panic. "Find them! Stop
them, Willy! They're going to do something stupid!"

Sir William stood quite still in shock, then sadly stared at
Miriam. "*Torscha.* That was what you meant, wasn't it? You love
Torscha."

"What? Well, yes—of course I do! Whom else?"

"Yes. Whom else." Willy swiftly turned and spoke without
looking back. "I'll find them. I promise."

And with that, he paced slowly out into the hall.

The king wavered between speechless shock and rapturous
delight. He stared at the dapper little creature on the table and
laughed for the sheer wonder of the moment. Mus bowed low, elegantly sweeping his little hat before him. His voice was by far the
loudest sound in the chamber.

"Mus of Kerbridge, your most dutiful subject, Your Majesty."

King Firined stood and examined this paragon through his
quizzing glass. "Are you indeed, sir?" He looked around at the assembled courtiers before turning back to the mouse. "I'm most glad to hear
it! My word, I thought the world had quite run out of surprises!"

The royal physician pulled at his beak of a nose. "Well, Sire,
there is the *gannet.* . . ." His limp interjection was swallowed up in

the general awe.

Mus looked gravely up at his king. "Pray forgive the intrusion, Your Majesty. I have no invitation, but I *so* wanted to meet you. I am the—the close friend of Lady Barbara and Damsel Miriam Jerrick of Kerbridge, Sir William Merle, and Colonel-Citizen Retter. Oh! And Baron Vardvere. I hope you're not angry at my presumption, Sire."

The king sat down once more, propped his chin on his hand and stared. His eyes shone with childish astonishment. "Angry? Ha! M' dear—er—*Mus,* I'm positively delighted. Delighted, sir! Retter, why on earth did y' wait so long to introduce us?"

The gigantic foreigner twitched in agitation; something about his clear blue eyes seemed reckless, almost self-destructive. He had an air of wildness that seemed quite at odds with his usual self-control. "This is our first true opportunity, Majesty."

"Quite so!" The king shook his head in wonder. "So, Retter, tell me of our friend Mus. You must give me an introduction!" King Firined brushed at his fashionable goatee. "He seems an honest fellow!"

Frielle stood miserably in Retter's shadow. She had followed along in Torscha's wake, hoping to prevent her friends from doing anything foolish, but had been too late. Now the whole world knew about Mus, and this was only the start of whatever they were up to. The little satyr chewed her knuckles and wished the night might be only an awful dream. . . .

King Firined had listened in fascination to Retter's account of Mus's heroics, and seemed duly impressed. "Well, Mus, it seems you have the honor of being my smallest subject! 'Tis a pleasure to meet any heroic gentleman. Pray, sit beside me and let us talk awhile."

The mouse seemed nervous. "I thank you for your kindness, Majesty. I have long dreamt of meeting you." The mouse flicked his eyes around the crowd, resting his gaze briefly upon Leymond. "Pray, Sire, may I beg a moment of *private* conversation with you? Uh—I would not presume, except that . . ."

"Presume! Faith, fellow—I'm quite atcha service!" King Firined extended one immaculately manicured hand. "Mount, sir! Mount, and we shall retire to my private study for a while. I'm sure we have much to speak about."

Leymond stepped hastily forward. "Majesty! Is this wise? We know nothing about this creature!"

The king gave the nobleman a wry look. "Concern for my

safety from *you,* Leymond? My, this *is* a night of surprises." The king looked levelly at his enemy. "Faith, Leymond, I have long smelled a rat at court. A mouse should be a positive relief!"

And with that, King Firined bore his surprise guest out of the room.

"Have you found them?" Miriam halted at the top of the palace stairs, her hooves clattering in agitation. She made a dark, frantic silhouette against the doors.

Below her on the gravel drive, Sir Willy screeched to a stop, stones showering in his wake. "No! The guards say that they've not passed the gate. I thought they might have gone off in pursuit of Pumbleby, but . . ."

"Oh, where can they *be?*" Miriam tugged frantically at her hair as her hooves pranced and shifted. Her voice trembled on the edge of hysteria. "I-I just want to say that I'm sorry! That I don't doubt them. I-I wasn't in my right wits—don't they understand?"

Willy surged up the stairs, his hooves clashing loudly on the stone. "Demmit if I can guess where they are. I fear for Torscha. If he gets in a state he might go wild. . . ."

Inspiration suddenly came; Willy's eyes opened wide.

"God, no! No, he wouldn't *dare!* Torscha would be ruined!"

Miriam looked up in hope and fear. "What? What?"

The stallion raced past her and dived back toward the ballroom, shouting over his shoulder.

"Quickly! We may still have time!"

Leymond let his cards fall, and an expression of extreme annoyance crossed his face. "Well done, Sir Mouse. You play a stimulating game."

Mus tilted his head and affected mild surprise. "And you, sir! Though I confess few players offer me any real challenge. You played quite well."

The two players were surrounded by a fascinated crowd. Frielle Delauncy sat unhappily beside the mouse, acting as his assistant. She raked in Mus's pile of winnings and glanced anxiously at Retter, who stood brooding nearby. The stallion hardly seemed aware of the room at all.

For the sake of her two friends, Frielle stayed close at hand. They were planning something—she felt sure of it, and perhaps the king was in on the plot as well. He had shuttered himself up with Mus for far too long. . . .

There had been several players in the game—even the king himself. That royal gentleman chuckled ruefully as he watched his money fall into Mus's paws. "Sink me if I don't seem fated to lose! First you, Leymond, and now this thumb-sized sharper!" He tugged slyly at his mustache. "Truly, Leymond, I fear our rodent friend may even be *your* measure."

Stung by the remark, Leymond jerked forward. His eyes had lost their veneer of laziness. "A few passes mean nothing! Come again, Sir Mouse! I would test your mettle!"

Mus ruefully looked at the pile of golden coins towering above him. "Fa, sir! Truly, the game lacks zest."

"*Zest!*" Leymond was becoming angry. "You beat me at cards thrice in a row and have the impudence to retire?"

Mus shrugged easily, and only Frielle seemed aware of the crafty twirl of his tail. "I think only of your nerves, sir. Another defeat might unduly upset you."

"*Upset!*" Leymond snatched up the pack of cards. "Come, Sir Mouse—I find you most insolent! I'll show you what makes a true card master!"

The mouse rubbed his little paws together. "Very well, sir. Perhaps I can show you a few pointers on technique. *My* deal I believe. Frielle—would you honor us?"

The cards were passed to the little satyr lady. Five players took their places, and initial bets were made. Mus watched the cards and slowly stroked his chin. There were two games being played here tonight, and Leymond cooperated beautifully with both.

Mus idly played through the game's first passes. Two of the players quailed and immediately folded, leaving the game in the hands of the king, Leymond, and Mus. The play flashed around the table, the Tarot cards making garish puddles of color across the dainty tablecloth.

Mus made his move; he deliberately discarded a vital card, innocently handing the game over to Leymond. Maliciously pleased, the nobleman played his trumps and raked in the winnings.

"Ha, Sir Mouse! Experience always tells in the long run! Inconsistency is your weakness."

Mus ran his fingers through his elegant whiskers. "I find predictability rather tiresome." With a casual air of interest, he looked up at the human. "You'll not trap me again."

Sneering in triumph, Leymond snatched up the cards and began to shuffle. He seemed childishly eager to best Mus once again; the mouse was the first serious challenge to his reputation. To be beaten by a rodent? Unthinkable!

The cards fell into Mus's hands; one by one the peripheral players dropped out of the play—some graciously, some ill-temperedly. The deck revealed all its little surprises, and Mus held the whole pack in his mind; it was almost too easy.

The king would not help overtly—he could not—but he and Mus had talked long and hard. Miriam would be saved, providing Leymond could be ruined and brought down.

It was time to bid for new cards. Leymond folded up his hand and gave a smile. "Well, mouse, we seem to be a match for one another. A shame we cannot test one another's coolness under fire."

The room suddenly became hushed and expectant. Watched by a crowd of whispering admirers, Mus looked up at Leymond with innocent little eyes.

"Why, sir, whatever do you imply?"

"A game for *real* stakes, mouse. You have had a fine run making a fool of me, but now it's time to see who is the better man. Offer me a wager worth my time and skill!"

Mus simply folded his hands. "Accepted, sir. I wager one thousand marks."

An excited shiver ran through the onlookers; Leymond sat back in alarm. "You . . . you can't have such a sum!"

"But I do, sir. Surely you are not backing down?"

Fairly caught! The nobleman's enraged dark eyes flickered across the crowd. The most influential folk in Duncruigh were watching him, measuring him by his actions; a whole reputation hung in the balance. "Back down? Never! But first I want proof that you truly own such a sum."

Torscha Retter swept forward, opening up a folio of papers. Before Frielle could intervene he had spread out a crisp, printed bill at Mus's side.

The paper shone with the crest of Welfland's parliament.

"A bearer bond for funds held at the bank of Duncruigh. One thousand gold marks."

"It-It isn't *his*."

Retter gave a chill smile. "Indeed it is, sir—I just gave it to him. And here are three more; that makes four thousand marks. The bonds are signed and countersigned. Legal tender."

With mild surprise, Mus looked down his nose at the four bonds. "Four thousand? Was it so much?" Mus gave a casual wave. "Well, why not? I shall wager four thousand."

The crowd grew quite still. Leymond looked at the bonds, painfully aware of the gaze of his peers; he had only one course of action.

"Very well! *Covered!*"

Mus looked quite apologetic, and tilted his ears forward. "*Ahem.* Not to put too fine a point on it—but do *you* have the funds, sir? I hesitate to ask of course, but then you were rude enough to question me."

Incensed, Leymond called for pen and paper. The scratch of the quill was loud, the air quivering with tension. The cursing nobleman finished writing and casually tossed the parchment into the center of the table.

"There! My note. If one of you gallant onlookers would be so kind as to witness it?"

The king himself coolly reached forward to witness Leymond's note. He admired his own handiwork for a little while, quite pleased with the effect.

"There! No one should argue with that, unless Aelis should care to dispute it." There was a dutiful little titter of laughter. "Gentlemen—the wager stands at four thousand marks."

Mus wriggled his tail and twiddled his whiskers.

"I say, Leymond! You're quite right! The excitement is extraordinary. So much hazarded at a throw. I feel quite—quite exulted." He leaned forward. "Don't you share the feeling?"

Leymond's dark eyes shone. "Indeed so, Sir Mouse. Quite extraordinary."

"I shall have a single card."

"Dealer takes two."

There was sudden chaos in the doorway as Miriam Jerrick erupted into the room with Willy Merle on her tail. The relief that flooded her gentle face gave way to horror as she saw the mouse playing cards.

"*Mus!* What art thou doing?"

The mouse flattened his ears, refusing to look around.

"Merely playing cards, my lady. You are just in time to see our final play."

Frielle leapt up to plead with the half-horse girl. "Miriam, stop them! He's wagering thousands!"

"Torscha! No—please!"

Retter looked at Miriam with the eyes of a wounded animal. "Madam, stand aside. You are interrupting play."

Willy Merle tried to tug at Retter's arm, but the bigger man simply shrugged him away.

The king looked from Mus to Leymond. "Play."

Mus turned to frown at his cards and indicated his discard. With a last despairing glance at Miriam, Frielle reached out to throw the card away.

Leymond drew his own card from the replacement deck and smiled. Mus glowed with pleasure; he knew exactly what the other man had in his hand. He asked Frielle to spread his cards and twirled his tail in glee.

"House of Death! King of Wands, Queen of Cups, Knight of Swords, Page of Pentacles—crossed by number thirteen. *Death*." The mouse sat back, enormously pleased with himself; the game was his.

Leymond slowly lowered his cards.

"King of Pentacles, Queen of Swords, Knight of Wands, Page of Cups. Crossed by number one—the Magician." He smiled slyly. "One beats thirteen. The game is *mine*."

The onlookers gave a chorus of groans and cheers. Retter swayed, looking quite ashen, and Miriam reached out to stop his fall. She surprised them both by having strength enough to hold him. Frielle slumped her face into her hands.

The noise died down. To everyone's surprise, Mus sat back enthusiastically applauding his opponent.

"How clever! An unusual ploy, sir! I should never have thought of it!"

The king leaned forward to hear the mouse better. "Lud, Mus, you're a gracious loser! What ploy do you speak of?"

The mouse shook his head in wonder. "Why keeping extra cards in the cuff of his glove! Truly—no one ever told me that there was such a rule!"

Dead silence reigned. Torscha Retter gripped Miriam's arm. "Wh-What was that, Mus?"

The mouse clearly did not understand. "Why he has cards hidden up his sleeve. He removed one from his hand when Miriam entered the room, hid it, and replaced it with another."

Leymond shot to his feet, his face livid. *"Preposterous!"*

Mus was mystified. "The *Magician* was removed from the deck sometime during the game before last. I rather wondered where it had gone." The mouse looked at the king and frowned. "I say—is that really fair? I don't have a glove to hide cards in."

Leymond shook with rage, and suddenly his hand flashed down to his rapier.

"You foul *vermin!* You dare to call me a cheat?" His sword half cleared the scabbard until a hiss of steel blurred past his eyes. Retter's sword hung before his throat.

"No, sir, he does not. He scarcely understands the term. The concept of treachery is quite beyond him." Retter flicked his sword. "Show us your gloves, sir! Let us check upon the deck!"

Leymond snarled and kicked over the table. Cards, notes, coins and a mouse went flying. Tugging his sword free, Leymond faced his huge opponent, muscles bunching as he readied for a lunge.

"HOLD!" The king's voice froze them. "Not here! Nobody move!" The king himself lifted aside the card table. "Mus, are you unharmed?"

"Pah!" Something stirred beneath a mound of fallen cards, and a little pointed nose struggled free. "Yes, Majesty! I fell upon Frielle's skirts."

The king gathered up Mus, then pushed back Retter's sword. "We will not check Leymond's gloves. It is an affair of honor. Settle it now." He looked across to his staff.

"Clear the main ballroom."

The dancers had vanished from the ballroom, and all the gaiety had left with them. The vast chandelier shone down upon a huge, empty hall. Perhaps a dozen people stood on the sidelines, with their eyes fixed upon the two combatants.

Retter tore off his sword-belt and handed it to Willy before starting to unlace his coat. His cold gaze never left Leymond, who

made his own preparations far across the room. "Willy—is there
any sign of Pumbleby?"

"No, Torscha. He's escaped us for now." Willy accepted Retter's
coat. "Not for long, though. He'll soon follow this traitor."

Torscha placed a hand on William's shoulder. "Thank you, my
friend. You have the papers?"

"Yes."

"Keep them close to hand."

There were few onlookers. Baron Vardvere had come to stand
by his young friend, his craggy face hard and set. Frielle hid beside
the curtains, too loyal to turn and flee. Mus sat upon her shoulder,
eyes wide with anguish. Suddenly his antics had put a loved one
into danger. He tried to make a brave show for Torscha's sake; the
mouse doffed his hat, and Retter saluted in return.

The king's majordomo appeared beside them, his gray-bearded
face stiff and neutral. "Gentlemen? With your permission, we will
begin."

Retter whipped his rapier from its sheath and tossed the empty
scabbard aside. He began to move forward, but suddenly became
aware of a presence behind him. He turned and stopped dead.

Miriam.

There she stood, staring at him with terror in her eyes. She
wept silently, tears trailing soft fingers down her throat. Torscha
faltered, then took a hesitant step toward her.

"Miriam! Miriam, I . . ."

The girl flowed forward, and soft hands reached out to take
Torscha by the neck. He found his face dragged down to hers as
she crushed him with a kiss. Torscha gave a brief grunt of surprise;
he returned the kiss in utter bewilderment, his mind in a dream.

God! The touch of her was like sweet fire in his veins. He
clutched her tightly, losing himself in the scent of her hair, the feel
of her skin. Her whole soul leaned into the kiss; long moments
passed until Miriam finally tore herself away, her chest heaving. "I
love thee, Torscha! I love thee!"

She turned and fled back to the sidelines. She stood beside Sir
William, clutching at his arm; her eyes never left Torscha's face.

With a long last look into Miriam's eyes, Retter turned to face
his opponent. The heat of her touch still stayed with him, and
Torscha thrilled to a strange new sense of power.

Stripped down to his immaculate lace shirt, Leymond seemed a picture of studied elegance. By contrast, Retter loomed like a vast tower of obsidian. The combatants faced each other off, rapiers lightly kissing as they sank en garde.

The air quivered with tension. Miriam drew in a breath and sent a frantic prayer heavenward as the majordomo looked from one face to another. "Begin."

The swords warily circled one another, the light licking reflections from the gleaming metal. A human and a half-horse are a fair match; where one held strength, the other had agility. Leymond settled back and forth as he tested Torscha's striking range.

"HA!"

Torscha lunged, only to have his blade coolly flicked aside. Leymond stamped forward in a lightning riposte, leaping back as a steel-shod hoof lashed out for his groin. Torscha had learned his art from fencing masters, but his practice had been on the battlefield. He fought to kill.

Retter crashed forward like a juggernaut as he pressed the human back. The air shivered to the ring of steel as the blades flashed back and forth. Sparks flew, and metal howled; the stallion jerked backward from a vicious swipe for his eyes.

With a flick of blades, they separated. Blood ran freely down Leymond's cheek. The nobleman touched his face, examined his bloodied fingers, then looked up at his enemy.

"You fight quite well—for a *soldier.*"

Leymond suddenly sprang into the attack. Sweat flew, and style began to slip as each man tried to savage his opponent. Hooves and hide, lace and steel—Retter was savage fury unleashed. Leymond raged forward, lunged, and his blade caught against Retter's guard. Suddenly Leymond came face-to-face with a quarter of a ton of enraged stallion. Retter rammed his body forward, and his enemy went tumbling to the ground.

Leymond's sword flew from his grasp and slid across the floor. The man scrabbled desperately toward his weapon, only to have a black hoof smash down onto the blade. The traitor found himself looking up into eyes of blazing ice.

"*Still!*" The stallion signed to Willy Merle. His voice hissed with fury. "Your life is mine, Sir Rodger. *Mine!*"

Leymond edged away, but was held by the threat of the steel at his throat. William Merle came to Retter's side bearing a wad of papers. Leymond's eyes widened as he saw what they were.

Retter panted. "Aaah! You *do* recognize them! Good. Confess that these papers are yours, and you are spared."

Leymond breathed wildly. He saw the king watching him closely. The king! So that explained it all! Firined had decided to play for blood. With this evidence in his hands . . .

Leymond slashed at the *carte blanche* with his hand.

"*Never!*"

The dark, savage half-horse narrowed his eyes. There was a clatter of steel as the stallion shoved Leymond's sword toward him.

"*Get up!* Pick up your sword and fight."

Leymond stared in disbelief, then scrabbled for his sword. With a shout, he surged back onto his feet. The man snarled and quickly circled his foe.

Torscha fought for breath; it had been a rash move, giving Leymond back his sword, but the traitor's death would not be enough. Leymond's entire treacherous network of supporters must fall with him; simply remove the head, and the body would sprout another like some foul hydra. With Leymond's confession, Aelis's agents in parliament were finished!

The human suddenly attacked with blinding speed. Retter desperately warded off blow after blow. Torscha fought a weakening defense, then slashed out at his enemy's sword arm. He saw Leymond's blade swerve aside, and a blinding tear of agony ripped into Retter's shoulder. Torscha kicked his opponent backward, then staggered back with blood running swiftly down his arm.

God! The pain!

His wound burned like fire. Retter lurched back into the fight, and Leymond's face shone with triumph as he closed in for the kill.

Half blinded by sweat, Torscha looked past his enemy and saw Miriam. The power came back through Torscha's soul in a giddy wave of heat. He reared high, kicked Leymond's blade and punched his hilt into Leymond's face. Torscha drove the human to his knees and plunged down with his hooves. Leymond rolled aside, gave a mighty shout, and hurtled himself forward in a single massive lunge.

Right onto Torscha's sword.

Leymond's mouth opened, and he staggered backward, his sword dropping from nerveless fingers. Torscha twisted his blade free of Leymond's guts and watched him fall.

The stallion reeled, then dragged his enemy back up from the floor.

"No, Leymond! Not dead yet! Not with a surgeon near." The stallion leaned over his opponent, his face ashen white. "The papers! Are they yours? Confess man! You'll be spared!"

Leymond clutched his stomach. His eyes still stared in disbelief. "N-Never!"

"Don't be a fool, man! You're beaten! *Finished!* But you can still have your life."

The human fell back and lifted up his bloody hand; his eyes blazed with hate. "I'll kill you!"

"You will not. You'll die in agony unless the surgeon reaches you. And he won't unless you confess."

Leymond sagged. He looked around in panic as Retter shook him by the throat.

"Come on, man! Don't be a fool."

The nobleman arched in panic, feeling blood leaking through his hands. "All-All right, damn you! Yes, they're mine! But it won't save your p-precious republic. Aelis will take you all!"

The audience had heard the confession, and Willy triumphantly passed the wad of papers to the king. Torscha turned his back on Leymond and staggered toward his friends.

Leymond's hand fastened about his sword hilt, and somehow he wove to his feet. He saw Retter's unguarded back and lunged.

"*Torscha! Look out!*" Willy shouted; Torscha whirled, his sword coming up too late to defend himself as steel ripped straight for his heart.

Suddenly a shot blazed out. Leymond's head snapped back, drilled clean through the forehead, and he spun backward with an unholy crash. Torscha stared at the body and then looked back to the crowd.

Miriam stood poised with her tiny pistol smoking in her fist. Torscha met her wide green eyes and blinked, then fainted clean away.

"*Torscha!*"

Miriam hurled her gun aside and galloped to him. She flung herself down beside him and ripped open his shirt. Blood flowed steadily out of his shoulder.

"Bandages! Probe! Mus—get over here!" Miriam roughly wiped the wound clean. An artery had been severed, and Torscha had lost an enormous amount of blood. Any lesser man would have fallen long ago. Miriam jammed the wound shut with a wad of shirt.

A presence loomed at her shoulder as the royal surgeon tried to intervene. Miriam slapped the man aside with bloody hands. "*Out!* Keep away from him, you pill roller!"

"Madam! This is not for a lady! You will soil your dress."

"To hell with my dress! And to hell with all ladies!" She called over her shoulder. "Mus! Get thy torch ablaze and heat me a probe and a needle."

"Very well!" The mouse sat right beside her, held in Frielle's little hand. "What's a probe?"

"A thin metal . . . Oh, go and show him!" She snapped at the royal quack. "You must be useful for something!"

The man hastened off to do as he was bid. Miriam found the king at her side and glared at him with outright hostility as she packed the wound.

"*Your* work, I suppose. I hope you're satisfied! One man dead and another nearly so!"

The king watched her hands as she stanched the bleeding. "Not so m' dear. Everything blundered onward despite my poor presence. A good shot, by the way. I've never seen anything quite like it."

"I'm glad you were entertained!" Miriam was uncommonly bitter. "We'll see whether we can kill some more for you later. Hold that!"

"Eh?"

Miriam grabbed the royal hand and pressed it up against the dressing. "Paddle in your handiwork! I'll rouse that fool of a surgeon."

The king was indignant. "Madam! You are insolent!"

"And you, Sire, are overripe for a dressing-down. Time your plotting got your hands dirty." Miriam stood up. "I suppose the twerp is actually qualified?"

"The surgeon? Why—yes. He mostly attends to my nerves. . . ."

"Wonderful. *Willy!* Fetch a surgeon from the college. And an alchemist healer—we'll need to replace the lost blood." She signed imperiously to the royal guards. "You oafs! Find a stretcher and get him to a table!"

Willy charged off with the guards on his tail. The king shook his head and turned back to his task.

"A whirlwind! I should leave running the country to her."

"... *It would ... be in ... good hands.*" Retter's eyes slid open, dazed with pain. The king gripped his other shoulder and smiled.

"Rest there, old chap. We'll soon see you to rights." He tightened his grip on the bandage. "She won't suffer anything else!"

Torscha awakened slowly to a strange sensation of inner peace. He heard his own breathing in a still, warm room; the tap and patter of raindrops on the windowpane; the swish of someone's tail. . . .

His left shoulder felt numb. A gentle hand caressed his face and tucked his hair back behind his ear. Retter sighed and spoke out his beloved's name.

She was there, his lovely Miriam. She knelt on the bed with her fine black legs folded beneath her, cradling his head. She had the wisest eyes in the world.

"Lie still, my love. Lie still. Thou'rt a stupid, courageous man, and I love thee." She wound adoring fingers through Torscha's hair. "The wound is healing. Just rest, and all shall be well."

Torscha tried to speak, and his voice sounded weak in his own ears. "I love thee, Miriam. I would make thee mine, if thou wouldst have me."

She stroked him, loving him with her hands. "I will have thee. I am thine forever."

The stallion sighed and closed his eyes; he lay content in her arms. Miriam. His lovely Miriam. Freckles and sunshine. For the first time in years, Torscha felt at peace.

Leymond. Parliament. *The bill!* Torscha opened his eyes and tried to rise. "*Parliament!* What time is it?"

"I told thee to lie still! The time is eleven of the morning, and parliament is over and done. Leymond's alliance has fallen. Parliament has passed an emergency act, and a royal commission is raising troops and taxes even as we speak."

Torscha struggled to get up, but Miriam held him firm. "Still!"

"But the baron . . ."

"Does not need you. It is all in hand. The king himself appeared before the house and rousted the traitors out. Lie thee here, or I shall tie thee up!"

Torscha scoffed. "Thou would not dare!"

"Every lady fantasizes about tying up a fine young man. Try me."

Retter lay back; he was weak as a kitten and in no condition to argue. He was forced to lie down and allow himself to be loved. It was no hard task.

Miriam seemed strangely silent.

"What is wrong, my love?"

Miriam's caress faltered. "News—from the continent. Our army is destroyed. Aelis smashed the Duncruighan expeditionary force before the walls of Welfland's capital. Your last city is under siege and our regiments are gone."

Torscha was not thinking clearly. He felt horribly sick. "How-How did this news break?"

"The survivors came in by ship this morning. Neither Father nor Roland were with them. They died at Lael."

Miriam crept into Torscha's arms, and he folded her against his heart. There seemed so little that he could do or say. They sat together in silence while the rain rattled against the windows.

They were in love, they were together, and the future would be theirs to hold.

Book Two
Invasion

Chapter One

Wooden Walls

 prancing devil raced across the sullen seas, crashing through foam and shouldering its way into waves. The sinister figurehead clove into a wintry gale, shrieking mindlessly at the coming storm.

His Majesty's warship *Nemesis* was a vessel of one hundred guns, one of the largest in Duncruigh's fleet. A towering monument of oak and iron, she made a sinister silhouette against the sky. Dull cloud met dull sea at an invisible horizon, and the *Nemesis* lumbered forward through a world leeched of anything but wind and icy cold. The vast three-decker shook to the blows of massive waves while bronze cannon creaked against their lashings.

A huge black figure staggered out onto the deck, its hooves skittering for purchase on the wooden planks. Torscha Retter hunched his huge shoulders against a fresh onslaught of spray. A ship is not a natural environment for half-horses, and Torscha's hooves were hard put to keep purchase on the slippery, rolling deck. He watched in silence as human sailors swarmed nimbly up into the rigging. What must it be like to have agility like that? To be that lithe, that flexible and sure of foot?

"*A wee strong blow, Colonel!*"

Torscha turned, keeping his hat clapped firmly to his head. A dark, suave little human stood at his elbow, seemingly enjoying the wild sea breeze. Mister Kelso, the ship's first officer, was quite clearly insane.

The wind made speech all but impossible; Torscha shouted to be heard above the smack of waves and groan of timber. "*Yes! Sooth—yes, indeed!*" Torscha scowled as spray lashed viciously across the deck. "*Is this-this weather usual for the time of year, sir?*"

The sailor shouted against the roar of the sea. "*Oh, aye! All quite normal for thissen place and season!*" He drew an eager breath and faced the waves. "*No need to worry y'self.*"

Retter and his half-horse regiment had been trapped upon this wretched ship for months, time spent without space to stretch, space to run, to feel freedom underneath their hooves.

Time spent without his Miriam . . .

The ship staggered as she rammed her way through another roller, and Retter irritably shook out his tail. "*Damnation! How long will this go on? I can scarcely stand!*"

The sailor shrugged, toying with one long tail of his mustache. He led the way into the shelter of the quarterdeck, where speech suddenly became easier.

"You're all the fighting contingent we have. Four-leggers or no, they'll not recall ye from shipboard duty. Not for months."

The half-horse turned away, drumming at the planking with his hooves. *Oh, Miriam—just to hold you in my arms again. . . .*

"Colonel? I'm sorry—I didn't quite catch that."

Torscha gave a guilty jump of surprise. "Ah—the sea is showing us its charms again."

"Aye—well, that it may be. P'rhaps you had best be going below, sir! This is not a good time to be slippin' and slidin' about the planks."

"The open air seemed . . . prudent for a moment."

Kelso turned and cast a questioning glance toward the aftercastle. "Oh, I see."

Beneath the decks, hidden utterly from view, Willy leaned against the windows, brooding out across the waves. The cavalier listlessly toyed with his wine as spray trailed past his face like bitter tears.

Miriam . . . Willy closed his eyes and wearily leaned his brow upon his arms. *Miriam, why couldn't thou have loved me?*

He thought of the feel of soft hair against his face, of the warm smell of her in his nostrils. In his mind's eye he could see how she would touch him, hold him—could see the love shining in those wise green eyes. He would have changed his ways for her. For once Willy could have been a lucky man.

Torscha. It was always Torscha! Always the one to be looked up to, the strongest, the suavest, the leader. Torscha had it all.

And now he had Miriam.

If you had died—if Leymond had skewered you, she would have been mine. . . .

"Willy?"

The young cavalier slowly rose and straightened his back.

"Willy, art thou all right, my friend?"

Torscha's voice, deep and mellow, with the rich spice of a foreign accent. Willy kept his face turned out to sea. "Indeed, Torscha. Yes—I am all right."

The great black stallion hesitantly moved into the cabin, seawater dripping from his burnished hide. The silence stretched, and Torscha seemed unsure what to do.

"Willy? Willy—something's wrong. This mood . . . it pains me to see you so." Retter reached a hand toward Willy's side."What's wrong, Willy? Can I help?"

Willy's fists clenched. Gambling debts, ruination, lost love! Willy jerked back from the touch and turned his back. "No! Just leave me awone!"

"Willy, I . . . "

"Leave me awone!" Willy whirled to stare at Torscha with savage despair, and his hand suddenly flicked down to his rapier. Torscha stood staring in shock at his best friend.

"Willy—*please!*"

The blond cavalier fought for breath for one long, fragile moment, then suddenly he turned and fled out into the storm.

Torscha stared after him in stunned disbelief. With faltering steps, the great black stallion backed away from his retreating friend.

The wind buffeted a sad, lonely figure on the hillside. She stood staring across the endless sea with her long hair and tail streaming out into the wind. Watery sunlight struck copper highlights from her hide as Miriam gazed out into the ocean's empty skies.

Ships returned to Duncruigh's harbors—but never *his.* Still Miriam came to watch and hope, climbing the hillside to hold her lonely vigil; the sea summoned her, and she followed the call. Miriam shivered and pulled her cloak closer about herself.

A small form with wise black eyes peeked out from her hair.

"I never tire of looking at it. This sea is a wonderful thing—so full of moods, so huge and wide. . . ." Mus stared at the horizon in awe. "Does it truly stretch across the whole wide world?"

Miriam's eyes were filled with sadness. "Yes, Mus. It does."

"How long has it been?"

"Four months, Mus. Four long months."

Silence reigned for long moments as the two friends regarded the tossing waves. There had been no news from the fleet, and Mus's search for Pin-William and the lady mouse had simply come to naught. Miriam leaned her head aside to nuzzle at her tiny friend.

"I'm sorry, Mus. I'm not very good company for thee, am I?"

Mus looked up at Miriam with bright, adoring eyes. "I'm pleased to be with thee. There's no need to talk. But if thou needest to know that someone is close, I shall always be here."

The girl dejectedly turned her back upon the sea.

"There's never any sign of them. Never any news. But I need to look, Mus; I need to hope." Miriam paused. "Am—am I being foolish?"

"He'll come back to thee, Miriam. He'll come back. Listen to the sand and water and be at peace. Worry solves nothing."

Miriam sighed once more. "I know, Mus. I know."

The friends passed the dockyards, where the unfinished ribs of a ship lay like the skeleton of some dead leviathan. A gull stood hunched in the shelter of a gigantic wooden beam, like a scavenger reluctant to leave a great, parched carcass. Miriam trailed to a halt and gazed back toward the harbor hills.

From the shore, a flock of sailors cantered on horseback, torches streaming behind them in the wind. The men pulled canvas from a pile of brush and swiftly set the wood afire. Mus and Miriam turned to watch as more beacons sprang to life all along the shore.

"What does it mean, Miriam?"

The girl turned sadly back toward the waves. "It means we must go home, my Mus.

"Aelis has finally come."

Chapter Two

Armada

lorious golden hair tossed in the wind, finer than silk, prouder than the snapping banners upon the masts. Aelis stood on the quarterdeck of the royal flagship, her four shapely legs splayed for balance as she examined the enemy fleet. The Duncruighan vessels had concentrated into a single wedge, and Nantierre's fleet deployed to swoop round and engulf them. Aelis had almost three hundred and fifty vessels to Duncruigh's two hundred. King Firined's navy would shatter like a rotten skull beneath her hooves!

Aelis lowered her perspective glass; her hooves danced, and her eyes were wild with excitement. "Now! All squadrons engage! I want close action—I want their fleet pulped!" Aelis slammed shut her telescope and whirled to face her officers. "They will attempt to break the line and fall upon us from the rear. This will *not* happen! Station a reserve division upwind of the fleet. If they break through, the reserves will sink them."

The younger officers' faces shone with adoration; they would not fail her—not while there was breath in them.

Hergon, chief admiral of Nantierre, was a tall specter of a human with a black patch set rakishly across one eye. A veteran of Nantierre's defeat in the channel five years before, he felt wary of underestimating his foe. On the other hand, Aelis did not seem to be making the rash mistakes that her father had. He folded his spindly arms and spoke into midair.

"General signal: *Close action.*" After a moment's thought, the admiral turned to his queen. "May it please Your Majesty, I shall withdraw this vessel for the reserve division."

"What! Why?" Aelis whirled about from the railings, and her
eyes had the hurt, yearning look of a child denied. "I'll not skulk
in safety while my men . . ."

"Majesty!" The admiral's face hardened. "I cannot control my
fleet from the thick of battle. The reserves are the critical element
of this battle plan. I prefer to be stationed where we can deal the
decisive blow!"

Aelis's cheeks blazed, and she refused to meet the admiral's
eyes. Long, hard moments passed before she spoke. "As you wish,
Admiral." Aelis's voice was bitter. "As you wish."

Over near the rails, the royal astrologer muttered darkly, scraping her talons back and forth across the decks. Aelis looked at the
old bird and irritably tossed her head.

"What art thou doing above decks? Get below, old hag. Go
where I know thou'lt be safe!"

The harpy stalked forward on lanky legs and tilted her hatchet
nose into the breeze. "It will be good today, Majesty. Your star is in
ascendance."

Aelis frowned."Go on—get thee gone, old crow. Move to the
orlop."

"Aye, Majesty."

The sails filled with a *crack* as the flagship tacked hard about to
join the reserve squadrons. Like a great, onrushing wave of doom,
the Nantierran fleet surged toward the enemy. Alone by the railing, Aelis shivered in anticipation.

Soon she would be fulfilled! *Soon.* Aelis fought for breath and
waited, her eyes bright and filled with hunger.

Duke Rorgeld, knight of the Order of the Dolphin and high
admiral of Duncruigh, stood at the center of his deck, his hands
clasped behind him. A short, slight figure in a sea-stained coat, he
swayed to the motion of the deck and, without a change of expression, watched the approach of the enemy fleet. He had made peace
with both his sovereign and his God; the day held no more fears.

He grimly surveyed the horizon; Nantierre's fleet had formed into
a huge crescent, the lighter vessels divided between the wings.
Landsman's tactics; Aelis's warships to the lee would be lucky to
engage. The admiral watched the skies and gave a calculating frown.

He turned to confer with his aide—a grim young man from a good, pious family. "What line of battleships do we have with the far windward division?"

The young man snapped back from memory: "*Kraken, Nemesis, Steadfast,* and *Vengeance.* All hundred-gun men-o'-war. Their consorts include another seven lesser craft."

The newest of the fleet's heavy ships-o'-war. Eleven vessels in total, all stationed across the horizon out of sight of Aelis's fleet. It was enough.

"Send an air courier to Admiral Horton on the *Kraken.* His squadron is to run downwind and attack the enemy reserve."

The orders were passed as the admiral's eyes remained locked on the enemy fleet. Four first-raters and seven consorts to engage Aelis's reserves? Impossible odds. Horton would go to the bottom, but the confusion would buy Duncruigh's fleet the time it needed to make its breakthrough. Horton's sacrifice would be remembered.

Satisfied, Rorgeld pulled his coat straight and nodded approvingly as his officers led the men in prayer.

"DECK THAR! ENEMY DIVISION TACKING TO WINDWARD!"

The *Nemesis*'s captain stamped over to the railing, gave a snort, and then simply turned his back upon the enemy.

"Very well, Mister Kelso, you may clear for action."

"BEAT TO QUARTERS! CLEAR FOR ACTION!"

Feet thundered across the decks as the sailors got to work. All through the ship screens were torn down and loose gear crammed below the waterline. The lower decks were suddenly transformed into vast, sinister caverns dominated by the crouching black beasts that were the guns. The gun crews stripped off their shirts and stuffed their ears with cotton waste, tying their scarves about their heads to block out the oncoming roar of cannon fire. The gunnery officers nervously flexed their swords between their fingers and stared up and down the lines of artillery.

The top deck had dissolved into a confusion of rushing men. Nets were strung along the sides of the ship to block enemy boarders, and yet more nets were suspended above the deck to ward the crew from falling spars. Pixie topmen flew up to the highest masts, their wings abuzz on the crisp dawn air as they doused the sails with fire-retardant alum.

The half-horse soldiers drove forward through the chaos, muskets held high above their heads. They stood-to with firelocks ready, taking cover behind the wadded hammocks that had been packed along the rails.

Nemesis formed the spearhead of a column of four titanic men-o'-war. The Nantierran reserve division had blundered about to face the threat, ships swerving as they dodged from one another's way. The enemy's lead vessel thundered forward through the water, foam surging up about her bows. Light glared from cannon, pikes, and armor as the ship drew ever closer. Behind the enemy came three more ships strung out in line astern.

Smoke puffed from the enemy fleet, and a cannonball plowed into the waves a cable length ahead of *Nemesis*'s prow. The half-horse musketeers nervously checked the cock of their weapons and flicked bright eyes in the direction of their officers. The men blinked as a vast black figure rose up into the sun.

The decks shivered as Retter stalked out behind his men. His entire body had been encased in a skin of midnight steel, the plates expanding and contracting to his every move. Sheathed from tail to crown, the colonel marched like a metal lobster, utterly uncaring of the armor's massive weight. A visor hid his face behind a savage, predatory beak. Retter turned toward the sea, posing like a pagan god of war.

A year ago he would not have been up to the task. Torscha reached under his sash to finger Miriam's locket, his mind far away. For long, precious moments, all fear faded as his mind caressed a dream.

With sword and pistols, warhammer and sword, the colonel seemed a fiend about to be unleashed. The musketeers turned back and began to load their weapons with anticipation shining in their eyes.

The captain leaned against the quarterdeck railings. He flicked his eyes briefly down the line of enemy vessels, already planning his second fight.

"Mister Kelso! Load and run-out, if you please. Chainshot."

Kelso bobbed into action. In honor of the day, he wore his finest motley, looking more like a pirate than an officer of the crown. Rumor held that he *had* served as a buccaneer, and had avoided the halter by opting for the navy; be that as it may, he was one of the finest gunners in the king's employ. The decks shivered as the huge guns glided forward through their gunports, while Kelso stood with one boot planted insolently on the rails.

The seconds stretched as water hissed beneath the beakhead. Torscha paced slowly back and forth behind his men, hooves crunching upon the sanded decks. Willy's company of half-horse musketeers were stationed on the quarterdeck high above, protecting the captain and the helm. Suddenly, from across the deck, Torscha felt his gaze lock with Willy's eyes.

—A chill spread from Torscha's sword wound. William stared at him with cold, unmitigated hatred.

It was as though Torscha had been slapped. He deliberately turned his back and faced the bows, feeling the bite of Willy's pain against his soul.

Once more there was a sudden puff of smoke from the enemy's bow, followed by the *bang* of a cannon shot. A ball groaned and grumbled high overhead, and the *Nemesis*'s crew jeered abuse at the enemy gunners.

"Mister Kelso! Show 'em how it should be done, if you please!"

Kelso squinted briefly down the barrel of each bowchaser, and then nodded to his men. When the ship poised on the uproll of a wave, both cannon slammed backward on their carriages. Great rolling jets of smoke shot from the muzzles to whip away into the wind.

Splinters erupted from the enemy's bow as *Nemesis*'s iron smashed home. The crewmen whooped and slapped at Retter's steel hide with joy. The captains of the bowchasers made elaborate bows to one another, sweeping their hats low across the decks and *Nemesis*'s captain joyously smashed his fist against the rail.

" 'WARE SHIP! HARD A' LARBOARD! STAND BY STARBOARD BATTERY!"

The wheel spun as *Nemesis* suddenly curtsied to the left, the wind slamming her stern hard around. The enemy ship tried to match the turn, and the wind slapped hard in her face and threw her sails back on their yards. Rigging tumbled as she found herself bow-on to *Nemesis*'s flanks.

"AT 'EM *NEMESIS!* FULL BROADSIDE!"

"TARGET: RIGGING! ON THE UPROLL . . . FIRE!"

Nemesis wrenched sideways as her cannon slammed backward in a mighty, stuttering roar. Smoke blasted through the air, and

Torscha saw the enemy's sails jerk as chainshot ripped into her yards. Spars exploded from her masts, sending her foresails thundering down into the waves.

Nemesis's gun crews roared as they hurtled themselves back to their guns; sponges hissed as fresh shot was frantically crammed home. Over it all the officers' voices chanted the monotonous litany of sea battle.

"STOP VENTS!—SPONGE OUT!—LOAD!"

Nemesis had spun back onto her original course, while her enemy wallowed in the water like a drowning beast. Duncruighan men-o'-war passed by the stricken vessel to concentrate on the next two enemy ships. The demasted vessel lost way to leeward and drifted downwind, where her bulk would block the Nantierran line of fire for precious moments to come.

Cannon flashed along the length of the stricken enemy ship. Although crippled, she still had vicious teeth. Stays parted with a *crack* like musket shots, and splinters erupted from the rails. The enemy vessel swung helplessly about as crews fought to cut away her broken masts. *Nemesis*'s course would take her hard beneath its stern.

"*Steady! Steady!*" Retter walked the line of his men as *Nemesis* crept across the Nantierran's counter. "*Aim for the quarterdeck! Kill the officers!*" He checked the range. A hundred yards. "*By platoon volley,* FIRE!"

Flame stabbed along the railings as soldiers smashed lead into the enemy decks. Ramrods flashed and bandoliers rattled; the poised, clockwork volleys barked like the pistons of some evil machine. There were answering flashes from the enemy ship; a bullet drove a splinter out of the rail by Torscha's side, and there was a violet flash as spells flickered through the air.

"*STARBOARD BATTERY, FIRE AS YOU BEAR!*"

The ship passed behind the enemy's unprotected stern, almost close enough to reach out to touch her gleaming windows. One by one *Nemesis*'s guns slammed backward, spewing smoke as balls punched home into the enemy. Wood and glass exploded inward, and round shot plowed the full length of the enemy deck, staving rudders, masts, and flesh into a gruel. The mizzenmast cracked and sank like a javelin through the crowded decks; sparks flew as guns burst beneath the strike of Duncruighan cannonballs. Her stern chasers tried to make a reply before they drowned beneath a wave of fire and steel.

Smoke cleared. The *Nemesis* slid past her victim. It seemed as though the other ship had been savaged by some ravening beast. Wood and flesh were riven, and blood dripped into the hungry seas.

"Oh, God . . ." Torscha stared at the ruined ship, mesmerized to profanity by the carnage. Blood streamed down the sides of the vessel—shocking red rivulets that splashed obscenely down the bright new wood, as though the ship herself were bleeding to death.

The crews rose to watch the enemy recede to stern as the first tongues of fire licked out from below her decks.

Nemesis closed on the next enemy ship; a vast vessel of one hundred and twenty guns or more. She would pass broadside for broadside and match *Nemesis* shot for shot. The vessel clawed arrogantly through the smoke with a huge banner streaming from her bows: a pure white rose upon a field of black. . . .

From far away, Torscha heard the thunder of guns as the main fleets engaged. It was another fight in another world. Here there stood only *Nemesis* and her gigantic foe.

"*Musketeers! By platoon volley*—FIRE!"

Torscha's sword swept down, and again the muskets began to fire across the bows. Huge bodies pranced backward from the rail to reload, hooves flashing, tails swishing. Men spun and cursed; sailors fell kicking from their guns as the enemy's bowsprit loomed alongside, her forecastle alive with rippling stabs of musket flame. Retter moved up and down the line of his men, calling the rhythm of fire. A man swore as his flint shattered in the pan; a sergeant passed him the bloodied weapon of a fallen man and moved on, dragging the wounded back out of the line of fire.

"*Keep firing! Kill the officers!*"

Torscha looked up to see the enemy ship almost side by side with *Nemesis*, three rows of gun muzzles yawning hungrily from her flanks. One of *Nemesis*'s gunners stood erect and solemnly removed his hat.

"Lord—for what we are about to receive . . ."

Kelso's voice scythed though the smoke. "STARBOARD BATTERY—FIRE AS YOU BEAR!"

One by one the guns bucked backward, blasting splinters from the enemy hull. The air cringed to the deafening bellow of cannon, and the gun crews began to cheer. . . .

Suddenly the world exploded into smoke and flame as the

Nantierran ship unleashed her guns. Gore vomited up across the decks, cannonballs blowing men to fragments. *Nemesis* quivered beneath the enemy fire; she took hits deep in the hull, blasting holes open to the waves. The hot breath of cannon seared across the decks, snatching men into bloody ruin, yet still *Nemesis*'s guns fired. The cannon crashed out one by one, punching iron into the hellish fog. The crews flung themselves at their charges, frantically reloading only to fire again and again. Metal howled maniacally as cannon were hit and tumbled backward to crush their crews to pulp. Torscha leveled his pistols and fired across the water, the noise of his shots quite lost among the din. He was rewarded by seeing an enemy sharpshooter come tumbling down out of the shrouds.

"Retter, move!"

Kelso hooked Retter's front hooves from beneath him as a Nantierran swivel gun blasted hailshot at the rails. The stallion felt a cloud of shot ripple past his hide. He staggered to his feet, and Kelso nodded at him in relief.

Standing close by, Willy stood staring at Retter's face, then licked his lips. Retter sketched a brief salute and then turned back toward his men.

The guns were still. The two ships had sailed past one another. The deck heeled over as *Nemesis* turned about to reengage.

The world was filled with choking, sulfurous fog, and axes thundered amidships as crews hacked shattered rigging free. The decks were strewn with ruined cannon, corpses, and wounded, shrieking men. Aelis stood on her quarterdeck, untouched amid the carnage. Long hair spilled out beneath her helmet to swirl golden in the smoke as the woman trod over the wreckage, wiping powder stains across her cheek.

"Where are they? Hurry, reengage!"

Powder smoke hung in filthy clouds above the water, hiding all from sight; of the Duncruighan warship, there was no sign. The queen whirled in agitation, prancing back upon her rear hooves and pawing at the air.

Where was she?

The ship's officers bellowed across the decks, bringing order to the chaos. Corpses were dumped overboard, guns uprighted while Aelis whirled about in search of her admiral.

"Captain! Where is Admiral Hergon?"

"Dead, Majesty!" The portly captain's eyes were wide with shock; nevertheless, he seemed the master of his senses. Aelis swished her tail and pointed a commanding finger.

"Reengage! We command you to put about and finish that vessel!"

"But, Majesty, we've lost our wheel!"

"*Repair it!* I want their squadron shattered before we fall on the enemy fleet's rear!"

The captain quickly issued orders. Below decks, men hauled at the rudder cables as the ship put herself about.

Suddenly there were huge masts looming overhead. A leering devil reared out of the smoke to snarl down at the gun deck. A ship's bowsprit lanced through the smoke and tore into the Nantierran shrouds.

Two hulls met with a splintering *crash;* the deck heeled hard over, and Aelis staggered for support as voices bellowed in a foreign tongue.

"AT THEM, *NEMESIS!* BOARDERS AWAY!"

Cannons lanced death through the smoke. Hail shot blasted across the Nantierran decks, snatching sailors back into the fog. A wave of half-horses fired at the Nantierran crew and then thundered down onto her decks in a savage wave of flesh and iron.

Aelis called for her guards and flung herself down the broad steps onto the gun deck. Hooves drummed at the planks as she raced into battle; she tugged free her sword, swept it toward the foe and charged.

Torscha smashed a man down with his sword while all around him soldiers and sailors from the *Nemesis* ripped into their enemy. Boarding pikes flickered in the fog while cutlasses clashed with musket butts and swords. All about were screams and confusion; high up in the rigging pixies and harpies tore at one another, sending bodies plunging down to slam into the battling crews.

Men grunted as they shoved blades home. Torscha looked across the decks to see *Nemesis*'s afterguard struggling aboard.

Willy led his men raging down onto the decks and tore into the enemy crew. Torscha saw him fire his pistols and then crash sword to sword with a Nantierran officer. The two battled back and forth, when suddenly a warning *crack* came from the rigging, and the spars began to sag.

"*Willy!*"

An avalanche of cord and canvas plunged down to the deck, and Willy disappeared from sight. Torscha gave a roar and hurled himself toward his fallen friend. An enemy sailor rushed into the attack; Torscha ran him through the chest and stamped his body underneath his hooves.

"*Willy!*"

The enemy parted as a wedge of armored half-horses fought through from behind—huge men draped in the blue and white of Nantierre. At their center whirled a blazing storm of fury; a terrifying warrior in unblemished silver-steel. The newcomers drove between Retter and his goal.

Retter ripped out his warhammer to smash an armored skull. Lesser men crumbled as the massive stallion gouged a path through the Nantierran Royal Guard. He turned aside a sword, blocked another blow, and hacked viciously downward with his pick. His victim screamed and reeled away, leaving Retter face-to-face with a snarling hellcat.

'D's blood, she was magnificent! Golden hair streamed out from beneath her helmet, and a silken tail swirled behind her in the wind. Her eyes blazed with battle madness.

Torscha bellowed in fury and flung himself at his enemy. Weapons shrieked in anger as they clashed. His opponent drove forward, ripping for his eyes. Torscha nodded his head and took the blow upon the peak of his visor, then lashed out with one massive hoof, smashing her aside.

The decks around them cleared. Hooves pounded loudly upon the deck as the two combatants duelled back and forth.

Aelis lunged home, only to be thwarted again and yet again! The warhammer blurred as the black stallion made a lightning backhand slash. Never had she seen such strength and speed! He towered before her like a god of polished jet. Aelis felt rage build in her even as a thrill flowed through her veins.

Damn you! Die! Die! Die! Aelis feinted, circled, and lunged, her hooves skipping across the deck. The stallion pranced backward onto his rear hooves and plunged forward; Aelis dodged aside, narrowly missing being crushed by a quarter-ton of armored foe. She whirled, her hair flying, and was just in time to smash aside a furious blow that drove her down to all four knees.

"*Majesty! Majesty, beware!*"

A shadow suddenly loomed from above, and Aelis saw her opponent flick his eyes upward. She leapt back just as a huge mast cascaded to the deck between them. Planking splintered and rigging avalanched around her. The queen whirled, and fresh cannon fire blasted the Duncruighan vessel from behind.

"RETIRE! RETIRE! BACK TO THE SHIP!"

Already the grapnels had been cut as the Duncruighans abandoned the fight. The enemy vessel began to drift away, the gap between the two ships ever widening. Aelis's opponent gave one last despairing glance at the wreckage farther up the deck, then tore open his visor and stared into Aelis's eyes.

The queen almost dropped her sword in shock. *Retter!* It was Count Retter; twenty years younger, yet it was he! Aelis started forward as the stallion whirled; hooves thundered across the deck as he sprang up over the rail. In one smooth, magnificent leap he sailed across to the enemy deck and was gone.

Aelis staggered across to the rail and leaned weakly against the splintered wood. Her legs shook as her sword tumbled from nerveless fingers. She stayed by the rail until *Nemesis* had sailed away and was gone.

The fog of war was shot through with flame. An explosion lit the sky, thundering on and on as debris splashed down into the sea. After two solid hours of hell, the sight scarcely seemed remarkable; the leviathans battled in the mist as corpses swirled upon the tide.

Torn beneath the waterline by endless rounds of shot, *Nemesis* slowly crept out of the smoke. Her single remaining mast held aloft a tattered scrap of sail—enough to barely give the ship steering way. The ship limped westward, trailing smoldering debris in her wake.

The crew, clanking monotonously at the pumps, wearily struggled to keep life in their vessel's body. Torscha stood by the starboard rail and tore off his heavy helm. The rush of cold air across his face was purest ecstasy.

The encounter with Aelis had frightened him. Torscha had too much to live for now; there was Miriam to go back to, a life to be lived.

Willy. Willy was lost. Dead? Injured and now held firm in the enemy's clutches? Torscha sighed and closed his eyes.

Voices murmured behind him; the captain and Mister Kelso, both still miraculously alive after all the ship had been through, stood at Retter's tail.

"Kelso—how much water in the well?"

"Six feet and rising, sir. We've crews set to caulking with plugs and sheets of lead. It'll not hold her." Kelso smeared blood back from an injured eye. "The fleet is lost, sir. We must retire."

"Thank you, Mister Kelso. Keep me informed of the work below." The captain drew a long, slow breath, and then turned toward Torscha at the rails.

"Colonel Retter? Are you able to give us advice, sir?"

The half-horse straightened with one great heave, dark and immaculate within his armored shell.

"I am your servant, sir."

"We're sinking, Colonel. The pumps cannot keep up with the flow. Inside of an hour or two, *Nemesis* will be finished; time enough to beach her on Duncruighan soil. You are a veteran of land wars—can you advise us as to our best course?"

With the fleet destroyed, Aelis would land in the capital by dusk. Alchester was unfortified; it would fall within a day, and the king would flee to gather up his army in the north. . . .

North—past the walls of a sleepy river town. . . .

Kerbridge. It had to be Kerbridge.

Torscha suddenly straightened; hooves stamped the deck as his body filled with power. "Very well, Captain, beach your vessel. We'll dismount as many cannon as our men can haul—powder, shot, and petty arms. The wounded we shall carry to some convent or hostel." Retter's face grew hard and set, his eyes lit by distant fires. "We march to Kerbridge."

Chapter Three

Fortress Kerbridge

Mus?"

The battlements were crowded with bustling figures; soldiers ran hither and yon, hounded by irritable officers while drummer boys played erratic tattoos beside the moat. Gunners hunched over telescopes waved signals as ranging stakes were emplaced along the hill. The fleet was beaten, the capital fallen, and the world edged with rising panic. Fear for Torscha ripped Miriam like an open wound; she dealt with it by living with each day as it came, lest worry make her wholly sick.

Miriam picked up her skirts and trotted along the crowded paths, her hooves tapping busily against the stone.

"Mus? Where art thou?"

Now where was that silly creature? Miriam had finally finished storing the garrison's medicines. It was a perfect time to snatch Mus and view the chaos, but now the little fellow had wandered far astray. His maps and charts were sitting forlorn and unattended where he had abandoned them. Mus had insisted that proper diagrams of the defenses be drawn, but it was a task he seemed to have small patience for. The little shirker spent most of his time peering out of the windows or exploring the castle. Mus had an insatiable lust for prying and fiddling. He had decided to investigate the workings of a fine wheel-lock pistol yesterday; the armorer was still trying to piece the wretched thing back together.

Come to think of it, Mus was also supposed to put an hour into spell practice today! As the castle's only sorcerer, he had a heavy responsibility. Miriam planted her fists on her withers and cast sharp eyes about her.

Where *was* that mouse?

Her eyes alighted on a curious sight: a crusty old gunner crouched beside one of the new cannon. He spoke down the barrel, looking for all the world as though he might have an adequate excuse for doing so. Miriam's freckled nose wrinkled in sweet seriousness as she trotted over to the guns.

On the windswept battlements, a tiny voice drifted from the cannon's maw. "Sooth! 'Tis very big! What sort of weapon did you say it was?"

The old gunner pulled at his lumpen, broken nose. " 'At's a *culverin,* Master Mouse. And a vurry handy gun it is!"

"A culverin?" A tiny pointed face suddenly peeked out from the muzzle. Mus's eyes shone and sparkled. "I thought that a culverin was a type of bird!"

"Eh?" The gunner cocked one ear.

"Culverins! Aren't they a sort of bird?"

"True it is, Master Mouse. True it is!" The gunner scratched at his patchy gray beard. "All ordnance is named after birds o' prey, y' see? Sakers and peregrines, falcons and culverins. Even muskets! A musket is a vurry small hawk, y' see?"

The mouse clambered up over the lip of the cannon's mouth, his tail twirling merrily behind him. Today Mus wore his sword and hat and a gorget made with the aid of Miriam's tin snips; quite the military gentleman he looked. The cannon had him quite in awe.

"Is it very loud?"

"EH?"

"I said—*is it very loud?*"

"To fire?" The old man shook his head contemptuously, making the tassel of his woollen cap dance and jiggle. "Nay, sir! 'Tis as sweet as a nightingale's song."

Mus pattered eagerly up and down the length of the cannon. "May we fire it?"

"Eh? Why, sir, thy mistress 'd have my eggs off with a blunt razor! We'un have precious little powder to waste! But you come by later when we range her in, an' ye'll see how she fires."

Mus gazed down with approval at the fortifications far below.

Ditches and earthen ramparts spread around the castle like a gigantic star. All the science of military engineering had been brought to bear. Mus struck a heroic stance upon the cannon's nose and regally surveyed his command.

From this high vantage, one could see all the hills and sleepy valleys that lay around the town. Kerbridge town had surrounded itself with earthen walls; backed hard into the river bend, the only approach now led straight past the castle walls. The old fortress stood high and proud above it all, her cannon covering both the river and the town. With the capital city fallen and Aelis's legions on the march, these strong old walls might see action all too soon.

Mus of Kerbridge, heroic defender of the crown, was interrupted from behind. "Mus, dear—may I disturb thee, or art thou being ferocious?"

The mouse looked up in embarrassment to find Miriam kneeling beside him. Her eyes sparkled with kindly amusement. "Personally conducting our defense again?"

"I—well, there is no harm in pretending. . . ." Mus blushed, and Miriam's warm smile did not help. "I like to pretend."

Miriam scooped him up into her warm hand. "And I also, my friend." She nuzzled him with her freckled nose. "Do the defenses meet with thine approval, Sir Mouse?"

In reply, Mus imperiously swept out one arm.

"Hang out our banners on the outward walls!
The cry is still 'They come!'
Our castle's strength will laugh a siege to scorn!"

Miriam laughed in delight. "Come, you wee poseur! Let's find Frielle and see what mischief's buzzing through her horns this time."

"Thou hast soot upon thy face."

"Hist now! Come along."

The two friends descended the stairs into the inner bailey, where the once-deserted gardens had been turned all atumble with livestock. Chickens chased one another through the dirt while pigs rooted through the waving parsley. Miriam's chapel retreat had become the forward magazine, its deep vaults now stuffed with barrels of powder and garlands of shot. Miriam sighed and promised herself that better days would come.

They found Frielle near the ruined bailey wall, tossing a small
ball into the air. Opal wheeled through the sky high above, catching the ball in midflight and then gleefully flicking it back to her
mistress. The little dragon flashed like a ribbon of molten sapphire, preening outrageously before her audience.

Frielle kept her eyes firmly fixed upon the dragon as her singsong voice danced out to greet her friends.

"Whenever I'm scared or lonely, this wee creature takes it 'pon
herself to play the buffoon! I soon forget what exactly was causin'
me fret." Opal swirled overhead in a clatter of gauzy wings, chirping with pleasure. "Are ye aware that there's soot on thy face?"

Miriam frowned and snatched up a corner of her apron. By irritably scrubbing at her cheek she managed to turn a sharp line of
dirt into a broad gray smudge. Frielle plucked a kerchief from her
sleeve and skipped over to the rescue. Wetting the cloth with her
dainty pink tongue, Frielle removed the offending stain from
Miriam's cheek.

Mus took the opportunity to flow across onto Frielle's bosom,
then lifted his nose, with his eyes slitted in ecstasy.

"O Frielle! Thou'rt beautiful!" Mus sighed. "And my favorite
perfume . . ."

"Why thank thee, Mus! I've had a perfectly awful time fillin'
cartridges all night. I changed into this before comin' out. If I'm
to be besieged, I'll at least be properly dressed." She crinkled up
her nose. "It might spark some o' the lads, anyway. At least that
might be somethin'. . . ."

Frielle's elfin little face fell, and dejection settled over her like a
cloud. Miriam took her by the arm as the satyr turned away.
"Frielle . . . ?"

Her friend remained silent, her eyes pained and sad.

"Frielle—is aught wrong?"

The satyr kept her head bowed. "I—I'm not clever like thee,
Miriam. I have nothin' to offer." She turned her face away. "I-I
can't even cook! Thou hast thy medicines; everybody looks up to
thee. All I am is in the way. . . .

"I'm frightened, Miriam."

They walked on. Miriam slipped her arm about her friend's
waist. "Frielle?"

Silence. Frielle's hands were trembling.

"Frielle—filling cartridges is no waste of time. Nor was

making sashes as field signs for the men. . . ." Miriam swallowed hard. "There—there's still time to leave. Go north to General Vardvere. . . ."

The satyr girl drew a deep, shuddering breath.

"You people are all that I have. Thou'rt everything to me. *Everything* . . ." She raised her face, and tears shone bright within her almond eyes. "I want to stay with thee."

"I can't ask that. Aelis is coming. We must surely fall."

"I know." Frielle's voice was hushed and quiet. "But all the same, I'll be stayin' with thee."

Mus crept beneath Frielle's hair and joined Opal in nuzzling at her neck. "I love thee, Frielle."

The satyr bit her lip. "I love *thee*, thou wondrous creature! I love thee both . . . !"

The silence was rudely broken by a joyous, thunderous shout from the gatehouse guards. The women looked up to discover the castle gone mad. Men charged over to the battlements and stood hurtling their hats into the air, their cheers shaking at the fortress like an earthquake!

Miriam's eyes went wide, and she took a faltering step toward the gates. Suddenly her heart hammered like a wild thing. "Is it them? Frielle—*it's them!*"

The satyr shot past her, her skirts hitched up and hooves flying. Miriam had a clear view of Frielle's woolly shanks before her own wits returned. With a squeal of joy she leapt forward, hooves gouging turf as she stretched out into the gallop.

"*Torscha!—Torscha!*"

The gateway thronged with footsore, bedraggled men. Sailors in woollen caps and soldiers in Duncruighan red had formed into draft teams, hauling dozens of massive cannons up the castle hill. Standing to one side was a huge black stallion in full armor. He dropped a load of powder barrels as his eyes hungrily searched the crowds.

"*Torscha!*"

The man whirled, suddenly light upon his massive hooves. Miriam flung herself into his arms and was lost to the world. His kiss felt like fire and wine, love and laughter; mere steel could not hide the pounding of his heart. Miriam crushed him close and wept for sheer joy, babbling words with no idea what she did or said. Torscha held her in his arms, and all seemed right with the world.

They drew apart to find a breathless Frielle awaiting nearby.

"Torscha! O Torscha, ye've come back to us!" She bounced up, grasped him by the neck and stole a kiss. "Oh!—Oh . . . !" For once the girl seemed utterly at a loss for words. Opal dived down from on high to swoop across their heads as the men from Torscha's ship flowed past to swell the garrison. The castle dissolved into utter mayhem as the newcomers were given a wild welcome.

A little furry ball sprang across to Retter's armored shoulder and perched between the two lovers. Torscha laughed with delight as he swept Mus up before his eyes.

"Mus! Mus, my dear fellow!"

The mouse turned wild with glee. "Torscha! O Torscha! You see, Miriam, I said that he'd come back to thee! Am I not clever?" The mouse danced upon the edge of Retter's hand and cast eager eyes about the soldiers. "Torscha, where's Willy?"

Torscha's face turned deathly pale as Mus looked up with innocent, happy eyes.

"I have *missed* Willy so! . . . Torscha?"

Retter looked back toward the sea, and Miriam's face fell in shocked disbelief. The stallion's expression said it all.

Mus bounced up and down merrily. "Where is he? I've so much to show him! Oooh, and a new card game, too!" Mus peered out over the milling teams of sailors. "Is he at the back with all the guns?"

There was a painful silence.

Miriam's eyes never left Torscha. When she finally spoke, her voice had fallen to a whisper.

"*He . . . isn't here, Mus.*"

Still Mus did not understand; all of a sudden his friends had gone terribly quiet. Miriam moved into Retter's arms, her face shining bright with tears.

Suddenly the truth became awfully clear; Mus rose to his back feet, his face draining of its life.

"NO! No, Torscha! He . . ."

Miriam cupped the little creature in her hands, and Mus fought frantically to break free.

"*No! No! He's coming! He must be!*"

"Mus!" Torscha's voice blew soft and firm. "Willy was lost during a battle at sea. I know not what became of him. We can only hope and pray . . ."

Mus wept as though his soul bled white, and Miriam folded him against her heart.

"There's a dear! We can't have you going thirsty, can we?"

The woman's voice purred like that of a well-fed cat, stimulating delicious tingles of delight. Lady Jessica perched herself upon a couch and flicked her tail about her haunches, sending a tantalizing waft of scent across the room. Her sly eyes regarded her guest as she lavishly poured him wine.

Her guest felt more than a little addled; the cavalier lay bonelessly upon a couch with all four legs drawn up beneath him, plied with wine and besotted by beauty. Even his freshly splinted arm seemed not to trouble him. His eyes kept wandering down to the low cleavage of Jessica's dress. The slippery satin hugged her body like a second skin, highlighting every pleasure that lay smoldering beneath. Jessica slyly stretched to show her charms to more advantage.

They sat in a drawing room in Aelis's headquarters outside of Duncruigh's conquered capital. Jessica lounged back and clinked glasses with her guest, satin whispering soft promises as she moved.

"Drink up, now! Drink up! We must celebrate! To think you have bested the officers of the guard at the tables!" Her lips pursed meaningfully. "You are quite the gamesman, sir. One wonders if there are *other* games at which you might excel. . . ."

"T-Twuly, madam . . ."

"Jessica! *Do* call me Jessica!"

"Twuly, *Jessica*—this has been the wuckiest evening I can e'er recall!"

The mare's muscles bunched as she changed position. "Well, Sir Cavalier, who knows? You may be luckier yet. . . ." The woman's tail lifted higher and shivered in anticipation. Jessica's eyes were dark and inviting, her lips soft and moist. . . . Her guest hastened to swallow his wine.

Her servant swiftly moved to top the empty glass. A strange, spry whip of a man, the satyr was fantastically decked out in clothes of riotous, clashing colors. At a signal from his mistress, the man faded out of view.

Willy shook his head and tried to clear it; 'd's blood, his ears sang as though they harbored swarms of bees! His brain swam through giddy mists of alcoholic fugue. Now what had they been talking of?

Winnings? Ah, yes, his winnings at the tables! Willy let the joy wrap itself around him like a warm yellow glow. The Nantierran royal guards lived a hectic life of gambling and carousing that left Willy Merle quite breathless. Here was the life: gaiety and laughter, the roll of the dice, the *chink* of glasses! Since getting his parole, he had been allowed to mingle about until he could be exchanged for a captured Nantierran officer of equal rank. He had signed on his honor not to attempt escape, and it was more than his life was worth to be cad enough to abscond! In any case, the Nantierran guardsmen had been more than cordial; truly he could not have fallen into better care.

Sharp nails traced their way along his flank. Willy's eyes opened in shock to discover Jessica nestling close beside him.

"Mmmmm, you are *beautiful!* It will be such a pity to lose you tomorrow."

Willy looked befuddled, and Jessica sweetly cocked her head. "Why, sir, did you not know? Tomorrow you are to be exchanged. We shall be all the poorer for the loss of your dear company." Her wandering hand became bolder. "I *so* wanted to give you a private farewell. . . ."

Willy was lost; he had fallen helplessly beneath the seductress's spell. "Well, I . . ."

Jessica's face fell. "Oh, Willy, it pained me so to hear that you are sorely in debt! We have become such friends!" She melted him with her wonderful eyes. "An acquaintance of mine would like to pick up your notes and free you from this plight."

Willy blinked, and suddenly his heart soared. Free from debt! Free at last from shame and penury. It was the chance of a lifetime!

"Wh-Who will do this?" Willy spoke in a hushed, drunken whisper. Something at the back of his mind tried to tell him that this was unwise.

"Why, simply some of the good friends that you've made here!" The woman's voice was sweet, her hands soft and exciting. "We simply ask that you remember the favor sometime in the future." She drew a paper out from beneath the divan. "Here's the silly thing! Why don't you just sign this—it gives your consent to pass all your horrid debts on to our friend."

Paper? Willy tried to focus but failed.

"It's all right. Sign! Sign and then let us celebrate. . . ."

Her smell swirled in his nostrils, setting his blood afire. God, what a woman! Willy somehow found a quill within his hand, beamed happily, and signed the paper, congratulating himself on his astounding stroke of luck. The pen was eased out of his hand, and he found himself stroking her.

Jessica's eyes met her servant's, and she gave a crafty smile. Her eyes flicked toward the door, and Pin-William quietly withdrew. The satyr brushed off his gaudy sleeves and rubbed his hands with glee.

"A sssuccess, masster?"

Snatch uncoiled from a mantelpiece and stretched like a languorous cat. Pin-William reached out to scratch his companion's furry ears.

"Success, Snatch! One might say he's rising to the bait. . . ." The satyr stroked his mustache. "Lady Jessica could put life in a corpse! A most admirable partner!"

Pin-William had finally fallen on his feet; in Aelis's ranks he had found fortune once again. Aelis had need of talented spies, and who else should rise to the task but Pin-William! Pin-William the bold, Pin-William the clever! A man who strode bravely forward where others feared to tread.

With his control of Snatch and the wretched, sniveling little lady mouse, Pin-William had become one of the queen's most valued agents. During the hard fighting for the capital and the reduction of the many little forts and enclaves that clustered thereabout, his creatures had proved their worth again and again.

Snatch touched his tongue to his wicked fangs. The stoat felt mischief on the air–a chance to kill again.

"And do we now to Kerbridge, Masster?"

"Oh, soon—quite soon. Brave King Firined skulks to our north. The river is the best road inland Aelis could ever have. We'll swat Kerbridge aside and then roust the good king from his lair!"

The satyr offered his arm, and Snatch flowed up onto his master's shoulders. Pin-William snatched up his hat and set it at a jaunty slant between his horns.

"Come, my good Snatch! Tonight you shall kill a sweet duckling for your dinner. Then we shall fetch that useless mouse up from the dripping dungeons and see what trivia the prisoners discussed today!"

They stalked off down the corridors, while behind them the parlor lights grew dim.

Light filtered through the lofty ceiling beams of Jerrick hall, where dust motes danced beside the ancient stones. It lingered upon shot-torn banners and stern-faced portraits, striking harsh highlights from the company below.

It was a grim gathering; Torscha Retter and Captain Brayberry of the *Nemesis* were hunched over a diagram of the town. There were ship's officers and gentlemen from the town militia, as well as country squires who had roused their men to arms. At the end of the table stood a grave-faced little pixie from the northern woods, who had flown in with fifty forest folk not an hour before. Miriam sat rolling bandages beside the surgeon, Doctor Freeps, and neither of them chose to speak a word.

Only Bishop Kaxter seemed light of heart. That worthy gentleman stood armed in a hunter's buffcoat, polishing a rifled musket fully seven feet long. He had greeted Mister Kelso like a long-lost child, and the two scoundrels had been sitting thick as thieves over a jug of rum.

Mus perched in the middle of the table, surrounded by a pile of tiny quills. Frielle stood close by, drafted by the tyrannical little rodent into copying out his maps. The girl squinted through a quizzing glass at Mus's drawings, biting her underlip as she carefully etched out measured lines.

Colonel Tyburn of the Kerbridge Trained Bands argued bitterly with Torscha, fighting against Retter's orders tooth and nail. "You waste our forces, sir! Waste 'em! It is futile to divide our men!"

With cold dislike, Torscha watched the militia colonel. Although his face stayed set in a martial frown, his rear hoof poised dangerously in midair. "I tell you, sir, it is no waste! Our best defense is to keep grips on both town and castle!"

"Futile!"

"Give me the benefit of mine experience, sir!"

Tyburn's face blazed red. "And give me benefit of my wits! We are Duncruighan gentlemen—not some republican rabble! The day some leveling foreigner . . ."

A little voice irritably interrupted Tyburn's tirade.

"Control commanding ground."

"Eh?" Tyburn whirled to find his speaker. "What! What nonsense is this now?"

"*Paloretto's Principles of the Siege.*" Mus measured drawings with his tail, scarcely looking up as he continued his vital work. " 'The engineer must needs be aware of commanding ground from which the assault may be prepared and supported by goodly use of ordnance. Such terrain must be secured and used to full advantage.' "

Tyburn gaped as though he had seen a frog in the milk jug; he had yet to come to terms with Kerbridge's shocking new resident. Mus frowned busily up from the tabletop and tucked his quill behind one ear. "The other books seem to agree. Deny the enemy their best advantage. 'Twould seem to be common sense."

Retter gestured with finality. "There you have it! We will hold on to the commanding ground." To Torscha, Mus was an unquestionable source. The militia colonel begged to differ, looking in horror from the half-horse to the mouse.

"You cannot be serious, sir? You intend to take tactical instructions from a mouse?"

"Indeed I do, sir; and if you ever speak as much sense as he, then we might heed your own words as well." Colonel Retter glowered at Tyburn from across his maps. "Colonel Tyburn, our dispositions are as I have ordered. The country contingents, ship's company, and half-horse shall remain within this castle. Take your 'trained bands' and go. Your station is within the town."

Tyburn departed, taking a swirl of militia officers with him, and morale noticeably rose once the wretched man had gone. Retter swiftly brought the meeting back to business.

"We have river cliff at the castle's east, and an open slope to the south. Horton and Keogh, your companies will hold the north and western walls, and the pixie bands the east. The south wall and gates shall be held by my men, the *Nemesis's* crew, His Grace the bishop's company, and the castle guard."

Retter leaned back from the maps. "My staff consists of my first lieutenant, Mus, along with any secretaries that he sees fit to appropriate. Victuals are in the hands of Hattie, the Jerricks' cook. Medicinary and surgery shall be undertaken by the good doctor Freeps and the ladies."

That was it; Retter drew on his heavy, lace-cuffed gauntlets. "Questions? No?—Good!" Everyone seemed firm unto their tasks.

The officers drew breaths and briskly reached for swords and hats.

Wineglasses were produced, and the company raised their cups. Retter stood beneath the Jerricks' coat of arms and called the toast.

"God save the king, and damnation to our enemies!"

"GOD SAVE THE KING!"

A young cavalier suddenly burst in upon the hall. Mud spattered his boots, and a bloody tear ran across the sleeve of his fine buffcoat. Retter clattered to his side.

"What now, sir! What report?"

The intruder slid hastily about to face Colonel Retter. "I bring orders from the army, sir! From the pen of General Vardvere." He breathlessly delved into his satchel and plucked forth a tight roll of parchment. "He advises that this p-position is untenable! He recommends that you flee northward to sanctuary with His Majesty's forces."

Torscha thoughtfully unrolled the parchment between his gauntleted hands, and the stallion's brow lowered.

Lady Barbara coolly crossed the room and put out her hand to receive the parchment. She flicked her eyes across the page without interest, then tossed it swiftly aside.

"So, Colonel Retter; do *you* believe that our position is untenable?"

"My lady, Kerbridge stands across Aelis's route to the kingdom's heart. I do not claim that we can survive; I say we have strength enough to make her pay heavy toll for her passage."

Mus suddenly leapt atop a helmet and looked around the company with blazing little eyes. The mouse's sense of drama had been challenged.

"Madam! You can't be thinking of abandoning thy home! Of turning tail in flight!" From atop his perch the mouse swept forth his tiny sword. "We stand upon the page of history! Let none say the doughty folk of Kerbridge were found wanting! I say stand firm!"

"Hear hear!" The bishop was well into his third glass of rum. "We'll stall her! You tell the king!"

The officers met the declaration with a storm of applause. Retter coolly handed the parchment back to the messenger.

"And there lies your answer, sir! Bid the king come in haste to Kerbridge. We defend his kingdom *here!*"

Chapter Four

Parley

ar came to Kerbridge bright and early with the dawn.

It started as a faint popping, crackling sound far off in the river mists. Mus perched upon the battlements with Frielle by his side and stretched up high on his two hind legs to listen. "I say, is it a *whole* army, or only part of an army?"

"Thou silly creature! However should *I* know? Part or whole, 'tis trouble enough, I'll warrant."

Mus moved closer to the edge of the wall. The eastern ramparts overlooked a sheer drop down into the river deeps below, and Frielle made haste to snatch hold of Mus's tail.

There was a renewed surge of small-arms fire in the distance, and this time Frielle's tall, pointed ears caught the direction. "There! Mus—d' ye see? Puffs o' smoke upon the ridge!"

"Odd's fish! They're way too distant!" Mus leapt up and down in agitation. "Frielle, I can't see!"

"Well p'raps if thou asked 'em nicely they'd come closer—seein' as they've nowt better on their minds."

Mus immediately went into a sulk. "Thou'rt being facetious. I only meant that I cannot see so far."

The satyr girl chucked him under the chin. "I mean nothin' by it. Hop up on my shoulder, and I'll tell ye what I see."

Frielle squinted prettily; it was hard to make out quite what was happening. "There's a small group o' men—p'raps four dozen or more. Fast, flash fellows on horseback. They've all dismounted to hide behind a hedge."

A fresh wave of crackling swept up on the morning air. Tiny

puffs of smoke drifted up from the skirmishers as they unleashed a storm of musket fire; Frielle blinked in amazement. "Whup! They're up and ridin' once again. An agile bunch o' fellows."

Mus bounced up and down in frustration, his tail bobbed furiously behind him. "Who are they fighting with! Tell me!"

"I can't see, ye bossy little creature! Be still!" The faun scowled as she rolled up her lacy sleeves. "They're shootin' at someone on the far side of the ridge—wait! I see now! Yes, there's a troop of horse in pursuit. Nantierran horse."

The mouse ran back and forth in agitation. "What now! What is the first group—"

"Mus! I've no idea, I tell ye! None of it makes any sense to me!"

Scolding her for a ninny, Mus raced across to one of the nearby cannon. A master gunner stood watching the distant fray through his perspective glass. Mus sprang onto the cannon's breech and politely doffed his hat.

"I say, excuse me, sir!" The gunner glanced downward in annoyance, then almost dropped his telescope as the mouse gave him a dapper bow. "Sir, I wonder if we might beg a moment's use of your glass. I should so terribly like to see the activity on the far hill!"

The gunner wordlessly passed his telescope across to Frielle, who graciously inclined her head in thanks. She made to hold the glass herself, but Mus threw up such a tantrum that she had to let him use it first. She found herself propping the glass upon the battlements while Mus crouched at the eyepiece calling directions.

"Left! Left—more! No, stop! Right . . ." His tail stuck up into the air like a skinny little question mark. "Oh! Well now it's all fuzzy!"

Frielle adjusted the tubes. "Better?"

"No—yes! Yes, that's it!"

Mus peered through the tube with one beady eye and watched the distant scene unfold. A line of dragoons were coolly fighting a rear-guard action against a troop of Nantierran horse. The dragoon's officer led his men back from road to road and hedge to hedge, dismounting to fire deadly volleys at the enemy. The enemy horse drew off, and the dragoons took the opportunity to cross the river and race toward the castle gates.

"Let me see now!" Frielle was fairly hopping with impatience.

"Just a moment more!"

"Mus—thou'st had it far too long!" Frielle snatched up the glass despite the mouse's whine of disappointment. She quickly fixed upon the swirl of troops below, ignoring the little creature that plucked irritably at her dress. Her glass fixed on the dragoon officer, a handsome satyr with a splash of white lace at his throat.

The dragoons raced through the orange orchard toward the castle walls. Behind them lagged a single dashing cavalier. He halted at the foot of the road, wheeled about and made a mock salute toward his foes. It was only then that Frielle noticed the man to be a half-horse.

"Mus . . . Mus! The officer at the rear!"

"Where! What officer! Oh, give me back my glass!"

Frielle almost dropped the telescope. "It's Willy! Willy Merle! Mus—he's come back to us!"

"WILLY!" Mus sprang for the battlements and leaned dangerously over the edge. "*Willy!*"

Frielle snatched up the mouse and charged off down the tower steps in a frothing foam of skirts. The master gunner bemusedly doffed his hat, wriggled his mustache, and went back to gazing thoughtfully out across the view.

"Willy! Willy, oh, Willy!" Mus rolled about in an ecstasy of affection, rubbing his nose against Willy's unshaven cheek. "Willy, I've missed you so!"

William laughed aloud; with Frielle hanging about his neck and Mus weeping in his ear, he must have made quite the picture. "Hush now—what's this? Surely thou didst not think old Willy wost?"

Mus simply ran tiny hands across Willy's face and wept for joy.

Frielle scrubbed at her eyes, clutching tight against the cavalier. "Oh, ye silly man, what e'er have ye done to thyself?" She plucked at Willy's sling. "What tomfoolery's this?"

William took Frielle's hands, keeping Mus perched on his shoulder. "Ha! A minor mishap caused by sev'ral tons of falling masthead." He fixed his audience with one sparkling eye. "I assure thee that it could have been far worse."

Willy suddenly remembered his companion of the dragoons, and waved the gentleman over. "Thomas! Come here and meet these people! Captain Sir Thomas Carpernan, may I present Damsel Frielle Dewauncy, and my dear friend, Mus of Kerbridge."

The young satyr had trotted briskly over, tail a-wag, to receive his introduction. Slim, dark, and golden-skinned, he had piercing golden eyes and the fine features of a hawk.

His gaze never reached as far as Mus. The captain turned from Willy to Frielle, where he stopped as though struck dead. The two satyrs locked eyes, their faces blanching ashen white; Frielle backed helplessly away, her pupils going wide with shock. Sir Thomas Carpernan removed his hat, freeing long black lovelocks as he numbly made a bow.

"*Madam . . .*"

"*Sir . . .*"

Frielle suddenly staggered backward and fled for the steps. Mus clasped adoringly to Willy's neck, barely even noticing that Frielle had gone.

"Oh, Willy—I've learned so much! And the place is so very changed. And then there's Torscha and the sailors. . . ."

Willy stiffened and swallowed.

Down the same steps Frielle had hurried up, Miriam was now whirling down in a great clatter of hooves, her arms outstretched to welcome Willy in. Mus whooped with glee.

"*Miriam!* I said he would come back!"

"*Willy!* Oh, Willy!" Miriam flung her arms about her friend and crushed him tight. "Oh, God! Oh, Willy, I'm so glad!" She looked back over her shoulder. "*Darling? 'Tis our Willy!*"

Torscha stood in the doorway, a massive shadow dressed in black and buff. He charged forward to clap his friend joyously upon the shoulder and grip him by the hand, while Mus leapt excitedly back and forth between all three.

"All my friends! All my friends together again!" The little mouse almost burst with joy. "Now we cannot fail!"

Willy could not meet Torscha's eyes. Behind him, Thomas Carpernan's hands shook as he trimmed his horse's bridle.

First came the cavalry—grim troopers encased in leather and steel. The light horse in their breastplates and long-tailed helms, and cuirassiers in full "lobster" suits of russet steel. Banners tossed while proud horses stepped high along the road, disdaining the humble earth on which they trod.

Next, the infantry stamped down the roadway, marching with the plodding ease of veterans. Pikes and muskets were held aslant and helmets hung casually from belt hooks. They were well paid and well fed, and the drive into Duncruigh's heartlands had brought victory after victory. With the sun shining and birds singing in their ears, the Nantierran army marched up the valley toward Kerbridge town.

Aelis stood on the flower-speckled grass, watching her men go by. The river gurgled sleepily by the wayside, caressing Aelis's soul with sweet dreams of contentment. The queen heaved a delighted sigh and plucked a succulent red apple from her apron pocket.

"Let us not waste time here." She repressed a yawn. "Encamp the men about the town, but don't bother with full entrenchment. We'll parley with the garrison before beginning investment."

A chill presence stirred beneath the trees as a black half-horse sheathed in sable armor drew closer to the road. Count Gerhard Retter, general of the royalist army of Welfland, stayed well clear of the shining queen. The massive black stallion remained a faceless juggernaut, forever hidden behind a visor of steel. The helmet slowly turned itself toward Kerbridge Castle.

"The castle is the key. Crush it, and the town will fall."

Aelis casually polished an apple on her breast. "The castle holds a goodly seat. A very pleasant place to live, I should imagine. Very pleasant indeed."

The first gigantic barges nosed around the river bend. Each vessel carried powder, shot and provisions to fuel Aelis's campaign in the north.

The river was Aelis's master stroke: a huge, smooth roadway leading far into Duncruigh's heart. The current ran slow, the river deep, and barges could move straight from Aelis's supply ships to Kerbridge and far beyond. All the way north—where King Firined skulked in hiding with his rabble of an army. *Kerbridge;* it guarded a swift highway to victory, and so the town must fall.

Frogs creaked to one another in the rushes. *Frogs!* Aelis cocked her head in interest as a sudden inspiration struck.

"We shall parley in a *civilized* fashion. Coax our erstwhile enemies into surrender."

The count hissed in contempt. "*Fear* is all an enemy understands. *Terror.* Sack the surrounding villages. Crucify every man, woman, and child before the castle garrison's eyes. Display the consequences of resistance."

Aelis sighed, then irritably took a bite from her apple. "*General.*
You can be so tiresome." Aelis finished her mouthful, then glanced
archly over her shoulder. "You are excused from our little levée. There is
a time for swords, General, and a time for words. I *never* fail to use my
every weapon. Diplomacy is one part of my arsenal; you are another."
Aelis thoughtfully took a bite. "I shall have my highway to the north,
General. Silken glove or iron gauntlet; it matters not to me." She gave a
saucy toss of the head. "But faith, a break in the violence would ease the
boredom. 'Tis spring! There's more to life than *war!*"

With a flirtatious flick of her tail, Aelis trotted off down the path
to seek out her staff. Behind her, Count Retter gazed up at Kerbridge castle with cold, dead eyes while behind him, siege cannon
rumbled down the country roads.

One way or another, Kerbridge would fall. Count Retter chafed
in the darkness and fed his ever-restless hate.

* * * * *

The Nantierran harpy wore the white garments of truce. He irritably paced the battlements, acutely aware of the Jerricks' sergeant
of the castle guard. The sergeant sat nonchalantly on the fire-step,
keeping a swivel gun casually pointed in the harpy's direction and
eating pickles from a jar. The harpy seemed less concerned about the
sergeant's swivel gun than he did about the dreadful stench of the
Duncruighan's lunch.

Miriam stood in the parlor, her eyes alive with excitement as
Torscha read the herald's scroll. The invitation to a parley seemed
like a dream come true.

Aelis! Queen Aelis! To meet her *at last. . . .* Miriam's mind raced.
*Lud! I shall need my best gown. . . . No! Too dressy! Heavens—it's to be
informal. Perhaps my good blue dress and a straw hat. . . .*

Torscha folded his arms and straightened, standing with his tail
held high. "No, I shall not parley, nor shall I break bread with the
despoiler of my homeland." That was that.

Miriam's face fell, and her underlip dropped in shock. "Torscha!
Thou can't be serious!"

"Yea—*very.*"

"But we need you, my love. You are our parliamentarian—our
orator. Please speak for us."

Torscha's tail lowered, and Miriam held his hands.

"Please?"

Retter sighed and nodded, the hatred suddenly washing out of his face; he was rewarded by a grateful squeeze.

Miriam's mother stood by Torscha's side, nodding thoughtfully to herself as she read Aelis's request for parley.

"We lose nothing by talking, and every hour we delay them is a godsend. Miriam, thou shalt go with the good colonel to represent our interests. Take one or two other officers with thee."

Torscha respectfully listened to her every word.

"Dost thou suggest any names, madam?"

"Frielle must certainly go, to show our unconcern. P'raps that satyr officer from the dragoons could partner her. They should make a handsome couple. Willy Merle—he has been in their camp and can possibly give us good report." The baroness made a quick total on her slim fingers. "Five. A party of five should be quite sufficient. Take the sergeant with thee as flag bearer and servant." She peered out of the window. "Though I think we shall bid him leave his pickles behind. . . ."

Mus burst out from a wall panel. He galloped across the sideboard with a fistful of bright ribbons trailing behind, then sprang up onto the table before the baroness. "Lady Barbara, canst thou advise me what to wear?" The mouse offered up his bunch of gay ribbons in tiny little hands. "Red, blue, green? Which collar would suit me best?"

The baroness reached out with one cool, thin hand and gently lifted Mus up from his perch. She loved little Mus and could not bear to see him disappointed.

"I'm sorry, Mus, but of all of us here, thou canst not go."

Mus made a little whimper of hurt dismay. "But—but I am Torscha's staff lieutenant. . . ."

"I know, my darling. But thou must remain here."

"B-But why?" Mus's whiskers trembled. "It isn't fair!"

"I know, sweet Mus, but thou art one of the aces up our sleeves. We must not advertise thy presence."

Mus hung his head, and his ribbons fell from his hand. "Bu-But couldn't I at least hide in someone's pocket?"

"Nay, sweet mouse. Everyone will be searched. You and I shall stay behind together, eh? Opal shall keep us company."

Mus slumped in misery, and the baroness tried to console him by scratching the root of his tail. Miriam knelt beside the mouse and offered sweet comfort.

"Ah, well, my friend. 'Tis all for the best."

"I suppose so." Mus sighed unhappily and settled into a sulky little ball. "But why is 'the best' never any fun?"

Aelis glowered at the cowering little figure before her.

"You are aware of the plan?"

The answering voice piped as sad and soft as thistledown. "Yes, Majesty."

"You know what to do?"

"Yes, Majesty." The little voice seemed infinitely worn and weary; without hope, without life. The mouse simply sat in her place and kept her eyes downcast. She appeared thin and sickly, and Aelis inspected the animal in alarm.

"Fellow! Do you feed this poor creature?"

"Indeed, Your Majesty! Indeed I do! A crust of bread from time to time." Pin-William posed with a long, admonishing finger held in the air. "A keen hunger keeps an edge on her enthusiasm."

"Keen edge? The beast's fading away before mine eyes!" The queen fixed the satyr with a distasteful glare, then signed imperiously to her cooks. "Bring her a biscuit and—and cheese!" She felt sure that mice ate cheese. "And some nuts and greens. I'll not have the beast dying on us. Feed her at once!" The queen looked at the mouse and swallowed unhappily. "Uh—*take her away* and feed her!"

A cook gingerly conducted the rodent to the kitchens while the queen paced irritably about her tent. A table had been set, all ready for luncheon with the Duncruighan delegation. Aelis frowned and moved a long-handled fork a few hairsbreadths to the left.

"You tell me that this mouse needs no papers, no pens, no charts and such?"

Pin-William swept down in another extravagant bow, brushing the floor with the plumes of his hat.

"O Queen of Queens, my servants have perfect memories. The mouse will be inserted into one of the visiting delegation's saddle-bags or pistol holsters. Upon the delegation's return to the castle, she shall come out and explore." Pin-William took a gleeful little skip and rubbed his hands together. "By tonight, we'll have their numbers counted and all their defenses mapped!" The satyr's plan obviously pleased him. Aelis tried to hide her disgust.

"Can this mouse be trusted? Why does she not merely take flight once she wins free of your tender loving care?"

The satyr gave a sly grin. "Aaaah, Majesty! She shall do *exactly* as she is bid!" His voice dropped to an evil whisper. "For if she displeases me, her mind shall burn like fire."

In the queen's commissary, the mouse sat staring wide-eyed at the food laid before her. Cheeses, sugar biscuits, fresh nuts, and salty pretzels! The mouse hesitantly reached out one hand to touch the nearest tidbit.

Real! It was real! The mouse felt a giddy rush of wonder. It seemed so hard to tell, these days. So very hard. Starvation and cruelty had reduced her world to a sea of pain and sorrow. But somewhere—somewhere there was a dream of safety—of belonging. There were bright black eyes, and a voice all full of kindness. . . .

Food. Eat! The mouse mechanically took the food, wincing as a hand savagely chopped her wrist, sending her morsel flying. *Snatch.* Of course it was Snatch. The mouse warily reached for food, and once again he slapped it from her grasp. The mouse drooped and quietly turned aside.

"They said I should eat. The queen said so."

"And sssso? But what of poor Sssnatch? But what shall *I* eat, I wonder?" Snatch's claw caressed her throat. The mouse closed her lashes and tried to ignore him. The stoat grabbed her by the neck and dragged her from the kitchens.

"It is time to go." Snatch hissed evilly in his victim's ear. "But if you beg, perhaps I might let you eat just a bite. Do you want to beg, yessss?"

The mouse dully closed her eyes and let him drag her as he willed. Finally she had a plan, a gloriously simple plan.

She needed her rest; she needed to be able to walk into the castle—far away from Pin-William's prying eyes.

And when she was safe, she would find a way to die.

The little group from the castle trotted through star-spangled grass beneath the shadows of the orange grove. A sergeant went before them, proudly holding aloft the Jerrick banner—a simple blue cornflower on a clean white field.

Miriam's head spun all abuzz as she rehearsed what she might say to the glamorous Queen Aelis. Torscha stalked through the grass at her side, casting a cloak of dignity about his companions. Treading silently on their heels came Willy Merle—conspicuously alone.

At the rear of the column rode the two satyrs, Thomas Carpernan laboring in the dusty wake of Frielle's mount. Frielle rode daintily upon a sidesaddle, her hooves all but hidden beneath frothing lace skirts. Unusually, Opal had remained back at the castle; the tiny dragon would not bear Carpernan's company, and went flying into a hysterical rage whenever he came near. Thus far she had managed to keep Thomas and Frielle well apart.

Angelic as her clothes might be, there was nothing soft in Frielle's expression. Slim golden hands held her reins in a death grip. She looked neither left nor right, excluding her partner as though he were less than a slug beneath her hooves.

Sir Thomas stiffly sat his horse, looking rigidly ahead, afraid of catching Frielle's eye. He drew beside the girl and kept his gaze fixed firmly on the dust. "Frielle?"

Frielle rode on as if she never heard.

Sir Thomas twitched his tail and tried again. "Frielle?" His voice held the rich dance of the Channel Isles. For all its soft music, it fell into silence. "Frielle, I-I have some things I wish to say. . . ."

Frielle gave a tap of her crop and stirred her horse onward. Suddenly abandoned, Thomas snatched out for the girl's arm. With a mindless snarl of rage, Frielle viciously slashed his face with her riding crop, and a line of bright blood burst across his cheek.

"*Don't touch me!* Don't you *ever* touch me!"

"Frielle! I . . . "

The satyr girl lowered her horns and hissed at Sir Thomas with contempt. "Don't *touch* me, don't *watch* me, don't think of me, don't speak to me. Not now—not ever!" She wrenched her horse about. "Now, begone!" With a dig of her hooves she cantered after Miriam. Thomas sat upon his horse and hung his head, slowly trotting on.

They were met halfway through the grove by a Nantierran colonel from Aelis's staff, an elegant human dandy with the tanned face of a soldier. The fellow gave an elaborate bow from the saddle, greeting them with the manners of a true courtier.

"Greetings from 'er Most Royal Majesty Queen Aelis of

Nantierre, Duchess of Arie and Lorrian, Regent of the Kingdom of Welfland." He elegantly swept his hat back upon his head. "I am Colonel LaVoisseur of 'er Majesty's Royal Guard, and I make you welcome."

Torscha doffed his hat, uncovering his face. He spoke in Nantierran. "Greetings, Colonel. I am Colonel Retter of the Castle Kerbridge garrison. Allow me to introduce the Damsel Miriam Jerrick, Damsel Frielle Delauncy . . ." Torscha's voice trailed off into silence as the Nantierran colonel stared at him with growing amazement. Retter scowled, irritated at having his words ignored. "Colonel! There is a problem?"

The Nantierran blinked. "I . . . M'sieur, I am sorry. Please forgive." He nervously shied his horse backward, hastily avoiding Torscha's eyes. "If-if you would follow me, *merci*. The queen awaits you."

The man wheeled his mount and led the way toward the enemy lines. Miriam leaned close to whisper in her lover's ear, never taking her eyes from the Nantierran's back.

"*Hisst—thine accent has improved.*"

"*Thank you,*" Retter hissed softly in Miriam's fragrant hair. "*Didst thou see the look on the fellow's face?*"

"*Aye, your countenance startled him. What can it mean?*"

Torscha's grip tightened as an awful, oppressive feeling stirred in his mind. "*I fear to guess. Come, let us meet this queen and make our way quickly home. My spine begins to crawl.*"

The castle's green hill had been encircled by grim lines of men. The legions of Nantierre had spread like ants across the quiet river valley. Their guide led the way toward a simple tent beside the river, where a picnic table had been laid out beneath the weeping willows.

A half-horse girl rose up from the fields of summer daisies. Glorious as the first wild breath of spring, she laughed as she came forth to greet them. The girl trotted gaily forward, riveting all to the spot with her eyes.

Miriam swallowed. *Aelis!*

Aelis of Nantierre could have been almost any young hoyden out to taste the sun, were it not for the air of majesty that surrounded her like a fiery cloud. Colonel LaVoisseur hastened to the fore. "Majesty! I present Colonel—Colonel *Retter* of the castle garrison!"

Aelis stalked forward and extended a hand; Torscha bowed over her fingers and brushed them with a kiss.

For her part, Aelis eyed the black stallion with rapt attention, her eyes full of wonder. "Colonel, a pleasure to meet you once again!" Her voice rang like music in a dream, high and pure as summer wine.

Torscha kept his face carefully neutral and responded in her tongue. "Majesty, you do us too much honor."

"Ahhh—the pleasure is mine, no?"

Torscha brought forth Miriam and bowed in introduction.

"Majesty, I have the honor to introduce Damsel Miriam Jerrick of Kerbridge."

Queen Aelis suddenly became interested; Miriam sank into a profound curtsy and spoke in a flawless Nantierran accent. "Your most Royal Majesty." Miriam kept her head bowed, but some of her adoration spilled out into her voice. "I am most *deeply* honored. . . ."

A slim hand took Miriam by the fingers and lifted her up. "Nay, nay, my dear! Grief! You speak with the accent of a courtier! Up! Up! Let me see you properly."

Aelis's wild blue eyes met the cool, wise green of Miriam's gaze. They were both of a size, and of the exact same age; similar, and yet utterly different. Intelligence and stubborn will lined each woman's brow. Each eyed the other in dawning wonder and respect.

Aelis's voice almost fell to a whisper. "My dear, it—it is truly a pleasure to meet you. . . ." She suddenly smiled. "It seems the Jerricks continue to carry their king's honor, no?" Aelis paused, somehow hesitant, as though afraid of a rebuke. "We must talk, you and I. Agreed?"

"I . . . why yes, Majesty. It should be an honor and a pleasure."

Queen Aelis reluctantly turned to the others. She accepted introductions to Frielle and Sir Thomas, and then waved the party's mounts aside. Still half under Aelis's spell, the folk of Castle Jerrick settled down to a picnic lunch.

Torscha seemed annoyed; he had come to throw the gauntlet of defiance in his enemy's face, and instead found himself taking a meal by the river. Miriam had laughingly entered the spirit, sighing with appreciation as she tasted the excellent cuisine. The girl listened spellbound to Aelis's stories about her past. She surprised the queen by the depth of her questions. In turn, the queen found herself fascinated by her partner's quiet wisdom. It was a quality that drew Aelis despite herself. It had been far too long since she had simply been able to relax and feel at ease.

The queen happily poured Miriam wine, waving away the servant that hastened to take over the task. "Oh, Miriam! 'Tis such a pleasure to meet someone who just simply wants to talk to me!"

Miriam blushed quite red. "Majesty, I . . ."

"Fa! You ought to suffer through a court one day! Ugh! It quite turns the stomach! Mincing courtiers and office seekers everywhere." She sneered in sudden contempt. *"Damn all ladies!*—Your phrase, I believe? I like it!"

Miriam pulled a rueful face. "Ah, Majesty—If only we'd met years ago. You make being called "unladylike" seem like such a compliment!"

"It *is* a compliment!" Aelis sipped her wine and encouraged Miriam to do the same. "Drink! Drink! Relax and be friends!" The food lay ready to hand; Aelis plucked a number of tiny, succulent drumsticks from a silver platter and indelicately ate with her fingers. She groaned in pure ecstasy. "Ooo—heaven!" She put down her plate and heaved a sigh. "If I have one vice, 'tis this. Colonel Retter, *do* eat something."

Torscha stiffly reached out to take a tiny joint of meat. Miriam and Aelis chattered away in Nantierran, and there would clearly be no business done until lunch had finished. Moving with his usual solemn grace, Torscha delicately nibbled on a drumstick, and it melted in his mouth like a stolen kiss. *Ecstasy!*

"Wonderful!" Torscha reached for another piece, then another three or four. "What is it called?"

Aelis licked sauce from her fingers in a most unladylike fashion. "Mmmmph! *Kermit au vin-blanc.* A wonderful dish!"

"Mmmmm!" Torscha mumbled avid agreement past a mouthful of food. "What does it mean, Your Majesty?"

Aelis turned to Miriam and spoke in rapid-fire Nantierran. Miriam answered, shaking her head in puzzlement. Aelis made little leaping motions with her fingers and pointed out to the lily pads by the riverside.

Miriam's eyes widened, and she hastily looked across to her fiancé. Torscha was just starting on his seventh piece.

"Delicious! Well—what are they?"

Miriam cleared her throat and pushed the platter closer to him. "Aaah, it's . . . it's from the river. I'll tell you later."

Aelis gave a laugh as clear and young as a summer's dawn. She eyed Miriam waggishly, and the girl whispered something in return.

The queen smiled and reached for her wine. "So, Colonel! It is a long way from Welfland, yes?"

Retter's face suddenly became grim. "It seems Your Majesty knows me well."

Aelis casually poured the wine. "Colonel Torscha Retter, once of Lørnbørg, once of Welfland's parliament, now with a commission in the armies of Duncruigh." She pronounced *Retter* "Rett-aire". A most endearing trait. "I 'ave seen you in your armor of black. Quite terrifying."

"Yes, Majesty. And I remember a she-demon in shining silver."

"Good! Well—it seems there are unseen depths behind any armor, no?" Aelis warmed him with her perfect smile. "A pleasure to see the man behind the warrior's mask."

Torscha pushed his food aside and stiffened his back. She was clever, this queen! It would be too easy to fall beneath the spell of those clear blue eyes.

Miriam now placed herself firmly at Torscha's side. "Your Majesty seems well acquainted with my *fiancé*." Miriam's hand tightened possessively on Torscha's arm. "How?"

The queen gave an easy gesture. "The colonel's father serves as a general with this army."

Torscha went quite rigid; although he remained outwardly calm, Miriam felt his muscles turn hard as iron. She suddenly noticed Aelis watching Torscha from the corner of her eye. The queen saw Miriam's gaze and nodded thoughtfully to herself.

Suddenly the queen sprang to her feet and dusted crumbs from her skirt."*Come!* Miriam, you and I shall talk."

The gentlemen hastened to struggle to their feet, and Torscha cleared his throat. "But Majesty! Are we to parley?"

The queen gave an artful wave of her hand. "To what point, dear colonel? You 'ave far too much of the fire! Will you surrender without a fight? I think not." The queen extended her arm to Miriam. "But it has been interesting to meet with you."

Miriam was firmly taken on the royal arm and steered toward the river. A Nantierran captain made to follow, but the queen seared him with a glance.

"A bodyguard, Capi'tan? No, I think not." Aelis looked at Miriam with cool, knowing eyes. "She may shoot my spies—but not me today, I think." Miriam paled, and the queen flicked out with her tail. "Come, come! Let us just stroll and make talk."

The two women walked arm in arm toward the river. The afternoon had mellowed into a warm, yellow haze, and they walked between the weeping willows and enjoyed the golden sun. Aelis and Miriam spoke about everything and nothing; it felt soothing simply to walk and talk. The queen had gone, and in her place remained a slightly lonely, lovely girl called Aelis. And so they simply took pleasure in each other's company—the wildflower and the rose.

The serenity ended as they rounded a grove of orange trees and the Nantierran main camp came into view once more. A forest of banners rippled on the wind, fluttering gaudy colors in the sun.

The size of the army! Miriam blinked as she saw campfires stretching out across the hills and valleys; the fields were black with men! Harpies wheeled and centaurs bickered. Regiment after regiment marched to swell the Nantierran ranks. Miriam stared out across the teeming legions with blank, unseeing eyes.

"You were always my idol, Majesty. For as long as I can remember, I have adored the shining queen of Nantierre."

Aelis looked out across the camp, the wind tossing her golden hair. She seemed lost and sad. "Why?"

"Because you were everything I ever wanted to be. A woman respected—a woman admired. Unafraid to match her wits against a world!" Miriam looked out across the camp, seeing the soldiers, the campfires—the whores and slatterns. Pike blades flickered in the light, piercing Miriam's heart with a chill of fear. "But you *hurt* things, Majesty. I-I don't understand the need. To kill and tear and burn . . ." Miriam put a hand to her head in confusion. "To be so gifted! So brilliant—and then to . . . Why do you have to do this?"

The blond woman reached out to lift Miriam's chin. There was taunting challenge in Aelis's blue eyes. "*You* have killed! You shot my agent. How did it feel—to do that to a man?"

"I-I was sick for days. I couldn't eat, couldn't sleep. . . . The moment haunts me every time I close my eyes." Miriam hid her face in shame as the memory brought her close to tears. "I pray for forgiveness . . . 'There is blood on my hands, and I shall never be free of it!'"

Aelis seemed taken aback; it was not the answer she had expected. She had been so sure that they were alike. . . .

"But—But then why did you do it?"

"*Torscha.* He would have killed my Torscha."

"Aaaah!" Aelis suddenly thought she understood. She leaned eagerly forward, her fists clenched and eyes flashing. "But to kill—

to defeat someone so utterly! To have done what even your huge stallion could not! The *power* in that moment!"

Miriam hung her head. "I feel only shame. I pray God will forgive me—*for I cannot.* But to save my love? Any price—even my life, my soul . . ."

Miriam raised her head, and green eyes looked sadly at the queen. "Why, Majesty? What is there for you to prove? Why must it be 'scribed in pain and blood?"

Aelis turned away, her tail slashing at the air behind her. Suddenly she whirled and wrenched Miriam about, pointing to the vast black shapes of the siege artillery. "*There.* There is power! Look—see and be afraid!" Aelis's eyes were wild. "Don't you understand? Those are cannon royale, the most powerful siege artillery in the world!" She half dragged Miriam toward the guns. "We have crumbled nations! Do you think your pathetic castle walls can withstand these?"

The queen seemed almost in tears. "Do you think courage is enough to beat all this? Well—*do you?* This is the science of war, and I am its master! *Aelis!*" Aelis turned to plead. "Your castle *will* fall! Why fight? It's lunacy! *Why must you fight?*"

She stood with her face flushed, her breast heaving.

Miriam simply shrugged. "It's my home."

Aelis's hide shivered; she had come out of the confrontation badly. Miriam had bared her soul and triumphed.

They returned quietly to the picnic ground, where Frielle and Sir Thomas mounted their horses. Aelis strolled with the delegates up into the orange groves and then turned to take her leave. The queen seemed loathe to let Miriam depart.

"We shall meet again, Miriam." Queen Aelis looked down at her perfect hands. "I thank you for this afternoon. There are so few people to talk to. . . ."

Miriam sank into a curtsy. "Good-bye, Majesty. May God one day bring you peace." Miriam slowly walked back to her friends and took her stallion's arm. The little group moved back up the hill to the castle, winding their way through the cool shadows of the orange grove.

Aelis stood in the roadside and watched after the delegates until long after they had gone. Her head hanging, the queen then turned and wandered back into her tent.

Chapter Five

Besieged

t was a cool, crisp spring dawn, and long tongues of fog coiled up from the dripping riverbanks to lap at the feet of sleeping soldiers. Siege cannon squatted like mighty beasts within the mist, muzzles gaping toward the distant castle walls. Twenty feet long, firing balls weighing eighty pounds or more, the vast cannon crouched awaiting bloodshed in the morn. Beneath one gun barrel, a patch of metal slowly turned bright cherry red. There was a sudden flash, a squawk of surprise, and then a steady drip of molten metal from the breech.

Mus sat upon the gun carriage whistling tunelessly between his teeth as he sabotaged the siege gun. Behind him lay eleven more gigantic weapons, each with a hole burned through its barrel large enough for three mice to pass abreast. In a single morning's work, Mus had destroyed the entire sum of Aelis's siege artillery.

Miriam will be so pleased! Just wait until I tell her what I have done, he thought. I am clever! And no one has been hurt. I can help my friends without hurting!

With the last gun finished, Mus had one more thing to do. The best part about being clever was boasting of it afterward; Mus unfolded a tiny scrap of paper and stuck it in the cannon's breech, then read the text with satisfaction.

Mus fecit: "Mus made this!"

Excellent! Aelis should positively curl her whiskers!

Mus teetered to his feet and lowered himself to the ground. Huffing a weary sigh of satisfaction, the mouse pushed up through the grass and made his way home.

Frielle looked out over the battlements to where dawn trailed threads of light across the hills. Mists lay thick upon the river-banks, rolling languorously about the timberline along the Nantierran camp. Frielle clutched the rough old stone of the bat-tlements and tried to calm her heart. She was Frielle Delauncy, sole heir to the laird of the Southern Isles—and she did not cry.

Tom . . .

Suddenly, gentle wings of memory fluttered at her heart. In agony, Frielle choked back the swarm. God! Why wouldn't it all just leave her in peace! A year! A solid year had gone by, and still it could tear her open like a knife!

I hate you!

I love you!

. . . Help me!

"Frielle?"

The girl stiffened, dragging tears back from her cheeks as a voice intruded upon her solitude.

"Frielle, may *I* help?"

Lady Barbara Jerrick laid a hand across Frielle's shivering shoulders, and the satyr pulled away in panic. "No. I-I'm fine. I just—" Frielle's voice choked. "Please—*leave me alone!*"

"It's all right to cry, my dear. I'll not fault thee." The older woman smoothed back a straying lock of Frielle's hair. "God knows—I've done enough crying myself these few months."

Frielle tried to turn away, then suddenly she found herself in Miriam's mother's arms. She shook with hoarse, racking sobs as the half-horse gently rocked her to and fro.

"Oh, love—I know it hurts. I know."

The baroness held Frielle against her heart and let the girl release her tears as the first cock of the morn began to crow.

It was dawn, and Castle Kerbridge lay besieged.

"*What do you mean, destroyed!*"

A crystal glass flew through the air, sending artillery officers diving for cover. "Majesty! It's not our fault. . . ."

"*Not your fault!*" Aelis gave an incoherent scream of rage and smashed a water jug with her marshal's baton. "Then in God's name whose fault is it?"

One officer peeked fearfully over the edge of a table. "The—the guards saw nothing. . . ."

"*Fool! Imbecile!*" Aelis clutched the tiny scrap of paper found by the ruined cannon, and with a roar she tore open the flaps of her tent. The queen snapped her fingers, bringing a colonel of her half-horse guards racing to her side.

"*You!* Take this—this *idiot* and inspect the area about the siege guns for signs of infiltration. Take a magician, take blood-hounds—take the whole accursed army if you have to!" The queen waved the little scrap of paper. "I want to know who did this! Who is this damned *Mus?*"

The colonel reared, wheeled, and galloped off in a fearful cloud of churning hooves. The rest of the staff stayed nervously engaged in their tasks as Aelis stamped her hooves in anger and snarled into midair.

"How long?"

A human officer made the mistake of looking up; this therefore elected him as spokesman. "M-Majesty?"

"How long will it take to bring new siege equipment from the continent?"

The officer tugged at his collar. Suddenly his lace falling-band seemed too tight. "Uh—well, Majesty, a—a relay of messengers could probably fly orders to Nantierre in five days. I-It would take about a week to gather the weapons and embark them on a ship, then two or three weeks of transit time. . . ."

"*Five weeks?*" Clenching her fists in fury, Aelis looked up at the castle. "Goddamn it! Goddamn it to hell! I want an assault! NOW!" Knife-sharp hooves stamped at the ground. "A petard attack on the gates—air assault on the walls! We'll do without the blasted guns!"

"An air assault will not work without ground support, Your Majesty." A creaky old voice drifted down from the trees. "Petards will not breach their gates while their artillery stands firm."

"Don't teach me my trade, old hag!" The royal temper was sadly frayed. The queen had been made to look foolish, and some-one was sure to take the blame.

The royal astrologer calmly weathered the storm and peered down from her knotty perch. "One suspects the hand of the half-horse girl.

No magazines destroyed—no men hurt. A remarkably gentle way to
wage a war."

"Gentle!" Aelis started to curse and swear—and then suddenly
stopped. "Yes—it seems we must be far more careful of these opponents." Aelis breathed slowly. "Cancel those assault orders! Commence investment—surround both castle and town with
earthworks. Begin to work with care and patience."

Aelis irritably tossed aside her charts and stared up at the castle
on its hill far above. "Damn it to hell. Who is *Mus?*"

The astrologer nodded thoughtfully. "Majesty, do you recall the
full tale of Leymond's demise? '*Mus*' is a mouse. An intelligent
mouse."

"A *mouse* did this?" Aelis whirled. "Well, where's our mouse?
What is that idiot satyr up to? *Where is my report?*"

Messengers scurried off to see to the queen's bidding. Quite
used to all the noise, the royal astrologer simply tucked her head
beneath one wing and went to sleep.

Inside the castle stables, a tiny figure stirred. The female mouse
rose from her warm nest at the bottom of Retter's saddle holster
and rubbed the sleep from her eyes. She blinked, then wondered
where the Tormentor might have gone.

FOOL! Idiot!

The hateful voice hissed evilly in her mind, scraping along
every nerve like a rusty chisel.

Why have you slept? Lazy, useless rodent! BURN!

Fire screamed down the mouse's spine. She squealed in pain,
eyes rolling madly as Pin-William's voice hissed with hatred in her
mind.

Get up! UP!

The pain retreated, and the mouse rose to her feet.

Yes, 'master'. She used the term with acid irony. *As you command.*
The mouse sobbed her agony, pulling herself erect. Her body had
been tortured once too often; a lesser creature would have been
unable to move, and yet the mouse drove herself on. She dropped
to the stable floor and staggered out into the open air. The mouse
swayed, and her back legs seemed to drag behind her as she
walked. It didn't matter. She had strength enough to do what she

had come for.

In full view of anyone who chose to see, the mouse dragged herself painfully onward in search of an executioner.

Where are you? What is happening?

Her Tormentor sounded pained, and the mouse felt a surge of satisfaction. Clearly his superiors were angry at the delay in his report. She looked unsteadily about herself and gave a smile.

She felt quite bright and aware. The castle courtyard stood out in startling clarity—every smell, every sound quivered with intensity. The mouse found herself in an open yard beneath a drifting rain of soft white plum blossoms. Fallen plum flowers made a carpet beneath her dragging tail.

How pretty. Why have I never seen beauty till now? The mouse felt tired and sad. She pressed a petal up against her cheek and gave a sigh.

It was time to go. The mouse regretfully put her flower aside and crept onward toward the waiting house.

Where are you going?

The mouse dragged herself beneath a wooden door. The room beyond was warm and dark and smelled of baking bread. Huge figures pounded back and forth across a wooden floor; ever-busy giants with their ever-busy lives. The mouse stepped out into the darkness. She fell down a step and crashed onto the floor, knocking out her breath. Her head spun as she felt her vision begin to fade.

Stop! What are you doing?

The floorboards shuddered as a nearby giant passed; the mouse fixed her eyes on the stamping hooves and hauled herself back onto her feet.

STOP! I ORDER YOU TO STOP!

The mouse laughed despite herself. Her mind blazed with triumph! *I have won! I've beaten you at last. . . .*

Hooves rumbled toward her, and the mouse deliberately dragged herself into their path.

The game is over. I have won! She collapsed in contentment as the darkness reached out to take her soul.

Miriam and Frielle were in the surgery, dragging a heavy table into place beside a wall, when all of a sudden a panel opened up behind the mantelpiece. Mus came sliding down a candlestick, quite beside himself with glee. The mouse danced across the woodwork as though he had not a worry in the world.

"*Mus!*" Miriam hurried across the floor with her skirts hitched high. "Mus! Where have you been? I've been beside myself with worry!"

"Ha! Oh, Miriam—Oh, Miriam, I've been so clever!" The mouse fairly puffed himself with pride; Miriam irritably began to pluck grass seeds from the little creature's fur.

"Oh, Mus—thou'rt a wreck!" Miriam plucked a piece of straw from behind his handsome ear. "What hast thou been up to? The armorer wanted you to help weld some seams."

The mouse leapt up and down in his excitement. "No, listen! *Listen!*"

Frielle drew her face into an indulgent little frown. "Mus, there are people who depend on thee for jobs 'n such. Thou should at least tell us what thou'rt—"

Mus bounced up and down in frustration. "Hist! Be still and listen! I've been down the hillside!"

Miriam blanched. "Mus—no!"

"What on earth were ye doin' down there, thou dozy—"

"*Ha ha!*" Mus crowed in triumph. He danced and capered along the edge of the table. "Clever clever! Sneaky tricks and crafty ways!"

"Mus! What hast thou been up to?"

"Aaaah! Mists and grass and scaly trolls. Prowling foxes, hooting owls. . . ."

Frielle put her fists on her hips. "There's nary an owl within five mile o' here! Thy pranks have seen to that! We could have cannonballs about our ears any moment now, an' all ye can be thinkin' to do is play silly games."

Mus clambered atop a bottle of purple tonic. "Cannonballs?" He peeked around the fat brown cork. "He hee! What cannonballs?"

"Mus! Get off that! Ye've dirty feet!"

The little mouse climbed upon the cork to perch on his hind legs. "The best trick of all, Miriam! The best trick of all! The queen of Nantierre's cannon are no more!" The mouse hung impudently upside down from the bottle neck. "So that—as they say— is that!" With a squawk of indignation, Mus found himself snatched firmly by the tail. He was held with his little feet splayed as he swung in front of Miriam's nose. "Madam! This is most undignified!"

"I'll give thee *dignified,* thou little pest! Now tell us what thou'st been up to."

Mus pouted. "I'll not tell thee anything if thou'rt going to be crabby."

Miriam pointed a finger at the mouse's nose. "*Speak,* small nuisance!"

"I don't know that thou deserve it." Mus sniffed as well as one can when upside down. "I went down to the Nantierran camp and melted holes in the breeches of the siege cannon."

Miriam's jaw dropped; Frielle laughed aloud, her whole face lighting with delight. "That's brilliant! That's the most . . ." The faun flapped her hands about in the air helplessly searching for words. She gave up and simply planted a great wet kiss on Mus's forehead as Miriam reared up into the air.

"Mus! Thou clever creature! Thou brave, brave fellow! Thou'rt a *genius!*" Miriam passed the mouse across to Frielle. "I must fetch Mama and Willy! You can tell us all at once!" The girl wheeled on her back hooves and lunged off down the corridor. "*Mus—I love thee!*" Miriam dashed past another figure in the doorway. Hattie, the waddling half-horse cook, dodged back out of the path of the flying filly.

"Faith, girl! Where's the fire?"

Mus sat on the table, happily soaking up Frielle's praise, when all of a sudden he looked up to see the cook leaning over him wagging a great wooden spoon.

"Mas'r Mus! I've a bone to pick with you."

Mus swallowed. The Jerricks' cook was . . . formidable. "Uh—yes, Hattie."

"As I recall, we had an arrangement, you and I." The cook held the mouse transfixed with her spoon. "There was to be no more mouse killing in this 'ouse, but you would see to it that the wild critters left the kitchen."

"Uh—yes . . ."

"Now you're one o' the fine folks in this 'ouse, so 'tis not my place to scold you; but there's mice in my kitchen, and I'm not havin' it!"

The cook held up a tiny dangling figure in her hand—the limp body of a mouse; Mus reeled backward in alarm.

"You—you haven't . . . killed anyone, have you?"

Hattie laid the body on the table. "Nay, I'll hold my bargain. This one's passing on without any 'elp from me. 'Tis up to you to . . . Mas'r Mus? Mas'r Mus!"

Mus *stared.* There in front of him lay a wasted young field mouse; gaunt ribs poked from her golden fur, and she was all but starved. But her face! It was the face of an angel.

An angel . . . A face that had haunted his dreams.

With a sob of anguish Mus scooped her up into his arms. She was thin! So horribly thin! Skin and bone and velvet fur. Mus crushed her to his breast and tried to warm her.

"Milady! Oh, don't die! *Please don't die!*" Mus frantically ran a hand over her face. "I beg you—*please!*"

Her long eyelashes lolled open, and great sad eyes tried to focus on Mus's face. *"One . . . last . . . dream."* The girl sighed and closed her eyes. *"Cruel . . . How cruel."*

"No!" Mus held the girl, but her body had gone limp. "Miriam!—MIRIAM!"

Frielle dashed out of the door to find her friend. "MIRIAM! MIRIAM! FER GOD'S SAKE, COME QUICK!"

Left alone in the room, Mus rocked the little body in his arms and wept.

By evening time, the castle parapet overlooked an ugly scene. The enemy had begun to dig their trenches, and the castle guns had made them pay for every yard with blood. Now the first tiny strip of ditch and rampart had been dug, the engineers hidden behind wicker gabions filled with earth. From behind this shelter came the constant sound of digging.

Miriam leaned over the battlements and let the clean wind blow through her hair. Siege warfare was a careful science—thus Mus had told her with grave conviction. The enemy trenches would eventually surround the castle to seal it off from the outside world. As weeks went by, more trenches would be dug, bringing the enemy guns ever closer.

It had a terrifying, inexorable progression. Miriam knew too much about military science to hold any hope for her little home.

The castle would fall, and then the town would follow; it was only a matter of time and resources.

A strong hand caressed Miriam's spine, and tired as she was, Miriam arched her back and sighed. Torscha's warm smell filled her nostrils, and his loving presence filled her mind; she leaned back into him and felt his arms gather her.

Torscha's voice sounded tired and strained. "How fares the lady mouse?"

"Dying." Miriam closed her eyes. "She won't save herself."

"Is she so sorely hurt?"

The girl shivered. "Starved and tortured. The physical harm might be treated given time, but her mind is quite decided. She wants to die. . . ."

They looked out over the hills and let the wind mingle their hair. Peaceful moments were so hard to come by. Torscha stood silent for long minutes before finally speaking.

"Wilt thou come with me and see Mus? He's in a sorry state. He hardly even hears what I say to him."

Miriam felt reluctant to leave her island of quiet—but Mus needed her. She stirred herself and let Torscha take her by the arm. He led the way into the castle—down toward Miriam's room.

In the bedroom, all was quiet. A tiny brown body lay stretched out at the center of Mus's bed, warmly covered up with scraps of woolen cloth. A little pile lay beside her; oats and almonds, cheese and cake. In the face of sheer helplessness, Mus offered all he had to give. He lay listlessly on his belly atop a cotton reel and watched over his charge with mournful devotion.

"Mus?" Miriam spoke quietly into the darkness, but Mus never stirred.

"Mus, darling?"

Mus kept his eyes riveted on the girl. She lay still and silent, her chest moving shallowly as she breathed. "She's dying, isn't she." The mouse kept his voice quiet and level. "I shall be going out again soon. Wilt thou watch her for me?"

Torscha carefully folded his four huge legs and knelt down beside the little mouse. "Mus—look at me. We must talk, thou and I."

"I'm going!" Mus never even looked up; a tear leaked down his face, and he simply let it fall. "He's here—he *has* to be. And now he'll pay."

"Who?" Miriam was mystified. "Who's here?"

"Pin-William." Mus's voice lacked all emotion. "*He* did this to her—the *Tormentor*."

Miriam knelt down beside the little mouse and ran a smooth finger along his back. "Mus, revenge helps nothing. She needs thee here to help her."

"I . . ." Mus suddenly sobbed for breath. "But she's *dying!*"

"Ssssh." Miriam rocked her little friend to and fro. "We'll not let her die. She's lost all faith, Mus. We must give her hope again."

Mus's heart hammered; his little chest heaved. Miriam stroked him with strong, gentle hands.

"That means that *we* cannot lose hope, Mus. We must believe in her, since she no longer believes in herself. She needs you here, Mus."

The mouse's voice became the merest whisper. "*What must I do?*"

"Care for her. Talk to her. Though she sleeps, she might hear thee. Tell her of the beauty of things, of how wonderful life can be; show her that she is not alone."

"She—she'll not die?"

"Nay, my love. Not unless we let her."

Mus peered over the edge of Miriam's hand and stared down at the sleeping patient.

"She's so *beautiful*. . . ." He closed his eyes. "How could he do this to her?"

"Mus—can he reach her again?"

The mouse slowly shook his head. "No, not while I live. His link is severed; I have closed the door on him."

Miriam placed the little mouse by his patient's side.

"I'll make broth for us to feed her. And she must take a droplet of potion from Doctor Freeps's store every few hours."

"I'll give it to her." Mus reached out to touch the sleeping field mouse. "She doesn't even have a name. . . ."

"Then we must give her one."

"Then I shall name her from a story." Mus ran fingertips across his patient's sleeping face. "I will call her *Lyssa*—the maid of dawn."

Miriam turned and quietly left the room, her hooves whispering softly upon the carpet. Behind her, Torscha and Mus settled down to watch their charge.

Chapter Six

Tying the Knot

y my hand, August Twelfth, 1642.

Mus tracked back and forth across the huge pages of his journal, writing with a microscopic hand. The top of his finch-feather quill bobbed and nodded busily as he wrote.

Five weeks since the siege began. Mus dipped his nib. *The enemy trenches advance despite our bombardment. Their second parallel is almost dug, and soon the reduction of our ramparts will begin. I can no longer creep into the Nantierran lines, since the mud is now too deep.*

The little mouse paused to look out of the shutters. The usual flock of harpies circled high overhead keeping the garrison under observation. Ugly rings of earthworks scarred the lovely hill, and figures toiled in the trenches, harassed by fire from above. The enemy engineers wore heavy suits of siege armor—enormously heavy breastplates and tassets topped by skull-faced burgeonets. Nevertheless, men fell with hideous regularity. Some simply sprawled, dazed from the impact of bullet on steel, while others were carried backward to safety.

Sir Thomas Carpernan, that most worthy and courageous gentleman, did sally from the defenses yet again last night. With the enemy trenches now compleat, I fear this raid shall be his last. . . . Damn! Mus scribbled out his misspelling and snorted with disgust. *Carpernan's dragoons returned with plunder from the enemy camp: sic—two cannon, eight barrels of powder, and a brassiere belonging to Queen Aelis.*

Morale remains high. Colonel Retter stays as steadfast as ever—he will brook no talk of defeat. If ever Nantierre had a mortal enemy, it is he.

He made another dip of the quill. *Our losses today are soldiers*

Toffler, Heenman, and Frochiss, all from the Welflandic ranks. Sailors Miller and Arnosson were slain at the guns. Lieutenant Palmer, also, died of his wounds.

The mouse's ears drooped sadly. So many names; he recorded each and every one faithfully, building his own monument to the fallen.

For my part, the siege drags on with awful monotony. Lyssa will eat if fed, but will not see or speak. Day by day she lies in place, staring from the window.

I cannot allow myself to lose hope.

Enough; Mus's own words had depressed him. He slowly washed out his pen and sat back to watch the ink dry across the parchment.

Mus wandered listlessly over to Lyssa's side. She lay as always—half dreaming and half awake, never moving or speaking. Mus patiently massaged her limbs, sinking clever fingers into her fragrant fur. He worked with a single-minded devotion to his task, talking softly to her all the while, then rolled the girl over to her other side and fluffed up the bed. He combed her fur, kissed her ear, and then settled down to read aloud from Miriam's storybooks.

Outside the little room, the walls shivered to another blow as the trenches ground toward the castle's heart.

A naval cannon roared, slamming backward on its trail to jerk against its tackles. Gunners from the *Nemesis* leapt to sponge out the barrel without so much as looking up while Mister Kelso ascended the battlements to watch the fall of shot. He ducked back behind the parapet even as a hail of musket balls cracked against the stones, then he reappeared to bite his thumb toward the enemy infantry.

The air rippled with the *snap* and *bang* of musket fire. Torscha paused in his slow tour of the battlements to watch an extraordinary sight; an untidy pile of sacking in the middle of the outer bailey suddenly gave vent to a titanic sneeze. The half-horse stepped closer and opened up the visor of his helm. "Hello?"

"Bless you, my son, and would you mind moving along?"

"Your Grace?" Retter blinked and tried to peer under the sacking. "Bishop Kaxter, are you injured?"

"Indeed not—now go away!" The sacking quivered as the bishop wound his wheel-lock rifle with its spanner. "Ah—here he comes!"

High above, an enemy harpy made a bombing run. The creature

clumsily lit the fuse of a grenade, heeled over into a dive, and streaked straight at Kelso's battery. Bishop Kaxter rose up from his hide, tracked the creature with his rifle, and casually gave fire. The harpy gave a squawk and crashed into the castle moat, feathers, bomb, and all.

Anything fool enough to invade Bishop Kaxter's See would clearly be in for a trying time. His Grace began the laborious process of hammering a new ball down the barrel of his weapon, then bustled off into the castle to lead the midday prayers.

A sudden blast of mortar fire rippled through the air. Fat black bombs rose from the Nantierran trenches, whistling demonically as they plunged over the walls. The garrison scattered for cover as the smoking spheres smacked into the ground.

The thunderous *boom* of explosions were accompanied by a clear feminine shriek. Soldiers sprang up in panic, only to find a shapely backside and two slender, woolly legs flailing upside down amidst a froth of petticoats. Beside the fallen satyr, cringing fearfully behind a ragged bush, Jane the maidservant attempted to cram her entire body into a single rabbit hole.

"Blast and bedamn it! That's the second time today!" Frielle was well and truly caught in a thorn bush. "Jane! Get me out o' here!"

The other girl covered her head with her hands as more bombshells meandered overhead. Fuming with annoyance, Frielle battled her way out of the brambles and glared down at Jane. "Oh, for God's sake, girl! Get up! You're makin' a spectacle of yerself!" The satyr saw Torscha Retter slithering down the slope toward her in a cloud of dust.

"Those bedamned things will be the death o' me yet!" The little satyr blew a straggling lock of hair away from her face. "God's blood, what a bang! Were any o' ye boys hurt?"

The growing audience of soldiers chorused "No," and more than one satyr trooper made haste to help brush the girl down. Torscha slewed to a halt at her side and took her by the arm, hurriedly checking her for damage.

"Frielle! You're all right?"

"Aye! Though this skirt'll never be the same! Aelis must have seen me comin'!" The girl passed a heavy keg to a soldier. "We've brought vinegar for the gun buckets and ale for the men—though which kegs are which I can't remember. Best take a sup and see."

Torscha looked out across the blasted ground. Shell craters and debris scarred the smoking grass; for a lady to venture out into this. . . .

"There's no need to take such risks! One of the men could have been sent for it. We'll not risk you with . . ."

"Oh, tosh! If you can be out here, so can I." Frielle busily rolled up her sleeves, then stuck an immaculate ivory fan through her sash. "Miriam's setting some poor devil's arm, or else she'd be doing the rounds as well. Lady Barbara's already served the northern wall."

"Frielle—I'll send some of the men . . ."

"Nay! I can do it!"

"Well—let me at least give you an escort. . . ."

"Stop thy fussin'!" The satyr began busily gathering up her gear. She saw to the unloading of her barrels from the pony cart, collected Jane, and stalked off in an imperious swirl of skirts.

Torscha found himself staring at the faun's retreating back as she led her little supply train off to the next bastion.

" 'D's blood! What a woman!" Torscha shook his head in wonder. "A month ago I'd never have believed it!"

Sir Thomas Carpernan stood staring after Frielle, a lost expression on his face. He radiated such mourning—such *yearning*—that it struck the heart like a blow. The satyr noticed Colonel Retter watching him, and swiftly jerked his gaze away.

Torscha slowly paced over to the other man's side. Too uncomfortable to meet Sir Thomas's eyes, he looked out over the battlements. "Captain—the morale of my officers touches us all." The stallion gave an embarrassed swish of his tail. "There is a . . . problem between you and the Damsel Delauncy."

"Aye. That there is."

The slender satyr folded his hands into the unbuttoned sleeves of his cassock as he closed his eyes.

"Once upon a time we knew each other. We met. W-We loved."

"Ah."

Sir Thomas flexed his fists in agony. "We were both new at the court, Colonel. It all just happened so fast. How could we have known?"

"Known?"

"Aye, known!" The man turned to Retter with stricken eyes. "Colonel—I'm from Hebdia, and she's from *Janis Isle!*"

Torscha's face remained blank with incomprehension.

Sir Thomas whirled, desperately trying to make Retter

understand. "It's the *Isles,* man! You can't . . . It just isn't . . ." The satyr blinked in misery. "My family made me leave her. They—they were my clan—my *family.* Nothin' matters more than family. Or so I thought then."

With unseeing eyes, Sir Thomas looked out over the river.

"So, there it is. They'd all but made me wall across the memories—until I saw *her* again." His voice dropped to a whisper. "I've nae face to show her."

They stood together in silence for a while. Sir Thomas kept his face turned away while his tail drooped sadly beneath his coat.

"There's nae problem, Colonel. None to hurt your men."

"And of yourself, sir?"

The satyr's sad eyes were filled with pain. "Should I fall, 'twould be no more than I deserve." He looked down at his cloven hooves. "But if it should happen, perhaps you would tell Frielle that my last thoughts were of her. . . ."

He turned away, and Torscha left the man to his solitude. His head bowed in thought, Retter silently paced the battlements.

The old man looked like a squat, gnarled little gnome. He stood by the banks of the river, bellowing insults at the crews who carefully unloaded massive siege guns from a string of barges. Each remark was punctuated by a wave of the man's lumpy, knotted walking stick. From time to time he cracked the staff against his wooden leg, startling the crews into greater care.

"You drop that into the drink, Gaston, and you'll be followin' it!" The stick poked straight out to fix one gunner's eye. "Get your handspike under it, boy!"

"My Lord Varre! You have recovered?"

The engineer whirled clumsily to see his queen floating down the pathway before him. He fumbled with the clasps of his helmet and tried to make a bow. Still unused to his wooden leg, he started to overbalance; to his surprise, he found himself caught and held by the slim white arms of the queen.

"My Lord! What foolishness is this? You should still be abed!"

" 'Tis but a leg! There's another one where that came from!" The old man found his footing and fought off the queen's helping hands. "I'll not lie idle while my queen has need of me."

Anton Varre was a veteran of three different rulers and untold numbers of campaigns. He had the distinction to be the foremost siege engineer of his time. Varre planted his cane in the mud and glared at the army's new siege train.

"We'll keep it hid until night falls, and then bring the guns up close. I'll inspect the digging myself." He stumped along the pathway at his queen's side. "So, Majesty! This wee paint pot of a castle has proved more trouble than we thought, eh?"

"Trouble? It's a hornet's nest! The garrison lashes out to sting us at every turn. Guns stolen, officers shot! Even the accursed *mice* see fit to attack us!" Aelis cracked her marshal's baton in the palm of her hand. "We'll not take the town without demolishing the castle. It commands a clear field of fire against the only approach to the town!"

The two soldiers had reached the river's bend, and suddenly the castle came into view. Even from this distance the *crack* and roar of cannon made the air jerk with shock.

"The Jerrick stronghold, eh?"

"Yes." Aelis stared up at the castle's simple flag, still fluttering defiantly from the keep. "Old Jerrick's brood are just as dangerous as *he* ever was."

"I'll take it for you, Majesty. With the cannon here at last, we'll have the wall down in nothin' flat." The engineer looked up the hill and nodded in approval. "Your men've done well on the trenches. We can take her in two weeks."

Aelis stopped short and swished her tail in indecision.

"There—there *may* be another way."

Varre's eyebrows rose casually. "Aaah—treachery? Excellent! By far the simplest method of assault."

The queen seemed ill at ease.

"I suppose it is simple—but a pathetic end to so grand a venture. No honor, no glory. Only an empty victory." Aelis sighed. "But if I must, I must."

She turned her back on the castle.

"Ready your cannon in any case. One way or another, that castle must be ours within fourteen days."

Each evening at six o'clock, the baroness presided over dinner for the garrison officers. Though she found herself trapped, besieged, and in mourning, Lady Jerrick still played the role of hostess. It felt somehow very calming to see the proud lady welcome her guests. Not even the thunder of the guns could shake the air of gentility and peace.

The guests seemed to come from a dozen walks of life. Willy Merle sat with his arm cradled in its sling, trailing patterns in his bowl of soup. Doctor Freeps drank only water, refusing all offers of wine, and looked more like a skeleton than a man. Of all of them, Bishop Kaxter seemed the most vigorously alive. He sat closeted with Miriam and Torscha, and positively *beamed*.

"Well of course *now* is the time to say it! Good God, girl, when did you think you should say it?"

Miriam blushed quite red. "I-I'm just not sure. I mean, is it right?"

"Well, of course it's right!" The bishop spread his huge hands wide. " 'Tis a perfect boost for morale! And think what a tongue-poke it will be at Aelis!"

"Your Grace—'tis too big a step to make it only to irk our enemy!"

"You were going to do it anyway! Why not now? Thy mother agrees!"

Miriam was flushing so brightly that she had to hide her cheeks behind her hands. "I-I want to. But only if it pleases Torscha. . . ."

The stallion held her and looked deep into her wonderful green eyes. "It pleases me. You know it pleases me."

The lovers gently kissed, twining their arms about each other. The bishop ignored them completely as he started to lift up napkins and search across the table. "Mus? *Mus?*"

A little furry face quickly peeked out from the biscuit bowl. There were crumbs on his whiskers. "They're doing it?"

"Aye! That they are!"

Miriam tore herself away from Torscha and whirled to face the little rodent. "Little wretch! How didst thou know?"

"Ha! I know everything! I'm clever!" The mouse leapt and danced across the table. "I'm saying it! Me! Me! I'm Torscha's lieutenant!"

"Mus! No!"

Miriam made a snatch, but Mus had leapt free. The mouse sprang up atop the silver saltcellar and whistled boisterously between his chisel teeth. *"Lords, Ladies, and Gentlemen! May I have your attention for an announcement!"*

Miriam was foiled; left with no way to gracefully withdraw, she subsided back into her lover's arms and tried to hide her blushing face.

The little mouse had drawn every ear. He perched perilously on the top of the salt and puffed himself up like a tiny, furry rooster. "Good friends! It is not often that we find pleasure in such a time of dark troubles; but it is now my joy to announce the forthcoming wedding of Damsel Miriam Jerrick and Herr Torscha Retter of Lørnbørg in the castle chapel tomorrow morning!"

There was a moment's pause, and then thunderous applause shook the table. The officers cheered their colonel and pounded on the table, and Mus was shaken from his perch to fall into the butter dish.

Miriam and Retter spoke quietly to a circle of friends as Mus struggled out of a mire of butter-curls. The mouse spied Willy standing in a corner, and immediately raced over to his side. "Willy! Willy! Isn't it just splendid?"

"You spoke beautifuwy, Mus. Quite beautifuwy."

Flattery was always guaranteed to snatch Mus's attention. He preened himself happily, hiding the butter on his rump.

"Why, thank you, Willy! I've been practicing in front of a mirror. A lieutenant has to know how to speak properly!"

A shadow fell over the table; Torscha and Miriam had come to see Willy, and Miriam's eyes shone with joy.

Torscha Retter cleared his throat. "Willy, you are my best and oldest friend. I-I would like to ask . . ." He seemed at a loss for words. "For tomorrow. Will you be my best man?"

To their disappointment, Willy did not answer at once, but instead looked down at his injured arm. After a while, he slowly answered. "I'm happy for you, of course. But—I must refuse. My arm . . . the pain has grown worse. I can hardly even stand. I'll be no good to either of you tomorrow."

"Willy!" Miriam looked up in hurt; Sir William winced without meeting her eyes.

"I'm sorry. But it really is for the best." He tugged carefully at his sling. "I'm sure Mus would be honored, were you to ask him."

The mouse looked up in sudden joy. His little black eyes sparkled in the light. "Oh, would you? Can I?" Mus was deliriously happy. "I can do it! I can, I can!"

"Mus—we should be honored if thou wouldst accept." Torscha shook the rodent's hand, then gave a frown. "Who's to give the bride away? We really must decide."

"Me! Me!" Mus hopped up and down on the table. "I can do it!"

"O Mus! Thou'rt already best man!"

"I can do both! I'm clever!"

Miriam pinched the little rodent's muzzle shut with her fingers. "Hush! Now don't be silly!"

"Mmmmph M h'm mmmph mmph mmmm!"

"Eh?" Miriam hefted the mouse and released his nose from captivity. "What didst thou say?"

Most put out at being so rudely handled, Mus irritably dusted off his whiskers.

"Why not Captain Brayberry of the *Nemesis*? He seems a nice man."

An excellent suggestion! This immediately met with everyone's approval; Mus settled back happily into the baroness's hand and let the satisfaction wash over him.

Everything was going to be just perfect! What could possibly go wrong now?

Behind him, Willy Merle poured himself another glass of wine. He gave the happy lovers one last, unreadable stare, and then settled down to drink.

"Is it straight! Is it straight?"

Mus pushed forward beneath Frielle's hands to plant himself square in front of her mirror. He began fussing about with his hat and getting right in Frielle's way.

"Mus, thy hat's jus' fine! Now push off, there's a good fellow! I'm *trying* to get dressed!"

The mouse sat up in front of her, looking quite splendid in his best collar and hat. "Ha! Well *I'm* ready!" Mus brushed fussily at his tiny bow. "I can't see why thou'rt always running late!"

"I take longer because I'm wearin' more!" She primped her hair, sending springy rolls of lustrous brown bobbing this way and that. "There! Now I'm done, ye daft rodent! We'll not be late." She cast about the dressing table looking for the small gold ring that had been her wedding present to the happy couple.

"Mus! Where hast thou put the ring this time?" He'd shifted it from spot to spot all morning.

"It's not lost! It isn't!" Mus resented the implication. "The sergeant said he'd place it in the chapel for me!"

"Well hurry on then, let's be off!"

In the chapel, all at last seemed ready. Miriam stood at the altar staring ahead of herself with great wide eyes. Her cheeks were pale with fright beneath their bands of freckles, and her hands clutched tightly at a bouquet of her mother's roses. Dressed in a gown made from satin drapes and an old lace tablecloth, she seemed more radiant than Torscha could possibly have imagined. The huge black stallion stood proudly at her side, his tail swishing grandly as he shifted his weight on ever-restless hooves.

The rest of the tableau was completed by the attendants. The bishop in his flowing robes of white and purple, and Frielle standing dutifully at Miriam's tail—the baroness, her face trembling on the edge of tears, propped up the copiously weeping Jane. Right in the middle of it all, Mus perched on the altar and preened himself like a sultan's prized peacock, his eyes alive with interest as he listened to the ceremony.

Ancient words were read, spreading their sense of *permanence* across the assembled crowd. Finally Bishop Kaxter turned to Miriam and spoke into the expectant hush. He fixed the girl's eye with his kindly gaze.

"Dost thou, Miriam, take this man Torscha unto thy wedded husband? To love, honor, and obey from this day forward—for better, for worse, in sickness and in health, as long as thou both shall live?"

Silence fell, broken only by the muffled sobs coming from Jane in the corner as Miriam tried to find her voice.

"*I-I do.* . . ."

The bishop smiled at her, and Miriam ceased her trembling. His eyes moved on to Torscha.

"Dost thou, Torscha, take this woman Miriam unto thy wedded wife? To love, honor, and cherish from this day forward . . ." There was a sudden howl of tears from Jane, and the bishop cleared his throat. "*Ahem!* . . . from this day forward—for better, for worse, in sickness and in health, as long as thou both shall live?"

The Colonel looked into Miriam's eyes. "I do."

Miriam and Torscha stayed lost in each other's gaze as the bishop gracefully turned to Mus. "Mus—you have the ring?"

The mouse suavely reached out to flick his whiskers, then dived one hand beneath the lace altar cloth. He reached deeper, a frown crossing his furry brow, then began to grope about in growing panic.

"The ring, Mus? The *ring!*"

With a hasty look left and right, the mouse quickly picked up the edge of the tablecloth and plunged beneath. Miriam closed her eyes and groaned while Frielle simply covered her face with her hands.

'D's blood, why had she trusted the little scatterbrain?

A tiny lump hunted to and fro beneath the tablecloth, until Mus's face popped out at the far end of the altar. The sergeant edged sheepishly forward, proffering the ring; it had been in his pocket all along! The man blushed and beat a hasty retreat before a dozen pairs of hostile eyes.

Mus rolled the ring like a hoop along the altar and then passed it to the colonel. Bishop Kaxter motioned Retter to take Miriam's hand, and Torscha held the ring poised above Miriam's trembling fingers.

The ring slid softly home, and they were wed.

Torscha tenderly drew back Miriam's veil. She craned her pale face upward and folded him in her arms. A cheer rose and swelled from the audience, thundering down the corridors to spill out to the battlements. The garrison stood to shout in acclaim, making the scarred old walls shake with joy.

Surrounded by well-wishers, the happy couple stood beneath the flowering plum tree in the courtyard. Fat kegs of ale were trundled out from the castle's precious hoard of stores; the whole garrison would drink the newlyweds' health. The monotony of the siege was broken, and hope shone brightly inward through the cracks.

Frielle leaned against a wall, fanning herself in the shade, when she suddenly noticed the sergeant riding for the gates with Mus perched merrily atop his helm. The satyr folded her fan and leapt up in alarm.

"Oi! Mus—what'rt thou doin'?"

Mus waved gaily from overhead.

"Shan't be long! We're just going visiting!"

"Mus! Come back here, thou varmint!"

Frielle hitched up her skirts and raced through the gatehouse, but the horse moved faster than her dainty hooves could go. The girl stopped at the edge of the gate and watched helplessly as Mus and the sergeant cantered out across the castle drawbridge.

White banner flying, the sergeant made his way downhill toward the Nantierran lines. The man licked his lips and nervously shifted his seat. "Mus! Who's to say they're not just goin' to take a wee pot-shot at me?"

"Well, you win some and you lose some." Mus did not seem particularly worried. "Here's a Nantierran now!"

A face peered warily over the edge of the enemy trench. Moments later an officer clambered painfully up over the lip, set his helmet straight and came to confront the sergeant. The young Nantierran made to speak, only to be interrupted by a little voice from the sergeant's saddlebow.

"*Good morrow!*" Mus swept off his hat and bowed; the Nantierran officer's steps faltered as his jaw hung down in shock. "Compliments of *Mrs.* Miriam Retter, and would Her Majesty be gracious enough to accept a slice of wedding cake!" The man made no move to take the proffered slice of cake; Mus pushed his hat back on his head.

"Odd's fish, fellow! 'Tis not poisoned! I helped to make it! I found the almonds myself!" The cake was wordlessly accepted, and Mus graciously doffed his hat once more. "That's it then! Do give the queen the best wishes of Mus of Kerbridge, and bid her enjoy the cake. I shall hope to meet her face to face one day under better circumstances." He merrily waved his little hat. "Cheerio!"

Man and mouse turned their horse about and rode away. The Nantierran bemusedly raised his helmet in farewell and wandered slowly back into his trench.

The young ensign's commander awaited him in the ditch.

"Hey! Who was it? Cartiere! What did they want?"

"Eh?" Ensign Cartiere seemed sadly distracted. "Oh—a talking mouse brought a slice of cake for the queen . . . "

The captain blinked in shock. "*What?*"

Cartiere shrugged. "It's all right, sir. He said he put the almonds in himself."

Chapter Seven

A Maggot in the Apple

us wended his way through the wall-space of the castle, heading for his comfy nest in Miriam's bedroom. Tonight Mus would have the place all to himself; Miriam had moved to the master bedroom with her husband to spend their first night of married life.

Mus would have been happier for her if he were not so tired. Now came the difficult part; Mus had to attend to Lyssa. He had to keep his spirits high enough for the both of them. Although she never changed from day to day, Mus never lost his hope.

The mouse pushed open a door in the wall paneling and slid down onto Miriam's bed. Frielle lay sprawled asleep across the covers, a book still open in her lap; she had nodded off while reading to Lyssa. Mus paused to admire her, his little black eyes shining in the dark.

A soft noise came from the far end of the room, and Mus's clever ears lifted high in wonder.

A giggle! *It was a giggle!*

Gaudy wings suddenly cartwheeled through the air. Opal swooped back down to the dressing table to slurp at something with her rough green tongue. Clear feminine laughter rang as the dragon pounced upon her playmate.

Mus raced down from his perch, bouncing off Frielle's bosom as he went. He dashed across the covers to perch dangerously on the bedstead.

A mouse rolled about in Mus's bed, kicking her heels in laughter as the hedge dragon tickled at her feet. The mouse turned her head, and her glittering black eyes suddenly met Mus's own.

Opal swiftly faded into the background as the two mice stared at one another. Hesitantly, Mus crept onto the table and approached Lyssa's side.

Lyssa's eyes were wide with wonder. She reached out with one frail hand to stroke Mus's cheek, and her hand came away wet with tears.

"*Mus.* Your name is Mus."

Mus could hardly speak. "*Lyssa . . .*"

"You wouldn't let me go . . . I so wanted to go. . . ." Lyssa looked clear into Mus's soul. "Why wouldn't you let me die?"

Mus swallowed. "Because I wanted to show you joy."

Lyssa hesitantly put a hand to her throat. In all her time since her *awakening,* there had never been kindness. Love had walked only in her dreams.

Mus fought back his fear. "You—you won't go? You won't leave me?"

"No." She looked up at him with dawning joy. "No, Mus. I think I'll stay with you."

Utterly exhausted, Lyssa began to slide back into slumber. She crept gently up against his side, gave Mus one last, adoring stare, and fell asleep inside his arms.

Up on the bed, Opal's eyes shimmered in the candlelight. The little dragon laboriously tugged blankets up about Frielle's shoulders, and then settled comfortably about her neck.

"Mus? Mus, wake up!"

The little rodent dangled in the freezing cold, held upside down by his tail. He blinked his eyes open and felt extremely annoyed. "Frielle, this is most unseemly!"

"Mus, Snatch is in the castle!"

Mus jerked awake, to discover Gus the pixie and Frielle illuminated grimly in the candlelight. The pixie took Mus into his hand. "We had elfhounds sniffing for him, as usual, but this time he has gotten past. A maid saw him creeping from a rain gutter heading toward the living quarters. He is somewhere here inside."

The mouse shook himself, then twittered down to find his hat and sword. "I'll go find him, then tell you where he is. We can trap the wretch at last!" Mus put on a hat, disliked the plume, and immediately changed it for another. "Frielle, could you guard my Lyssa? He might be after her."

Frielle pulled a gigantic mace out from underneath the bed and stood holding it like an ogre's club.

"She'll be safe enough. You just be careful, Mus! That stoat is deadly"

"Ha! All he has is teeth—but *I* am clever!"

Mus doffed his hat and made a swift exit through a gap in Miriam's skirting boards. Safe and sound inside his own personal highways, the mouse slid quickly down to a lower floor. Finding his first spyhole, Mus anxiously peered though into the room of Captain Brayberry.

Nothing; the room lay dark and still, with not a sniff of stoat upon the air. Mus twittered on, trying to guess his enemy's moves. Would he try for the stairs, or perhaps slither up between the wooden floors? Mus's mind raced all the while he scampered from knothole to knothole, but never once did he see sign of his foe.

Suddenly it hit him; the thick acrid stench of a stoat or weasel. The low murmur of voices drifted through the walls; left without a spyhole, Mus pressed his ear against the skirting and gave a little smile. He was Mus, and he was clever!

Mus pressed himself close to the wainscotting and listened: "It would be sssso easy. . . . Jusst sssay yesss."

Snatch's voice; Mus flattened his ears. There was a sigh.

"I-I just need to think. . . . " The second voice seemed tired and slurred. "You're sure no one will be hurt?"

"Of coursssse not! Not if you act sswiftly. Thisss way it all endsss peacefully." Snatch's voice grew oily and cajoling. "Surely you want the bessst for all your friendsss?"

Mus's heart went cold. *Treachery!* Someone was talking treachery! The little mouse swallowed, trying to choke back his rising horror.

"Sssso—we have a bargain?" The stoat's voice was sly.

"Just bwow up the magazine, you say? That's all?"

Mus went cold. He knew that voice! He knew it as though it had been his very own.

"Yessss—just one little bang. One little bang and it'ssss all over. The garrissson mussst conccede. With no powder, they have no choice." There was a long moment's silence; the stoat seemed in no hurry. "Sssso—isss it agreed?"

"How—how much?"

There was a hiss of stony laughter. "All your debtsss gone, and ten thoussand markss in gold."

"Ten thousand!" The voice had filled in awe. "But . . . to betray so much . . ."

"No! Not betrayal—not when it'ss the besst for everyone." The stoat's voice coiled in the dark. "Just think; you will be saving her. . . ."

"All right! I'll do it! God damn me—I'll do it."

"A brave decisssion. A wise decision."

"Tomorrow night at midnight, then?"

"Yesss, midnight tomorrow."

There was a whisper of sound as Snatch left through the window, and Mus made no move to stop him. The little mouse huddled down in the dark and wept as though his world had ended.

The wooden paneling levered itself open in silence, and Mus slowly plopped out onto the bedside table. Frielle hefted her mace, then set it aside and frowned at Mus in consternation. "Mus? Mus, darlin', are you all right?"

Mus gave a strange twitch. He glanced about the room in a panic, almost began to speak, and then somehow seemed to catch himself.

Frielle blinked. "Mus?"

The mouse swallowed; for the first time ever, Mus of Kerbridge lied. "He ran away—never entered the buildings."

"Ah, well, that's all right then. We scared him off again, eh!"

"Yes." Mus shivered. "Yes, I suppose so."

The little mouse sat quietly beside Lyssa and watched her as she slept. Her brow creasing in a frown, Frielle moved out into the halls and quietly slipped away.

Early next morning, Mus sat on Miriam's desk reading from a gigantic volume of plays. He read with avid attention, dashing down from his seat to laboriously turn the pages as he finished each one. His eyes were wide and frightened, lit with a sickening fear.

The door whispered open, and Miriam stood in the doorway, beaming in upon her favorite friend. The new bride danced in on feather-light hooves, whirling through the room in a swirl of lace. She was singing sweetly, without a care in the world—despite the roar and thunder of Nantierran guns.

"Mus! I just heard! Isn't it wonderful?"

Mus gave a jerk of surprise. He looked up at his friend with sick, hollow eyes.

"Wha . . . ?"

"About Lyssa! I brought her flowers and some food. . . ." Miriam faltered. "Mus, art thou all right?"

The mouse blinked. "I—I think so. . . . Maybe."

Miriam took the mouse into her hand, then peered down at the book he had splayed open on the desk.

"*The Viper.*" Miriam made a face and shuddered. "O Mus, what dost thou want to read a miserable story like *that* for?" She plucked him up and cosseted him. "Enough of that! Come along! Breakfast time."

Miriam walked out onto the balcony and set Mus before a plate filled with crumbs. She perched the little fellow on her knee and combed his fur with a tiny brush, letting the morning sun spread its warmth along his side.

The girl waited patiently, knowing he would talk to her. Sure enough, Mus finally chose to speak.

"Your wedding night. Did it . . . did it go well?"

"Yes, Mus." Married; she was really married! It still seemed difficult to believe. "It was *wonderful.*"

"Yes . . ." Mus twitched miserably. "Miriam?"

"Yes, Mus?"

"I have been reading *The Viper.* You know—the play where a minister betrays his king?"

Miriam's voice remained carefully neutral. "Yes. I know it."

"Miriam—they cut his head off. . . ."

"Yes. They did, didn't they."

The mouse squeezed his eyes shut. "Must traitors always die? Couldn't—couldn't you just let them go? What if they only did it because they were very sick?"

"Oh, Mus . . ." The mouse trembled, and Miriam stroked a soft fingertip along his back. "Mus, dost thou want to talk with me about anything?"

"No. I-I can't. There's duties; Torscha needs me."

Miriam nodded. "All right, Mus—but not now. We'll eat together and sing to Lyssa. We have half an hour yet."

"Yes." Mus blinked. "I don't suppose half an hour will make any difference."

"I love thee, Mus."

"I love thee, Miriam. I love thee."

The companions nestled down in the sun, and Miriam explored private thoughts as she shared breakfast with her little friend.

The dungeons of the castle keep ran deep beneath the ground, well away from the fortress walls themselves. Black old tunnels burrowed past the rose garden and out under the bailey. Cleaned and caulked, they made a perfect central powder magazine. Tons of powder had been stuffed into the ancient cells and chambers; the ammunition supply for the entire garrison.

Lamplight shone down the broad old stairwell, bringing with it the slow, measured sound of hooves. Two guards stirred, hefting the blunderbusses they had been issued as a deterrent to wandering stoats. Both men smiled as Captain Willy Merle came slowly around the stairs.

Captain Merle's face seemed pale, and his eyes were sunken back beneath his brows. The senior guard doffed his leather hat, then started forward as he saw Sir William's sweating face.

"Sir! Are ye feeling well, sir?"

Willy licked at his pale lips. "I'm well enough, thank you." He could not meet the soldier's eyes. "I have been asked to inventory the pistol powder. For—for tomorrow."

"Well certainly, sir. The left gallery holds all the pistol powders." He made haste to replace Sir William's lantern. "No burnin' lights beyond here, sir. Ye'll have to use a pixie light, and felt slippers for your hooves. Can't risk sparks, y'see?"

Willy shook the pixie light into a glow, then accepted the help of the soldiers in tying thick felt sheaths about his hooves. Willy leaned against the wall till all was done.

"Thank you—uh . . ."

"Doby, sir! Trooper Doby and Trooper Friant!"

Willy closed his eyes. He had never wanted these men to have names. . . . "Thank you, Doby—thank you, Friant."

A thick leather curtain hung across the door, designed to muffle any blast that roared along the corridor. Willy shoved the curtain aside and walked through into the darkness.

Moving slowly, he paced through a long, vaulted hall. Boxes of bullets were piled high on either side. There were barrels of matches and baskets of flints—all the stores needed to fuel a tiny army. Willy's muffled hoofsteps echoed as he advanced deeper down into the magazine.

He reached another leather curtain; beyond that would be an empty room—the junction that led to the powder galleries. Willy reached into his pocket and felt for his tinderbox and a fifteen-minute fuse.

Fifteen minutes and the siege would be over. Miriam would be safe.

Willy stared at the final curtain, his hide twitching in indecision. Finally he stepped forth and moved into the open room. Feeling more confident, the stallion drew out his length of fuse.

A quiet little voice shattered the silence. "Hello, Willy."

The huge half-horse skittered backward, hooves prancing in terror. Wild eyes searched the dark, trying to pin the mouse down. "M-*Mus?*"

"Yes, Willy, it's only me." The mouse felt very sad; if only Willy hadn't come. Mus kindled a little light on the end of his tail. "Only me."

Willy edged backward as he saw the mouse sitting square in the middle of the room. Willy quickly shielded his eyes with his wounded arm. "Mus! How—how did you learn to do that?"

"I know lots of things, Willy. I always told everyone that I was clever." The mouse miserably closed his eyes. "Sometimes being clever hurts. I've only just learned that."

Willy licked his lips, then edged cautiously closer.

"Mus? I'm going to go down into the powder magazines."

"No. No, Willy, you're not."

Willy could finally see Mus's face. The mouse was crying—silent, hopeless tears that ran down his little cheeks.

He knew. Willy felt a sick wave of regret. "Mus?"

"Please go away, Willy! Go home! You're sick!" Mus sobbed. "Maybe—maybe one day you'll be well again. . . ."

Willy's eyes blazed in the unwavering light. He fought for breath. "Mus, don't be stupid! I'm just . . ."

". . . going to blow up the magazine. You arranged it with Snatch." Mus turned his face away in pain. "I-I heard you."

The stallion swallowed. "Did you—did you tell anyone?"

"No, Willy. I love you! How could I tell anyone?"

"I see . . . " Willy fingered the pistol in his pocket. "So that's it; I just go away, and nothing ever happened."

"Please, Willy. Please go away."

Sir William slowly paced closer. "I'll be a hero, Mus! She'll see that! It's an act of love!"

"Willy—*go away!*"

Willy snarled in bitter hate. "Who's to stop me, you?"

"Yes." Suddenly the light changed; the tiny mouse sat outlined in a crackling aura of fire. Willy trod closer, but Mus stood his ground. "Stop, Willy!"

The stallion sneered. "You can burn potted plants, Mus! You can light candles! But you're no sorcerer!" He snatched out his pistol. "There's not . . ."

Fire lanced out to splash across the pistol in Willy's hand. There was a *crack* as the bullet buzzed harmlessly off into the dark. Sir William cradled his scorched hand, staring at Mus in shock. The mouse was panting.

"No, Willy. I'm only half a sorcerer. There's only fire in me. Only love." Mus shaded his eyes, pleading with his friend. "I love you, Willy. *Don't make me do this!*"

Willy gathered his muscles for a leap.

"*Please, Willy!*"

Mus wept even as he drew his power about him. He had never hated it until now. The mouse blazed with light, making the air boil with force. Willy stared, and then suddenly turned and fled. His hooves echoed down the passageway as he staggered back into the darkness.

Mus closed his eyes and cried, his body racked with helpless sobs. A loud *click* came suddenly from behind him, and Mus whirled in disbelief as a shadow emerged from the halls. There was a smell like wildflowers and fresh bread on a rainy day. . . .

Miriam lowered her pistol, swept up the little mouse and cradled him against her heart. From behind another curtain, Torscha Retter moved slowly into the room. The pistol in his hand trembled as Miriam's had not.

Mus wept helplessly against Miriam's breast. "You—you heard! No one was supposed to know. . . ."

"We guessed, little one. Frielle, Torscha, and I all guessed." They had lain in wait long before Mus had arrived.

Mus swallowed. "There—there was no need. I wouldn't have let him in."

"I know, but we feared for thee, Mus. We love thee."

Mus squeezed his eyes shut and burrowed close. Miriam held him tight, reaching out for Torscha with her other hand.

There was comfort in togetherness. The three companions embraced in the darkness and wept for friends long gone.

Chapter Eight
A Withering Bloom

ime! What time is it?"

An aide hastened to open up a pocket watch, blinking at its face in the light of a glim.

"Twenty minutes past midnight, Majesty."

"*Damn!*" Aelis whirled clumsily in the trench, her white hide shimmering in the darkness. "Varre?"

"Majesty!"

"Their magazine has held. Open fire!"

Goblins leapt to obey; powder was ladled into the guns by squawking imps while spindle-legged trolls plied their ramming staves. Aelis waved a gun-captain aside, snatched a linstock from his hands, and set fire to the cannon's fuse.

The gun slammed backward with a numbing roar, punching its massive ball toward the castle wall. One after another, cannon fired all along the line. From the castle ramparts came the sound of shattering stone as the night lit up with flame.

There was a wild cheer from the goblin gunners. The odd creatures turned handstands, shrieking insults as the loaders rushed to sponge out the guns. The toadlike gun-captain slobbered a great draft from a wineskin, then danced a dangerous, hopping jig atop a stack of powder kegs.

Aelis looked about her in confusion; she had to shout above the racket. "*Is this really necessary?*"

The hobgoblin held aloft a stuffed hedgehog on a stick.

"*Borchiocha! Go ballum-ballum!*"

"Eh?"

Varre coughed. "He says yes—he's very much afraid it is."

From the next battery came the crash of other guns. The night trembled to the might of Nantierran artillery blasts, growing faster and faster as the crews settled down into their rhythm. The enemy earthworks erupted in a shower of dust, red-hot ricochets plowing high into the air. Mortars sent shell-bursts tearing down into the castle roofs. Aelis watched, breathing heavily as the fires shone in her eyes.

Able to see the fall of their own shot in the dark, the goblins would crew the guns by night, while human artillerymen would maintain the fire by day. The castle walls would dissolve like sand before the wind.

A presence loomed behind Aelis in the darkness. Death drew Count Retter like a moth unto flame.

"You have waited long, Majesty."

"I wait no more!" The queen stamped at the mud with her hooves. "Varre! How long?"

"One week—perhaps nine days, depending on the temper of their stone."

Aelis stood posed against the gunfire. The flashes outlined her perfect figure against the chill night sky. One week. One week, and Castle Kerbridge would be gone.

"Count Retter—you may plan your assault."

* * * * *

Wind swept across the purple heather, making it ripple like a strange alien sea. Tents flapped as the wind plucked its icy fingers through the army camp, and banners slapped sullenly at their staves.

In the royal pavilion, the mood was glum. King Firined irritably paced back and forth, a shimmering vision of military fashion. In an etched suit of cuirass, helm and bridle gauntlet, the scholar-king of Duncruigh was sure to be quite safe from shot and shell. No weapon would *dare* mark such perfect clothing, nor ruffle his gleaming hair. He kept his back straight and his brow furrowed.

"Where are they? Demned fools! What in hell's name made me trust 'em?"

General Vardvere wearily removed one boot and poured out half a pint of water from the offending footwear.

"*Hemmm-haw!* Northerners! I never trust 'em! Never!"

The king had put command of his field armies in the hands of his most experienced general. Old Vardvere had risen to the task as best he might, but the troops were simply not to hand. The newly raised regiments would have been chaff before the wind had they tangled with Aelis's veterans. They had needed training, and they needed leavening with experienced men.

Kerbridge had bought him time, and finally the troops were ready. They were outnumbered, but drilled to a standard that continental troops seldom met. Their musketry was second to none—but morale was doubtful if a fight came down to pike point.

The army was ready. They waited only for the contingents from the Northern Isles—wild lancers, savage warriors—even ogres from the fens. And yet, as always, Vardvere counseled patience. Firined paced and cursed, slashing his magnificent sword behind him.

"Peace, Majesty! Peace! *Hemmmm*—p'raps they are delayed upon the road."

"Delayed? Delayed!" The king was at the end of his tether. "First we need to buy time to find an army! Then we need time to fetch Erliken's troops from Aurey! And meanwhile, the Bitch lays waste to half the kingdom with none to stop her!"

"She is being stopped, Sire. She is being stopped at Kerbridge."

"*Kerbridge.*" The king stared toward the south. " 'Tis a hard thing when the fate of a kingdom rests on the shoulders of a mouse." The wind blew fine rain across the hills as King Firined gazed out across the empty fens.

* * * * *

The walls of the great hall trembled, making dust drift down from the ceiling. Miriam winced, but carefully refrained from looking out the window. The morning sun shone down to light her hair with a thousand gorgeous flecks of copper red. She sat with Mus and Lyssa in her hand as Lyssa carefully read aloud from a gigantic yellow book.

> "*Of all their company, he was the truest knight.*
> *Enamored of truth, and grace and light.*
> *He knew no bounds to loyalty,*
> *Truth, honor, and courtesy.*
> *A knight who worshiped chivalry from the time he first began:*
> *He was in every inch a gentle-man.*"

Lyssa sat back and twirled her tail in wonder. "It sounds like Mus!" Lyssa's voice had a sweetly sensible quality that had captured Miriam's heart. "He is a *gentle*—man. All fine and full of life."

"Well . . . all fine and full of *pose*." Miriam fondly stroked her little friend. Mus arched his back in pleasure and sighed. "We shall certainly keep him just as he is."

Lyssa was recovering. A deep sleep, food, and love had roused her from her stupor. Although weak, she had at last found strength enough to see and hear and talk.

With glittering eyes, Mus peered over the edge of Miriam's hand. "I *so* want to be a gentleman. I try so hard." The mouse's fine black whiskers quivered in the air. "I'd like to be a knight! Wouldn't it be fine?"

Lyssa pulled a little frown.

"We shall have to ask the king to make you one. You have been so terribly brave!"

"I'm brave?" Mus's eyes shone; there was no one from whom he would rather hear praise. "You really think so?"

Mus danced and capered upon the table, then leapt up into a potted plant and hung upside down in the branches.

"Lyssa can read! She is clever! Ha ha! Thou canst see what a wonderful, magical world it is?"

Miriam irritably reached out to evict Mus from the potted plant. "Mus! Get out of there! Thou'st already eaten half the leaves off my poor little geranium."

"They're crunchy! It tastes like cinnamon."

"Out!" Miriam plucked the mouse up by his tail; Mus dangled upside down and squawked in outrage. He called Miriam a rude name, and was dunked into the water jug for his trouble. The mouse clambered up over the lip, looking half drowned, and chittered like a mad thing.

Suddenly all argument stopped as sweet laughter welled up from the tabletop. Lyssa rolled on her side, weak with mirth, and Mus pouted down from the lip of the water jug.

"Well, you could help! You like geraniums too!"

The lady mouse mopped at her eyes. She had caught a thorough case of hiccoughs, and Miriam gently rubbed at Lyssa's belly with one finger. The mouse quickly went droopy about the eyes; she tired so very easily.

Lyssa heaved a sigh and curled into a fluffy ball.

"Thank you, Mus. Thank you, Miriam. You—you're both so very kind to me. So very kind. . . ."

And with that she simply fell asleep. Mus slid down the side of the jug and noisily shook off his fur, drenching Miriam in the process. "Is she asleep?"

Miriam irritably dried her face with a handkerchief. "Aye. Shhhh—we'll put her to bed and let her snooze. It's been a tiring morning for her."

Miriam instinctively hunched over her small friends as a rapid series of blows hacked against the southern wall. The shutters trembled to the shock of distant cannonballs while Miriam carefully transferred her little patient into bed. Mus assisted the whole procedure, plumping up pillows and offering unneeded advice.

"She laughed. She really laughed!" Mus gave a lovesick sigh. " 'Tis like sunshine on flowers."

The pair of friends carefully left the room, closing the door behind them. They walked down the corridor toward the staircase, Mus clinging quietly to Miriam's hair.

"Miriam?"

"Yes, Mus?"

"About—about last night . . ."

The memory was painful; Willy had been locked in a sickroom, and no one had yet found courage enough to visit him. Mus looked down at his little paws. "I lied to Frielle. It is very wicked to lie."

"Not always, Mus. Sometimes a gentleman has to know how to lie—when it's all for the best." Miriam tucked the mouse up onto her shoulder. "But we shall go and talk to her about it. She understands."

Miriam bore the mouse downstairs. The castle walls shivered once more as the ramparts slowly weakened.

They found Frielle beside the castle gatehouse, just within the shadow of the drawbridge. With grim determination, she was loading spare muskets. The weapons were much taller than she, giving the dainty satyr an awkward time working the ramrod; even so, a pile of loaded muskets attested to her skill.

Thomas Carpernan and his men collected armfuls of the loaded weapons. Sir Thomas edged warily around Frielle, who made an elaborate pretense of ignoring his existence.

A mortar bomb warbled through the sky to explode harmlessly in the middle of the bailey ruins, throwing water weeds high into the air. Frielle looked up as Miriam approached, wiping a dirty fist across her cheek.

"Miriam! Hast thou come to help, then?"

The half-horse felt more than a touch guilty. Here she was, idling the morning away with the mice while Frielle had made herself useful.

"Uh—I didn't know. No one told me!"

With her teeth, Frielle pulled the cork from a fresh powder horn. "Well—ye know now." She spat out the cork. "Come on, grab a bundle and pitch in, there's a lass. There's two hundred to get through!"

Mus waved a cheery greeting to Frielle and then leapt down to inspect the muskets piled at the gate. The mouse poked his head right down one gun barrel to peer within, and inevitably found himself stuck.

"*Miriam! Help! Help!*"

"Get out of that!" Miriam plucked Mus free. "We'll pull the trigger next time! That'll get thee loose in nothing flat!"

Mus sulked. "I only wanted to see inside. . . ."

Miriam fetched his hat and placed him down upon the steps. "Now just sit there and cause no more trouble!"

Frielle finished another musket and placed it on the pile beside Mus. She picked the rodent up and kissed him on the nose. "Mornin', Mus! How's thy patient?"

"She can read!" The mouse swelled up with pride. "She can read—and walk! And she said that I was brave!"

Another mortar shell warbled overhead. Miriam winced, then edged closer to the pile of muskets. It was not a task that seemed attractive. "Well—I suppose it will help to . . ."

The howl of the shell grew louder. Miriam's eyes grew wide. "DOWN!"

The shockwave hit them like a giant's fist. Miriam felt herself picked up and slammed against the stones. Debris showered down over her back. Miriam spat and opened her eyes as the others climbed back to their feet. Mus and Sir Thomas rose dazedly from a ditch, and Miriam looked across to Frielle in relief.

"Well, that was our piece of excitement for the day!"

Frielle tottered to her feet and stared out across the moat. She had the expression of a little lost girl.

"Frielle?"

The satyr blinked, looking strangely pale, then lifted one hand up from her stomach to look stupidly at her palm. Blood spilled from her fingers and soaked down her skirts.

"FRIELLE!"

Sir Thomas caught her, staring into Frielle's horrified eyes. The girl clutched at him with bloody hands and began to shiver. Blood soaked through her dress to spatter down onto the officer's sleeves.

"M-*Miriam!*"

"*Oh, God!*" Miriam hastily ran a hand across the girl's face. Already she was pale and stiff. "Quick, put her on my back! I'll get her to the surgeon!"

Mus made a spectacular leap from his perch on the ledge and caught Miriam's hair in passing. Together the group raced into Jerrick hall, leaving a splash of blood behind them as they ran. They burst into the empty surgery to be met by the stench of brandy, gin, and herbs. Though a small man, Thomas somehow found the strength of ten as he lifted Frielle and laid her on a table. Jane peered hastily in through the door, gave a gasp, and clattered off in search of Doctor Freeps.

"Mus, the lamps!"

Lights sprang into life all across the room as Miriam stripped the blood-soaked clothes from the little satyr's body.

Frielle panted, pressing her head back onto the table, still too proud to scream. "Tom! *Tom!*"

Thomas held her. "I'm here, love! I'm here!"

Frielle clutched at him, crushing him tight. The man desperately ran his fingers through her hair, helpless to choke back her pain. The girl lay naked on the table in a sea of blood. Miriam hastily wiped a towel across a hideous, ragged hole in Frielle's waist, just above her fur.

There was no exit wound. . . .

Jane burst in through the door. "*Miriam!*"

Miriam whirled, her hands stained with her best friend's blood. "Where is he? Is he coming?"

"He—he . . ."

Miriam desperately tried to stop the flow of blood. Panic rose to choke her. "*I told you to bring him!*"

The maidservant pressed her hands to her cheeks and wept. "He's *drunk!*"

Miriam stopped and stared. The words simply made no sense . . .

"The doctor, my lady—he's dead *drunk!*"

Miriam was light-headed as she felt Frielle dying under her

hands.

Dying!

"Jane, fetch the potions! Mus, translate the labels for her!" Miriam tried to think. "I-I need a probe and a scalpel!"

Frielle's skin shone slim and white against her lower body's fur. The satyr stiffened as Miriam set to work; a fragment grated against Miriam's probe, wedged too deep to reach with the tongs. The half-horse hastily clamped arteries shut, trying to remember what to do.

"*Mus!* Darbrett's surgical procedures! Do you remember the sections on abdominal surgery?"

The mouse hopped up atop the table, his horrified eyes never leaving Frielle's face. Mus chanted the precise pages of the medical manuals back at her, word perfect. Miriam listened, and her hands began to move of their own volition.

She bent to cradle Frielle's head in her arms.

"Frielle? I-I have to *cut* you, my love. I have to! There—there's nothing for the pain. . . ."

The fawn fumbled out to draw Miriam close, then buried her face in Miriam's hair. "*I-I love you!*"

The little satyr fumbled a leather strap between her lips and looked at Miriam with bright, frightened eyes; she then pulled Thomas close and hid her face. Whispering a prayer, Miriam reached for her instruments.

Miriam was acutely conscious of the precious life beneath her hands. It was the longest few minutes of her life. Finally a jagged piece of bomb casing lay upon the table, all glistening with Frielle's blood.

Somehow, Opal had appeared in the room. The little dragon sat perched on the edge of the drug shelf staring at Frielle with glittering, intelligent eyes. She looked from the satyr to Miriam and back again before throwing back her head to give a plaintive moan. The mournful song rang through the room, making Mus's hackles rise.

Miriam slowly laid her instruments aside. Thomas wept as he cradled Frielle's brow. "Will—will she live?"

Miriam's fingers combed through Frielle's soft wool. "I . . . There will be fever . . ." Miriam could not meet Sir Thomas's eyes. "It may kill her. . . ."

"*Fever.*" Sir Thomas swallowed. "Why fever?"

"Her gut was pierced. There'll be infection." Miriam's voice was toneless, and Mus crept over to nuzzle against her neck. "Th-The alchemists with the army might be able to save her, but I cannot. It's far beyond my skill."

Miriam stood. "Without aid, she'll be dead within a week—ten days at the most."

Frielle whispered Thomas's name. The cavalier folded her against his breast and wept.

* * * * *

In the black moments before dawn, the castle's eastern walls stood still and silent. Cannon gouged and chewed at the southern battlements—the background noise now seeming common as summer thunder.

A slender figure froze and stared back toward the castle keep, the gunfire reflected in his eyes. Below the walls, a cliff dropped a sheer hundred feet into the river Fandin. The figure drew off its shirt and stood naked in the gloom—skin shining pale as milk against legs sheathed with handsome fur. The man paused, took one deep breath, then launched himself out into the void.

He clove into the water like a supple fish. Moments later, he surfaced and struck out toward the distant shore. Naked and alone, the tiny figure struggled to the north.

Toward King Firined.

Back in Frielle's sickroom, a sealed envelope lay upon her pillow. Inside there lay a small gold ring, and a letter written in a smooth, elaborate hand.

It read:

My Darling Frielle,

I know what thou must think of me. I can never ask forgiveness for my betrayal—for my cowardice. It has only been now that I have discovered how deeply I truly love thee.

For the hurt I have done thee, there is no excuse, but perhaps in some small way I can atone for my wrongs. I shall try to pass the enemy lines to take message to the king. He must come soon, or we are lost. . . .

If by life or death I can serve thee—then I am happy.

I enclose the ring that I promised thee so very long ago. It is thine to keep in troth, or to throw back at me.

I love thee.

Tom

Chapter Nine

Miriam's Bargain

ET BACK!"
"SHE'S GOING!"
Across a three-yard section of rampart the rock
began to slide. The battlements slowly collapsed
backward only to disintegrate as a massive cannonball
slammed into the stones. The garrison soldiers dodged wildly
aside as the rock face cascaded to the ground.

From the enemy lines came a wild cheer; the beginning of the
end had come. A breach had opened, and the guns ripped it farther
open with their claws.

Colonel Retter danced backward, rearing high to paw the air
with his hooves.

"*Kelso!* How long has it been?"

"Sir?"

"How long since the siege guns started firing?"

The sailor pulled at his gold earring. "Five days, sir."

Had it really been so long? Five days. Sir Thomas might have
reached the king, if he had somehow found a horse and had ridden
like the wind. How long to move the army two hundred miles
downstream? Ten days? Twenty? The wall would have fallen long
before then.

Torscha stood tall and proud as another enemy shot carved a
furrow in the battlements. They would be through the wall within
the next few days. Two, perhaps three at the most. "Tonight we'll
mine the back of the breach with bombs. Detail ten men from each
company to fall in for sapping."

He calmly turned his back on the damaged wall and walked

away. Retter's men stirred with confidence as they saw him fold his hands behind his back and calmly make his rounds.

Torscha found Miriam in the dining room with her mother. The women both wore patient expressions as Mus and Lyssa raced frantically back and forth among an incredible pile of mechanical cogs, springs, and gears. The baroness tried to remain calm.

"Mus?"

"Uh—I have it! I have it!" The mouse dived into the back of an open clock, and a rain of tiny parts showered out behind him. "Never fear, I have it now!"

Torscha took the baroness's hand and brushed it with his lips, then moved to quietly take Miriam in his arms while Lady Jerrick stood over the two mice tapping her hooves.

Lyssa's tail waved from somewhere beneath a pile of gears. "No no no! The big wheel fits over the little one—thus and so!"

Mus's voice was indignant. "*I* took it apart! I tell thee it goes the other way around!"

"Cheese thief!"

"Ninny!"

"Give me that!"

Mus squawked. "Let it go! It's mine!"

Lady Jerrick sighed. "*Children!* If that clock is not working again within the next five minutes, I shall personally load thee into a cannon and fire thee across the walls."

Lyssa's head peeked up over the edge of the clock.

"How can we know that five minutes have passed if we no longer have a clock?" She disappeared with a squeak of outrage as Mus tugged her tail. Lady Jerrick folded her arms.

"Just get thee busy, young lady! I'm waiting!"

Torscha frowned. "What on earth are they doing?"

"Ah." Miriam carefully ignored the sounds of cannon fire and breaking stone. "Mus decided to show Lyssa how a clock worked. . . ."

Oh, no. Torscha could see it all just as it would have happened.

"Give it back!"

"It goes *here!*"

"Nay, thou feather brain! It fits beneath the spring!"

"*Feather brain!* I'll give thee feather brain!"

The stallion sighed. "Was it a valuable clock?"

The baroness grimaced. "It was a wedding present from old

Queen Margerie!"

Oh, dear.

"Well—I shall take it to the shop in Harpot Row to have it fixed next week."

Miriam looked away; the likelihood of their ever being able to visit the clockmaker was not high. Miriam feared for her husband; every minute seemed precious, and every night was a priceless gift. She lived moment by moment, trying to ignore the choking waves of fear that almost overwhelmed her. Frielle had begun to fade away before her very eyes, sweating in a fever Miriam could never seem to break. . . .

Torscha listened to the squabbling mice and smiled. "An evening at the theater would be nice. I shall take thee to the theater when all this is over. We shall laugh and dance, and never look at bombs and muskets for as long as we live."

He seemed quite content with his vision; Torscha smiled and closed his eyes, oblivious to the roar and fury of the cannon at the walls.

The mice began to squabble bitterly, and clockwork parts bounced across the table until the baroness clapped her hands. "*Children!*"

The two mice poked their heads out of the ruined clock as Lady Jerrick sternly shook her finger.

"If thou canst not work nicely together, then there is no point in working at all."

The mice shuffled their little feet and looked down at their hands.

"*Mus,* what should a gentleman do?"

The little mouse played with his tail. "I'm sorry I called thee a ninny, Lyssa."

The baroness nodded in approval and turned to the lady mouse. "Lyssa—how should a *lady* respond?"

Little Lyssa ashamedly kicked her feet. "I'm sorry I called thee a cheese thief, Mus."

"Excellent!" Lady Jerrick reached out her hand and the two mice skipped gaily across the table to jump into her palm. As was characteristic of the little creatures, all grudges were forgotten the minute the incident had passed. Lady Jerrick placed the mice upon her shoulder.

"Now! We shall call the clock a disaster, I'm afraid." She

ruefully swept up the bits and pieces with her hands. "We'll fix it another time. Pray, do not tinker with complex mechanisms again."

"I'm truly sorry." Mus peered down toward the wreckage. "It all seems to rely on just one vital piece! Once you take it out, it all just collapses!"

Miriam gazed blankly at one wall, her face draining white. Long moments drew by, until she felt Torscha lifting up her hand. "Miriam? Shall we look in upon Frielle?"

"What?" Miriam slowly stirred, her eyes still gazing far away. "Yes . . . Yes, I suppose so. . . ."

The little party rose and wandered off into the gloom, while somewhere in the distance, cannon roared.

In the ancient castle gardens, the air smelled pure and clean. The awful crash of cannon fire was forgotten in the caress of nature's hand. Almost—but not quite. The mice leapt and played in the grass, calling happily to one another as they romped in the sunshine, guarded by the castle sergeant's ever watchful eyes.

Miriam wandered with slow steps and a face turned pale and wan. The air swirled with the sharp scent of aniseed as fennel plants brushed velvet-soft against her hide. The whisper of the wind through their stalks seemed like the quiet chatter of old friends.

A little mousy gasp of wonder came from underneath the bushes. Mus watched in awe as a beautiful blue butterfly drifted down to settle on his back. He laughed for joy, making Miriam turn to stare in his direction.

"It's *beautiful!* Oh, it's beautiful!"

Lyssa had her eyes screwed shut, looking strained.

"*Uh*—is it blue?"

"Oh, *yes!* A lovely shimmering blue!" The butterfly flapped off between the weeds, and Mus followed merrily in its wake. Lyssa gave a gasp of effort, struggling against some fearful barrier, and suddenly the butterfly faded from the sky. Mus gave a little "Aaaawww" of disappointment.

"It's gone!"

"I-I couldn't keep it there!" The lady mouse sighed unhappily.

"The door just seemed to close."

The sergeant's jaw dropped almost to the ground. "Madam Lyssa! Did *you* do that?"

Mus's head popped out from behind a toadstool.

"Well of course she did. Why not?"

"Bu-But *how?*"

Lyssa vigorously scratched her ear with one hind leg. "I *like* butterflies!"

Miriam simply accepted it all, as though Lyssa's talent did not surprise her. Illusion; another creative magical talent. She gently bent down to kiss the little mouse and place her safely on a rock.

Mus ran all the way up a primrose bush. Perched absurdly high off the ground, he reached out to try and pluck a tiny, perfect bud that hung just out of reach.

Miriam sighed indulgently.

"Mus! Don't fall, my sweet!"

"Ha!" The mouse plucked the bloom and waved it in triumph. "I have told thee I am clever!"

"That thou hast, my love." Miriam looked at him fondly, with something strange and mournful in her eyes. "That thou hast."

Mus slithered down the primrose to leap back to the ground. He proffered the tiny rose to Lyssa, whose ears turned positively pink in embarrassment. She buried her nose in the flower and sighed.

Miriam stared at the mouse while she called out to the sergeant. "Oh, sergeant? Sergeant? Would you keep an eye on these two while I wander off—I just wish to do something in the—the magazine."

"Aye, milady! I'll keep watch till you get back."

The woman turned and paced her way down through the wild parsley. Broad pathways had been worn through the rich green weeds. Miriam reached the ruined chapel—now the forward magazine—where four human soldiers stood on guard. Miriam nodded to the men as they swiftly doffed their hats. No one dared ask why the Colonel's lady needed to visit the powder stores.

Inside, all lay hushed and silent; Miriam breathed in the scent of ancient stone—cool, heavy, and full of peace. The girl's hide shivered as she felt the chill.

Here, in this place of comfort, Miriam reached her final commitment. The filly looked up into the shadows with grave, wide eyes, and then slowly bent her head in prayer.

To freely give a gift can never be a loss.

Let them understand, I do this because I love them. . . .

With tears in her eyes, Miriam turned and slowly made her way out of the chapel.

It felt like leaving a younger self behind.

She walked out into the red light of sunset. It would be a precious evening, and she must make the most of it. Few people were as lucky as she had been; Miriam looked out at the glorious sunset and was at peace.

With calm, soft movements she walked to the old yew tree that grew at the bottom of her garden. Miriam carefully drew on leather gloves and took a billhook from her belt. With one smooth chop, she clove a young branch cleanly from the tree.

"Miriam?"

The girl reached out to stroke the yew needles. They were tough and springy, rattling against the palm of her glove.

"Miriam? Shall we go in now?"

Miriam looked down to see Mus perched on a rock before her. Lyssa sat nearby, stealing shy glances at Mus through the petals of the primrose.

The half-horse put away her billhook, picked up her little friends, and gave a silent smile. With sunlight shining from her hair, Miriam Retter turned away from her regrets and wandered back into her home.

Hooves thundered on the evening air as troops cantered down the small back-country lanes of Duncruigh. Troopers of horse bore infantry behind their saddles; cuirassiers had discarded cuisses and arm harnesses to increase their traveling speed. Half-horses lumbered forward with lighter races perched unhappily on their backs. The royal army surged through the evening with grim determination as King Firined led them to Aelis's lair.

"Thomas! How far to go?"

"Forty miles, Sire! Forty miles!"

The king nodded. His helmet plumes were bedraggled and his armor stained with travel. All about him the army lunged forward at a breakneck speed. The cannon and wagon trains had been abandoned, along with any man who could not beg a lift upon four hooves. The men had only the food and ammunition that they carried in their pouches.

In two days, they had covered more than a hundred miles. Far from being downhearted, the men stamped on with wild, ferocious vigor. The king drove them on with his boundless energy, galloping up and down the line to stir up the laggards with his banter. This was a most extraordinary king.

Thomas Carpernan reeled in the saddle of a borrowed horse. The satyr had ridden three horses into the ground, reaching the royal presence with Kerbridge's plea for help. Naked, pale, and bleeding from a pistol wound, the cavalier had fainted at his monarch's feet.

It had been enough; his ride had inspired the king, and so the army hurled itself at Kerbridge.

A troop of Royal Life Guard cantered past, throwing up a shower of mud as General Vardvere reined in at King Firined's side.

"Majesty, the village of Faxter lies ahead. I suggest we spend the night athwart the crossroads."

"*Stop?* Stop now!" The king was angry. "Forty miles to go, Vardvere! Forty miles! And y' want us to stop?"

The old general pounded his fist against his saddle pommel. "Damn it, Sire! They'll not march in their sleep, nor are dead-tired men worth tuppence in a fight! We must rest!"

One hundred sixty miles; it was a miracle that they had managed to come so far. Aelis could not possibly suspect. With luck, they would catch Aelis's army between the hammer of the army and the anvil of the castle and destroy her utterly. If they were unlucky, Duncruigh's massively outnumbered army would be shattered at a blow.

It all rode on a single cast of the die, and Firined felt strangely liberated; win or lose, a decision would be forced.

He owed everything to Kerbridge. They had taken up the gauntlet on his behalf, gambling on giving him time enough to save his kingdom. Was a king to abandon his loyal subjects? That would not be how history would remember Firined. They were all but actors on a deadly stage; it was time to play the final scene.

Forty miles; the king's horse pawed at the ground.

"Very well, Vardvere, we shall stop for the night. Send patrols out to gather stragglers." Firined jerked hard upon his reins. "But we march at dawn, Vardvere! We march at dawn."

The evening seemed strange and strained as the officers gathered for what must surely be their last dinner in Jerrick Hall. Tomorrow evening the enemy would attack, just as the sun went down. The breach would be wide enough for Aelis to assault the castle.

It made no difference to Lady Jerrick; she played the hostess with cool, unhurried calm, stopping to talk with each officer and make each man forget his worries. Her body stood straight and proud inside its black mourning gown, and her hands moved smoothly as she talked.

Miriam Retter sat happily in her husband's company, talking softly to him, adoring him with her eyes. The girl filled the halls with light and laughter, lifting up the flagging spirits of the men. Tonight, Miriam had dressed with incredible care, with hair arranged in little rolls and ringlets that bounced about her oval face.

There was something strange about Miriam's manner; she seemed too at ease—too loving. Her eyes were bright, her pupils wide, and her breathing strangely fast, as though she were living the evening with unearthly intensity.

Miriam sought out her mother once the dinner had come to a close. The girl took her mother's hands and drew her aside into one of the sitting rooms.

They stood in silence as Miriam stared at her mother with loving, trusting eyes. She reached out to take her mother's face and kiss her, making Lady Barbara blink in surprise.

"Why, darling! What ever was that for?"

"Just for being thee. I love thee, Mama."

"I love thee, Daughter."

Miriam looked strangely sad.

"I wish Papa were here for thee. Or Roland. It must be lonely for thee, Mama."

Lady Barbara smiled. "Oh, love . . . no. It's not so very lonely. Not with thee here."

Miriam stared. "Yes—yes, that's right." She touched her mother's face. "Not with me here."

Miriam's mother tucked her daughter's curls back into place.

"Oh—I know thou'rt married, and I cannot keep thee forever, but Kerbridge is not a lonely place. God has been very kind to me."

Not so very kind, Mama. He has taken away so much. . . .

"Mama—I have been so happy with thee. So very happy. There has never been a better mother. Never a better friend."

Lady Barbara held her daughter tight.

"Why, darling, thank thee. Thank thee for saying so."

"Just as long as thou knowest. I—I needed to tell thee."

"Why, Miriam! Thou'rt crying!"

"Nay, Mama!" Miriam kept her face buried deep within her mother's curls. "Nay—I'm not crying. But hold me a while; just hold me."

Mother and daughter held each other close. Eventually Miriam drew away, and Lady Jerrick followed after, feeling strangely ill at ease.

Willy sat locked in his room, silently eating his dinner. He lived a strange and hollow life, trying to hide himself away. Though no guards stood outside his door, he was a prisoner in everything but name. Willy's movements were listless and drained—utterly without hope or pride.

He looked up in shock as Miriam came through the door into his room. The man erupted up onto his hooves and crowded fearfully away. He backed into a corner, with nowhere else to run.

Miriam slowly paced through the door to stand before him. She held his sword and scabbard in her hand, toying with the hilt. Willy shrank aside, but Miriam gently took his hands and held them in her own. Hesitantly, reluctantly, he looked up to meet her eye and found the one thing he had hoped for . . . and feared.

Forgiveness.

"Oh, Willy . . . Willy, I'm sorry."

He had to struggle to find his voice. "*S-Sorry?*"

"It was all my fault. I should have seen how deeply I had hurt you." Miriam gripped his hands. "Canst thou ever forgive me, dear Willy? I never meant to cause thee pain."

Willy shivered and hid his face, weeping tears of shame.

"*I betrayed thee. . . .*"

"I'm sorry that it ever came to this, Willy. I'm so sorry. If we had but talked . . ." She sighed. "But my only thoughts were for mine own happiness." Miriam looked into her lap. "Say that you forgive me. It's important to me, Willy. It's important for me to know. . . ."

Willy sobbed, hiding his face. "That thou canst ask me if I forgive thee—after all I have said and done?"

"Please, Willy!"

"I-I forgive thee." The words made no sense; there was nothing to forgive her for. Willy had been given a test of friendship and had *failed*. He shuddered. "How can I ever atone for what I have done to all of thee?"

Miriam reached out to take the stallion in her arms. She held him as he wept against her breast, rocking him like a baby. "Shhhhh, be at peace. At peace." She kissed his cheek. "We love thee, Willy. We love thee. Look after them for me. Look after Torscha. He's your friend—he always has been."

Willy's trembling quieted as Miriam drew him up into her light. The man felt her gentle goodness and knew why he loved her.

The awful need—the shame—had gone.

The girl whispered from the room, and Willy was alone. He stared after her, feeling strangely at peace. She had absolved him through her own confession.

She had left his sword upon the table, and the door stood unlocked and open. From outside, he heard the crash and thunder of the enemy guns. Willy rose and threw off his sling, then dressed himself with extraordinary care.

He wheeled about and walked slowly down the corridors. Sir William Merle marched out into the courtyard, through the gates and toward the sound of guns. He climbed the battlements and stood in the open night, backlit against the cannon fire.

A lieutenant dashed forward from the dark and stared at Sir William in shock.

"Captain! Sir William, you're back!"

Willy nodded. "Aye, wad! That I am." Willy's lisp came as smooth and casual as ever. "We'll make the siege more wivewy now, eh?"

The lieutenant relaxed, happy to have a firmer hand in authority once more. He doffed his hat and ran off to inform Colonel Retter of the captain's recovery.

Willy placed a hoof upon the battlements and stared out across the hillside. He turned his face into the breeze and closed his eyes.

Few men are given a second chance.

He would earn Miriam's forgiveness. Somehow he would pay her for her trust.

She had loved him with incredible, yearning passion; Torscha held Miriam's naked body close and breathed the wondrous scent of her hair. He thought he knew why she had made love with such intensity. She feared for the morrow—feared what might happen to him. Curled close against his wife in the darkness, he listened to the slow rise and fall of her breathing, and felt at peace.

Miriam rested Torscha's head upon her breast and held him tight.

"I love thee, Husband. Thou'st made me so happy. So very happy."

Torscha nuzzled his wife and smiled in the dark. They were together—and it was all that mattered. "I love thee, my Miriam. My love, my life. . . ."

Her hand stroked his hair, winding its way down into his beard. It is the way of things that men fall asleep after making love. Miriam stared into the dark and kissed her husband's face, content to sit and watch him in his sleep.

The time passed all too quickly; as the clock hands swept toward two, Miriam began to feel a strange sense of unreality settle down upon her. She felt herself rise from bed and silently dress, drawing on a cloak to keep away the chill.

Miriam went to kneel beside her sleeping husband. She kissed him, trying to remember this smell—this touch. There had been so much she wanted to give him; so very much. . . .

Any price—My life. My soul. . . .

"Forgive me, Husband. *Forgive me . . .*"

Miriam rose and whispered from the room on stealthy hooves. She shut the door behind her and did not look back.

Dawn brought a frenzy of fire from the Nantierran guns. Sensing that the last day had come, the crews hurled themselves into their work. Stones and earth erupted as the breach in the curtain wall grew ever wider.

Torscha clattered from the keep and trotted down the stairs, making ready to inspect the battlements. Retter sought out Mus and lifted him up before his troubled eyes.

"Mus, hast thou seen Miriam this morning?"

"Nay, Torscha! I came straight down to breakfast."

Torscha had desperately wanted to talk to Miriam. The enemy would be coming with the setting sun, and he somehow had to convince Miriam to hide in the cellars with the other women. The likelihood of Miriam's listening to reason was virtually nil. It was both a relief and a puzzle to have escaped the inevitable argument.

Still—he yearned to speak with her. There were things yet to be said between them; important things. . . .

"Well—let me know when she reappears. I need . . . I need to talk to her."

The soldiers all looked up as a fresh wave of cannon fire swept out across the walls. The gun crews of the southern bastion were whooping and cheering, tossing their caps into the air; an enemy gun must have been hit. Torscha carried Mus down the slope toward the southern walls. It would be a frantic day, and there was much to do.

They met on the battlements of the bastion; Torscha's hoofsteps slowed and faltered as he saw the other man waiting for him.

"Hello, Willy."

The blond cavalier swallowed.

"I-I'm here to help. I—If thou'lt have me."

They stood looking at one another. Sir William Merle stood straight and tall, unafraid to meet Torscha's eye.

Torscha reached out to take his hand. It was not enough; the men embraced, crushing one another tight. Torscha gripped his friend and felt his spirits soar.

"Oh, Willy! Oh, God—it's good to have thee back!"

"I'm sorry, Torscha. I'm sorry . . ."

There was a stir in Torscha's pocket, and a tiny pointed face peeked out to stare up at Willy with wide black eyes. William faltered; this was a meeting he had feared. Of all the people he had wronged, this had hurt the most.

"Mus . . ."

The mouse scrabbled frantically out of Torscha's pocket and

flung himself clean through midair. He landed on Willy's sleeve to race up onto the cavalier's neck.

"*Willy!* Oh, Willy, you've come back to us!" Mus ran his hands across his friend's skin. "Oh, Willy!"

Sir William held the mouse and closed his eyes.

"Mus! Mus, I'm sorry. . . ."

"No! Nothing happened. Nothing at all." The mouse looked up at Willy and wept for joy. "You came back to me! I love thee, Willy."

"I love thee, Mus. I love thee."

Torscha put his arm about Willy's shoulders, and the three friends stood on the ramparts and let the wild wind blow about them. Willy felt their trust, their love, and felt his resolve strengthen.

But it did happen, Mus. It did happen. Somehow I shall redeem myself. I will not be found wanting again. . . .

Aelis stood within the orange grove and switched her tail from side to side, hardly daring to breathe as she tried to hold her perspective glass steady.

Excellent!

The castle's southern ramparts were gashed wide open. Cannon fire had gouged a deep rift clean through the sloping wall, filling the castle ditch with rubble. As she watched, fresh shot plowed into the breach, chipping it ever wider; by evening, the gap would be viable.

With Kerbridge gone, she would begin her advance to the north. Once Firined's head had fallen, Duncruigh would be hers! She would inherit a colonial empire, trade routes, navies. . . . All Mittelmarch would bend knee to Aelis of Nantierre! Flushed with excitement, Aelis lowered her telescope and felt her spirits *soar*.

Soon . . . Soon it would fall. The rest would follow in time. Aelis breathed hard, contemplating the glory of it all!

Founder of an empire!

"Majesty?" The sound of feathers rattled in Queen Aelis's ear; she frowned and opened up her telescope, knowing what was coming next. "Majesty? I beg thee—keep back from the assault! Let someone else take the risks."

Aelis stamped her hoof in annoyance. "More portents?"

The astrologer knew better than to offer misgivings as argument. "Nay, Majesty. Common sense. A siege is the most dangerous of battles, and we cannot afford to lose thee."

"Stars and comets! Mumbo-jumbo!" Aelis grumbled sourly. "Rot and nonsense!"

The astrologer sulked. "Mere common sense. You will remember I once advised you to give birth to an heir. The dynasty ends if you should fall!"

"Later, old hag! Later." Aelis sighed and smoothed the old harpy's feathers straight. "You worry too much."

Aelis and the ancient harpy walked slowly down the hill, weaving their way through the orange trees. All about them spread the bustle of the camp; galloping horses, soldiers sharpening weapons, squabbling camp followers. The queen passed a loud gaggle of washerwomen and then made her way back toward the royal tent.

One of the girls by the water looked up, wringing out a dirty shirt. The young half-horse stared at the queen with a cold, deadly intelligence.

Miriam scowled; her disguise was less than perfect. Dirty clothes and a few smudges of soot did little to hide a lady. Only her country girl's brawn and freckles had saved her thus far. She waded ever farther down the stream, fearful of losing sight of the queen.

Miriam had followed in Sir Thomas Carpernan's footsteps; there were ways down the eastern cliff face of the castle—secret ways she had explored with her brother when they were both wild and young. Passing the enemy pickets by the riverside had been all too easy. A woman was met with delight and obscene propositions rather than suspicion. To the Nantierran soldiers she was just another washer-girl.

Miriam fingered the little pistols in her apron pocket. Castle Kerbridge might still fall; the enraged Nantierrans would still carry on their assault, but the Nantierran empire would be doomed. It would take but a single shot to change the flow of history.

One shot.

Two deaths.

It is fairly simple to guard against assassins, unless the assassin cares nothing for her own life. No power on earth will ward away an attacker who is utterly content to die.

There was no fear, no anger, and no sorrow. Only a vague regret
for all she would never see and do. Miriam had given life one last
caress, and let it go.

The royal tent stood just as it had when Miriam had last been
there. Her sharp, hard mind measured distances and numbered
guards. Servants were carrying platters of food in from the kitchen
tent; it was a busy scene, full of comings and goings. Miriam carefully wiped her face and hands, then proudly ran a comb through
her hair. She stood and moved into the kitchen, and the cooks were
too busy even to look her way. The girl wordlessly lifted a plate of
tarts and bore them off toward the royal pavilion. Miriam's hoof-
falls were strangely loud in her own ears. Hollow, steady steps taking her closer and closer to the end.

The guards never even looked her way. Miriam passed right
beneath their eyes just as she knew she would; it seemed as though
she had lived these moments all before.

And there stood Aelis, pure and white and strong, wearing a
sweeping black hat across her hair. Miriam stared at the woman
she had admired so long, then set aside the plate of food and
turned to face the queen. Time seemed to slow—moving with the
crystal clarity of a mountain stream. The crowds parted to either
side as Miriam reached beneath her skirt and pulled back the hammer of her little pistol.

"*Your Majesty.*"

Her voice rang loud and clear across the tent. Aelis stiffened in
shock, then whirled about, eyes staring wide.

Miriam looked at her with sad, calm eyes. "I'm sorry. . . ."

Miriam drew her pistol and fired, and a hole cracked through
the forehead of Aelis's hat. The queen never even had time to
scream. She stumbled backward, crashing through the table to collapse upon the ground.

Miriam turned to face the guards with her strange, gentle gaze,
then bowed her head and simply closed her eyes.

"Kill me."

Chapter Ten

Rodent Rescue

iriam heard the vicious *click* of musket locks. They would blast her to fragments; at least the pain would not last long.

"H-HOLD!" There was an excited stir of movement, and someone sobbed in relief. "HOLD, I SAY! SPARE HER!"

Miriam opened her eyes and stared without understanding. Aelis had woven to her feet, held up by an age-old harpy. The queen had her hands pressed over her forehead, letting blood trickle through her fingers—but nevertheless, she stood!

Aelis's hat had been knocked aside, revealing a steel skullcap underneath. The queen's "iron secret" had deflected the bullet.

She was alive! *Alive!*

Miriam lunged for her unfired pistol, but strong arms held her back. She collapsed to hang in her captor's arms, trembling with shock.

Failed. You've failed them all!

"*Lea-Leave us!*" Aelis's voice, dazed and weak. "Keep her . . . her guards, but leave us."

Miriam found her head being roughly lifted up. Looking pale and weak, Aelis sat on a bench with a pad of cloth pressed to her head. In the background, a surgeon bustled with bandages while his alchemists prepared a potion.

In hurt confusion, the queen stared at the girl.

Miriam looked away. She felt so tired—so very tired.

"Miriam—why? *Answer me!*"

The girl sighed, hardly having the strength to raise a whisper. "Your empire dies with you."

Aelis closed her eyes; she understood. "Yes, of course. Elegantly simple. A single, perfect shot. . . ." Aelis nodded thoughtfully. "You were close, Miriam. Very close . . ." She sighed, then turned her head aside. "Take her away."

A guardsman tightened his grip on Miriam's arm. "Your orders?"

Aelis met Miriam's eyes and found no fear, no regret. They both knew there could be only one decision.

"Garrote her tomorrow, dawn."

It was a cool and lazy afternoon, with just enough hint of cloud to give the sky good texture. Pin-William lay back upon the grass, obscenely at ease, and luxuriously puffed his pipe while Snatch curled in the grass beside him, gnawing a pheasant chick. The assault had been postponed one day until the queen could recover, and so until tomorrow at dawn, the campsite lay quietly at ease.

Snatch tore through flesh and bone, chewing noisily on the gore, then cocked his head in thought. "Will they crack?"

Pin-William sucked slowly on his pipe and rolled the smoke about his mouth.

The stoat sat up higher, flicking blood from his paws. "Will they *crack*?"

The satyr pushed his hat back to fix the stoat with one beady eye. "Eh? What's that you say?"

"The bonesss in her neck! Will they *crack*, or will she choke sssslowly?"

"Snatch, if you are going to make your way in the world, you must learn to state your case clearly! Now whose neck do you talk about?"

Pin-William knew perfectly well—he was supposedly part of the detail guarding the assassin captured this morning—but it was in his nature to be exacting.

"Why, the girl, Massster! The soft, sweet girl with the long brown hair! The one with skin ssso white, and breassts ssso plump!" The stoat grew excited as he tore strips of feathers from his sad little meal. "They will sssstrangle her with a rope and ssstick!—How delicccious!"

The satyr drew his face into a sour pucker.

"Really, Snatch! Must you go on so? There's no sophistication to it. The rope tightens, the eyes bulge. . . . Quite unspectacular! The Nantierrans have no idea of theater." He smiled in evil remembrance. "Now a beheading . . . there's a death! Great jets of blood, the thud as the head hits straw, the sharp, harsh scent of death upon the air." Snatch listened in breathless silence as his master spoke. "The *fear,* Snatch. The overpowering fear! The horror in their eyes as they see their executioner. The panic as they cling to their last few moments! They plead! They cry, but all hope fades in that awful instant! Always the same! Always *good!*"

"Thisss one will be good, Massster! I can feel it in my bones!" Snatch coiled about his master's legs, and Pin-William gave a smile. He was right! It would be good to see that bitch from Kerbridge throttled! To revel in her torment would be some small payment for all that he had lost!

"*Yes,* Snatch. Yes—it will be good tomorrow. We'll watch and laugh and feel her die. . . ."

The stoat hissed in anticipation. "And her friends?"

"Soon, Snatch. Not until dark." Pin-William knocked out his pipe and smiled a vicious smile. "Revenge is sweet indeed!"

The two evil creatures nestled down in the grass to wait. Soon it would be dark, and their real work would begin.

Miriam sat with her head leaning against the cold stone wall as the day wore on with slow determination. Sunset had almost come; the shadows had lengthened into sad curtains of purple, drawing the day to a close.

And after the night would come the dawn. . . .

But the assault had been delayed; at least she had achieved that much. Kerbridge would hold for another night.

She supposed it was not such a bad sort of prison, as far as prisons went. Miriam had been locked inside an old stone farmhouse by the riverside. There were guards outside the window, and another in the room outside the door; but it had a bed, and a little table—more than enough comfort for what Miriam had to do.

Aye, comfort enough.

She would not tarry long, but the chance to write some final letters was a priceless gift. Miriam stared down at the paper spread before her and tried to think of what to say. The words simply refused to come. Her mind wandered, lost on strange, lonely paths as she prepared for death.

Her life was hers to keep or throw away; she would let no one take it from her. No Jerrick would ever suffer the shame of execution. She caressed the vial with her fingers; her final escape. She had sewn it into the lining of her chemise, where it would not be found. No one would strip and search a noble prisoner.

The oil of yew leaves; death in thirty seconds.

Miriam felt cold and calm. All her choices had long been made. She would wait until dawn—just to see one last sunrise across the winding river, and then she would die.

The pen dipped into the ink. Miriam looked down at the paper and began to write.

My beloved husband,
By now thou wilt know that I am dead. . . .

What to say? How to tell someone what you wished could have been? Just to have loved him—to have cared for him. To lay her firstborn child in his arms. . . .

I did not leave a message behind to tell thee what I went to do—for it had to be done, my love, and I would ask no other to go in my place.

The pen shook, and Miriam angrily wiped away a tear. She had built a wall against emotion, and now it was slowly breaking down.

Know that I have loved thee so deeply—so totally—that I could not tell thee what I planned. Forgive me, my love. I saw a choice between our future together and the life of my country—and I have chosen in the only way I could.
There was so much I had yet to give thee. There was no time for us, my love. No time . . .
Take care of my lovely Mus, and preserve thy lives, that thou may live in peace. What I have done, I have done for love, for I hold thy lives more precious than mine own.
Thine adoring wife,

Miriam

And it was done. Miriam carefully removed her wedding ring and placed it atop the letter. She weighed the poison in the palm of her hand and watched night fall across the gentle riverbanks.

The search had ended in the infirmary, and Torscha was beside himself with panic. They had torn the castle apart from top to bottom, and there was no sign of Miriam. None had remembered her at lunch, none had seen her at dinner.

Torscha hammered his forehead with his fist. *Oh, God, what if a mortar shell has maimed her? What if she's lain out there crying for help for hours! What if she is dead?*

Miriam dead; the thought struck Torscha like a blow to the heart, and he staggered down onto an empty bed. How would he live without her . . . ?

Lyssa sat in thought upon the infirmary workbench, as though sheer deduction would produce her missing friend. Mus meanwhile paced up and down, trying to sound controlled for the others' sakes.

"Now be logical! Be calm!" Mus's eyes were anything but calm. "Now where did we all see her last?"

Torscha answered first. "She went to bed late. Sh-She tried to tell me she loved me, but I fell asleep in her arms. . . ." The stallion swallowed his guilt, and Mus hurried swiftly on.

"Milady Jerrick? Thou sayest that thou'st not seen hide nor hair of her since last evening?"

"Aye." Lady Barbara had turned pale with fret, desperately trying not to think of the worst. "We had dinner. We talked. . . . That's all I have seen of her."

Lyssa broke the stems off a tiny sprig of herbs, unconsciously shredding the leaves between her fingers.

"Well *we* last saw her at dinner. We'd spent the hours before with her. She read books with us and played cards and chess and told us she loved us. . . ." Lyssa's voice caught. She looked down at her feet and could not go on.

There was a soft stir of motion from the nearest bed. Frielle lay pale and sweating with fever, weakly cradling Opal at her breast. "She said beautiful things. . . ." The satyr sighed, slipping back into sleep. "Such lovely things . . ."

The baroness picked up her skirts and hastened to the girl's side, then ran a hand across Frielle's brow. "Frielle? Frielle, darling? Tell us! Tell us what she said."

Frielle smiled softly. "She said good-bye. . . ."

Good-bye . . .

Good-bye!

Mus felt a cold hand clutch his heart. *Oh, God—please no!*

He babbled in panic. "Lyssa, what are yew tree leaves used for? D-Dost thou know?"

Lyssa's eyes went wide. "Poison. A deadly poison. . . ."

Torscha didn't understand. He put his hands to his eyes in frustration. "Mus, I don't see what all this is leading to! We have no time. She could be anywhere! We have to . . ."

Suddenly he stopped short. Mus was crying. Mus had never really known how much she loved them all; not until then. . . . "She was saying good-bye! She said good-bye, and none of us ever saw it! " He sobbed with fear. "Miriam is going to kill Queen Aelis!"

Torscha reared up and lunged toward the door, and the baroness hurtled herself into his way.

"*Torscha!* Torscha, what art thou doing?"

The stallion tried to press past her, too shocked even to fight. "Stop her! I-I'm going to stop her!"

As the two giants struggled, Lyssa shook Mus's arm. "She can't have succeeded! You and I must find her. We're her only hope! Only a mouse could slip into the camp unheeded!"

The lady mouse stuck her fingers between her lips and gave a piercing little whistle. Opal flew up onto the table to stare at the weeping half-horses, following all that was said. The little creature whirled and spread her wings as Lyssa leapt up onto her back. "Mus, quickly!"

Mus never hesitated, but bounced atop the tiny dragon. With an almighty spring, Opal shot into the air. Magic sparkled all about them as the hedge dragon arced up toward the open window.

"Mus, Lyssa! Where art thou going?" Torscha stared amazed as the dragon buzzed overhead.

Mus held on for dear life, too frightened to look down.

"W-We'll find her! We'll save her! We're *clever!*"

And with that, they were gone.

Outside his tent, Ensign Cartiere sat glumly nursing a bottle of wine. Another day had gone by, and he was in trouble once again. Ever since claiming to have spoken to a mouse, his officers had treated him with a wary kind of caution. They had carefully eased him out of strenuous duties and put him in charge of counting the picks and shovels. Day after day—shovels, bloody shovels! It was enough to drive a man stark raving mad!

This morning the axe had fallen; he had seen a mouse sitting atop the cavalry feed sacks. There, in view of half the army, he had taken his hat off and tried to say good-day to it. Captain Harrot had relieved him of his duties and sent him packing off to see the surgeon.

Cartiere solemnly jerked the cork from another bottle of cheap red wine and simply wished the world would go away.

"I say!"

The soldier frowned, then looked about the darkened tents but saw no one.

"I say! Up here! Hello there, fellow!"

Cartiere looked up to where a small blue dragon hovered over-head. Two mice sat upon its back—a pretty little girl with a ribbon around her neck, and a bright-eyed little fellow with a hat and plume. The male mouse politely doffed his hat. "Excuse me, you wouldn't happen to know if any prisoners were taken today, do you?"

Cartiere nodded; his eyes stared, and he immediately developed a nervous tic.

The mouse sighed in relief. "Really? A half-horse girl?"

The ensign nodded once again and slowly set aside his wine. The mouse clapped his hat back upon his head.

"Do you know where she is being held?"

A finger was pointed at the solitary house that stood near the river. The mouse seemed overjoyed.

"Thank you! Thank you so very much—and a good evening to you, sir!"

Cartiere grew dimly aware of the mice chattering to themselves as they whirled away.

"See, it always pays to ask politely."

"But he never spoke! Do you suppose he feels all right?"

"I think so. Perhaps it's my accent. Nantierrans never seem to want to talk to me."

Cartiere solemnly corked his bottle of wine, pulled off his boots and went to bed. In the morning, it would all be better.

Miriam had heard the guards talking outside. They planned to take her to the scaffold long before the day had dawned, so she would not see one last sunrise after all. Not that it really mattered; she had a few hours grace before they came to disturb her.

Time enough.

She had smoothed her dress and combed back her hair as best she could. The girl sat propped up against the corner of the wall, rolling the tiny poison vial between her fingers. Slowly she drew the cork from the bottle.

Though her hands did not shake, her heart hammered and her breast heaved; she held the vial before her mouth and slowly closed her eyes. . . .

"Miriam!"

She stopped. Suddenly she began to pant in fear.

"Miriam! It's us!"

"Mus?" Miriam opened her eyes and fought for breath. "*Mus?*"

Locks on the shutters instantly burnt through, and Opal swirled into the room. The mice tumbled down onto the bed and leapt into Miriam's lap, sobbing deliriously with joy. Miriam dropped her poison and swept the creatures up into her hands. "*Mus!* Oh, Mus!"

"We thought thee dead and gone! Torscha is beside himself with fright! Thou brave, silly girl!"

Miriam had trouble standing up; it took three tries to find the strength to rise.

"Miriam! Art thou well?"

"Aye." Miriam felt the room whirl as she slowly pulled herself back from the brink. "I-I think so. . . ."

Mus quivered against Miriam's skin. Lyssa pulled his tail until he ceased his crying and sat up to look around himself.

"Mus! We must escape! Hast thou any idea how to pass the guards?"

"Aye! We'll blast any man who tries to stop us! Run for the river and . . ."

Suddenly the door crashed open. Pin-William stood in the doorway with a leveled pistol in his hand, Snatch coiled about his neck, and gave a laugh.

The mice stared in shock as the satyr raised his pistol to point at Miriam's would-be rescuers.

"We knew you would come. So heroic. So . . . *predictable.*"

It was a blunderbuss pistol—loaded with duckshot, chains and nails. Mus's fur crackled with sparks, and Pin-William aimed his pistol straight at Miriam's face.

"*Don't!* Or I'll shear her face clean off!"

Opal flashed in from above and sank her fangs into the satyr's nose. In one smooth blur, Miriam smashed Pin-William's gun aside. Her huge weight lunged forward as she slammed him up against the wall. The pistol fired with a *crash* that filled the room with shock, then Miriam leapt up over the sprawling satyr and galloped through the door. A guard bowled aside, his matchlock musket spinning from his hands as Miriam and the mice raced out into the night. Pin-William gave a roar.

Miriam raced for safety. A bullet hissed viciously past her ear, knocking the mice with the hard *slap* of its wake. Mus held on to Miriam's hair and twittered in her ear. "The river! Hide in the reeds by the river!"

There were shouts from the dark as soldiers erupted out from their tents. Bullets plowed into the rushes, smashing twigs and reeds in two. Miriam dived down between massive piles of barrels. A ragged fusillade of shots came from behind until a hysterical voice in Nantier-rese brought the firing to a stop. Miriam stumbled deeper into cover, her flanks heaving as she tried to catch her breath. She leaned against a huge black barrel and felt sparks dance before her eyes.

Mus tugged frantically at her hair. "Miriam! Miriam—quickly! They're coming!"

"Wh-Why have they stopped firing?"

Lyssa's voice was suddenly filled with fear. "Gunpowder! The barrels are full of gunpowder! This is the magazine!"

Oh, my God! Miriam jerked aside, spilling and crushing a tiny powder keg. Boots pounded the pathway behind her as soldiers closed in on all sides.

Miriam skittered slowly back onto a pier, then looked out across the water and ripped away her dress. "Mus! Where are they?"

"They're coming! Pin-William's in the lead. He has a matchlock! He sees us!"

Miriam stripped herself, and then took the mice into her hands. "*Hang on!*"

The girl galloped down the pier, and with one almighty leap she hurtled herself out into the water. Her huge body plunged beneath the river to throw up an enormous gout of spray. Miriam broke the surface, her hooves churning as she lunged across the current.

Swimming by the river; she remembered Father teaching her, Roland laughing in the sun as he showed off before the girls.

Powerful legs kicked out into the water as Miriam drove toward the distant banks.

Pin-William ran through the maze of barrels, holding his musket high overhead while one end of the sputtering match-cord dangled crazily above the ground. The satyr raced to the banks and planted one foot upon a bulging keg. Snatch perched upon his shoulder, hissing with delight as he saw the half-horse girl striking bravely out across the stream.

Pin-William raised his musket to his eye and gave a smile. A clear shot; not more than ten yards separated them, and the moon outlined her perfectly. Pin-William drew careful aim between the swimmer's shoulder blades. The air was thick with the stench of saltpeter and burning match. Snatch sniffed, then suddenly he stiffened in alarm!

"Masster!" *Gunpowder! It was gunpowder!* "MASSSTER!"

The glowing cord brushed a shattered keg of powder.

Snatch hadn't even time to squeal.

Miriam was twenty yards from the bank when the blast thundered overhead. In one almighty blaze the powder magazine exploded, barrel after barrel blowing the night asunder. Miriam struggled up the opposite riverbank, coughing hoarsely as she combed the mice out of her hair. Two mice, a half-horse, and a dragon all dropped into the reeds, staring at the raging hellfire across the stream.

Miriam wiped mud back from her eyes as a column of flame ripped up into the clouds. "Come! We'll hide down in the brambles until this dies down, then double back and hide on their side of the bank. They'll never search their own side of the river!"

Mus and Lyssa were silent. They both sat staring at the place where Pin-William had stood.

"Mus? Lyssa?"

The fire sent sharp reflections flashing across Mus's eyes.

"It's all right. We can go now." He stared at the flaming ruins. "He's finally gone. We're free of him."

The distant hills were bathed with flame. Men sat up in shock as horses stamped and whinnied in alarm. The king burst from his rough bed of bracken and blinked with surprise. "Arthur, what is it!"

"Eh? What's this, what's this?"

The king grabbed General Vardvere by the arm and pointed up into the sky. There, reflected off the clouds, hung a bloody orange glow; faintly on the breeze there came the rolling thunder of explosions.

Vardvere rose to his feet and snatched his sword.

"Powder magazine." He snatched up his helmet, trying to turn the thing the right way around. "Someone's lost their powder!"

King Firined whirled. "Trumpeter! To arms! To arms!" He reared back, his hooves pawing wildly at the air. "We march at once! To arms!"

The camp burst into activity as troops tumbled out of bed. The king stared at the distant flames and called for his standard. "Mount! We march to Kerbridge!"

The day of reckoning had finally come. Men snatched up pikes, swords and muskets, and marched to the rumble of the guns.

Torscha closed his eyes and reeled backward in relief. Lady Barbara snatched a tiny scrap of bark from his grasp as he let it fall. She read the tiny script through a quizzing glass, blinking tears back from her eyes.

> *Miriam is alive and rescued. Our suspicions were correct. Aelis wounded but not dead. We are hiding down the riverbanks where no one shall find us. Enemy assault is planned for dawn.*
>
> *Didst thou like the explosion?*
>
> Regards,
> Mus
>
> P.S.—*I told thee we were clever!*

The baroness blinked. Dumbfounded, she dropped the scrap of bark and looked over at Opal. The dragon lay curled on Frielle's sleeping breast—a touch sooty, but none the worse for wear. She looked at Lady Jerrick with unreadable golden eyes and then quickly went to sleep. Lady Barbara wound her arms about her son-in-law, and the huge man trembled in relief.

Alive! She was alive!

Whatever happened, Miriam would be safe. The stallion drew himself erect; he was Torscha Retter—last member of his country's parliament, and the enemy were coming.

Torscha gripped his sword hilt, his hide rippling with muscle as he strode for the door. "I will issue the orders. We meet Aelis at the breach at dawn."

Chapter Eleven

Assault

OR GOD, THE QUEEN, AND NANTIERRE!"
Thousands of voices roared in anger as the assault troops thundered forward. Musketeers screened dense blocks of armored grenadiers as the Nantierran infantry stormed up into the breach.

Men howled like banshees and flung themselves toward the massive castle walls. The ramparts erupted into flame: hundreds of muskets crashed out from above, and hundreds more followed moments later in a great rolling volley. Cannon fire blasted from the ramparts, gouging furrows through the attacking infantry. Nantierrans screamed as lead crashed through their lines, ripping into flesh or earth to fill the air with terror.

The front ranks shrugged off their casualties, reached the castle ditch, and hurled down their fascines. The bundles of sticks clattered down to fill the bottom of the ditch, and men leapt into the shelter of the moat, desperately scrabbling aside as more men poured in from above.

The hollow offered no respite from enemy fire. Muskets flamed, ripping bullets down into the milling soldiers. Duncruighan infantry fell into their fearsome, clockwork pattern of volley fire, muskets stabbing from the walls in an all-destroying rhythm.

Aelis's troops were veterans of a dozen sieges. Skirmishers struggled forward up the shifting rubble of the breach, screening the dense formations following behind. Suddenly the Nantierran musketeers split to either side, punching bullets up into the choking smoke as the assault wave passed them by. Grenades bounced across the breach, fuses sputtering, and explosion after explosion rocked the walls. The grenadiers vaulted up the slope to tear at the defenders' makeshift palisades. A cheer roared out from the Nantierran ranks. . . .

The rubble bucked underfoot and split asunder as hundreds of mines blew themselves apart. All up and down the breach, canisters of nails and musket balls exploded with incredible violence. Men were ripped to bloody ribbons and flung into the air.

"ONWARD! KILL THE BASTARDS!"

Pikemen bunched together and flung themselves back up the slope. With a roar, the banners of Nantierre disappeared into the castle's heart.

Hundreds of men lay in cover beneath the bailey ruins, too well hidden for an overflying harpy to observe. They watched as the dragoons pulled back from the breach, having made good use of the hundreds of loaded muskets prepared so long ago by Frielle. Nantierrans spilled over the crest, swung their banners high, and stormed down-slope toward the open ground. They milled into a churning mass as their enemy simply disappeared.

Torscha rose up from the bushes like a monument of glittering iron, and a forest of men sprang up around him, pikes and muskets glittering in the crimson sunlight. The gunners rose up behind their cannon and blew their slow match into life.

"PRESENT!"

Hundreds of matchlocks slammed down onto their forked musket rests. Sergeants raised their hats to signal that their men were ready.

"GIVE FIRE!"

Muskets and cannon roared, spitting a storm of shot into the breach. Hundreds fell, while still more surged across the castle walls. The Nantierrans were flailed by devastating fire, falling backward to tumble screaming out of sight. They came on again and again, disintegrating in the meat grinder of the breach. The Duncruighans gave a cheer as they felt the enemy crushed in their grasp.

Suddenly there were explosions all around as feathered pinions roared through the sky above. Aelis squandered her air troops in attacking the defending lines. Wall guns coughed from the castle battlements, the huge blunderbusses blasting harpies from the heavens. The fliers lost heart and fled, flapping off into the distant south, far away from siege and battle.

The confusion had allowed the Nantierrans to race down the rubble in their hundreds. Torscha looked across to Willy, who led the half-horse soldiers.

The chestnut stallion fired a borrowed musket up at the breach and whirled to face his colonel. "It's no good, Torscha! We'll not hold 'em!"

Enemy mortars now found their targets, smashing into the right side of Torscha's line. Torscha looked back to the solid walls of the keep. "BACK! PULL BACK!"

The units leapfrogged backward, half the men running for the ruins while the second half stood to punch bullets at the enemy. Shot whipped through the parsley to smack into the ground, and a drummer boy screamed in horror as lead ripped through his spine.

Torscha walked slowly backward with the front line, listening in approval as Willy directed fire on the left; it was as though their partnership had never broken. The armored stallion kept pace with the humans, tail twitching as a bullet ricocheted from his gorget.

A rhythmic ripple of fire echoed in the distance—regular, paced platoon volleys in the Duncruighan style. Torscha tried to track down the source, but his helmet blocked his ears.

Willy reared and pawed the air as he pressed his troops into cover. "We'll not hold them! Ten minutes more and we must withdraw to the keep!"

Torscha turned to shoot his pistols into the thickening powder fog. All around lay death and chaos as blood splashed across the ancient stones.

The defenders were losing.

Miriam stood at the bottom of an old windmill, listening in terror to the storm of gunfire from the castle walls. She held an old scrap of sacking about herself, cradling Lyssa as she shouted above the din to Mus. The tiny mouse had perched himself at the very tip of the windmill's broken sail.

"Mus, what's happening?"

Mus's small voice twittered down from on high. "The town militia!

They've abandoned the town and have come out to fight! Three—four regiments in the fields! Aelis's reserve is engaged!"

Miriam screamed for joy and reared high into the air. "Are they winning?"

"Aye! Aelis's trenches have been overrun!"

It would not be enough to stop her—but by God it was something! The town garrison had suffered enough watching and waiting. Miriam leapt and cheered; Kerbridge still had teeth!

There was a squawk from above. "Rats! There's filthy rats up here!"

"Oh, Mus—don't be such a baby!"

"There's movement in the woods to the north!"

Movement? Miriam's tail shivered. "What movement? How many men?"

"I don't know." Mus was getting short-tempered. "I can't see!"

"Well, look, Mus! Look!"

Miriam and Lyssa held their breaths as they waited for news from above.

"Retter!—General Retter!"

Queen Aelis skidded to a halt and reared high, her tail streaming in the wind. She shifted the bandage under her hat and flicked a glance toward the castle walls.

"Retter, continue the assault! Don't lose your momentum!" The queen's sword flashed in the light. "I'll deal with these idiot militia! With luck we'll follow their rout through their own gates and take the city!"

The vast black half-horse seemed to expand. The faceless figure in its visor turned to look up at the breach, and something like a sigh of anticipation quivered on the air.

"Retter?"

Count Retter weighed a massive poleaxe in his hands. "It shall be done, Majesty. The castle will fall."

The queen whirled off and led her reserves down the road toward town. Count Retter turned to face his enemies and growled. "Signal the attack. Raise the red banner."

An aide smiled evilly. "Aye, sir. No quarter."

General Retter led his troops up the glacis. They trod over the corpses and the wounded alike as they stalked their way through the gaping castle wall.

The Royal Life Guard reined to a halt at the edge of the trees as harpies swirled down to make their report. Their leader clattered forward on ragged wings and knelt before his king.

"Sire, the castle's all but overrun! The town garrison has sallied forth, and Aelis has taken the bulk of her troops to attack the town!"

The king ripped open his telescope and stared down into the valley. Aelis's army lay strung out along the road as she raced toward the Kerbridge town militia. The brave little garrison was outnumbered perhaps twelve to one.

"There's no air scouts? We're undiscovered?" The royal voice was incredulous.

"Indeed, Sire! Not a feather in the sky!"

Firined closed his telescope with a *snap!* "Vardvere! What now?"

The old general slapped down the visor of his battered brown armor, swept his sword from its scabbard, and stood in his stirrups. "We charge, Sire! We *charge!*"

The army swept forward, pouring down the hill into Aelis's unguarded flanks.

"Beware the left! Beware the left!"

A shock wave plowed into one of Aelis's regiments, and the queen whirled about from her scrutiny of the embattled town militia and stared. A wave of cavalry stormed down from the flanks and charged across the valley, crushing Nantierrans under hoof.

Firined!

The Duncruighan horse blasted through the Nantierran ranks with a horrific *crash.* The cavalry trampled the infantry beneath their all-destroying hooves as if wading through a bloody sea.

Aelis ran her eyes over her battle lines and reached for her perspective glass. "Send four regiments to hold the line against the Kerbridge militia!" The queen's mind raced, watching the ebb and flow of imaginary troops across the field. She was the most brilliant tactician of her age—and she had been caught between a hammer and an anvil! "Leave the flank units to their fate! Draw back to align on the guard . . ."

"Majesty!"

Aelis reared back as a line of horsemen smashed into her guards. Nantierran half-horses were crushed underfoot as human troopers threw their weight behind their blades. The elite guard of Nantierre—the pride of an empire—reeled backward, splintered, and then fled south in alarm. Aelis snarled and fought against the storm.

"Come back, you fools! Cavalry can be beaten!" The queen drew her blade and reared high into the air. "I am Aelis! Stand! Stand with me and fight.. . . ."

Men swept past the windmill on foam-flecked horses and hacked at Nantierrans with their blades. Lyssa, Mus, and Miriam watched in awe as the banners of Duncruigh came sweeping down the hills.

"The life guard! The king's life guard!" Miriam nearly shouted. "The army—it's here!"

The mice leapt and danced for joy, shivering their little tails. They kissed Miriam, and then gleefully kissed each other. Miriam held her friends in her hands and burst out onto the road after the last of the enemy had passed. She breathlessly reared up and waved to the royal troops.

"Hello! I say! Hello!"

A tall, slender man sawed at his horse's bit and wheeled from the ranks. He jerked open his visor to stare dumbfounded at the disheveled girl with the two little mice perched on her shoulder.

King Firined's eyes widened.

"Dame Miriam? Mus—Mus is that you?"

The mouse squealed for joy as he recognized the king.

"*Majesty!* Majesty—thou'rt here to save us!"

King Firined hurried forward, swirling off his cloak to proffer it to Miriam. The king held the mice while he waited for Miriam to dress.

"*Mus!* Mus m' dear fellow!" He shook his head in wonder. "This is a rescue, old chap! Queen Aelis's days are done!"

Behind them, the sounds of battle rose to a deafening storm. They walked into the shadow of the royal banner while Mus introduced

Lyssa to the delighted king. Behind them, the cavalry roughly wiped their bloody broadswords and fell into ranks about the flags.

The enemy poured through the outer breach and swept like a blackened tide toward the castle keep. The forward magazine detonated in a blast of fire, spreading carnage through the Nantierrans like ripples in a pond. Muskets fired from the walls, stabbing holes into the ocean of enemies, and still the Nantierrans came on. Half-horses raced forward through a hail of shot, crammed powder kegs against the Jerricks' gates, and blasted a path into the castle yard.

Nantierran infantry and Welflandic traitors instantly surged toward the gap. Torscha's musketeers killed them in their droves, still unable to turn the charge aside. Men screamed and fell from the castle walls as enemy shot ripped out their lives. Torscha's men fell back pace by pace into the courtyard.

"Avast and hold! All ranks—kneel!"

The walls were lined with sailors from the *Nemesis,* armed with cutlasses and pistols as they abandoned their guns. The seamen snatched at ropes and halyards as though climbing rigging out at sea. His Grace the bishop drew a massive, rusted blade and placed himself at the fore while Torscha and Willy galloped underneath.

"Your Grace! Get into cover! We cannot risk . . ."

Bishop Kaxter tied a silken scarf about his brow.

"*The king, boys! The king!*" He bellowed the news to all the courtyard in a voice more at home at sea than in a pulpit. "The king has come! Aelis's troops are driven back!"

From down the hillside, the men heard a ferocious battle. The defenders cheered in wild elation as the bishop's blade was waved on high. "Hold 'em, lads! Hold 'em for the king!—Aelis is destroyed!"

Torscha stiffened, and his tail lifted with new hope. William Merle paced steadily by his side, his sword held beneath one arm like a silver swagger stick as they dressed the ranks. Kneeling men found it difficult to retreat.

A new wave of shots began as the enemy stormed into the gate. Torscha swept up one hand, and the musketeers leveled their pieces like a mass of automatons.

"FIRE!"

Guns crashed out across the courtyard. Attackers screamed,

attackers died, and the charge was stalled. The Welflanders gathered again, massing behind a hurricane of their own musket fire as Torscha drew his men back into the yard. "This time let them in! Charge pikes! Charge pikes!"

Armored pikemen locked their ranks; high above the courtyard, the bishop leapt among the sailors, stepping over the body of their dead captain. "Kelso! Show these buggers how a seaman fights!"

The sailor snapped his cutlass up in a salute. "Aye, sir!"

The bishop looked round at his men. As good a crew as any he'd sailed with! "GO, BOYS, GO!"

Welflanders poured through the gatehouse, slamming pike to pike with Torscha Retter's men. Into the melee swung the seamen, crashing down into the brawl. The world dissolved into chaos as men grappled hand to hand. Men staggered and swayed, fighting sword to sword and knife to knife. Musket butts clubbed, halberds chopped, and the wide courtyard filled with cursing crowds of men.

Nantierrans raced up the stairs onto the battlements, trying to drop down behind the defenders. With a snarl of rage, Torscha flung himself up the steps to bar the way. He lashed out with his hooves, hurtling men down into destruction.

The enemy turned and fled. As suddenly as the chaos had begun, it swept away and left Torscha at the eye of the storm.

The wind blew through Torscha's tail, lifting it out upon the breeze. Torscha slowly turned, tossed aside his sword and drew the battle hammer from his belt.

"Hello, Father."

His enemy paced slowly from the shadows of the stairs. Black armor glittered—a perfect twin for Torscha's own. Blood marked Count Retter's hoofprints, and a mask of steel hid away his eyes. Count Retter's hooves struck sparks on the ancient stones as he closed the distance.

Torscha remember how deeply he had once desired this moment—before Mus, before Miriam. He looked at the evil creature his father had become and felt a wave of sadness.

"I'm sorry, Father. . . ."

He hurtled all his massive strength into a savage, crushing blow. The count's ax whirled up to meet the hammer in a shower of sparks. Both stallions crashed chest to chest, hooves lunging as each tried to ram the other man aside.

The stallions fought with blinding fury. Count Retter made a ferocious backswing at Torscha's face. The young stallion leapt inside the blow, catching his father's arm and slamming him back into the wall. The count's gauntlet clawed at Torscha's face, gaining a grip on the visor and smashing Torscha's head against the battlements. Steel groaned beneath the attack. With a savage roar of defiance, Torscha hammered his fist against his father's throat. Sparks flew, and the count staggered back in shock.

The count fought with superhuman strength. Armor plate buckled as his ax hacked at Torscha's arm. Torscha roared and smashed his hammer down onto his father's helm. The count reeled away to collapse against a wall, nearly falling over the corpse of a dead grenadier.

Both men stood with chests heaving, clutching the battlements for support. Torscha's father tore open the visor of his battered helmet and raggedly sucked air into his lungs.

"*. . . kill you! I'll kill you!*"

Torscha turned his hammer so the vicious pick became the leading edge. With a mindless howl, his father flung himself forward, ax sweeping in a blur of steel. Torscha reared sideways, hacking back with the pick as his enemy lunged past. Hooves lashed out to slam into Torscha's side, and ribs splintered, sending Torscha tumbling to the ground.

Count Retter staggered on, the pick jutting out from his shoulder blades. He stumbled over the body of the dead grenadier and fell, blood spilling down his backplate in a mortal stream. The man lay dying, snarled and hunched over a dead man's corpse. Torscha tried to move, but bones shifted deep inside him, ripping him with pain.

Count Retter laughed in triumph and lunged to his feet. He lurched and staggered, somehow managing to turn about. In his hands he held a smoking, lit grenade.

"NO!"

Something blurred between Torscha and his father. Willy Merle hurtled himself at the huge black stallion, smashing him aside. Count Retter staggered, carrying both men to the wall.

"*Willy!*"

The explosion roared out across the fire step. Count Retter disappeared in a blast of flame, and Willy spun aside. The cavalier crashed to the ground, stiffening with pain. Torscha desperately fought free of the wreckage and somehow reached Willy. "Willy—Oh, God—

Willy!" He gently lifted his friend's head, and Sir William somehow opened up his eyes.

"D-dead? He's . . . dead?"

"Yes! Don't talk! Sa-Save your strength. We'll get a surgeon. . . ."

"*No!*" Willy fought for breath. "It's all right. Really—it's all right. *You* might have forgiven me, Torscha. Bu-But not I." The stallion coughed blood onto the stones. "It had to be paid for. I had to buy . . . redemption."

Willy convulsed in agony. "W-We're friends?"

Torscha sobbed helplessly. His voice was a choked whisper. "Yes. We always were. . . ."

Willy gripped Torscha's hand. "Tell Miriam I'm sorry." He searched for words as his breath rattled in his throat. "And tell Mus . . . tell Mus it's been an adventure. . . ."

Willy smiled. He stared into the sky with fine blue eyes, and his hand slackened in Torscha's grasp.

Behind them the sounds of battle ended. The Nantierrans were in retreat, and the day was won.

Torscha folded over his dead friend's face and wept.

They found her beneath a tree beside the river, lying amidst the remnants of her guard. The dead lay strewn across the road in ghastly tangled drifts, filling the air with the stench of blood. It was not yet noon.

Miriam knelt beside the wounded woman and took her head into her lap. The mice slowly crept forward to peer down at the pale, exquisite face.

Aelis looked up at them and smiled a rueful smile .

"You . . ." She closed her eyes. "I'm glad. It's good thou art alive. . . ."

Miriam ran horrified eyes across the queen. Wounds gaped in Aelis's side, and her pure white flanks were drenched in blood.

Aelis coughed, and the action hurt. She fumbled for Miriam's hand. "It's over. It's finally over."

Miriam softly pushed the queen's hair back from her face. "I'm sorry, Your Majesty. I'm sorry."

The mice wrung their little hands in distress and pattered down to touch the queen. Her eyelids flickered open, and she saw the mice and smiled. "The mice! How beautiful. How clever . . ." She raggedly fought for breath. "Mus of Kerbridge, I presume?"

Mus removed his hat and made a little bow. "Yes, Your Majesty. Your most humble opponent. . . ."

A tear slid down Mus's eye. Queen Aelis gathered him onto her breast and idly dried the little mouse's cheeks. "Now, now. No tears! No one else will shed them."

Miriam wept, and Aelis looked up at her in wonder as her breathing grew more labored. "Miriam? I'm glad thou'rt here." She closed her eyes, her voice grew soft and sad. "There were never any friends, you see. Never any friends. . . ."

Miriam's voice was a whisper. "Nay, Majesty. There was always me."

They sat quietly together. Miriam stroked Aelis's face and tried to ease her pain as the queen grew ever weaker. "Will they write about me, Miriam? Will they remember?"

"Aye, Majesty." Miriam held the queen's small hand. "I shall write the words myself."

Aelis weakly tried to turn her head. "Mus, there is a—a banner hidden beneath the tree. A white rose. Thou've earned it more than most. Wilt thou keep it for me?"

"Yes, Majesty." Mus's eyes were wide. "None shall ever mock it."

The queen shivered, and her breath came hard. "It—it won't be long, I'm afraid." A tear escaped her eye. "Wilt thou stay with me. *Please . . . ?*"

"Aye, Majesty." Miriam held her close. "We'll not leave thee."

"Put my sword in my hand, then. We'll wait together. . . ."

They sat together in the cool shade beneath the trees. The grass was long, and the river breeze blew sweet. Lyssa made butterflies dance upon the air as Mus quietly began to sing.

And that was how they found them: a weeping girl and two small mice, cradling the corpse of Nantierre's queen.

Aelis had achieved her legend at last. And in the end, she had found three friends to weep for her.

Epilogue

ime had passed, and wounds had healed. Spring was gone in a whirl of gun smoke; summer withered as the invaders were driven back into the sea; but the autumn saw Duncruigh finally free of war.

Free.

The palace became the center of a marvelous celebration. They had come from every corner of the nation; human and half-horse, satyr and harpy. Pixies and hobgoblins from the deep, dark woods. There were islanders from the channel and boisterous chieftains from the north. In every ale house across the land the scene repeated itself upon a humbler scale. A royal holiday had been decreed, for Nantierre had gone!

In the palace, ball gowns sparkled with satin and lace. Silk rustled sensuously as the dancers swept across the floor. Men posed grandly in their coats of velvet and brocade, laughing loudly and fingering sheathed swords. If the fates were willing, they need never bare their blades again.

At the great oaken entry doors, the seneschal banged his ivory staff against the ground. "COUNT AND COUNTESS RETTER! GENERAL OF THE ARMY OF WELFLAND, COMPANION OF THE ORDER OF THE DOLPHIN!"

Torscha stood at the head of the stairs, posed magnificently against the open doors. Miriam stood serenely at her husband's side, coolly looking out across the crowd. Her ball gown was of champagne satin, spilling down across her hooves in a dazzling cascade of light. About her slender neck there sparkled a small medallion of plain brass taken from the cannons of Kerbridge.

They were gifts from a grateful king to all those who had been most valiant in his kingdom's defense. Only three had been awarded; the rest would be kept for future generations.

It had been a long, hard fight. In the six months since Aelis's death, her empire had thrashed in self-destruction. Like the body of some awful hydra, it sprouted new heads that snapped and bit at one another. A dynastic war still held the continent in a grip of steel.

Torscha Retter could not yet lay aside his sword. He must return to his homeland to rebuild a new ideal—and Miriam would stay there by his side.

Torscha had accepted his noble titles after painful argument and deliberation. Duncruigh had pointed them the way; where a republic failed, a constitutional monarchy could succeed. The tiny child that Aelis had crowned king of Welfland would remain upon his throne; now a proud, free Parliament would make the nation strong.

Torscha and Miriam graciously stepped down into the swirl, and the courtiers came forward to meet them. Heroes were in fashion this week, and it was likely they would stay so.

"SIR MUS THE MOUSE, KNIGHT COMMANDER OF THE ORDER OF THE DOLPHIN!—AND THE LADY LYSSA MOUSE!"

Gus the pixie stood grandly in the doorway, proudly holding high a velvet cushion. There, perched upon the pillow, were the mice. Mus had made sure that his medal sat prominently displayed on the cloth. He was inordinately proud of it, and had been parading the wretched thing about ever since he had received it that afternoon.

Lyssa stared with wide wondering eyes out at the ballroom. She held Mus tight and gaped in amazement at the dazzling parade of light. They descended into the chamber, celebrated as the heroes of the age.

"Miriam!"

Courtiers were roughly pushed aside as a little figure excitedly fought her way across the room. Frielle Delauncy picked up her skirts and battled over to her friend, towing Thomas Carpernan behind her.

"*Miriam!* Now where'st thou been hidin' thyself?"

"Frielle! Oh, lud, Frielle, 'tis good to see thee!"

The little satyr brimmed with life as only Frielle could. Something new had filled her face with light. Miriam thoughtfully examined her, mulling over a strange new intuition.

Frielle gave Miriam a last excited hug and then nestled back in Thomas's arms. Sir Thomas Carpernan doffed his hat to Torscha and gracefully kissed Miriam's hand.

"Count-Countess . . ." Candlelight glittered from the medallion at his throat. "There's somethin' you might do for us." Thomas seemed a touch nervous. "We'd appreciate the moral support. . . ."

Frielle struck him on the hat with her paper fan.

"Oh, bosh! Y' do talk daft, man! 'Twill be good fer laughs!" Her brown eyes flashed. "Let's collect those no-good mice an' set the fun in motion!"

Mus was found hanging upside down from a flower arrangement, trying to snatch the cherry from the center of a cake. Lyssa was very partial to cherries. Mus swayed dangerously close to an ocean of sticky cream as he edged ever closer to his prize. Frielle snatched him up moments before disaster could overtake him.

"Mus, thou dizzy creature! Come out o' that!" She picked up Lyssa and passed her to Miriam, plucking off the cherry to pass into the mouse's paws. The little party approached one of the private drawing rooms, and Frielle gripped Thomas by the hand. "Ready?"

"Aye!"

Frielle rolled her eyes expressively. "Well, then—here we go!" She shoved open the door and swept inside in an imperious swirl of lace. With Tom beside her she boldly strode into the room. Two satyrs stood in the chamber, pointedly ignoring one another's presence; one was stout and dark, and another thinner than a racing hound. Both gentlemen stared from Frielle to Thomas in shocked amazement.

Frielle stood with one arm clutching her sweetheart's waist as she defiantly clopped a hoof upon the ground.

"Pa, I'd like t' introduce thee to my lover, Sir Thomas Carpernan. We're gettin' married in a month!"

It was like setting off a gunshot. The dark, burly satyr whirled to face Sir Thomas, his face blazing red.

"*Villain!* Y' bloody *Carpernan!*—If thou'st touched her, I'll . . . !"

The other man stared at his son with hatred. "You bloody fool! So her claws are back int' ye again, eh?"

Thomas lowered his horns in anger. "I love her, Da'! She'll take me back—and the likes o' you won't separate us again!"

"Well, I forbid it!"

Tom's thumb eased his dagger in its sheath. "Let's just see y' stop us."

"HOLD!" The voice barked out through the room, snapping like a whip across the satyr men. Torscha Retter stamped between them, his black presence dominating the room. "Enough!" His hooves crashed upon the floor. "How long will you persist in this useless feud? Hundreds of years of bitterness over nothing! Let it heal—let it heal, or be damned, the lot of you!"

Frielle's father gave a venomous glance toward Sire Carpernan. "No daughter o' mine'll shame me with a *Carpernan!*"

Miriam walked slowly in from the doorway, then calmly looked from Frielle to her father. "Well now. And what will you say when the wee one is born?"

The men all blinked. Lord Delauncy looked at Frielle in pale dismay. "Wee one?"

Frielle's cheeks blazed red "Aye, I'm up the duff—so there!"

"Oh, m' God! Y' canna—ye wouldna. . . ." Suddenly he glared at Thomas, ripping his dagger from his sheath. "Y' damned villain! You've soiled me precious daughter!"

Old James Carpernan went for his knife.

"Touch me son an' I'll have thy tripes across the floor!"

"I'll cut thy lights oot! Swear to God, 'tis time I did!"

Torscha kept the old men apart by forcing in between. Without him there they would have torn each other to pieces. Sir Thomas noticed none of it. He seemed to sink down like an empty sail.

"W-Wee one . . . ?"

Frielle bit her lip, scuffing with her hooves.

"Well . . . I'm six weeks late. . . ." She swallowed. "But—I'd not meant to worry ye."

"Oh, my God!" Thomas looked about to faint. "I'm goin' ta be a father." The words seemed to take a while to soak in through his shock. "*I'm goin t' be a father!*"

The old men ceased their bickering as the news sunk properly in, and Miriam came over to take her husband by the arm. "For heaven's sake—get them off somewhere, sit them down, and bid them drink! They'll handle this far better when they've had a while to think."

Torscha collected the satyrs, one under each arm, and began to lead them off. "Later on, thou'lt have to explain how thou knew."

Mus's head popped up from beneath Miriam's hair. "Because she's clever!"

Thomas held Frielle as though she were something precious made of porcelain. "Uh—dost thou need to sit down? Is there anythin' I should be bringin' thee?"

Frielle hesitantly took him about the neck. "Thou—thou'rt not angry?"

Thomas was looking pale. "Oh, God. I'm the happiest man in the world!" He didn't look it.

Frielle dived a hand beneath her skirts and came up with a flask of whiskey. "Well just get a stiff shot o' that in ye, and we'll talk all about it, eh?"

The poor bemused fellow stared into her face with worshipful, adoring eyes, and Frielle kissed him. "Art thou happy, my love?"

"Yes. Yes, I'm happy! Thou dozy female—why didst thou not speak out before?"

Frielle looked down at her dainty hooves. "Aaah—'tis still too early t' say."

"A daughter! 'Twill be a daughter!"

Frielle frowned. " 'Twill just as like be a boy!"

Miriam smiled and collected up the mice, softly crossing to the door. Behind her, Frielle and her Thomas snuggled down to talk.

The hour grew close to midnight, and on a marble table, two little mice gaily danced the night through. Each graceful swirl— each poise and sway—was made with perfect harmony.

The music drew to an end, hanging upon the air like some strange and delicate flower. Mus and Lyssa walked beneath the shade of a potted fern to catch their breath. Mus held his lady's slender hand in pleasurable silence. They sat together and listened to the bubbling rise and fall of talk.

Lyssa moved slightly away to sniff at the overhanging flowers, then looked shyly back at Mus from the corner of her eye. Mus leaned yearningly toward her, his heart hammering frantically in his breast. "Lyssa?"

The lady mouse walked on, gently trailing leaves past her tail. "Yes, Mus?"

"I . . . I would like to go to Welfland with Torscha and Miriam. There's so much for them to do. I would like to help."

Lyssa bit her lip. "Then I'll go, too. I-I want to be with thee. . . ."

Mus edged closer. He reached out to touch his Lyssa, and then knelt softly at her feet.

The little fellow's ears blazed cherry red. "Lyssa?"

"Yes, my love?"

"*Marry me.*"

Lyssa caught her breath in surprise.

"*M-Mus?*"

Mus almost dropped dead with fright. "That is . . . I-I most humbly beg thy hand in marriage. . . ."

"Oh, *Mus!*" Lyssa made happy little noises in her throat, running fingers through Mus's fur. She wept against his neck, hardly daring to breathe. "*Oh, Mus!*"

The little mouse's ears stood up in wonder. "*Yes?* Thou—thou wilt?"

She looked into his eyes, weeping for sheer joy.

"Silly, silly man! Of course I'll marry thee!"

"Thou wilt! I . . . *Really!*" Mus panted in disbelief, then suddenly gave a little shout of joy. With a whoop of delight, the mice skipped and danced across the table. Faces turned to stare in wonder as a thousand blossoms of fire popped and crackled in the air.

"Miriam! Miriam, come and hear!"

The mice pranced off to share their wondrous news. All about shone light and color, love and laughter. It was a wonderful, magical world!

Far above in the chandelier, Opal peered down at the mice and purred. She coiled about the candles, closed her eyes, and smiled a secret smile.